BONANZA
THE PIONEER SPIRIT

BEN CARTWRIGHT—A man of strength, a man of adventure, a man of vision—he would follow his dreams wherever they led ... to the sea, to the woman he loved, to the wide-open spaces of the American West, where his true destiny lay.

CAPTAIN ABEL STODDARD—He never forgave Ben for choosing to stand with honor rather than bow to his own will; home from the sea, Stoddard hated young Cartwright nearly as much as his daughter loved him.

ELIZABETH STODDARD—The belle of Boston and the joy of Ben's life, nothing could take her away from him—not the sea, not her father—nothing, that is, save a cruel twist of fate.

ADAM CARTWRIGHT—A child of love and tragedy, as sturdy and strong-willed as his father, he was a boy who would someday be a man, a partner in Ben's pioneering dreams.

INGER BORGSTROM—In a small midwestern outpost, Ben saved her from a bullying brother and found a kind, decent, gentle companion, a mother for his son, a wife whom he would come to love ... but would he realize the depth of his feeling too late?

HOSS CARTWRIGHT—Ben's second son, a baby of the wagon train, born with a smile—and a heart—as big as the great Rocky Mountains.

THE PIONEER SPIRIT

STEPHEN CALDER

BANTAM BOOKS
NEW YORK · TORONTO · LONDON · SYDNEY · AUCKLAND

THE PIONEER SPIRIT

A Bantam Domain Book / September 1992

ISBN 0-553-29041-X

Published simultaneously in the United States and Canada

*Bantam Books are published by Bantam Books, a division of Bantam
Doubleday Dell Publishing Group, Inc. Its trademark, consisting of the
words "Bantam Books" and the portrayal of a rooster, is Registered in
U.S. Patent and Trademark Office and in other countries. Marca
Registrada. Bantam Books, 666 Fifth Avenue, New York, New York
10103.*

PRINTED IN THE UNITED STATES OF AMERICA

OPM   0 9 8 7 6 5 4 3 2 1

Dedicated to the memory of Michael Landon (1936–1991)

CHAPTER 1

The small ship raced down the back slope of a huge, storm-driven swell, then with a lurch and a shudder was driven to her knees by a monstrous wave that rose as if by malevolent design to meet the *Wanderer* and break over her bows. White foam and green water boiled across the deck, and the impact was enough to bring the ship nearly to a halt.

She wallowed for a moment, her bows almost fully submerged, then slowly, miraculously lifted, rising out of the surging sea like a great, spiny whale breaching the surface. The conflicting forces that raged and tore at her, pushing and pulling and striving to break her apart, made her shake and shudder like a dog in cold rain. But rise she did, the buoyancy of her oaken hull overcoming the tons of water that would have buried her, and the drive of her storm-shortened sails finding purchase enough on the air to once more send her slicing forward in close-hauled defiance of the elements.

Stoic seamen with clenched teeth and grim expressions huddled tight against the lee boards that surrounded the helmsman's cockpit. All of them had been drenched for so long by now that their flesh was wrinkled from the constant near immersion. One of them fingered the beads of a rosary and muttered quietly to himself. If the wind became even worse—if indeed it were possible for wind to become any worse—if sail had to be shortened even farther—there was little canvas in place *to* shorten lest they strip away the last vestiges of sail to stream a sea anchor and ride with bare sticks, trusting to God and to good fortune that the storm would abate before the plunging *Wanderer* was driven onto an uncomfortably close lee shore—if a shroud parted or an order was given, these were the men who would have to go aloft and try to work under truly impossible conditions. And no sane man, not even a seaman, would want to find himself aloft under conditions like these.

The ship creaked and groaned, yawed wildly and rolled. But somehow, slowly, she once more righted herself and drove on, quartering into the force of the storm just as stoically, just as reliably, as the men who worked her—and who depended upon her stoutness to preserve their very lives.

Another great sea broke over the bow and swept a flood of foaming water over the foredecks. The *Wanderer* shook herself and lifted herself yet again.

In the midst of this, while green water sheeted half a foot deep on the deck, a rectangle of bright light flashed yellow in the gloom as a companionway leading up from the forecastle was flung open.

A man's figure appeared there. He leaped onto deck, teetered off balance for only a moment and then raced for the safety of the shrouds. The fury of the wind was nothing compared to the awesome power of the water. Better to risk the heights than the deck while water flowed so deep and so swift.

Close behind this first man came a second scrambling in pursuit. He too flung himself out of the companionway, his tall figure silhouetted stark against the bright light from belowdecks. He too ran for the safety of the shrouds.

The first man, though, plucked something from his waist and flung it at the second. For an instant lamplight flickered on a slim needle of steel spinning through the air. A knife or sharp-pointed spike sought flesh.

The man on deck threw himself sideways to avoid being impaled by the blade of the other. He succeeded in ducking underneath that threat, but his foot slipped and he landed heavily on his back amid the wash of onrushing water that covered the wooden planks. He skittered and slid, borne swiftly along by the force of the water, borne toward the scuppers and the sea and a certain death, for no man could long survive a storm like this one.

A cry rang out, sharp and startling and quickly whipped away by the wind. Yet, oddly, it was not the man who faced a death by drowning who yelled. Rather it was the man who hung clinging in triumph in the shrouds who shouted, and his voice was loud with joy.

The man who was down and seemingly helpless only knitted his brow in concentration and waited for a split-second opportunity.

Just as his feet reached the scuppers and it seemed that he was surely lost, he twisted his body, gathered himself, and lunged for a handhold.

His fingers encountered the base of a rail and clamped down with the strength of desperation. If he lost his hold . . .

The rushing water carried him inexorably to the edge of the wet, slippery decking and beyond it. His legs dangled over the side, suspended above oblivion, yet the concentration in his face never wavered. He clung tight with the one hand and turned his torso so as to take hold of the rail with his other as well.

Then, his own strength meeting that of the now lessening flow of water, he pulled, regained the deck and came to his knees.

He looked up with grim intensity, and the man in the shrouds gasped, the pallor of fear bleaching the deep seaman's tan from his pinched features. The seaman retreated up the ratlines a dozen feet, but his effort was futile, and he had to know that it was. On a ship at sea there is nowhere to run. Nowhere to hide. Nowhere at all.

"Come down, Judas," the much younger man below him ordered.

"My name—"

"I know what your name is. And I know that you are a Judas. Now do you want to come down on your own or shall I fetch you down in my own way?"

The seaman's answer was to come down the lines hand over hand, agile as a monkey but sullen and of a sudden petulant. "I never meant to—"

"Close your mouth, Judas, and lay aft. Quietly and at once."

"Yes, sir, Mr. Cartwright. Just as you say, sir." The voice was an ingratiating wheedle now, and the man's head bobbed and nodded.

Benjamin Cartwright, third officer of the barkentine *Wanderer,* scowled and followed close behind as ordinary seaman Watts trotted obediently aft along the heaving, rolling deck.

CHAPTER 2

Abel Morgan Stoddard, master of the good ship *Wanderer,* fixed his third officer with a challenging glare. Cartwright, Watts, and First Mate Hiram Truesdell were all crowded into the tiny cubicle that served Captain Stoddard as quarters and office alike, Abel Stoddard not being a man to waste space or specie on foolish comforts. And in the *Wanderer* all things were cut to Stoddard's measure, for the man was owner as well as master of the vessel.

"Sir?" Ben Cartwright asked.

"It is a simple question I asked of you, mister. It is a simple answer that I require. What was it you were doing snooping about in the crew's quarters?"

Cartwright continued at a loss for words. The request—no, demand, for that was clearly the tone that was present in Captain Stoddard's voice—was so completely unexpected that he was having difficulty comprehending the weird direction this confrontation was suddenly taking.

"But I—I—I saw Watts there pilfering from the men's seabags, sir. I saw him, sir. With my own eyes, I did." Cartwright could hear himself stammer, could hear an unwelcome note of uncertainty in his voice. His confusion tied his tongue in knots and secured it firmly to the roof of his mouth, and knowing all of that, hearing it in his own ears, did nothing to calm him nor help him adjust to this twist of accusation.

Of a sudden even his personal appearance was working against him, particularly as the thought of that very drawback brought heat into his cheeks and ears and no doubt put color there as well.

If the captain saw that—of course the captain would see that—however could Ben expect to be taken seriously?

Probably he looked like a baby to begin with, Ben thought. An ungainly scarecrow of a baby, but a baby nonetheless. And standing here in the captain's quarters making accusations against a seaman who was twice Ben's age and likely more. And a man moreover with whom Stoddard had sailed for many years past, while young Ben Cartwright was on his first voyage aboard the *Wanderer*.

Not for the first time in his twenty years, Ben Cartwright wished himself a more imposing figure than truth allowed. He was man-tall, that was true enough, standing several inches above the height of most men at five feet ten and a fraction. But his frame had not yet filled out, and he was so lean and lanky as to appear weak. Which he was not, his muscles being wiry and corded like good hawser. But from any distance his slight build made no good impression.

And his face? Hopeless, that was all it was. A baby's face, he acknowledged, beardless and wide-eyed and innocent. Not that there should be anything wrong with that, but . . . if a man wanted to be taken seriously among men, well, perhaps something more than a beardless youth was called for.

But not now, surely. Surely that should have no bearing on an eyewitness account of theft. And theft from the man's own shipmates. That made it all the worse, didn't it? Ben certainly believed that to be so. Surely the captain understood . . .

"I am well aware of what you claim you saw, Mr. Cartwright. You have stated it loudly enough and often enough that I would have to be completely deaf in order to have missed it. But what I asked you, sir, and what you fail to confess to me, is what *you* were doing in crew's quarters to have seen—if indeed you did see—Seaman Watts take anything from one of the men."

Ben tried to stand boldly upright but only succeeded in knocking his head against the overhead. Captain Stoddard had standing headroom in his cabin only because the man was five feet six inches in height and not a fraction more.

In any event, the impression Ben wished to create proved impossible. Instead of coming across as bold and determined, he feared he was only making himself a laughingstock as the sort of bumbling officer who cracks his own noggin.

"I was there, sir," Ben said slowly, determined to see this thing through as best he could, "because I overheard members of the starboard watch complaining about the thefts, sir. And knowing that the starboard watch was on duty, sir, I thought it best to see if I could find the miscreant and bring him before the mast, sir. I know the high regard the men have for you, sir, and the pride you take in your—"

"Mr. Cartwright."

"Yes, sir?"

"Leave the butter in the cask, sir, and stick to the facts, if you please."

"Yes, sir. As, um, as I was saying, sir, I deliberately secreted myself in a locker so as to keep watch over the men's personal belongings. It was then that I saw Watts come in and steal from his shipmates, sir."

"Seaman Watts claims he was borrowing an object with the full consent of its owner, Mr. Cartwright."

In fact Ben had heard Watts utter no such explanation.

"A silver locket from one man's bag, sir, and a quantity of coins from another?"

Stoddard frowned and said, "I have not asked Watts for an inventory of the items in question, Mr. Cartwright."

"No, sir, I daresay you have not."

"Don't get snippy with me, mister."

"No, sir. I apologize." But Ben noticed that now the captain was no longer meeting his eyes. Captain Stoddard was giving close examination to a chart pinned onto the table that filled most of what little floor space there was in the rocking, lurching cabin. All four men in the cramped room swayed from side to side with the motion of the storm-tossed vessel, none of them having to make the adjustments by acts of conscious will. The ability to remain upright regardless of the canted, tilting attitude of a deck was simple second nature after one was so long at sea.

"The fact remains, sir," Ben persisted, "Watts was stealing. I was there. I saw him do it, and I know that he is a thief. On top of that, Captain, may I remind you that Watts threw a knife at me when I pursued him. I regard that as attempted murder, sir. No less."

Stoddard scowled and tugged at his beard. The ship's captain was thick of body, with a closely trimmed spade beard that partially hid an accumulation of scars earned in the performance of duties on many a sea and over many a year. He had dark eyes, large and bright and intelligent, set wide over a nose that had been many times flattened.

Captain Stoddard's eyes, Ben often thought with a mingling of irony and wistfulness, were very much like those of his daughter Elizabeth. But that was a subject that should best be avoided at this particular moment in time, Ben chided himself, lest he become distracted from the tasks at hand.

"Does the captain suggest, sir, that I disregard an attempt made upon my life?" Ben insisted.

Watts spoke up for the first time since being hauled into the cabin. He snatched the knit cap off his balding head and knuckled the place where a forelock would have been had he retained the ability to grow one. In some ways, Emmanuel Watts was a sailor of the old school, having learned his trade as cabin boy and powder monkey aboard a British man-o'-war before finding his way to America. It was said that he'd been taken prisoner along with a prize ship during the conflict of eighteen and twelve and that he'd opted to remain in America when his shipmates were repatriated. Ben understood that the man had been with Captain Stoddard ever since, signing articles with the captain aboard Stoddard's first command and following him into Stoddard's own bottoms as the master's fortunes improved.

Ben understood that there should be loyalty between master and seaman. That was only right and proper. But this? No, this was more than could be deemed right or proper, either one.

"Beggin' the cap'n's par'n, sir?" Watts said.

"Yes, man?"

"Mr. Cartwright, he thinks I tried to stick 'im, sir. I can see as how he'd think that true as true could be. But what happened, sir, I flung my spoon at him. That's all I done, sir. T'was only my spoon. I 'as tryin' t' distract 'im, like. Tryin' t' get higher inta the lines so's he couldn' catch me, see. An' then, sir, I figured t' have one o' me mates explain, sir. How it 'as all a misunderstandin', sir. That's all. Just me borry'in' from some o' me mates, sir. No more'n that. But I never tried t' murder Mr. Cartwright, sir. No, t'was only me spoon 'at he saw an' handily ducked under. As I knowed he easy could, sir." Watts bobbed his head to emphasize the sheer honesty of his explanation, then jammed his watch cap back over his naked scalp.

Ben's mouth dropped open to protest this utterly outrageous invention. Why, the enormity of it was an insult to the intelligence of anyone within hearing. To think that Watts could believe he could make such a claim ... to think that he would think anyone might believe—

Ben hadn't time to voice his disgust.

"You heard the explanation, mister."

Ben gaped. Then clamped his mouth closed.

"It was only a spoon. Hardly attempted murder for someone to throw a spoon, eh?"

Ben's hands clenched and unclenched, knotting into fists against his will and then quivering as he tried to force them open again.

"Mr. Truesdell."

"Sir."

"Kindly take Seaman Watts forward, Mr. Truesdell, and verify with the men the accuracy of his claim that he had permission to borrow the, um, items in question."

"Sir," Ben injected, knowing he should keep his mouth shut but unable to do so and yet maintain any shred of self-respect, "have you knowledge of just which crewmen Mr. Truesdell should interview?"

"I do not, Mr. Cartwright." Stoddard slyly smiled. "Can *you* identify the belongings of individual crew members?"

"No, sir, I cannot, but—"

"Carry on, Mr. Truesdell," Stoddard snapped. "Watts will tell you who it was that gave him permission to borrow property."

Ben had intended to suggest that the members of the starboard watch be shown the objects Watts claimed he borrowed. That could be done with neither Watts nor Third Mate Cartwright present. Spontaneous reactions by the owners of the items in question might have been illuminating indeed. But it seemed the captain was in no humor to receive suggestions.

"Yes, sir," Truesdell said. The first mate jerked his head toward the cabin door. The expression he gave Watts would have been as murderous as Watts's knife—spoon, as it was being called lately—had only the sharp glare been given solid form. But the first mate did not argue with his captain nor in any other way show that he might—or indeed might not—disagree with Stoddard's judgment.

Watts knuckled his forehead again and followed the first mate out into the passageway.

Ben too turned to leave.

"Mr. Cartwright."

"Yes, sir?"

"You are young, sir. You lack experience. I suggest you refrain from forming judgments until you understand all the many aspects of a question. And I suspect you will find, Mr. Cartwright, that that is advice that will stand you in good stead through all your life. Never judge until you know all the facts. Mmm?"

Ben hesitated. Swallowed. Honestly tried to understand what the captain was driving at, but failed. "It was not a spoon, sir, nor was Watts borrowing with anyone's permission."

Captain Stoddard sighed. His expression was firm but not unkind. "You are dismissed, Mr. Cartwright."

"Aye aye, sir." Ben Cartwright turned and departed. Unlike Watts, the young third mate did not salute the ship's master.

Ben found Mr. Truesdell at the foot of the short ladder leading from the after passages to the helmsman's station on deck. The men of the starboard watch were up there now trying to stay low and thus find relief from the wind and blowing spray; they were not welcome in the dark maze where the officers lived. The first mate, who had spent forty of his forty-seven years at sea and knew when to share his men's discomforts—or when not—leaned against a bulkhead, tamping tobacco into his pipe. The task of filling and lighting a pipe would have been impossible on deck so long as the storm continued

Cartwright stopped beside Truesdell in the T-shaped area where the passages connected. He looked first to port and then to starboard. He knew Seaman Watts hadn't doubled back to the captain's cabin. So where . . . ?

"First officer?"

"Yes, Mr. Cartwright." Truesdell grunted as he

packed the tobacco down tight, pressing on it with the ball of his thumb. Then he took a small lamp down off its gimbal and applied the flame of it to light the pipe, pale smoke quickly wreathing the first mate's head and filling the passageway with a honey-sweet aroma.

"Surely you haven't allowed Watts to go on alone, sir."

"He told me which men I should talk to," Truesdell explained.

"But sir, if Watts has time to see them first he can, well, prime the pump, so to speak."

Truesdell drew on the pipe for a moment, his expression one of great satisfaction. His eyelids sagged languorously, and whatever tension might have been in his frame disappeared. "About Watts, Mr. Truesdell?"

Truesdell sighed and for the first time looked directly into Ben's eyes. "You wish to remind me that seaman Watts now has opportunity to till his garden and plant the seeds as he wishes, mmm? And of course you are correct, Mr. Cartwright. My response to your entirely accurate assessment, sir? It is that I certainly hope Watts has sense enough to do exactly as you say. For I shall question those men. Indeed I shall, sir. The captain so instructed me, and so I shall perform." The first mate was smiling.

Ben Cartwright was not. "I don't . . . I do not understand, sir. Not a bit of it."

Without slackening his smile, Truesdell pushed away from the bulkhead and approached Ben. The much older and more experienced officer put a comforting hand on Ben's shoulder and gently squeezed it as if in encouragement. "I like you, Cartwright. I daresay Captain Stoddard does also. You show great promise. You are intelligent, no doubt about that. And no slackard, sir. You fall to, regardless of the burden. That is to your credit. And you are honest." Truesdell squeezed again, smiled again. The smoke from his pipe curled around Ben's nose and made him want to sneeze, but he fought the impulse back.

"Honesty, Cartwright," the first officer rambled on as

if musing aloud. "A wonderful quality, honesty. Invaluable in man or officer, either one. But one must be practical as well as honest. If you know what I mean."

"No, sir, I do not."

"Take Captain Stoddard, now. He is a fine officer, our captain, and a wise ship's master. A practical man too. Let me tell you, sir, I've sailed with him for the best part of these twenty years past, and I can tell you. Abel Stoddard gave as honestly to distant ship's owners then as he does now to himself. Like I say, Cartwright, he is an honest man. Just as you yourself are. But the captain has learned to be a practical man as well as an honest one. As, um, in this business with your seaman Watts."

"But that is what I fail to understand, Mr. Truesdell. Does the captain not believe me? Does he think Watts really was borrowing from those men? Does he not believe there was a knife?"

"As for the knife, lad, that is a serious charge, and you admit that you got no good look at whatever was thrown. It could have been a spoon, as Watts said. It could have been anything. It could have been a knife thrown to delay and not to harm."

"And the thievery?"

"That is quite a different matter, Mr. Cartwright. And it is here that the captain's practicality must be brought into play. You are familiar with Watt's, shall we say, shoreside services?"

"No, sir."

"Seaman Watts, Mr. Cartwright, is the reason Captain Stoddard has had such exemplary crewmen through all these years. The man is a genius at . . . well, pressing a crew is not a lawful method in most places, Mr. Cartwright, but one might say that Watts has a certain capacity to convince his fellow man of the, um, desirability of sailing with a captain so fine and upright as Abel Stoddard. And the crew, for some reason they regard themselves as being under Watts's protection and, um, discipline. So to speak. I've even heard that a great many of them give the man gifts in the form of a percentage of their wage."

"In exchange for which?"

"Oh, I wouldn't know about that, Mr. Cartwright. But then a first officer must necessarily keep himself at arm's length from his crew." Truesdell smiled and puffed at his pipe.

"What you are saying, sir, is that Watts is allowed to get away with whatever he wishes aboard this ship, in exchange for which the captain is assured that he will have no troubles with the remainder of the crew?"

"That is not what I said, Mr. Cartwright." The first mate winked. "Not precisely, that is."

"The captain is wrong, sir. And so are you." Ben was not smiling. A wink and a pat on the shoulder were hardly enough to turn wrong to right, no more than they would turn night to day. Not in his view, they were not. "To be practical is one thing, sir. To allow unchecked criminality is another. I submit to you, sir, that Watts is a thief and a would-be murderer, and he should be brought to port in irons at the very least. Better he should be flogged first and then discharged at the next landfall."

"You are a hard man, Mr. Cartwright."

"No, sir, only an honest one. And no believer in the bending of rules for the sake of convenience."

"Not even the small rules, Mr. Cartwright?"

"Not even the small ones, Mr. Truesdell. Not that I consider murder to be a small rule."

"I'm trying to remember something, Mr. Cartwright."

"And what would that be, sir?"

Truesdell smiled again. "Whether my hackles came up so quickly and so thoroughly when I was your age."

"I don't believe right and wrong have changed much in that time, sir. I hope you once were able to discriminate between the two."

The smile was wiped away from the first officer's face. He held himself stiffly upright, his expression and posture grim and threatening. "You overreach yourself, sir."

"Yes, sir. If you say so, sir."

"Have you no duties to perform, Mr. Cartwright?"

"Not until the next bell sounds."

"Then perhaps you should lay below and rest while you can, Mr. Cartwright. This storm may be with us for a time."

"As you wish, sir." Ben turned away from the first mate but stepped not down the passageway that led to his dark and cell-like quarters, but onto the ladder.

"Cartwright."

"Sir?" Ben stopped on the ladder but did not look down at the glowering first officer.

"You will be free to make your own rules when you are master of your own vessel, Cartwright. Not before. And for your sake I hope that by then you will have learned that not everything is black or white. In this life there are shades of gray too. Remember that."

Ben waited until the first officer was done, then went topside. He found it more comfortable confronting the lash of whipping winds and salt spray than he had been below.

The helmsman, clinging to the spoked wheel but unable to see anything ahead beyond the bare foremast, saw the young officer climb into the partially sheltered cockpit. Ben saw the watchkeeper's eyes shift to the glass, then quickly—and with no small degree of disappointment—drop again as the man realized it was not yet time for his relief to come on deck. The men of the watch did not even look up to see who it was.

Ben nodded to the helmsman and made his way carefully forward.

It was one thing to have sea legs. Every man aboard could be said to have that. But sea legs were not enough when a deck was slick with running water and the ship was plunging and yawing so madly. Some quirk of current was working in opposition to the wind, one force building swells from one direction, the other creating conflicting

waves across those already massive storm swells. The result was a sea that jumped and spiked in crests and spurts
and leaping, disjointed confusion.

Ben left the scant protection of the helmsman's low
cockpit and made his way forward from one handhold to
another. He sprinted from the mizzen to the thick bole of
the mainmast, hesitated there a moment while he waited
for the pitching deck to stabilize. Overhead a storm staysail sheeted close on the fore-and-aft main moaned and
thrummed with the force of the wind. Much more strain
and the sail could break loose. If that happened, they
would lose their ability to make way and would risk being
driven around into a broach. Ben hadn't seen the second
mate, who was the officer of the watch at the moment, but
someone needed to order the hands to set a smaller staysail.

He looked up toward the staysail, trying to judge if
the slender strip of tough canvas would hold, or if the incessant wind would shred even that rugged cloth, perhaps
rip the eyes out. He could hear the low-pitched hum of the
vibrating sail even over the howl of the wind. The tone of
the noise was different, much deeper, than the higher,
sharper whine of the shrouds and the stays. Ben wanted—
needed—to go forward to where he'd been when Watts
threw that knife at him.

But the ship came first. Always, above all else, the
ship came first. He turned and made his way back the way
he had just come, wobbling from handhold to handhold,
pausing to wait for the few moments of relative calm and
then dashing on while he could.

When he reached the cockpit, he had to raise his
voice to make himself heard. "Sanderson, where is Mr.
Thom?" he asked the man on the helm.

"Below, sir. Second officer is b'lowdecks."

Ben tapped the elbow of the crewman huddled closest
to him.

"Aye, sir?"

"Go below, Marcum. I want you to find Mr. Thom

and tell him I sent you. Tell him I think we need to reduce sail."

"Sir?"

"I know, Marcum. I don't like it either. But tell him."

"Aye, sir."

The seaman scurried away, likely grateful for a chance to get out of the cold, wet wind and go below even for a few moments. He was back in less than a minute. "Mr. Thom's compliments, Mr. Cartwright, and you have permission to reduce sail if you please."

Ben grunted but of course said nothing to Marcum or any of the other men. Although they knew. They knew as well as he did that if the sail had to be reduced, it was the watch officer's place to see to it. It certainly was not the responsibility of the most junior officer aboard, and an off-duty junior officer at that. Still and all, the ship came first. Ben could take time to think about Thom later if he wished. In the meantime there seemed little for it but to do what needed doing.

"All right, lads. Everybody up now," he said loudly. "Marcum, you and McFee go for'ard to the locker and break out the smallest stays'l we carry. The rest of you come with me." He turned and started forward once again, not bothering to look to see that the men were following. He had complete faith that they would be and so went on without looking back.

Nor did he stop when he reached the base of the mainmast. Motioning half the crew on to the foremast where the foot of the staysail was secured, Cartwright took hold of a tarred line and began climbing, leading the way up the lines himself. He climbed past the clew and on to the head of the taut, thrumming sail, taking the highest and most dangerously exposed position instead of asking a crewman to do it.

"Not yet," he shouted down as one of the men, anxious to be done with this task and back to safety, began unfastening the shackle that secured the clew. "We'll set the new stays'l first, then take off the old."

"Aye, sir."

It seemed forever but actually required only minutes before Marcum and McFee came hurrying back from the sail locker, both of them bent low to avoid the force of the wind. They dragged a slim roll of tightly bound canvas between them, and it occurred to Ben that he hoped one of those two knew the contents of the sail locker much better than did the third officer of the *Wanderer*. Otherwise they might yet be in trouble.

At one point Marcum stopped, almost dragging McFee to his feet. Marcum dropped to his knees and fumbled on the deck for something. Ben could see that clearly and was sure the man hadn't fallen. After only a moment Marcum was back up and the two seamen hustled the last few steps to the foremast where sure hands were waiting to take the foot of this new and smallest sail and secure it. Then aft, and the crewmen burst into swift, controlled motion, setting the new sail and stripping off the old almost before Ben had time to open the shackle at the head of the old sail and jam it onto the eye of the new.

The loose canvas of the old staysail cracked and snapped like a bullwhacker's whip as a gust of wind caught it and streamed it alee. Strong hands grabbed and pulled, bundling the sail into a wad and hurrying it away lest it be lost overboard. It would have to be stored free for the time being. Lord only knew when there would be opportunity to dry the canvas and lash it into a proper bundle, Ben thought.

As he climbed back down to the deck, he noted with satisfaction that the ship remained stable in the wind with the smaller staysail and that the strain was much less intense with so much less canvas aloft. There was little danger now that the wind would overpower the sail and send the *Wanderer* out of control.

The men went about their business—which at the moment consisted of returning to the cockpit and finding what shelter they could—and Ben Cartwright continued forward on the errand he had set for himself when he came on deck.

His search was fruitless, though. He was unable to recover the knife—and it was a knife, he was sure of that—that Watts had thrown. It must have failed to stick into the planking and been washed overboard by the cold, green water that kept periodically flooding the forward decks.

Ben searched in and under every niche and crevice, continuing the hunt until he heard the bell announcing the change of watch. He had to leave his search then and go aft to relieve Mr. Thom.

There still was no sign of the object that Watts had thrown.

CHAPTER 3

Ben grimaced, braced a hip against the side of the heavy table in the officers' mess and dipped his spoon into the mug of greasy coffee. He fished out two of the tiny, wiggling objects with his first attempt and got the third and last one out with his very next try. Not bad. The results of his efforts he tossed into the slop bucket that was secured to the bulkhead nearby. He knew he was considered something of an oddity because he preferred to soak the weevils out of his bread and discard them. No one else aboard seemed to pay much mind to the unintended additions to their bread ration, but Ben still balked at the thought of eating the bugs along with the hard, crusty bread. Besides, the bread was so much easier to chew once it was thoroughly soaked in coffee or broth or whatever hot liquid might be available at the moment. So the soaking was a twofold benefit as far as the young third mate was concerned.

Cartwright used the spoon to finish the soaked and softened bread, then dropped the utensil into the appropriate bucket and drank off the last of the coffee. The empty mug followed his spoon into the bucket.

"No moah, mistuh?"

"No thank you, Jo-Jo. No time for more right now."

"Yes, mistuh, plenty time." Jo-Jo, the ever smiling boy from far Owyhee pointed to the glass mounted on the wall. The hourglass in the mess was an unofficial instrument that no one bothered to keep in time with the real ship's glass in the cockpit, an oversight that Jo-Jo never seemed to comprehend.

"Thank you anyway, Jo-Jo, but I'll be going above now."

"Yes, mistuh." Jo-Jo smiled and bobbed his head agreeably. It had taken Ben some time to realize that he was not being discriminated against just because Jo-Jo did not know his name. Jo-Jo referred to all officers from Captain Stoddard down as "mistuh" and to all seamen of whatever stripe or ability as "hey-you." This was not a question of indifference, Ben eventually came to realize, but of efficiency. Jo-Jo seemed to like everyone and had neither favorites nor foes.

Ben was wearing his heaviest sweater. He considered putting his coat on too before going on deck, then decided it would not be necessary. The storm continued and the temperature probably was little different now than it had been through the night, but daylight lent a perception of lessening the storm's discomforts, whether justified or not. So the third officer settled for leaving his heavy woolen coat below and pulling on oilskins over boots and trousers and sweater. "What's for supper tonight, Jo-Jo?" he asked as he struggled into the awkward but necessary oiled canvas trousers.

"Stew, mistuh. Ver' good." Jo-Jo grinned and smacked his lips.

Ben grunted. Very good. They should be so lucky. It was all the worse when one considered that the men were fed even poorer than the officers. The officers were given porridge and coffee for breakfast, the men only biscuit and water. If Ben Cartwright were master of this ship— He caught himself and ruefully smiled as he finished fastening the toggle closures of the oilskin jacket. He was being foolish again, the error no doubt encouraged by the disappointments of the night before. Well, all of that was behind him now. The captain might not always be right, but the captain was always the captain. And third officers are expected to learn, not to instruct. He really needed to take a grip on himself, Ben thought, and learn to accept Captain Stoddard's judgment about these things. No doubt the captain would control Watts in his own good time and his own good way. Of course, Ben decided now upon reflection, that was all it was. The captain had his own plans in mind here, and it was not Third Officer Cartwright's place to interfere.

"Ver' good stew," Jo-Jo chortled as Ben left the mess and made his way to the ladder.

"Right," the third officer muttered.

Once he reached the deck, Ben decided that it wasn't merely perception at work here. The storm truly had abated somewhat. The continued harsh motion of the ship was caused by the course the captain was steering as much as by the force of the wind, although that remained high. Since Ben's last watch, the course had been altered considerably. A pair of trysails had been set on the foremast jib stays in the stead of the small storm stays'l, and aft there was now a spanker to balance the drive of the trys'ls. Ben pondered that for a few moments, wondering why the captain would choose to make them all deliberately uncomfortable when a small alteration of course back as it had been would so greatly ease the motion of the ship, especially now that it was possible to carry added canvas.

Then he realized. There had been concerns through the night about the nearness of a lee shore. Not that there was imminent danger of the *Wanderer* being driven aground, but then a prudent seaman does not wait for an imminence of danger before he acts. Which explained what Captain Stoddard was doing now. The captain was driving his ship farther offshore lest the storm renew its force and once again threaten. Very sensible, Ben realized.

Very smart. That was the sort of thing he needed to learn under the tutelage of a ship's master like Abel Stoddard.

Pleased now, Ben made his way into the cockpit, standing behind the helmsman and checking the glass. He had some time yet before his port watch was called to duty. Jo-Jo had been right after all. There would have been time for another cup of coffee if he'd wanted. Ben yawned—sleep was a scarce commodity on a storm-tossed ship—and ducked his shoulders to protect the lower part of his face from the cold, driven spray. With his nose inside the oilskins like that, he could smell himself. The odors were of waterproofed canvas and wet wool and that salt-tinged mustiness that comes to pervade any cloth or clothing after being months at sea. But to a seaman those odors are not all unpleasant.

"Shall I call the port watch on deck, Mr. Cartwright?"

"Not till the turn of the glass, Carter."

"Aye, sir." The helmsman grinned to show that he was fairly caught and didn't mind it. He'd only been trying to shorten the watch by a few minutes.

There was no sign of Mr. Thom in the cockpit. But then there hadn't been through the night either. The second mate or the captain or possibly both would have been above earlier or their course and canvas would not be as they now were. And Thom would appear in time for the change of watch. He was required to do so in order to pass along the master's instructions to the relieving officer.

"S'pose I should call them two down anyways, eh, Mr. Cartwright?"

"What's that, Carter?"

"Them two aloft, sir." The helmsman pointed.

Ben had quite naturally paid close attention to the working rigging when he came on deck, but he hadn't bothered to inspect the bare yards on the square-rigged fore. The *Wanderer* being a barkentine, she bore three masts, the main and mizzen rigged fore-and-aft and the fore rigged square. Now that Carter was directing his attention toward the foremast, Ben could see two figures riding the spreader beneath the tightly furled fore topgallant. The men were perched, apparently in comfort enough, two thirds of the way up the foremast structure. "Who the devil ordered them up there?"

"No one, sir. They just . . . I dunno. Nothing against it, is there, Mr. Cartwright?"

"Certainly not. It seems strange, that's all."

"Yes, sir." The helmsman acted like he wished he hadn't brought the subject up, and Ben decided against asking who the men were. From the cockpit he couldn't see. He was, however, curious as to who in the crew would be daft enough to go aloft on a whim under conditions like these. With no particular design in mind, he left the cockpit and drifted forward, bracing himself against the plunge and roll of the deck beneath his feet so automatically that he was not conscious of having to do so.

By the time he reached the mainmast, Ben could see that the man nearer him in the tall rigging was the sailor Marcum. The other man was on the far side of the thick doubling where the topmast and topgallant mast were joined; he was obscured from Ben's view. Whoever he was, he and Marcum seemed to be arguing. Marcum took something from beneath his oilskins and reached toward the other man. Then recoiled as if in sudden alarm, and without warning plunged backward off the spreader.

Marcum made a blind, desperate grab for the footrope dangling beneath the topgallant yard. Ben could see his hand close on it. But only briefly. Only long enough for it to alter but not break the force of his fall. Marcum's hand slipped off the footrope and he plummeted screaming to the deck.

Ben felt his gorge rise in shocked rejection of what he saw, and more than that in response to what he heard when Marcum's body smacked wetly onto the unyielding planks.

"No!" The third mate went pale and for just a moment was dizzy. Then—there seemed no need to hurry—he started toward Marcum, who must surely have been killed by the force of the impact.

Too late Ben realized that he should have been quicker to act. *Wanderer*'s bow plowed deep into a massive wave, and water sheeted across the deck. Ben had to grab a shroud line to keep his feet from being swept out from under him as the water was carried off the now rising deck. Before Ben could do anything to stop it, Marcum's body was plucked off the decking and spun swirling away with the cold, foaming waters, disappearing into the scuppers and on into the slate-gray, storm-churned sea.

Powerless to call back that which was done, Third Officer Ben Cartwright squeezed his eyes tight shut for a moment in a mute and anguished apology to the lost seaman who now could not even be granted decent burial.

When he opened his eyes again a moment later, Ben saw Emmanuel Watts calmly descending the ratlines from the fore topgallant, as calm and unruffled as if he were coming down to dinner.

"Pity 'e had to go an' fall like that," Watts said casually. He used the edge of a grimy fingernail to probe for something lodged between his teeth. "But you seen it clear, Mr. Cartwright. An' accident, that it was." The man gave Ben a smug look.

Ben opened his mouth. Then, his face set and stern, closed it again. For what, after all, had he really seen. Murder? Probably. But what proof had he? None. He saw Marcum hand something to Watts. He saw Marcum recoil. He saw Marcum fall. At the time Ben hadn't even known who else it was who'd been aloft with the seaman. Now what proofs could Ben offer to a court of inquiry? If indeed Captain Stoddard would wish to convene a court when port was made. Third Officer Cartwright had damn-all for proofs.

Still, though, Ben couldn't give it up without reminding Watts that, proofs or no, he *knew*. He knew the truth of this even if he could not in good conscience swear to that truth. "Is that what you're claiming, Watts? An accident?" He shrugged and added, "If you wish." And Ben turned and walked away, returning to the cockpit where Carter had just then turned the glass and taken up the brass hammer to ring the hour and the changing of the watch.

"Beggin' your pardon, Mr. Cartwright, but can I ask somethin' o' ye?" The port watch seaman, Timmerman by name, knuckled his forehead but met his watch officer eye to eye. Ben felt it something of an accomplishment that the men of his watch felt free enough with him to do so. There could be no affection or camaraderie between officers and men on a tautly run merchant ship. But this sort of respectful yet relaxed approach was closer to it than any other officer aboard could claim. Or, Ben thought ruefully, than any other would wish for. Still, it pleased Ben regardless of what anyone else might think or feel. "Ask whatever you please, Tim."

"Aye, sir, thankee, sir. Would it be true, sir, what we been hearing, that Isaac Marcum be dead now, an' that Emmanuel Watts were wi' him when he fell?"

"Sadly true, Tim. Marcum fell to the deck from the foretop just before you were called on watch. I saw it happen."

"An' Watts, sir? Were he the one that—I mean—"

"Seaman Watts was aloft with Marcum at the time. I make no claims beyond that fact, however."

Timmerman's broad, weathered face darkened with anger. He looked fit to burst.

"What is it, Tim? You know something. Say it, man. What is it you aren't telling me here?"

"I . . . the crew is a-scared, sir. Bad things can 'appen aboard a ship, sir. An' none t' protect the innocent."

"Watts, Tim? Is that what you mean?"

"I ain't sayin' that, Mr. Cartwright. You never heared me say no such."

"Nor would I claim otherwise. But what is it you know, Tim?"

The seaman hesitated, glancing over one shoulder and then the other as if to assure himself that they were not

overhead. " 'Ave you looked at Isaac's body, sir? T' see
was 'e cut, like?"

"Cut, Tim?"

"Aye, sir. T' see was 'e bit by a knife, sir."

"I don't understand, Tim."

"Marcum was a special chum o' mine, Mr. Cartwright. Close, we was. An' I warned 'im. I warned 'im not
t' be comin' crosswise wi' Emmanuel Watts. But he
said—sir, Isaac was on deck las' night after Watts tried
t'—that is, sir, after th' incident in the fo'c'sle an' . . . you
know."

"Yes?"

"Isaac found the knife, sir. The knife Watts threw?"

"The knife he named Spoon," Ben said dryly.

Timmerman smiled a little. "You do unnerstand, I
see."

"Yes, I'm beginning to."

"My friend Isaac found the knife, Mr. Cartwright.
An' he, uh, was gonna give it back t' Watts t'day, sir. An'
ask for, well, for a favor. If you take my meaning, sir."

"Marcum intended to blackmail Watts into granting
certain favors, else he would give the weapon not to Watts
but to me. Is that it, Tim?"

"Aye, sir. Sumpin' on that order o' things, sir."

"Which explains why the two of them were aloft in
this weather, doesn't it. Both would have been desirous of
privacy for that particular discussion."

"Aye."

Ben sighed. "It went badly for your friend, Tim. I'm
sorry for him. I saw him hand something back to Watts. It
must have been the knife."

"An' after that, sir?"

Ben gave Timmerman a tight, thin-lipped smile but
no answer beyond it. The truth was that he really had none
to give, unless he would be willing to perjure himself. He
hadn't actually seen Watts stab Marcum, nor even jab at
him so as to make him lose his balance and topple from

his perch. And now with the body washed away before anyone was able to inspect it . . .

But why let the crew know all of that?

As surely as God made the winds blow and the seas heave, the crew would soon know the essentials of this conversation between Adolphus Timmerman and Third Mate Ben Cartwright. Ben saw no reason why he should grant Watts the comfort of knowing that he had indeed gotten away with his murderous game.

"Call the watch into the lines, Tim," Ben ordered, changing the subject. "I think we can bend on a bit more sail and see can't we make more way to the east before the change of watch, just in case the captain will be wanting to shorten sail again for the night." Ben was explaining it more to himself than to Timmerman, who in any event did not care about an officer's reasoning, only about the degrees of discomfort that might result from an order.

"Aye, sir." Timmerman tapped his forehead again and turned to trot aft for the other members of the port watch.

Ben relayed the current orders, signed off the watch log and handed the responsibilities of the ship over to Mr. Thom. By the time the officers completed their rituals, the men of the crew had long since finished their less complicated ones, the port watch crewmen hurrying below for a few hours of sleep in their canvas hammocks, and Mr. Thom's starboard watch standers taking their places huddled inside the protection of the cockpit.

"You are relieved, sir." Thom's statement was a welcome one to Ben, but not for the obvious reasons. Four hours on and four off, day after day, sapped a man's strength. But not so badly now as it had at the start of this voyage. Ben was fatigued, true. But his thoughts now were as roiled as the pitching, churning surface of the murky Atlantic.

It was midnight, and he had completed two full watches since having that discussion with Timmerman. The plain truth was that he was no nearer an answer to his dilemma now than he had been then. In the hours since, he had sat at the mess table with Captain Stoddard for supper and several other times had occasion to speak with the captain regarding course and sail. But so far he had not raised the matter of poor Marcum's death.

Ben felt morally certain that Emmanuel Watts this day committed murder. He himself was a witness to it. But he himself was unable to swear to it.

The captain had made it clear enough the previous night what he thought about Seaman Watts. Proof against the schemer would have to be drum-tight ere Captain Stoddard would accept it.

And that was the rub.

Ben's conscience cried out that justice be done.

His Yankee practicality warned there was nothing that could be done.

And the most disturbing of all was Ben's fear that he might be fooling himself, that he might be giving in and allowing justice to miscarry out of considerations not of true practicality but of self-interest. Was he remaining silent in the interests of his own career and allowing an innocent man's death to go unnoticed and unimportant? That thought was repugnant to Third Officer Cartwright. Abhorrent to him. Yet he could not in good conscience actually *swear* to what he truly believed Watts did, because he had not actually and truly seen Watts stab or otherwise dislodge Marcum from that spreader. Ben's doubts, with those doubts of self foremost among them, had been torturing him throughout the dark hours of this latest watch. Now he was much too agitated to be able to sleep, and so when he was relieved of the watch he remained on deck while Mr. Thom immediately went below to seek sanctuary from the continuing storm.

Ben was in no humor to share the company of others, though, in particular the company of the seamen of another's watch. He left the men in the relative protection of the cockpit and made his way forward along the slippery, tossing deck until he found the isolation he desired. He crossed over to the windward railing abreast the forward cargo hatch and braced himself there with his face to the storm.

Cold wind whipped the hood from his head and sent oilskin and hair streaming back off his face. The wind was strong enough to bring tears to his eyes and a sting to his flesh. Salt spray picked off the caps of the waves dashed into his face and ran down his collar. He could taste the sea and smell it. The sea was primal, implacable and impersonal in its power, but there was no dishonesty in it. The sea would rend and destroy, but never corrupt. It would take life and property, but it could not lie. Meet it fair and it would return the same. Ben only wished life were as clear and straightforward as the sea.

He sighed. Wishing, he long ago learned, has remarkably little result.

His best course now should probably be to go below. If he could not sleep, he might at least grant himself the comforts of a cup of broth, because soon enough the watch would change and again he would be responsible for a ship and a cargo and the lives of thirty-odd men.

Deliberately he willed the tension to leave his shoulders, then let go his hold on the rail and turned his back to the force of the cold wind.

Ben jumped a little, startled, as a shape loomed close to him in the night. A man was standing not five feet away.

"Who are you? What do you want?"

The dimly seen shape came closer then, and Ben could see that it was Watts. Ben felt a chill in his spine that had nothing to do with the cold wind at his back.

"You can put the knife away, Judas, now that I know you're there. Your kind needs a man's back to make you feel brave."

"Shows what you don' know, mister," Watts said, coming nearer. "I was facin' that fool Marcum straight on, weren't I? That never saved 'is skin, did it, na?"

"You admit to murdering him, eh?"

"An' why not, I say? Though it ain't murder that I'd call it. Protectin' my interests is what it was. Damn fool wanted me t' pay 'im money t' keep his silly mouth shut. That was stupid of 'im. But I knows I can't trust the likes o' you t' understand that, mister. You won't leave things be. Not you. If you can't convince the cap'n now, you'll wait till we're home an' blab t' the bailiff. Oh, I know your kind, mister. Fancy yourself better'n others. I know you, all right. I know how t' handle you so's you won't be tellin' no lies on me too." He cackled. "Nor tellin' no truths, which 'ud be worse than the lies, wouldn't they? Ha."

"You're being foolish, Judas. You—"

"It's Watts, damn you. My name is Watts."

"You are a Judas, Watts, and I shall call you that if I please. You rob from your own watchmates. You are a thief and a murderer. And of course you are right. I shall indeed bring you to law. I have your own confession now, for which I thank you. Obviously you can't have known that I never saw you stab Marcum. If I had, man, you would be in chains now. The funny thing is that you would have been safe from me except for coming out here now and trying to creep up on me from behind. Like the coward you really are."

"I'm facin' you now right enough, ain't I?"

"Precisely why I feel safe from you now, Judas."

Watts snarled and lunged forward, his hand sweeping up from his side with the speed of a striking snake.

The knife in his hand sliced toward Ben's stomach in a vicious attempt to disembowel.

Ben skipped backward on the wet, slippery deck. He felt a tug as the hook-billed knife encountered the treated canvas cloth of his oilskin coat. But cloth was all Watts cut.

The force of Watts's own lunge carried his arm past, and Ben stepped in behind it to deliver a hard right fist.

Had it landed as Ben intended, the fight might have

ended there and then, but when he braced himself, Ben's leading foot slipped a little on the deck and the punch flew wide, battering Watts's shoulder but doing no real damage.

And there was no time for a second blow.

Ben had to jump back and spin away as Watts's knife swept through at belt level again in a backhanded slash. Ben could hear Watts grunt with effort. Ben grabbed hold of the rail and used it to regain his balance. He pulled himself back along it, wary of the raging seaman who was so intent upon his death.

This was no rough-and-tumble game. Emmanuel Watts clearly intended to murder the third mate of the *Wanderer,* and no less. There would be no second place finisher in this contest. Nor was there any realistic hope for rescue. The men of the watch were far abaft and had no cause to be peering into the rain-lashed darkness of the deck before them.

Watts lashed out again. Again Ben was able to dodge the ripping blade. But how long could he continue to do so with the uncertain footing and the repeated attacks? Watts could miss and try again over and over and yet over again. Ben could err but once and he would be lost.

Carefully watchful of Watts and his knife, Ben began crabbing sideways, sliding his hand along the rail as a guide so that he could concentrate his attention solely on Watts, thinking if he could reach the forward shrouds—take up a belaying pin—he needed a weapon, anything, and had nothing.

"Ha!" Watts barked, leaping to place himself and his knife between Ben and the heavy pins that could so easily serve as a bludgeon or cudgel.

Ben backed away, avoiding another hacking cut of Watts's knife, and thought about the rigging lines of the main. With only the foremast carrying broad sail on the *Wanderer,* the few belays needed elsewhere were all at the mast trunk tables. To reach them Ben would have to leave the relative security of the railing, where he could find support if he slipped and where Watts's movement was limited, and cross the slick, pitching deck in a rush. But he had to have a weapon, else sooner or later Watts's blade was sure to find flesh.

Ben let go of the railing and rushed forward.

With a grunt of effort and an amazing turn of speed, the wiry little seaman leaped to intercept Ben's course.

"Not that easy, damn you," the murderer snarled.

Watts hacked and slashed, his face contorted with rage and his knife darting and dancing in a blurred frenzy of motion as he stabbed and slashed and thrust like a maddened swordsman even though the knife in his hand had a blade hardly more than four inches in length.

With a groan of despair Ben had to give way and once more retreat toward the railing.

Watts paused for a moment in his mad attack and stood there gasping for breath. "Damn you. Damn you," he muttered.

Ben braced himself. He could sense that Watts intended now to rush him. To batter and cut and to kill.

"Damn you," Watts said again.

Ben waited. He needed to do so for only an instant more.

Then Watts launched himself hard and fast with his knife held low, its hooked blade poised to rip Ben's belly open from belt to sternum.

Ben intended to duck quickly to the side so that Watts's momentum would carry him past, allowing him to make a run for the rack of belaying pins at the mainmast, but Ben's foot slipped on the sea-slick decking. He slipped down to one knee and, with a cry, skidded again and felt himself overbalancing, falling backward even as Watts was on him.

Ben chopped the side of his hand onto Watts's wrist. The knife was jarred free from the man's grip and went flying onto the deck with a clatter.

At the same time, Ben was being bowled over backward by the sheer force of Watts's charge.

Instinctively Ben kicked out, trying to ward off the

assault. His right foot caught Watts in the stomach and was driven back by Watts's weight so that Ben's knee was doubled and shoved hard into his chest.

Ben was still trying to kick Watts off of him. He pushed Watts off even as the momentum of the charge carried Watts past. Watts flew into the air, Ben's kick launching him high while his own charge provided the impetus of the motion.

Ben heard a short, abrupt scream. But no sound of Watts striking the deck.

Quickly Ben twisted and spun, desperately trying to regain his feet and at the same time trying to turn and face the deadly sailor.

He ended on his knees facing the ship's railing. There was no sign of Watts. Only the windblown spray striking Ben in the face and an empty, storm-riven sea beyond the rail. Ben hadn't realized that he had been forced to retreat so far, nor that the railing had been so very near. Watts's own charge must have carried him overboard.

Slowly, suddenly weary, Ben crawled the last foot or two to the rail and pulled himself upright.

Somewhere out in the night a man would be drowning. But Ben could see nothing, hear nothing. There was no point in trying to come about. In weather like this and with visibility like this, such a maneuver would only risk the ship and the lives of the men aboard her without purpose. And even an officer as inexperienced as Ben Cartwright knew better than that.

With his heart heavy—for Marcum, for the other crewmen, perhaps also for a certain loss of innocence, but with no regrets whatsoever concerning Emmanuel Watts— Third Mate Cartwright stumbled aft toward the warmth and the comfort of his bunk. In a very few more hours his watch would take the deck again, and he had to be rested enough to fulfill his duties.

CHAPTER 4

To your good health, Mr. Cartwright."

"Thank you, sir."

The captain raised his pewter tumbler in a toast, and Ben mimicked the motions.

They were seated in the captain's cabin, taking a private dinner there, only the two of them seated at the table where normally Captain Stoddard spread his charts. Ben had no idea why he had been singled out to dine in so familiar a fashion. It was not an expression of the captain's fondness for him. He was certain of that. In the six days since the loss of the two seamen, both incidents duly recorded in the log and attested by way of the third officer's signature, the captain had not once found occasion to speak to Third Mate Cartwright. Until now.

Even more mystifying, really, was that the unusual invitation was made at a time that was in conflict with Ben's watch schedule. First Mate Truesdell himself had relieved Ben from his duties on deck so that he would be free to join the captain in his cabin now.

Stoddard drank deeply of the watered brandy he served. Ben's draught was more sparing. He was unaccustomed to spirits, and this would not be a night to make exceptions, he suspected.

"Dig in, Cartwright. Help yourself." The captain motioned to the bowls that crowded the already small table. The captain's fare was no different from that served in the officers' mess. Fried salt pork, boiled rice covered in lumpy gravy, boiled turnips. The men ate much the same except they received less pork and the gravy prepared for the crew's mess was mostly water with only enough drippings and flour to give it a tinge of brownish coloration and perhaps a hint of flavor. The meals seldom varied, month in and month out. And the *Wanderer* had the reputation of a ship that fed her crew well. Ben could not imagine how the ordinary seamen on one of the poorer ships fared.

"Thank you, sir." That was, he suspected, a response he should adopt as standard throughout the course of this evening. Better yet, he should have the good sense to limit his end of the conversation to that and no more. He helped himself to healthy portions of the meal. The captain was sparing in his selections. But then Captain Stoddard was sparing of most things.

"I misjudged you, Cartwright," the captain said when the near silent meal was close to its logical conclusion.

"Really, sir?"

"Aye." Stoddard nodded in affirmation of that unfortunate fact and mopped his face with a napkin, discarding the cloth afterward on the remains of his meal. Ben took that as a signal and laid his own fork down.

"Go on, please. No need for you to stop eating. I remember the appetites of youth, you know."

"Yes, sir. Thank you, sir." Ben retrieved his fork.

"Yes indeed," Stoddard rambled on, fumbling in his pockets for his pipe and then lighting a bit of straw from the gimbaled bulkhead lamp so he could set the tobacco to burning. "I've learned from you this voyage, Cartwright. I should be grateful to you for that."

"If you say so, sir." Ben kept on with his meal.

Stoddard puffed on his pipe for a while, the smoke from it wreathing his head like a halo and drifting slowly toward the overhead. "You have no intention of asking what it was I learned from you, Cartwright?"

"If you want me to, sir."

"Don't bother. I shall tell you regardless."

"Yes, sir." Ben laid his fork down again. He was no longer much interested in the meal.

"I have learned, sir, not to trust to appearances. Nor even to impressions gained through months at sea. Because you see, Cartwright, I believed you an open, honest, able young officer with little in the way of vice or guile."

"Thank you, sir."

"Oh, don't thank me for that, Cartwright, because that is where I misjudged you so badly. And it is from this error that I take my lesson."

"I . . . don't follow you, sir."

"But you should, Cartwright. Think about it. There I was, believing you to be an innocent, and all the while you were hiding a somewhat more passionate self behind that boyish facade. Should I commend you for the deception, Mr. Cartwright? Forgive me if I do not. I should have been wise enough in the ways of men to recognize the zeal of one who feels impelled to appoint himself as jurist and jury combined. Yes, and executioner too if that need be. And he not the master of his vessel but merely a stripling who has not yet learned his trade. Do you begin to follow me now, sir?"

"I . . . believe I do, sir. But please, if I may explain—"

"Explain? What is there to explain, Cartwright? No need, sir. None. It was I who erred. It was I who believed my orders on the subject in question, which I do not believe we need elaborate upon, would be heeded. And before you speak up, sir, I freely concede that the letter of my command was most stringently adhered to. There is no basis for charges to be levied against you, Mr. Cartwright. You have witnesses in support of your log entry. Did you know that, Mr. Cartwright? It is true. I have made inquiries. What you claim is indeed the literal truth. What I object to, sir, is your failure to bring these new facts to me. But no, rather than grant me my rights as master of this vessel, Mr. Cartwright, you chose to exact your own dire penalties upon an enrolled member of this crew."

"But sir, I—"

"You will kindly do me the courtesy of silence, Mr. Cartwright," Stoddard snapped.

"Yes, sir."

"Thank you." The captain nodded and paused for a moment to suck on his pipe. The tars that had boiled out of the tobacco hissed and bubbled in the bottom of his pipe bowl. Soon enough, too soon for Ben's comfort, he resumed. "As I stated before, sir, I have no basis to charge you in the matter of the said crewman's death. If inquiry is made, which is unlikely in any event, the ruling will stand as a common 'lost at sea.' Which, technically, one would have to admit that it was. That much was observed and attested by three separate witnesses who were not members of your watch."

"Yes, sir." Ben felt cold and curiously hollow. He braced himself upright and motionless in his chair and reminded himself over and over again that he must remain quiet at all costs while the captain had his say. Anything less would be discourteous. And that, he was sure, Captain Stoddard would not tolerate in the slightest measure. But, dang it, if only the captain would *listen. . . .*

"I have no basis to charge you, sir, but I have no fondness for you either."

"Yes, sir. I'm sorry, sir."

"With a fair wind and God's will, Mr. Cartwright, we should arrive at Boston harbor in the forenoon tomorrow."

"Yes, sir."

"I intend to return your papers to you at that time, Mr. Cartwright. I shall give you a reference as to your competence as an officer of the deck, which I have witnessed and which I concede has pleased me. But I intend to offer no comment as to your character, sir. I trust you will find this to be fair and agreeable with all parties."

"As you wish, sir."

"Very well, Mr. Cartwright. May I take it then that we are in agreement?"

"You may, sir."

"And have you finished your dinner, Mr. Cartwright?"

"I have, sir."

"Then please excuse yourself, sir, and present yourself to Mr. Truesdell to resume your watch."

Ben stood at the railing and watched the beehive activity with mixed emotion. There was a lump of sadness weighing heavy in his chest at the thought that he would no longer claim the proud title as a mate aboard the good ship *Wanderer*. There was also a sense of deep shame that weighed and pulled at his normally ebullient spirits now that the Boston quayside was within sight. And that was not at all a common thing for him to feel.

Ben Cartwright loved Boston. More particularly, Ben Cartwright loved—he blushed at the thought but did not turn away from it—certain inducements peculiar to the *Wanderer*'s port of origin.

But on the occasion of this particular homecoming, nothing was as he had expected it to be. In particular he was torn by a conflict in his feelings toward Capt. Abel Morgan Stoddard.

The captain had discharged Ben from this ship for reasons with which Ben could not fully agree. The captain had that power implicit within his authority. Ben had neither question nor quarrel with that. But he did not believe it morally right of the captain to have exercised the power in this particular case, and therefore Ben could not help but feel a certain amount of resentment toward the man.

Yet at the same time Ben could not help but admire Captain Stoddard's abilities as a seaman. Just today, approaching the wharf, the captain displayed a truly masterful command of his ship. Where normally one would expect a vessel the size of the *Wanderer* to heave to in the roadstead and make a final pull to her berth with the towing power of small craft and hard muscle, Captain Stoddard had elected to carry way under sail until they were within a cable's throw of the wharf. Granted that wind and current had been ideal for the maneuver, it was nonetheless an outstanding display of skillful seamanship. Captain Stoddard was a man from whom a young officer could learn much.

There were also, it was true, other matters causing Ben Cartwright discomfort on the subject of Capt. Abel Morgan Stoddard, but this seemed hardly the proper time to be thinking about that. In fact, with his personal circumstances so perilously altered, this was anything but an appropriate moment for him to be weighing such thoughts, he realized. Accordingly, Ben leaned upon the railing and tried to bring to the fore of his thoughts as much joy as possible in this homecoming and to ignore the negative view of things.

He watched as the crewmen swarmed over the rigging and the quay, securing the thick hawsers to the bollards on shore, furling all sail and stopping off the lines as the ship was allowed to come fully to rest for the first time in all the months of the voyage. There was no slacking in the work today, though; no seaman is a sluggard when shore leave in his home port lies at the end of the day's labors.

Ben watched the members of his own watch—that is, his former watch—scamper over the yards and the footropes for this one last time while still he served as their officer. He was proud of his men. He even liked them. Which, had they known it, the other officers would have considered an aberration if not an outright betrayal of caste. Nonetheless, Ben did like these men of his watch. He would miss them.

He stood like that, pensive and uncertain, until the ship lay at rest and the plank was ordered to be brought up from the hold. Then, sadly, he went below to fetch up his seabag and chest. Those things would not be needed aboard the *Wanderer*. Not ever again.

When finally the gangplank was laid and the crew brought into line to be paid off, Ben held himself proudly erect and saluted Captain Stoddard. He would not demean himself by a show of disrespect at this late date. He simply would not.

"By your leave, Captain."

"Very well, Mr. Cartwright. Good day to you, sir." There was a cold nod but not the courtesy of a handshake. Not that Ben had expected one.

He gave Captain Stoddard a final sketchy salute and turned away with the intention of departing the ship this last and final time. He balanced the chest upon his shoulder and picked up the seabag. And then, his heart in his throat, he made his way slowly to the shaky, swaying plank with the intent to leave the *Wanderer* behind him.

Instead he found himself stopped short, frozen into position like a spaniel brought to point.

For there, not two hundred feet distant at the edge of the wharf where a host of Boston's loveliest ladies were gathered to see the ship home, there standing with her pretty face shaded by a pale green parasol, was the girl who owned Ben's heart. Not that she knew she had captured that particular possession. There were no declarations between them. Ben Cartwright was much too shy in her presence for there ever to have been the slightest intimation of his feelings for her. But the fact remained. Elizabeth stood there, certainly in his mind the brightest jewel among all those who were gathered, and watched beside all the rest of the wives and the daughters and the simply curious.

Remorse and shame suffused Ben. His discharge from the *Wanderer* was disgrace enough, but to have Elizabeth witness it now. And further to know she would be hearing all the gossip that was sure to be bandied through the par-

lors and the drawing rooms after this miserable day was
done . . .

He could not bear the thought of facing her. Not just
now. Not, at least, until there had been time for her to hear
of his shame from other sources. Then she would have the
opportunity to preserve her own sensitivities by turning
her back upon him if she wished, which she most assur-
edly would choose to do. How could she do otherwise?

A hard and bitter lump formed in the back of Ben's
throat at that thought.

Yet how could things be otherwise?

Elizabeth would shun him in future. She would be
bound to. After all, how could she allow herself to be seen
in company with the young man who was discharged from
the *Wanderer* by Captain Stoddard? Discharged, that is, by
her own adored and adoring father, Captain Stoddard? Ben
could not expect anything else from his now-lost love
Elizabeth Stoddard.

A new wave of grief swept through him. This realiza-
tion that Elizabeth was denied to him was far, far worse
than the loss of his berth could ever be.

And until this moment his loss of the right to ever
court Elizabeth Stoddard was something he had not permitted himself to face. Now there was no longer time to
pretend or to deny.

Now Elizabeth stood right over there, among all the
other fine ladies, and if he were to march ashore now, she
would see him, might even feel impelled to speak to this
least of her father's officers. For so she would think him
to be until the truth of his shame was related to her. That
was a humiliation Ben was sure he was not strong enough
to endure. And so, as close to weeping as he had been in
a very long time, he set his things down beside the ship's
rail, turned and made his way slowly below once more.
There was nothing there for him to do. But he could wait.
He could allow the ship to empty and the happy throngs of
welcoming spectators to dissipate. Then, and only then,

would he permit himself to go ashore in his beloved Boston.

And after that?

The future would simply have to take care of itself.

Almost any future would be acceptable, he supposed. Now that he knew Elizabeth could be no part of his life, there was no spice or flavor to living anyway, so one measure would be as good as any other.

Probably, he thought, his best bet would be to simply wait until the crowds left the vicinity of the *Wanderer* and then seek out the first berth that might come available to him, no matter where that ship might sail or in what capacity he might be allowed to serve her.

Better that, he thought, than to find himself ashore and have to parade in disgrace before Elizabeth and her father day after day.

Better anything than that, he thought sadly.

And so he sat upon the bunk that no longer was his and waited in anguished silence for the sounds and movement above to fade away.

CHAPTER 5

"Señor?"

"Mmm?"

"You would like another rum, señor?"

Ben shook his head. "I'm fine, thanks."

"A cigar, then," the fat little man persisted.

"No thanks."

"My daughter, perhaps?"

Ben scowled so hard the proprietor of the nameless little cantina gave up and turned away. Thank goodness. For a moment there . . .

Ben shuddered and used a kerchief to mop away some of the sweat that was inescapable in this hot and humid climate. His forehead was greasy with sweat that collected and ran, tickling and irritating, across his cheeks and down his neck and into his shirt. It was the humidity that made it so bad. Even nightfall brought scant relief from the discomfort of it. Nightfall did no good. Nor did distraction.

Ben sighed and glanced around the crowded, smoky, boisterous cantina. As far as he could determine, he was

44

the only one in the place who was not having—or striving to have—the happiest night of his life.

The *Pandora*'s entire crew was here or had been. Along with men from half a dozen other ships and probably some local fishermen too.

He was a hell of a distance from Boston now, Ben reflected as he took up his mug of watered rum and sipped from it. How many ports had there been since last he saw Boston? He couldn't come close to remembering.

Lord, he would be lucky if he could remember the names of the ports they'd made on this journey alone.

New Orleans to Key West, Key West to Santiago de Cuba, Santiago de Cuba to Kingston, Kingston to Cartagena, Cartagena to . . . to—it took him a moment to call the next one to mind—right, Cartagena to Colon, Colon to Campeche, and now Campeche to Tampico. And from Tampico . . . where? New Orleans again? Back to Cartagena? They wouldn't know that until the captain found a cargo. Not that it mattered.

Ben's scowl deepened. Damn little mattered. Now that was the truth of things.

As if sensing the young officer's mood, the cantina man was back. "A little more, yes? On the house, yes?" Without waiting for the Yankee to respond, the little man tipped more of the grog into Ben's mug and smiled. "You have seen my daughter, señor?"

Ben turned quickly away. Too quickly, perhaps. He did not want to betray to this insulting fellow the fact that, despite himself, he was tempted.

The girl—Ben knew better than to believe for a moment that she was kin to the degenerate man who wished to sell her services—was young and slim and pretty. And from a certain angle, when the light was just so and her hair was drawn back away from her throat, she had a heart-stopping resemblance to Elizabeth Stoddard.

Elizabeth. Good Lord, Elizabeth! He hadn't thought of her in . . . Ben smiled ruefully into the depths of his mug. Truth? All right. The truth was that he hadn't thought about Elizabeth in all of six hours. Or was it closer to four? At least two, though. He was sure he hadn't thought of her in the last two hours. Maybe.

He sighed. Wasn't he supposed to be over Elizabeth by now? Surely he should be. It was a year and more since he'd fled Boston in the night that last time, drummed off—not literally, but close enough to it so that the difference hardly mattered—drummed off the old *Wanderer* and signed onto the *Hartisbeake* as an able seaman in the middle of the night like that.

That had gotten him as far as New Bern. And then there'd been that wallowing, miserable coastal lighter on to Charleston and another almost as bad to Savannah and finally a decent berth aboard the *Preston L.* The *Preston L.* had been a fine little ship, engaging in trade between the Carolinas and the Bahamas and on down through the Windwards as far as Martinique. A fine ship and a fine berth, the captain impressed enough to name Ben Cartwright as his second mate after so few months aboard, and Ben would have stayed with her except the captain lost her—to a wager, not to the sea—and the new owner wanted no part of the old crew with their baggage of old loyalties. And since that there'd been other ships, other ventures, and now the *Pandora* and Captain Dawson, and why in *hell* did he see Elizabeth Stoddard every time he looked in the direction of that cheap little Tampico bawd . . . ?

If there was any one thing Ben Cartwright learned in this past year, it was that love does not have to be returned by its recipient in order for its flame to burn hot and true.

Because the sad truth was that even after all this time, he remained as much—if as hopelessly—in love with Elizabeth Stoddard as he'd been the last time he saw her, standing on that Boston quay and awaiting her father's return with the dear old *Wanderer*.

Why, for all he knew, after all this time, Elizabeth might by now have married already. She was pretty enough, God knew. Elizabeth was surely the toast of Boston now. By now she could even have a child. Very well could have. Dear Lord, what a thought that was.

If only . . .

No, dang it, he was *not* going to fall into that most useless of all emotional traps. "If" is an empty word. He would not apply it. He absolutely would not.

He took another swallow of his rum and pretended to not even see the girl who looked like Elizabeth. Did she truly appear so much like his beloved, or was that only his own fervid imagination at work? Elizabeth had hair dark and glossy as a raven's wing just as this girl did. But Elizabeth's dear flesh was pale, not dusky and foreign. Elizabeth Stoddard was true beauty, not some pathetic substitute for loveliness. Ah, but Elizabeth was distant. This girl was here. And this girl was smiling at him.

"Señor? Would you not wish—"

"No!" Ben barked. He pushed his mug away, sloshing rum onto the bar, and turned to stalk out through the curtain of fly beads that hung at the door.

Captain Dawson, he saw, was just then leaving the cantina too, was tacking into rum-driven headwinds with the assistance of a dark and buxom lass whose face was pitted with the scars of some long gone pox, but who had a sturdy form and a willing spirit. Or so, at least, the captain seemed to think as he allowed her to help him along the rutted and uneven street. The captain's legs were rubbery, and it was the woman who seemed to be doing the navigating for the both of them.

Ben chuckled, unwilling himself to participate in such, but just as unwilling to judge the conduct of others on the subject. The captain, bless him, had little enough opportunity to unwind. When they were at sea, even a first officer, which Mr. Cartwright was proud to be under Capt. Emil Dawson, could unbend himself in conversation with his captain. But a captain had no one upon whom he could lean. Not even his first mate. So the captain was entitled to whatever diversions he felt appropriate, Ben believed. Even a diversion as basically homely as this one, who was no temptation in Ben's view, certainly not when compared with— Quit that, he chided himself. Why—

He blinked. Stopped. The captain and the bawd had been walking ahead of him not twenty paces distant. Now the street—so narrow it was little better than an alley— was empty save for a scrawny dog. The mongrel, though, was peering into a shadowed recess that Ben took to be a doorway. Ben increased his pace. The dog tucked its tail and slunk nervously away at his approach.

The depression Ben had thought a doorway proved to be an alley barely wide enough to admit his broad shoulders.

Surely the woman hadn't taken Captain Dawson in there.

Had she?

Ben hesitated, trying to see inside the alley where there was no light.

Then his heartbeat quickened as he heard a series of muted thumps and a groaning whimper of pain.

There was a woman's voice and a sharp and snippish response by a man. But the man's words were Spanish, and to his own certain knowledge, Captain Dawson knew even less of the Spanish tongue than he did.

Ben felt a curious sense of joy that now, at last, he seemed to have something against which he could vent his frustrations.

He balled his hands into fists as hard as keel oak and without hesitation plunged forward into the darkness of the alley.

The alley opened into a tiny, trash-strewn area that might once have been intended to serve as a courtyard. Or as easily could have been the accident caused by the irregular shapes and sizes of the buildings nearby. However it came to exist, the small patch of level ground was a perfect accommodation for the cutpurses and sneak thieves who inhabited the night in this and all other sea ports.

Ben burst out of the alley to find three people stand-

ing over Captain Dawson's supine, and quite limp, form.
One, the woman, Ben recognized. The others were familiar as to type, even if he had never seen these individuals
before.

The others were men. But in his mind they were little
better than vermin. Quick, cowardly skulkers who prowled
by night and hid by day, too lazy and inept to earn an honest living or even much of a dishonest one. With the help
of a woman to lure victims into their trap, they preyed
upon drunks and fools. The only thing that amazed Ben
here was that Captain Dawson had been so unwary as to
be caught in their snare.

When Ben came upon them, the nearer of the two
men was just then bending down to rifle the captain's
pockets. There was light enough for him to see that much
because here beyond the alley there was a spill of yellow
lamplight from windows in the surrounding structures.

Without giving thought to his own safety, Ben allowed the momentum of his rush to carry him forward. He
lashed out with his foot to kick the thief's hand away from
Captain Dawson's lapels.

Taken by surprise, the thief grunted and ducked away.

"That's right, damn you, keep going."

Both men looked quite willing to accept that advice,
but an angry and probably demeaning snarl out of the
woman's mouth stopped them. Ben wished he could understand what was being said. As it was, he had no idea
if the men could speak English or not, although the
woman was sure to.

"Break this up and leave be now," he said calmly,
"lest somebody end up hurt here."

The woman said something short and sharp to the
men. Ben had the impression, possibly imaginative, that
her translation was a distortion of his words, that she was
deliberately forcing a confrontation where none need happen.

But then, why not? If these two stood and fought, it
was they who would feel the pain of defeat should they

lose, but the woman who would reap profits from two Yankees at once if the thieves should prevail.

"Just back off," Ben urged. "Just, uh, vamoose, okay?" He gestured as if to shoo them away.

The woman's voice, derisive and sarcastic, intruded once more.

"Leave us alone and I won't have to hurt you," Ben told them. The English words had no more effect than he might have expected.

The woman spoke again, and the men laughed and looked at each other, obviously taking courage from the fact that there were two of them but only one Yankee. One said something to the other, and Ben could see a change in their eyes as something dark and deadly simmered there. The two men separated and began moving to flank him so that when he turned to defend himself from one, he would expose his back to the other.

Both now were reaching beneath their shirts, their hands coming back into sight with slim, long-bladed knives.

Ben Cartwright looked at them almost sadly and grunted. Did these silly Tampico sneak thieves think he would tremble and run from so slight a threat as two inept cutpurses with skinny knives? That seemed awfully silly of them. And leave his captain in the bargain? That was sillier still.

Ben felt once again a joyous strength as his senses quickened to danger.

In spite of himself, his lips drew back in a devilish grin, and rather than waiting for the two men to trap him between them, he attacked them while they were still fairly close together.

He dashed forward and launched a massive right fist into the face of one man. In almost the same instant he backhanded the second man with his balled left fist. The first one's nose buckled flat under the force of Ben's blow. The second was knocked backward two steps to collide with the shrieking, yammering woman.

Ben laughed and plunged forward again, the sound of his own wildly racing blood loud in his ears.

The Latino, trapped with his feet tangled in the bawd's skirts, had no choice but to stand and fight. He cut circles in the air with the blade of his knife, but Ben could see that his heart was not really in this. Ben helped him out of his predicament by plucking the knife out of the fellow's fingers and tattooing him with a pair of quick blows to the midsection that drove the wind from him and left him bent over and gasping.

By then the first man had recovered enough to take a stab—literally—at Ben's back.

Ben heard the shuffle of the fellow's feet behind him and turned in time to parry a viciously hard underhanded sweep of the man's knife. Ben chopped at the incoming knife hand and caught the man on the wrist hard enough to make him howl with pain and to dislodge his grip on the knife, which clattered to the ground somewhere in the shadows of the little courtyard.

"Naughty, naughty," Ben chided, and punched the man in the face again. If the fellow's nose hadn't been broken the first time Ben hit him, it certainly was now. The thief staggered backward.

The woman was still screaming, but neither man seemed to be paying her much mind at this point. Both males were considerably the worse for wear already.

"Hush!" Ben told the bawd.

She paused long enough to give him a glare, then once more raised her voice in a prolonged cry.

"C'mon, Ben, we'd best be getting out o' here."

"Cap'n?"

Captain Dawson was looking somewhat the worse for wear too. But he was conscious again and was on his feet. Unsteady, perhaps, but upright and able to navigate. More or less.

"C'mon, Ben, 'fore she brings the guardia down on us. You know whose story they'd believe if they got into this." Dawson took Ben by the coat sleeve and tugged him in the direction of the alley.

One of the thieves, perhaps sensing a last second opportunity for victory or perhaps only wanting a chance to get a lick in against this tall young Yankee, slipped forward while Ben was paying attention to his captain. The Latino jumped at Ben's back and began digging punches into Ben's kidneys just as hard and fast as he was able. Which, in the event, proved to be not nearly hard or fast enough for success.

Ben stepped backward into the assault and jabbed hard with the sharp point of his elbow. The bony protrusion landed flush on the fellow's breastbone with all of Ben's weight and muscle strength driving behind it. There was a loud pop as cartilage, and possibly bone as well, gave way, and a rasping gasp as all traces of breath were driven out of the man. The man, suddenly quite pale, collapsed onto the ground and began to writhe in pain.

"How about you?" Ben asked the one Latino who was still capable of combat, even if he was bleeding and somewhat battered already. "You want any more?"

The thief probably spoke not a word of English, but that did not prevent him from comprehending the tone of Ben's offer. He gave Ben and Captain Dawson a wan smile and a shrug. *"No mas, eh? No mas."*

"Yeah, if that means what I think it does. Right."

Ben looked at the woman, who was alternating between bloodcurdling screams and viciously angry glares, but Dawson tugged at him again.

"Leave her be, Ben. No point in starting something you can't finish."

"If you say so. Are you all right, Cap'n?"

Dawson chuckled. "Better'n I had any right t' be, thanks to you. C'mon now, quick, before the guardia gets here."

It was the captain who led the way back through the alley and off toward the anchorage where the *Pandora* lay at a mooring.

*   *   *

For a few pennies a Mexican with a leaky dory rowed them out to the *Pandora,* and Ben helped the captain aboard.

Dawson's powers of recuperation were little short of amazing. But Ben nonetheless felt it was better to give more of a hand than might be strictly necessary than to risk losing the ship's captain overboard. Especially since, like most seamen, Dawson could not swim a stroke.

"Here you are, sir. Mind the rail there. That's right, Cap'n. Watch you don't bump your head, sir." Ben made sure the captain had his legs beneath him and seemed in control of his faculties before he released his grip on the older man's arm. He leaned over the rail to wave the oarsman away from the side of the ship, but the dory was already a good dozen strokes distant from *Pandora*'s side and was pulling strong for shore. Ben turned back to the captain. "Good night, sir."

"In a hurry are you, Ben?"

"No, sir."

"Join me for a brandy in my cabin, then. It'll clear the fog o' this Mexican rum."

"Are you sure . . . I mean to say, Cap'n—"

Dawson smiled. "I'm all right, Ben. Really. Didn't have all that much, y'know. I think the woman slipped a powder into my noggin. But I'm all right now. Let me pour you that drink as a way o' thankin' you."

"I'd be honored, sir."

Dawson led the way to the captain's cabin, which was little larger than a landlubber's pantry, but which by seaborne standards was luxurious indeed. There was room enough for a bunk, a chest, and a chart table. Mostly there was privacy, that most rare and most valuable of all commodities when at sea, especially on a ship as small as *Pandora,* which was only a topsail schooner and no behemoth of the seas. The captain sat on his bunk and motioned his guest onto a stool at the chart table.

"The brandy's in that locker, Ben. Would you hand it

down, please, and a pair o' the tumblers, the little ones? No, the door to your left. That's it, thank you."

"So many books," Ben commented when he peered into the locker. "I wouldn't think you could find the time for reading." He found the flask of brandy and selected two of the small pewter glasses from the crowded wall locker as directed.

"Oh," Dawson was saying, "there's always time for a good book, just as for an old friend. Do you read, Ben?"

"Yes, sir. That is to say, I enjoy it, sir. I haven't had much of a chance to, um . . ."

Dawson smiled. "You don't have to explain. I understand how it is with a young man of your age and vitality. Reading is for those of us too old t' do, eh?"

"That isn't at all what I intended to imply, sir, and if I've given offense, why—"

"Oh, calm down, Ben. You haven't given any offense. Nor have I intended any of you."

"None taken, sir."

Dawson handed Ben a glass of the brandy, which proved to be raw and biting but at the moment welcome in spite of that. Ben was feeling awkward and shy and was grateful for something to occupy his hands and his thoughts.

"I must say, Ben," the captain was rambling on over his brandy, "that this evening's little adventure in the alley was the first I've seen to support your reputation. And at that you let the dastards off without maiming them. Good for you. I must say I like a man that doesn't lash out more'n he must. But you're all right, Ben. You hide your ferocity behind a velvet mask."

"Sir?"

"Oh, you needn't be so modest with me, Ben. I knew all about you before I ever signed you on to the *Pandora*. Liked what I heard too."

"Whatever could you have heard, sir? If you don't mind me asking."

"Don't mind at all. But surely . . . the nickname, o'

course. That's what gives everyone the impression that you must be a wild man."

"Nickname, sir?"

"Oh, you know."

"I assure you, sir, that I do not. What nickname are you talking about?"

Dawson scowled and rubbed at the side of his neck. "Damned if I can recall the Spaniard lingo for it. Means, I dunno, something like the Devil from Boston or Boston Terror. Something like that. You can't tell me you never heard 'bout that. Everyone else most certainly has."

"No, sir, I swear to you I never have, not before this moment."

"Oh my, yes. Haven't you noticed how docile the crew is with you? Huh. Last first officer aboard *Pandora* got himself whipped one too many times. That's why 'e signed off. Wasn't up to the job. It takes a real man t' handle these lads. Which is why I was pleased t' sign you an' why they been so easy t' get along with, see. Your reputation, Ben. We all been hearing stories about you for the better part of a year now. Lots of 'em. Let's see now. There was one—let me think—something about conducting a raid on some garrison in Nicaragua ...?" The captain paused and lifted an eyebrow.

Not that he was asking. Exactly.

Ben blushed. "That, uh, really wasn't much to speak about, sir. Not really."

"No?"

"No, sir. It was just ... you don't really want to hear all this nonsense, do you?"

Dawson refilled Ben's glass. "I have to admit t' being a mite curious. An' now that we're on the subject—"

"It really wasn't anything, sir. The commandant of the garrison there put some of our boys into his brig. Quite unjustly, really. Put them in under false charges and wanted us to ransom them out again. Or sit at anchor with the port charges piling up and too shorthanded to leave."

"I know that game, believe me," Dawson put in.

"Yes, sir. But it really wasn't anything special. I got the lads out. And we, um, sailed. And that's about it. Sir."

Dawson smiled. "Getting them out, 'least the way I heard it, involved blowing up an entire shore battery."

"It was just the magazine, sir. So they wouldn't have powder to shoot at us when we sailed under the guns, you see. I mean, we needed a diversion anyway, and it just seemed efficient to, well . . . no one was hurt, Cap'n. And there really wasn't all that much to it."

Dawson laughed. "And something about a dispute with customs officers on the Rio Bravo?" he asked.

"Oh, that. It wasn't—"

"I know. There really wasn't all that much to it."

"No, sir. There really wasn't."

"And there was something said about you serving as a mercenary down south somewhere?"

"That whole thing was blown way out of proportion, sir. There really wasn't—"

"All that much to it," Dawson finished for him.

"Well, uh, no sir, there wasn't."

The captain of the *Pandora* threw his head back and roared. "No wonder I like you so much, Ben. You have a reputation that's spread through all the southern seas, and yet you don't seem to so much as know it."

"But really, sir—"

"I know." Dawson grinned. "You don't have to say it again. But still and all, sir, my original point was well taken. A young and vital fellow like you hasn't time for sedentary pursuits like poring over musty books."

"I really did mean that, sir. About liking books. I must say that I envy you your library here."

"If you mean that, Ben, we must turn this into a library indeed, and you must borrow from it."

"You wouldn't mind if I did that, sir?"

Dawson smiled. "Oh, I think I'd be inclined to trust you with them."

"That's very kind of you, sir."

"Huh. Small recompense for saving me a lost purse

tonight. Or worse. Never know what fellows like that will do once they have you. They might've sliced my gizzard open just so they could admire the pretty colors. No, I'd say that the loan of a book or two would be small pay indeed for so large a favor. Feel free, son, to enjoy anything you can find in that locker. Except, ahem, for the brandy."

"Thank you, sir."

"My pleasure, believe me."

Ben set his drink down on the chart table and admired the selection of titles in the captain's locker. There must have been, he thought, two dozen books or more. One struck his fancy, and he took it down.

The title, he thought, certainly seemed appropriate enough to his circumstances. It was that which captured his interest.

"Are you familiar with Milton, Ben?"

"No, sir, I can't say that I am."

"Wonderful stuff there. If you haven't already read it, then I envy you the pleasure of this first reading. No, it's all right. Take it. Put it in your pocket this instant before you let it slip your mind."

"Thank you, sir."

"Before you go off to your own quarters and the pleasures of Milton, though, Ben, I should enjoy hearing some more of your adventures so far from home. And anything else you might care to tell me 'bout yourself."

"Yes, sir. Not that there's all that much to tell, really."

"So you insist, Ben. Although the tales in the grog shops of half a hundred ports give the lie to that modesty, I tell you. Now put Milton into your pocket, sir, and tell me the truth behind a few more of these tales of the Devil from Boston."

Ben shrugged and slipped the clothbound volume into the side pocket of his coat as he was bidden. Captain Dawson once again tipped the brandy flask over their glasses, and Ben began shyly responding to his captain's curiosity.

Peeking out from beneath the flap of the young offi-

cer's pocket was a line of block lettering in fading gilt, the
name of the book that to Ben seemed so appropriate to the
peculiar state of hopeless, helpless near-ennui that had
overcome him since last he saw Boston:
Paradise Lost.

Ben tapped on the door frame—the door itself was already open to facilitate a flow of air through the small
cabin—and waited for Captain Dawson to motion him in.

The captain smiled when he saw what the youthful
first officer was holding in his hand. "Finished it, have
you?"

"Aye, sir, and I want to thank you."

"Wonderful stuff, isn't it?"

"Yes, sir. I would have to say that it is."

"You look . . . awfully solemn, Ben. Are you all
right?"

"Fine, sir, thank you. It's just . . ."

"It's all right, Ben. You can speak freely with me if
you like, whatever you have to say."

"It's just . . . Milton's work is awfully powerful,
Cap'n. Thought provoking."

"I agree that it is."

"It's set me to thinking, sir. Stirred me up something
terrible."

"Milton can do that, yes."

"I mean, there is beauty in there, sir. And power. But
an awful lot to think about too. About humanity, I mean.
About right and wrong, good and evil. Decency and value
and . . . oh, I don't know exactly what it is that I'm trying
to say, sir. Just that this book has got me all stirred up in
my mind. It's set me to thinking about, well, about what
happens if a man should see his paradise and then turn
right around and let himself lose it without ever even trying to set things right."

"Somehow, Ben, I don't think we're talking 'bout a
book here."

"No, sir, I suppose we aren't."

"Do you want to tell me what it is that's on your mind, son?"

"I'd rather not, Cap'n. No offense."

Dawson grunted and reached for a pipe. He took his time filling and tamping it, then lit a taper from the whale oil lamp hanging in gimbals on the wall over his chart table. He lighted his pipe and extinguished the taper flame with a puff of breath. For several moments he sucked on the stem of the pipe, until his head was wreathed in pale smoke. The tobacco smelled almighty good in the stagnant air belowdecks. "A man is entitled to the privacy of his thoughts, Ben. But you act like there's something you're wantin' to say."

"Aye, sir. I expect that I am."

"Something to do with trying to find your own private paradise, son?"

"You could say that. Yes, sir."

"You're leaving the *Pandora*." Captain Dawson was wise enough to the ways of men that he didn't bother making a question of the words. They were more appropriate as a statement.

"Yes, sir."

"You're a good officer, Ben. Someday you'll make a master. I can think of nothing finer that could be said about any man."

"You'll not try and hold me, sir?"

"Could I? No, don't answer that. I know that I could. If I plead need, you will stay on. But your heart wouldn't be in it, lad. So no, I'll not try an' bind you to a berth you no longer want. *Pandora* got along before you. An' for that matter, before me as well. She'll get along without you now, an' without me when that time comes, for ships have lives o' their own. So no, *Pandora* an' me will wish you Godspeed an' goodwill, son, an' hope you find this paradise o' yours."

"Thank you, sir. Thank you very much."

"You'll leave us in N'Orleans, Ben?"

"Aye, sir. If that's all right with you."

"All right? No, I cannot say that it is all right. But you have my permission and my best wishes. That's the best I can do for you, my young Devil from Boston."

"Thank you, Cap'n, it's been . . . an honor, sir, sailing under your command."

Dawson waved the compliment away. But he looked pleased by it nonetheless.

"Oh, yes. Before I forget." Ben extended the volume of Milton's epic work to the man who had introduced him to it, and who thus so powerfully affected Ben's entire life and outlook for possibly the remainder of his days.

Dawson looked at the squat and diminutive but thick little book with true fondness but also with a shake of his head. "No, Ben, I'd like you t' keep that. It's plain it means much t' you. Take it with my blessings, son, an' think o' me now an' then when you turn back to its pages."

"I couldn't—"

"Bah! 'Course you can. Now put it back in your pocket. Then go above an' see to the set o' the sails. The quicker you see N'Orleans—an' then that cold an' dreary Boston o' yours, if my guess is a'right—the better 'twill be for you."

"Thank you, sir. Thank you *very* much." When Ben turned away from the captain's cabin, he felt so light and free he could have floated up the ladder.

For good or for ill, he realized now, demons must be faced before ever they might be overcome.

And Ben Cartwright's demons, as well as his hopes, were all to be found in far distant Boston.

CHAPTER 6

Homecoming. That was supposed to be a special thing, gay and joyous and uplifting. This homecoming was . . . gray. Not scandalous, exactly, but hardly cause for excitement or rejoicing. Mundane, he supposed, would be the most charitable way to put it.

Ben stood in the waist of the coastal lugger *Manhasset,* not the proud and distinguished ship's officer he would have hoped on this arrival, but a mere passenger. And on a coaster at that. He watched with mixed emotion as the little *Manhasset* picked her way daintily through a squadron of tubby fishing boats and into the familiar waters of Boston harbor.

He was pleased to be home again after so very, very long. His heart lifted to the so-familiar scenes and scents of this port that still held his loyalties. And his loves.

But he was trepidatious too, because soon he would have to face Elizabeth and expose himself to her scorn.

He had sailed thousands of miles to reach Boston today. From Tampico through New Orleans and Cedar Key and Key West and Fernandina and New York and finally home now. He had come all that way both as officer and

61

hand, finally as passenger ... and he was so unsure and fearful now that he was tempted to turn and take ship south once more without ever seeing Elizabeth or speaking to her.

Would she despise him? Hate him? Vilify him? Any or all of those might be possible. For, after all, her own father had seen fit to discharge his former third officer and send him away in disgrace. Could Elizabeth possibly feel any different than her father?

And yet ... And yet Ben could not face the idea of leaving now without at least ... He hadn't come these thousands of miles, dang it, just to turn and run again now that Boston was in sight.

Remember the lessons gleaned from *Paradise Lost,* he reminded himself, as he had, in fact, been doing almost constantly through the two and a half months it had taken him to reach Boston from Tampico. Remember those lessons and the resolution he had made based upon them, he told himself. That was all he needed to do. Just make sure he didn't throw his last chance for happiness away without at least trying to ...

But what if Elizabeth scorned him? What if she sneered at him? What if she ...?

The truth, of course, was that it wouldn't matter if she did *all* those things. Because if she did scorn and sneer and vilify him all at the same time, why, in truth he would be no worse off then than he already was at this very moment.

And his situation of the moment—bereft of any hope that Elizabeth Stoddard might someday find him acceptable—was unutterably, inexpressibly intolerable.

And that, sadly, was the truth of the matter.

He was caught. Trapped. With scant hope that Elizabeth could ever care about a man whom her father mistrusted.

And yet, he knew, scant hope is preferable to none. And so he must face down his fears and make this attempt to see Elizabeth. Even to speak with her.

But not ... *quite* yet.

Not today. Today there was yet time to ponder and fret and gird himself for the tasks ahead.

And so he watched the little *Manhasset* wear closer to the quay where once the *Wanderer* was tied, the quay where ... It occurred to him to wonder if his old ship, Captain Stoddard's proud ship, might be in port at this moment, but she was not; Ben looked 'round the roadstead and found no sign of *Wanderer*'s distinctive trimasted barkentine rig. This quay that reminded him now both of shame and of promise.

There was no sign of *Wanderer,* but again today, as there had been before, there was a gathering of ladies and children and even some merchants and midday malingerers come to watch the arrival of a ship in from the sea, the event a matter of consequence even if it was only the *Manhasset* and even if she was only making port after a voyage that was barely longer than overnight.

Today though, as before, Ben stood among the other passengers and observed the townspeople on shore who were gathered there to observe him and all these others debark.

At least, he thought, none of these shoreside layabouts were apt to remember Ben Cartwright nor single him out from the other passengers.

Once the coaster was warped safe to the quay and her cables secured, the plank was set and the other passengers began to debark, shuffling forward slowly like so many sheep mounting a chute. Ben waited patiently until the others were clear of the deck, then hoisted his sea chest and balanced it atop the point of his shoulder. He took a fresh grip on the canvas sling of his seabag and made his way easily down the swaying, bobbing plank to shore. Without pause he began walking quickly toward the house where he customarily took a room when here in his home port.

"Benjamin."

He turned so abruptly that he nearly lost his balance. "Elizabe—I mean, Miss Stodd—" His mouth was dry and his heart was pounding. She stood among the crowd of spectators not a dozen feet distant from him, her lovely, dimpled face framed within the protection of a delicate pink parasol. He hadn't suspected her presence before, hadn't been looking for her, but now, without warning . . .

Ben found himself frozen into immobility by the shock of this most unexpected encounter. He had come all this way for the sole purpose of seeing her. But he wasn't prepared to see her *today*. He needed time to prepare, to adjust, to plan out what he might say or do. But . . . this? He just wasn't *ready*.

Elizabeth was in no such state of bewilderment. She left the company of the proper ladies of Boston who surrounded her and rushed on ahead. Which she should not have done. It was not seemly for her to do that. Not at all. But she did not hesitate so much as a moment. She dashed quite boldly forward and planted herself directly before a startled and frowning Ben Cartwright.

"Benjamin. Aren't you glad to see me, Benjamin?" she insisted.

"I . . . yes. Of course." He cleared his throat loudly and glanced beyond Elizabeth—beautiful, lovely, exquisite Elizabeth—to the staring eyes of all the important ladies of the town. They appeared quite as surprised as he himself felt at this moment, Ben thought. The tongues would be wagging tonight, he was sure. As for himself, his own reputation, he did not truly care. But as for Elizabeth . . . "I . . . didn't expect to see you here."

"Nor did I expect you, silly. Imagine my surprise after all this time. Why, the last time you were home, Benjamin, you didn't speak to me at all. I resolved then and there not to let that happen again. If you ever came home again." She stood square in front of him and distressingly near. Twirling her parasol. For all the nervousness she displayed, they might as well have been at a church social.

Ben had no idea what he should or could say. His tongue was as thoroughly paralyzed as the rest of him. He stood mute and oafish and felt, inexplicably, like a toddler caught with his hand in a cookie jar.

"I was beginning to think you would stay in those warm seas forever, Benjamin. Not that I would have blamed you. I am told the ladies there are very beautiful. And they must have swooned dead away at the appearance of the Devil from Boston." There was a sparkle in her eye now and a smile on her pretty lips. Yet there was some slight undertone in her voice that Ben could not quite fathom.

"I never—that is to say—"

"No need for you to deny it, Benjamin. Your reputation precedes you, sir. The Devil from Boston, indeed."

Ben felt his cheeks commence to burn, and he shuffled uncomfortably from one foot to another. He might have wrung his hands except that he was still holding onto his chest and seabag. "It wasn't really—I mean—"

"Don't try to deny it. We've heard stories about that dashing young man from Boston. Just imagine my surprise to learn he was the same Benjamin we've known all these years. Can you imagine that, Benjamin? Can you?"

He shook his head. That seemed what she wanted of him, and so he complied.

"Of course you cannot, silly. But here I was, listening to all these tales about the gallant and handsome ship's officer in those faraway seas. And then we come to find that he is our very own Benjamin. Footloose and gay. And those dark-eyed women. Are they truly so beautiful, Benjamin? Are they? Did you leave your heart with one of them? With many, perhaps?"

Ben hadn't much experience in treating with women. But he would have had to be a complete fool to not recognize that there was no good response that could be made to a question like that one. He at least had sense enough to maintain his silence for the time being.

Benjamin. It occurred to him that she was calling him Benjamin. Not Mr. Cartwright, as would have been appropriate, but Benjamin. Never before had she spoken to him so familiarly.

In truth it had been a rare enough occasion in the past when Elizabeth Stoddard was permitted to speak to Ben Cartwright. For her to use his given name now was unthinkable. Yet she was doing it.

For one instant Ben had the fleeting thought that Elizabeth Stoddard might return the depth of feeling that rushed through him whenever he thought of her.

But that would be impossible, of course. It was crude of him even to think such a thing. Delicate, highborn ladies had no such thoughts or feelings. He knew that. Everyone knew that.

"I didn't—that is to say—" he said, forgetting the wisdom of silence in the face of Elizabeth's unrelenting inspection of him from such close quarters. His cheeks burned all the hotter and he knew they must surely be bright and red as beacons.

"Are you sure you are all right, Benjamin? You didn't come down with malaria in the southern climate, did you?"

"No, I'm fine."

"Did you know that I missed you, Benjamin? Do you care?"

"Oh, my. You can't—I mean to say—" This was too much. Too sudden. Ben felt hollow and slightly unreal. Elizabeth Stoddard missed him? Impossible. For practically as long as he could remember, he had been hopelessly, distantly in love with this bright and beautiful maiden. But he hadn't the slightest thought that she might return any of his feelings. Why, it would be miracle enough just to think that she remembered who he was. And now this?

"You are too shy, Benjamin," she declared. "You always have been. At least you were until you became the Devil from Boston. Did you know that?"

Mutely he shook his head.

"Well that is a truth, sir. And looking at you now, I do not believe you've greatly changed. You are much too shy. And you don't think highly enough of yourself. You must stop that, Benjamin, truly you must. You must learn to trust in yourself and to take initiatives. Even when that means going against the grain of convention."

"Yes, um, I'm sure you are quite right, Miss Stoddard."

"See there, Benjamin? That is exactly the sort of thing I mean. You are addressing me correctly, yet I've made it quite clear, sir, that what I want from you is something much more familiar than that."

"But—"

"Oh, Benjamin." Her eyes were huge, even pleading. "There is so much you don't understand. So much I want to teach you. If you will only allow it."

"I would allow you anything, Elizabeth," he said softly. There was no more sincerity possible within him than was expressed in that simple and wholly honest statement of fact. He would in truth grant her any boon up to and not excluding his very life's breath.

"You do feel something for me, then, Benjamin? Tell me you do. Please tell me."

He nodded. He was unable to speak the words. A sense of inflexible propriety simply would not permit that. But no way could he have denied the truth.

"Someday I shall have to explain all this to you, Benjamin. In the meantime, please understand that I do not intend to squander my youth on the altar of convention nor turn my back on the hopes and dreams of a lifetime. Will you grant me that much, Benjamin?"

He had no earthly idea what the girl was talking about. But if Elizabeth wanted it, well, Ben Cartwright wanted her to have it, whatever it might be. Again he nodded.

The girl's solemnity of purpose dissolved with almost magic suddenness and she flashed a joyous, impish grin that was perhaps even more startling to him than her incomprehensible statements already had been.

Without further warning, Elizabeth Eloise Stoddard, daughter and only child of Capt. Abel Morgan Stoddard of Boston, Massachusetts, in the full view of all the good citizenry of Boston who had chosen to come to the quay this day, stepped boldly in front of Ben Cartwright and lifted herself onto her tiptoes.

And there without warning—without opposition too, if the full truth be told—Elizabeth Stoddard boldly and unblushingly kissed Benjamin Cartwright full on the mouth.

Ben felt his head swim dizzily, felt his heartbeat race and his breathing quicken. The heavy seabag dropped unheeded from his suddenly nerveless fingers, but he did not care about that in the slightest. He was numb and disoriented. And as thoroughly, as completely happy as he had ever been in his life. No, he was more happy than he had ever been before this moment. Much more.

Yet he was apprehensive too.

For Elizabeth, not for himself. For her reputation and her happiness. Because Elizabeth and he were standing, after all, in the full view of all of Boston. In full view of all of the Boston that counted that is, the portion of the city that was devoted to the sea. In the Stoddards' circle, that was the only part that was worthy of consideration. And in Ben's view too, for that matter.

But now Elizabeth Stoddard was seen kissing a young man. Publicly kissing him. And the two of them not married nor even betrothed.

Her act was shameful.

Or it was a declaration.

Even while he was still reeling from the impact of her unexpected kiss, Ben was realizing the full and awesome extent of this step Elizabeth just now took.

Without ever having been allowed the intimacy of a private conversation between them, Elizabeth plunged boldly forward and committed herself to this man by her display of public affection.

If Ben Cartwright chose to reject her shameless advance, Elizabeth Stoddard would forever after be regarded in polite company as a common hussy and little better than a trollop.

She would be ruined.

Or he could accept this greatest of all gifts that she so freely, if unexpectedly, placed before him, and they two would be as good as engaged. Never mind that banns had yet to be posted nor a dowry discussed. Never mind, even, that the girl's parents had yet to be consulted on the subject—and wouldn't that have been an exercise in futility, Ben realized—the choices were just that clearly defined. By this act Elizabeth placed herself at his mercy to do with as he pleased. He could destroy her. Or he could accept her troth forever more. No possibilities between those extremes any longer existed.

Ben understood that even as he tasted of Elizabeth's sweet breath. Even as he felt the trembling, fluttering, light as a moth's wing touch of her lips upon his. Even as he felt the touch of her fingertips at his chest as she steadied herself. Even as the warmth of her closeness seared his senses. Even as, the brief kiss ended, she dropped back away from him and suddenly, furiously, blushed.

"Elizabeth, I—" He wanted to tell her, to assure her, to let her know that he would not forsake her, that he would never dishonor her. The words wouldn't come.

Ben gaped. Cast madly about for control of a tongue that seemed trapped within the fences of his own teeth.

Elizabeth's eyes were wide and her cheeks even redder than his own must be.

"Someday—" she started to say. And then the enormity of her act seemed to overwhelm her, for she turned unnaturally pale and, spinning in a whirl of skirts and flounces, ran blindly away to disappear into a buzzing and bemused crowd of onlookers.

Ben stood where he was in a stunned and wondering silence.

Finally, after the passage of long and uncomfortable moments under the critical eyes of the crowd, he retrieved his seabag and once more set off onto the streets of Boston.

Just that quickly Ben Cartwright's world was turned upside down.

CHAPTER 7

I t isn't locked," Ben called in response to the tapping at
his door. "Come in." He was standing at the open
wardrobe with his seabag on a chair immediately before him. The sea chest was already unpacked and positioned at the foot of the tiny cot that was to be his bed for
the foreseeable future. This room hard under the eaves of
Mrs. Adlington's boardinghouse would be hot and stuffy
and uncomfortable, but it was cheap and the best he felt he
could manage, at least until the question of his future—
and Elizabeth's—was settled. He had no resources to
squander, particularly now that he faced a new depth of responsibility.

The door squeaked open on hinges that were in need
of oiling, and a seaman named Nevin came inside. Ben
knew the man, a pensioner no longer fit to put to sea, who
now did odd jobs throughout the waterfront. Nevin was
not particularly old, perhaps in his late thirties, but his hair
was graying and his limbs permanently twisted from a
combination of ancient injuries and disfiguring rheuma-
tism, both common enough among lifelong sailors.
Nevin's eyes cut from side to side as he took in everything

there was to see, no doubt seeking to compare the shore quarters of a gentleman to whatever rat's nest he himself was accustomed to.

"Hello, Nevin. What can I do for you?"

Nevin cleared his throat. "Beggin' your pardon, Mr. Cartwright, but Cap'n Stoddard asks you t' call on 'im tonight for dinner, sir. He, um, says ye're t' be there prompt by eight. At 'is 'ouse, sir."

"Captain Stoddard, Nevin? But the *Wanderer*'s not in port, is she? Surely I would've seen her if she was."

"*Wanderer*'s not 'ere, sir, but the cap'n be. At 'is 'ouse, sir, like I said."

Ben frowned. The *Wanderer* was not in Boston but Captain Stoddard was? How remarkably odd. He would have liked to grill Nevin for some answers, but the man grunted something unintelligible and knuckled his forehead as he backed and bobbed to the doorway and through it. The messenger was gone before Ben had time to pose his questions.

He left Ben with little choice but to comply with the summons or to allow Elizabeth to think he was abandoning her.

But . . . Captain Stoddard here? And his ship not?

There was something very wrong about that. In a way, it was even more puzzling than Elizabeth's inexplicable behavior on the quay this afternoon.

Still and all, the answers would be forthcoming soon enough. All Ben had to do was present himself at the Stoddard home promptly at eight. Whenever that might be. Ben owned no timepiece. But then he knew few men who did. Aboard ship the turn of the glass determined time. Here he knew of no glass to watch. Nor would anyone be striking the bells.

Eight o'clock, he decided, would happen just about as quickly as he could wash and change and walk the three quarters of a mile to the Stoddard house.

And if he happened to be early, well, perhaps the excess time could be spent in Elizabeth's company.

But whyever would Captain Stoddard be here and the *Wanderer* not?

The question nagged at him while he laid out his very best suit of clothes and hurried through his preparations for an evening under the critical eyes of Elizabeth's parents.

Ben was scarcely able to conceal his shock. He'd been greeted by the Stoddards' Negro servant Luther and led into the parlor where Mrs. Stoddard and Elizabeth were seated primly upon high-back rockers while the captain—Ben hoped his feelings did not show—sat between them in a basketlike wicker chair that had tall wheels on either side of the seat, and a push handle like those on perambulators attached to the back of the device. The captain's legs were concealed beneath a woolen robe, although the house was more than adequately warm. Ben gasped and struggled for control, fighting to maintain a normal outward appearance and to refrain from blurting the obvious questions.

"Well, Cartwright? What've you to say for yourself, eh? Cat got your tongue, boy?"

"No, sir, but . . ." Ben looked bluntly in the direction of the wheeled chair and the obviously useless legs.

"That's better, dammit. Out in the open where things belong, right? 'Twas last fall off Hatteras, beating into a norther with the spars bare and storms'ls set. Damn tye broke, a chain tye too—you remember how the ol' ship's rigged, always best quality chain for the tyes, but this one busted, snapped clean through, an' somehow the jackstay came loose. Damn thing caromed off the rail an' whipped low 'cross the deck like a scythe. Cut me down like a stalk o' wheat, it did. Hamstrung me, dammit. Just that quick, Cartwright. Damn link o' chain breaks and a man can be turned into a worthless old cripple. Just that quick."

"Daddy!" Elizabeth chided gently.

"I know, I know. I promised. An' it's right you are, child. This is not a time for sorrow, but for cheer." Stoddard forced a smile that he quite obviously did not feel in the slightest. "Good to see you again, Cartwright. Glad you've come t' your sense, eh? Never could understand why you signed off the old *Wanderer* before. Caught hell from Liz'beth here and her mother for letting you get away then. Won't allow it t' happen again, right? Ha ha."

Ben coughed into his fist in an attempt to cover his confusion. What was this about him signing off the ship? Surely Captain Stoddard hadn't . . . but, oh, surely Captain Stoddard had. Why, the old scoundrel. Ben never would have thought it of him. Abel Morgan Stoddard was in fear of his wife and daughter. How very unexpected. But did the man think he could conceal the truth from them?

Well, apparently he did. And likely right about it too. If Ben went along with the deception and kept his mouth shut, no one else was apt to bring up the question of whether the *Wanderer*'s one-time third mate was discharged or chose to leave.

And in light of this afternoon's display of public affections, well . . .

Ben coughed into his fist again.

"Sir." Luther provided a most welcome distraction, bowing to Ben and presenting a tray of wine goblets for his selection. "Madeira, sir. Very nice."

"Thank you, Luther."

"Yes, sir." Once the guest was served, Luther went on to the ladies and finally the captain.

"To the young people," Mrs. Stoddard said when all had their glasses. "To their happiness." She lifted her goblet high, first toward Elizabeth and then to Ben.

"Hear, hear." The captain put in with a show of false cheer.

Elizabeth blushed. Ben bowed in acknowledgment of the toast. The elder Stoddards sipped from their glasses. While they were thus occupied, Ben was able for the first time this evening to devote his attention to Elizabeth.

He saw she was peering any- and everywhere in the room except at him.

Was she embarrassed? Quite probably, he realized. For by now it was clear to all of them that the bridges had all been crossed. And now burnt as well.

Elizabeth's actions of the afternoon required a declaration in one direction or the other. And his appearance here this evening made it clear which path he had chosen.

Further, the invitation extended by the captain made the family's position equally clear. Benjamin Cartwright and Elizabeth Stoddard were now, to all intents and purposes, betrothed. And with the full consent and approval of Captain and Mrs. Abel Morgan Stoddard.

Lordy, Ben thought. Good Lord above!

Whoever would have, could have believed—

". . . May," Mrs. Stoddard was saying. "It is such a lovely time of the year, and the flowers are so lovely then . . ." Ben found himself practically reeling from the enormity of it all. He was fairly sure that Mrs. Stoddard was talking about plans for a wedding. In May. Beneath a brush arbor if the day was fair. Indoors at the Middlesex Congregational Church, if not. Ben knew she was discussing all that. But of a sudden he felt detached and slightly apart from all of this.

It was all so simply overwhelming.

His head buzzed and his hearing blurred.

There was so much to take in here.

Elizabeth. Dear Elizabeth. And the captain crippled, and Mrs. Stoddard smiling, and he himself swaying from side to side. Ben blinked. Helped himself to a seat. Took a swallow of the Madeira.

What?

He managed, barely, to avoid spewing out a mist of wine, regained control of himself and quickly swallowed. "What was, uh, that again, Mrs. Stoddard?"

Elizabeth's mother smiled as sweetly as if all of this were oh so very normal. She nodded benignly. Leaned over and patted the back of Ben's wrist. "I was saying, dear boy, that Mr. Stoddard and I shall miss Elizabeth once she has become Mrs. Cartwright."

Mrs. Cartwright. That *was* what she'd said. Ben was a little better braced for it this time. He was able to conceal the sense of alarm that ran cold fingers up and down his spine.

He was pleased. Of course he was. But . . . it was all coming so quickly. Why, they'd scarcely spoken before this afternoon. Oh, a word here, a remark there. Certain inflections in one's voice when reading aloud at a social, perhaps. Certain glances half hidden from those who were around them at this gala or that affair.

But . . . Ben swallowed. Hard. He felt slightly dizzy, and hoped he was not noticeably pale. He smiled at Elizabeth's mother and took another drink of the Madeira in an attempt to wash away the blockage that seemed to be lodged in his throat at the moment.

"Shall we take it that May would be satisfactory with you, dear boy?"

"Yes, um, yes, ma'am." The dizziness was replaced by a rush of heat into his cheeks. He felt quite sure he was about to topple off his chair and make a spectacle of himself.

He glanced at Elizabeth, who was pretending to concentrate her attentions on the pattern in the carpet.

He looked at Captain Stoddard, who was glowering silently into the crystal stemware in his massive hand. The goblet was empty of Madeira, the captain apparently having gulped his down immediately upon receiving it.

Luther hurried forward with a carafe to fill the captain's goblet once more, then came around to Ben and filled his glass also. Funny, but Ben didn't recall emptying it, although obviously he had done so.

The captain tossed off his wine as if it were a shot of common spirits. Ben found himself doing the same. Luther refilled both glasses.

". . . a brush arbor would be by far the better if possible," Mrs. Stoddard was saying. ". . . so many guests, and of course . . ." Ben was losing track of the conversa-

tion again, although he was fairly sure that Elizabeth's
mother was continuing with her inane talk. Which, it suddenly occurred to him, was quite likely a sign of the poor,
startled lady's own nervousness more than anything else.
After all, the Stoddards no doubt were as shocked this afternoon and as apprehensive this evening as he himself.

Ben looked down at his wineglass—the thing was
empty again, although it was beyond him to comprehend
how that might have happened so very quickly—and felt
just the least bit woozy.

Luther poured for him again, but this time Ben set the
glass firmly onto a nearby table.

". . . the Reverend Mr. Wickstrom to read the service,
and Esther Moore to sing the hymns . . ." Mrs. Stoddard
was mumbling. Or perhaps she wasn't mumbling so much
as that Ben was not hearing her.

Ben felt heat gather beneath his collar and radiate up-
ward into his cheeks. He wished he had a fresh kerchief
with him so that he could mop his forehead, but he hadn't
had time this afternoon to see to his laundry after the journey. And he certainly had not foreseen anything remotely
like this when he planned this homecoming.

He looked at Elizabeth.

And felt a melting warmth within his breast.

Oh, she was beautiful.

Words could not describe . . .

She was so tiny. So delicate. Dark hair. Huge, dark
eyes. Slender as a foil blade. Pale. Rounded cheeks with
dimples framing a rosebud mouth. Strong and proud in
spirit if not in body. Oh, Elizabeth. So beautiful, he found
her. So dear.

It seemed incredible. Beyond incredulity. To think
that Elizabeth Stoddard was to become his bride.

But of course after that display of public affections,
what choice had he? What choice had any of them? They
would marry or Elizabeth would be disgraced. The girl
had understood that when she approached him on the quay
there. Her mother understood it every bit as well.

As for Captain Stoddard, well, Ben was not so sure about what the captain understood. Or wanted.

One thing sure. Understand or not. Want or not. The captain's wife and the captain's daughter had things in hand now. The captain's likes and dislikes were unimportant insofar as this planning unfolded. Elizabeth *would* become Mrs. Cartwright. The only thing capable of stopping that now would be if Ben himself were churlish and cruel enough to withdraw.

And that he would never do. Could never. For that would involve hurting Elizabeth Stoddard, and bringing harm to her was something he could never do, not do himself nor allow at the hand of any other.

He began to smile. He looked at Elizabeth boldly and openly for the first time in their lives. He grinned. He retrieved his glass and drank off the Madeira from it and motioned to Luther for more.

May. Yes, May was a most lovely month indeed.

Mrs. Stoddard was still yammering, although yammering about what, Ben hadn't the faintest notion.

Ben chuckled. Laughed aloud. Tried to drink from a glass that had become mysteriously empty once more. He looked about for Luther, swaying only slightly. Grabbed hold of the arm of his chair for support. Laughed again. Ah, good, there you are, old fellow. Good man, Luther. Fill the cup again, eh? Mine and the captain's, that's right.

Ah, such a wonderful time this was proving to be, ha ha. . . .

Ben heard someone giggle, realized he was making the sound himself. That seemed quite funny, so he laughed a little more. Had another wee and tiny sip of the Madeira. Good stuff, Madeira. Damned good, ho ho.

"Thank you, Luther, thank you very much." He giggled again. "Did you know, Luther, that I've had more than one glass of this wine? Know how I know that, Luther? I deduced it. Yes, I did. Because the end of my nose 'as—excuse me, *has*—gone numb, y' see, and my cheeks too. See there? Pinch 'em if you like. 'S all right.

I won't feel it. Numb as hazelnuts, they are. No more feelin' than salt cod, Luther. You ever open a box o' salt cod, Luther, an' see those eyes staring back at you, all caked in salt but not feeling a thing? Did you? 'Course you have. Well, that's what my face is like right now, Luther. Whole thing 's like that. You haven't put salt on me have you, Luther? No? Let's drink to that, Luther, you an' me. Pour me s'more of that . . . you know, whatever it is . . . pour me s'more and—*thank* you, Luther, it's *so* nice o' you to carry me to . . . where we going, Luther, hmm?"

Oh, Luther, don't jostle me so, he thought wildly. Don't bounce me around like that or I think I'll be . . . bucket, Luther, hand me that bucket there!

Ben groaned in agony.

And smiled in beatific ecstasy.

May.

Elizabeth.

May and Elizabeth.

Elizabeth in May.

Oh, dear.

"Thank you, Luther, I'm feeling much better now."

en circled carefully wide of a mound of refuse on the side of the cobbled street, mindful of the state of his shoes. He wished he'd had the wit last night to be equally mindful of the state of his head. Mid-afternoon of the infamous Day After was proving too late for anything more constructive than remorse and recrimination, the worst of which was a nagging fear that Elizabeth and her parents might think that thoroughly disgusting behavior to be normal for him. Never mind that the experience was a genuine first—and last, he now vowed—in his lifetime. He could hardly expect Elizabeth or the captain or Mrs. Stoddard to believe protestations of past innocence. Not after the display he'd put on last night. He shuddered just from thinking about it.

He also gagged just a little as his travel took him past the open doorway of a café. Scents of hot grease and stinking cabbage made his stomach churn and gurgle in mad rebellion. The thought of any sort of food was repulsive at this moment. So far today he'd been unable even to down any coffee. A tot of sweet tea with milk and half a dry biscuit of hardtack had been all he'd been able to force down for lunch. Breakfast had consisted of a mumble, a belch, and the act of drawing a limp and sweat-soggy pillow over his eyes. He had not, in fact, risen today until near noon.

Now he was on his way once more to the Stoddard home. And, as before, he was making the trek at the express command of Capt. Abel Morgan Stoddard.

He hoped the captain did not intend to offer foodstuffs today. Or any beverage more potent than spring water. Ben's queasy stomach would not accept anything beyond that, he was sure.

His steps took him past the last of the shops and houses of commerce and onto the shady, tree-lined street where the Stoddards' trim dwelling sat amid a blocks-long run of similar houses, all of them built tall and trim and spare like the ships that paid for them. The houses all seemed stern and uncompromising, like their Yankee masters. Ben felt his nervousness return and redouble. He licked at lips, which were suddenly dry. As he turned in at the Stoddards' gate he felt almost faint, and for the first time since waking was not immediately conscious of the state of his stomach, that being a matter not so much of improvement as of distraction.

"Good afternoon, Mistuh Cartwright. Might I take yo' hat, suh?"

Luther either had been watching for his arrival or heard his footsteps on the porch because the servant had the door open before Ben had time to knock. Luther, Ben noticed, accepted his presence without any outward display of disapproval.

"Thank you, Luther," Ben said, surrendering the salt-crusted, short-billed cap that was a symbol of his status as an officer and not a mere seaman.

"Cap'n is in his office, Mistuh Cartwright. Follow me if you please, suh."

"Miss Elizabeth is . . . ?"

"The ladies be out o' the house fo' the afternoon,

Mistuh Cartwright. Now if you be so good as t' follow me, suh?"

Ben caught a hint of mild rebuke in Luther's tone. He accepted it and, chastised, followed close behind, as he'd been told to do.

Captain Stoddard's office proved to be a small area that might once have been a sun or reading room. With so much glass all about, it would no doubt be so cold as to be uninhabitable in winter, but there was no sign of a stove or of a flue or chimney where one might be emplaced on a seasonable basis. Nor would there really have been room enough for one. The captain's large and clumsy wheelchair occupied most of what floor space there was. The rest was taken up with a cluttered rolltop desk, a few bookcases, and an ornately carved table—Ben recognized the style as having come from China—that held a flagon and the same pewter tumblers that Ben once saw, and had been invited to use, in the captain's cabin aboard the old *Wanderer*. Ben hoped the captain would not again suggest they share a brandy or—

Safe. Oh, he was definitely safe from having to join Captain Stoddard in a toast. Ben recognized that instantly in the captain's expression upon his appearance at the doorway.

Funny how of a sudden now he would actually have welcomed an invitation to imbibe. For surely that would have been preferable to having to receive this look of—it was unmistakable—of loathing that he was sure he saw in the captain's dark and hooded glare.

"Cartwright." The name was acknowledgment, not welcome. There was no hint here of last night's familial goodwill.

"Sir."

"I suppose you'll be wanting to talk 'bout the dowry you can expect, eh? Is that your game, Cartwright? Or is it that you expect me t' buy you off? Mm? Which, man? Either way it's wanting into my pockets you are, mister." There was contempt apparent in the man's eyes now.

Ben felt his neck swell and his shoulders rise as if to a challenge. "If you were a whole man—" He bit back the remainder of the retort.

If Captain Stoddard were still a whole man, Ben would pulp his face for saying such a thing.

But Stoddard was *not* whole. And he *was* Elizabeth's father.

Ben drew himself upright so that he towered tall and rigid above Abel Stoddard in his wheelchair. Ben kept his mouth closed and, insofar as he was able, his dignity intact.

"Huh. You deny it. 'Course you do. And o' course you've the upper hand, haven't you, you damned whelp. Know it too, don't you? Well, so d' we both. An' I'll pay. But not t' buy you away from my little girl, Cartwright. If I must choose 'tween two evils then, sir, I shall choose the one that promises t' bring her the most joy. It's you she wants an' you she'll have, mister. So I'll pay you a dowry. But not a bribe, eh? You'll get your money, Cartwright, but you'll have t' stay on as Elizabeth's husband. You'll have t' *earn* it, see."

Somewhere deep within himself Ben found a measure of restraint, a pool of calm and unroiled tranquillity. He looked down at the bitter and crippled man who was so soon to become his father-in-law and paused for long moments before speaking.

"It will be my privilege and my joy to marry your daughter, sir, but not because of your money. I shall take her to be my wife because of my deep and abiding respect for her, indeed my love for her. My only regret, sir, is that she has a father who cares so little for her that he sees only plots against his purse and not the true pleasures of life that are Elizabeth's due. It is your daughter that I wish to court, sir. Not your fortune."

"Nicely said, Cartwright. If you lie as smoothly to the child as you do to the da, then she'll never see the truth." The man cleared his throat and scowled down at a sheaf of papers on his desk. "Here is what I have to offer. Hiram

Truesdell is serving as captain of the *Wanderer* now. Upon his return, Cartwright, you will be enrolled as first mate. You will serve in that capacity for as long as I see fit. Which for all practical purposes means until Captain Truesdell chooses to leave my ship either in retirement or to accept another berth. At that time, Cartwright, I shall make you captain of the *Wanderer*. I trust you are bright enough to undertake the qualifications. At least there is that to be said in your favor. And certainly you have ample time in which to prepare yourself for the examinations. I'll inform Captain Truesdell 'bout all this and instruct him to assist you in your study. I cannot do fairer than that, eh?"

"That would be—"

"Do not interrupt me, Cartwright. Bad habit of yours, that. Always interrupting. I remember that about you, sir. It's burden enough that I have t' say an' do all this. I don't care to suffer through your holier-than-thou posturing too, nor will I listen to any more o' your lies."

Once more Ben was required to bite his tongue and swallow his pride lest he say much, much more than he ought to his beloved Elizabeth's father.

Stoddard grunted. "So as I was saying before you interrupted me, Cartwright, the child's dowry will come to you in the form of employment far and away above your worth or value. You will be first officer aboard one of the finest ships afloat, an' if you live so long, will one day become her master. But you'll ne'er own my ship, Cartwright. Don't for one minute ever think that you will. I'll scuttle her before I turn her over t' the likes o' you, mister. I swear I would, sir. Scuttle 'er dead away, damn you. Damn you." The captain's face had been turning redder and redder during that last outburst, and by the end of it he was shouting and leaning forward in his chair. "You'll ne'er own *Wanderer*, Cartwright. Ne'er so long 's I live."

Luther must have heard the outburst because now he appeared with magical efficiency to lean over the captain and pound him upon the back to quell a spasm of coughing that erupted from deep in the crippled seaman's chest. "There there, Cap'n, it's all right now."

Luther motioned toward the brandy flagon, and Ben quickly took the hint, grabbing up one of the tumblers and splashing a swallow of spirits into it. Luther held it to the captain's lips and practically forced it down the man's throat. Soon the spate of racking coughs subsided.

The captain groaned and rolled his eyes in a glare that was directed toward Ben, but when he tried to speak again, he only coughed instead.

"I think, Mistuh Cartwright, you might bes' be leavin' now, suh."

"Yes, Luther, thank you." Ben turned to go.

"Mistuh Cartwright."

"Yes, Luther?"

"You be knowin', suh, that you expected fo' suppa t'night, suh?"

"No, Luther, I was not aware."

"Oh, yes, suh. Seven o'clock sharp, if you please, suh. The Rev'rend Mistuh Wickstrom be here, suh. An' the Wyants an' the Tillys an' mayhap the Lewises, suh. Lots o' introducin' t' be done, suh, befo' the banns be posted. Lots o' lookin' at an' lookin' out for, suh."

"Seven o'clock, Luther?"

"Yes, suh."

"Thank you, Luther."

"An' Mistuh Cartwright."

"Yes, Luther?"

"The cap'n here, he won' be sayin' nothing in front o' them folks that the ladies wouldn' want heard. You c'n be sure o' that, suh. Everything be fine by supper t'night. You'll see."

Stoddard squirmed a little in his chair, but Luther was standing between him and Ben at the moment. Deliberately? Quite possibly so, Ben realized. And so Ben could not see the captain's expression when all of this was revealed.

"Good day, Captain."

Stoddard coughed a little, although whether he was trying to speak or not, Ben could not discern.

"Good-bye, Luther."

"G'day, suh."

Ben let himself out of the house and walked back toward the waterfront in a state that verged somewhere between deep shock and simple bewilderment.

He was to have the wife of his dreams. He was to command the ship of his dreams.

And Able Morgan Stoddard detested him, utterly and truly and without hope the man might ever relent.

Aye, Bobby, he thought, 'tis a tangled web indeed.

"Papa likes you. I can tell."

Ben smiled and declined to correct that misinformation. Talk about so serious a subject—and this evening was too wonderful to admit to seriousness—would only lead to frowns upon Elizabeth's lovely countenance. And if there was one thing Ben Cartwright wished, it was for Elizabeth Stoddard, soon Cartwright, to possess only smiles forever and ever more. He settled for patting the hand that rested so lightly, so warmly on his wrist.

"Would you like to see something, Benjamin?"

"With you? Anything."

"It is my very favorite view in the whole world."

"Then it must surely be mine as well."

"That would be a silly thing for you to say, Benjamin, if it weren't so gallant. You don't, after all, know what it is that I shall show you."

He smiled again and rose, offering his arm to help her to her feet as well.

"Would you excuse us, Mother?"

Mrs. Stoddard nodded. She was seated in her favored parlor chair, her hands busy with thread and tatting shuttle, and her eyes carefully avoiding the young people with their surreptitious but frequent touching of hands and wrists. The dinner guests had stayed their welcome and then departed, the Stoddards' purpose of introducing Elizabeth into polite company as the betrothed of First Officer Benjamin Cartwright having been satisfactorily begun. Luther had long since wheeled the captain away into some self-imposed solitude, and now only Ben and the two Stoddard ladies remained in the formal little sitting room. "Mind your step, dear," Mrs. Stoddard said without looking up from the lace she was making. "But I needn't worry now, I suppose. After all, dear, you have Ben to catch you if you should trip."

"Mother!" The exasperation in Elizabeth's voice rang false. In truth she sounded pleased with her mother's gentle teasing.

"Enjoy yourselves, dears," Mrs. Stoddard said.

"Yes, ma'am."

Ben was prepared to find his hat and escort Elizabeth off somewhere to this unspecified favorite place in the whole world. Instead of turning toward the vestibule, however, Elizabeth led him upstairs and the length of the second story hallway to a narrow door that might have concealed a broom closet but which in fact gave access to a gloomy, twisting set of stair treads as steep as a ship's ladder, and so narrow that Ben barely fit between the walls. Ben could appreciate now Mrs. Stoddard's warning to avoid a fall.

"Mind this last step, Benjamin," Elizabeth said from ahead of and slightly above him, "there is a high sill over the threshold to keep the rain from seeping in."

"Then you be careful too, please."

"Oh, pooh. I've been up here a thousand times. A thousand thousand times."

"That doesn't make you any the less valuable to me, Miss Stoddard. Please be so kind as to mind your step."

Elizabeth paused on the staircase and reached back. Her hand lightly caressed Ben's cheek, and he was glad for the gloom on the stairway so she could not see the bright flush that unexpected gesture caused. Almost at once she lightly mounted the last few steps and flung a low door open to expose starlit sky and invigoratingly fresh night air.

The stairway ended at a tiny cupola surrounded by railed decking and a Widows Walk, also railed, that led atop the house's roof peak to a second platform that was surrounded by rails and capped by a gazebolike structure. The gazebo—if such it should be called when situated a good thirty feet above ground level—was an octagonal-shaped dome protecting narrow benches and trelliswork sides that would provide a measure of shade and privacy while admitting passage of the sea breezes.

Much more interesting than this widow's walk, however, was the view of Boston harbor in the distance. At this time of night the dark waters lay spread out like a sheet of black velvet, and the mooring lights and watch lights and yellow-gleaming port lights of ships at anchor shimmered like miniature stars brought down from the sky and sprinkled across that majestic swatch of velvet.

The beauty of it captured Ben and stopped him short even as he straightened to full height after emerging from the stairwell.

"Do you like it, Benjamin?"

"It's wonderful." He smiled. "But not so beautiful as you."

"You're being silly again."

"Oh, no. I am very serious about that, I assure you."

"Oh, Benjamin, do you—" She stopped.

"What?"

"I . . . nothing."

"Tell me."

She shook her head. After a moment more she took his hand in hers and led him out onto the widow's walk and on to the gazebo. She sat close beside him. "You really like it here, Benjamin?"

He nodded. There was little light to see by. But what there was he intended to use for a purpose much more interesting than looking out at Boston harbor.

"I spend ever so much time here," she said. "Ever

since I was a little girl." She paused, swallowed, looked away from him. "When I was little, Benjamin, I attended Mrs. Carrecker's Academy for Young Ladies. Did you know that?"

He shook his head.

"We were all much more young than we were ladies." She giggled and hid her face for a moment. "Mrs. Carrecker would have been shocked if she'd known how impure some of our thoughts were. About boys in particular. Most of the girls had fantasies of being found by dashing princes on white chargers and being carried off to live in a castle and have tons and tons of servants and be rich and gay forever more. Do you know what I always dreamed, Benjamin?"

"No, I'm sure I don't."

"I shouldn't be so forward as to tell you."

"If it makes you uncomfortable—"

"Benjamin! You are supposed to beg me to tell you."

"Sorry. I, uh, please tell me what you dreamed of then."

She looked away from him again. "You'll think I'm lying."

"No I won't."

"Promise?"

"I promise."

She sighed. "This was just after your family moved here. Do you remember that summer? Your father had the shop in Janus Common, and Mama shopped there for the first time on a Wednesday afternoon. It was in July, I think. A Wednesday afternoon in July, yes."

"However can you remember that?"

"Because you were standing at the shelves. Putting something on them, I don't know what."

"Such a memory . . ."

"That was the first time I ever saw you, Benjamin. I saw you and I thought I was going to melt clean away. I thought sure I would melt into a little puddle and drain through the floorboards and seep into the ground underneath the shop. But I couldn't let that happen because if it did then I would never see you again. And I knew right then and there, Benjamin, that someday I would be your wife or else I couldn't bear to marry anyone, ever. And that, you see, was my dream when I was a little girl at Mrs. Carrecker's Academy. And ... and that is still my dream, Benjamin. It is and it always has been, ever since that very first day."

"You can't be ... You're serious, aren't you?"

"Yes. I am very serious. I've been in love with you, Benjamin, ever since that Wednesday afternoon in July of that very first year your family came to Boston."

"I never knew, never suspected—"

"Of course you never knew, silly. Why, I would have perished, simply *perished* if you'd ever even *suspected*." She rolled her eyes and took his right hand between both of hers. "That is why I ... did what I did. It was awful of me. But I couldn't stand not to. Why, just think how happy I was when you became one of Papa's officers. I thought everything would all come true, Benjamin. All the dreams I'd ever had. And then the two of you came home from that voyage and Papa fired you. I was crushed."

"I thought you weren't supposed to know about that. I mean, judging from the way your father spoke and everything—"

"Oh, Mama and I know more than Papa thinks we do. But we don't let on. He's just trying to save face with us. Mama knows about my feelings for you, Benjamin. She has known for a long time. So when Papa fired you, Mama let him know that he shouldn't have. And believe me, if you hadn't run off to the Caribbean so quickly that time ... but never mind all that. The point is, dear, I've been quite desperately in love with you since we were children. And so when I saw you coming down the plank right there in front of me ... well, I hadn't planned to, you know, make a scene or anything. I swear to you that I hadn't. It was just that, well, there you were and I was so excited and so happy and so hopeful and ... well, I just did it. I just ran over to you and made a spectacle of myself and, if you must know, I am very glad that I did. Because tonight you are sitting here at my side and we are as good as betrothed and—and—" she grinned, "and *everything*."

He squeezed her hand. "May I be so forward, Miss Stoddard, as to tell you that I . . . care for you."

"Do you? Oh, Benjamin, do you truly? You aren't just—"

"Elizabeth, never doubt that. It is the one thing I can think of that is undying, and that is my regard for you, my respect for you, my . . . love for you. Whew! That's hard to say. I don't know why, but it is. Perhaps because I've never said those words before. Nor ever thought that I would be able to say them. Because you see, dearest Elizabeth, I've hidden a secret love for you for quite as long as you say you've hidden one for me."

"Really, Benjamin? Ever since that first meeting in your father's shop?"

"Every bit that long," he swore. Which was a mild stretch of the truth perhaps, but not an actual lie. He had loved Elizabeth Stoddard for a very long time. For so long that he could not now remember or identify the exact moment when that love had blossomed. And not remembering any *other* moment made the one as good as any other for the purposes of discussion. And so, why not accept as the launching point the same moment in time that Elizabeth remembered so well and cherished so fondly?

"Elizabeth, would it be too bold of me . . . that is to say . . ." Awkwardly, fearful of giving offense, he touched first her shoulder and then her cheek.

And then she was in his arms. Her lips were touching his. Their very life's breath was shared, and her slight and trembling form was pressed tight against him. It might have been an exaggeration, he really was not sure, but he thought that even their heartbeats were racing in perfect coordination one with the other.

CHAPTER 9

As the daughter of a seafaring man, Elizabeth Stoddard knew what it was, or would be, to be the wife of a seafaring man.

And that was a very good thing because Captain Stoddard seemed intent on keeping First Mate Cartwright as diligently at work as possible. And as far from Boston while he was at it.

Ben and Elizabeth had less than three weeks to spend in their first-love idyll before Captain Truesdell brought *Wanderer* home with a cargo of raw hemp destined for the rope makers' lofts and coffee beans that would be distributed throughout the northern tier of states. Within hours of her arrival, *Wanderer* was ordered to sea once more.

So anxious was Stoddard to see young Cartwright out of his home in the evenings—and Ben had no doubt that that was precisely the motivation behind Elizabeth's father's haste—that he sent the ship out with only ballast in her hold. He did not allow Captain Truesdell even to seek a cargo before *Wanderer* was again under sail. There could have been no more telling indicator of the truth than that, because after sailing with the man, Ben well knew Abel

Stoddard's nickel-squeezing parsimony. It must have torn at Stoddard's gut to order his own ship away with the crew drawing wages but her bottom empty.

Still and all, he'd done it. And Ben had neither seen Elizabeth nor heard from her since, although he faithfully mailed thick packets, letters running to many pages, which were added to each night without fail, from every port they touched.

Seven months' worth of letters, seven months' worth of ports. Seven years, it seemed to a young man in love. Seven eons. Seven months of restless nights and fond re-memberings. Seven months of hope and plan.

Now, by jingo, the time apart must surely be nearing its end. Because now, in February, it must surely be time soon for *Wanderer* to point her bowsprit north. After all, the first mate had an appointment in Boston come May. Captain Truesdell surely would have been given orders to have the ship home before that time, because while the ship's owner might want Cartwright kept away in the in-terim, he was unlikely to do anything that would distress either Mrs. Stoddard or Elizabeth. Crusty and unpleasant though Stoddard might be in many ways, he was as mal-leable as clay for either of those ladies.

Ben was hoping they would steer a course for Boston as soon as this next cargo was loaded. Whatever the cargo might prove to be. Captain Truesdell had gone ashore in Port-au-Prince to find a broker and secure one or, barring that, perhaps to use ship's funds and purchase a cargo of their own. As a first mate Truesdell had always been sup-portive of his captain and industrious in his labors—an ex-ample Ben tried his best to emulate now—but as a captain the man proved, at least in Ben's opinion, somewhat on the tentative side of things. Instead of risking ship's capital to buy cargoes—and hope to earn large returns there-after—Truesdell tended to load goods belonging to others and thus settle for haulage fees rather than outright profits. Ben, with his background in commerce as well as the sea, already planned to conduct the affairs of the *Wanderer* more aggressively than that when someday he occupied the captain's quarters.

In the meantime, though, he did his best to serve at Hiram Truesdell's, and Abel Stoddard's, will.

"G'day, Mr. Cartwright," a seaman from the starboard watch called as Ben came on deck late in the forenoon of a warm and sunny—warm in February, incredible—Haitian day.

"Hello, Talbot."

"Something I can do for you, Mr. Cartwright?"

"Yes, Talbot, there just might be. I'm looking for Jo-Jo. Can't seem to find him anywhere belowdecks. You don't happen to've seen him, have you?"

"Aye, sir. Jo-Jo went ashore an hour ago t' buy provisions. Cap'n told him just this morning t' lay in enough for a four months passage."

Ben frowned. Four months passage? Even with adverse winds, Boston couldn't be two months distant from Hispaniola. If the captain ordered the buying of provender for four months . . . well, Captain Truesdell simply was not one to spend more than was required. Particularly when their course should carry them close to a friendly shore where restocking could be readily accomplished. And frequent purchases were always to be preferred over large ones. There was money lost to spoilage whenever large quantities of foods were loaded. Captain Truesdell had lectured Ben on that very subject shortly after Ben rejoined the ship and as first mate suggested buying twice as much rice as usual so a little money could be saved off the hogshead rates.

Four months provisions. Four months passage. Ben tried to work out the possibilities. There was no part of the Caribbean nor the Gulf of Mexico so distant that four months of provisions would be required in Jo-Jo's lockers.

Why, even if Truesdell intended a southerly course to or around Cape Horn, the ship would not want four months' provisions taken on here because that voyage would surely require a layover in the Argentine to refit and prepare, and the water casks and food stocks could be replenished then.

There were only two possibilities that Ben could think of that might require provisions for four months at sea. No, really only one. The winds being what they were at this time of year, a course for Europe would mean first driving north and therefore running parallel to shore and close to home. The *Wanderer* would not likely strike for England or any European port without first putting in at Boston.

So the only real likelihood if indeed so much provision was being purchased would be a crossing in the southern latitudes to West Africa.

Ben scowled. That was impossible. Wasn't it?

Surely he was only thinking that because Haiti reminded him so very much of West Africa. The people, the markets, the happy-go-lucky way of life here all reminded him of the ports he'd touched and the people he'd seen on those few occasions in the past when he'd made that South Atlantic crossing.

Surely that was all it was that brought West Africa to mind now. Why, whatever need could there be for *Wanderer* to go there? Cargo fees? Humbug. It would take payment for far more than *Wanderer*'s holds could accommodate to justify a passage to West Africa. Whatever could the captain hope to find as cargo for a return trip if they did go there? Slaving was outlawed and had been for years. It was still done, of course, but . . . no, Ben could not believe that. Not of Hiram Truesdell. Surely not that. Not for any amount of profit.

And all of that aside, what of the captain's instructions to touch home port again before the wedding date in May? What indeed about that? Truesdell couldn't be planning . . .

Ben grunted and tugged his cap lower onto his forehead. "I'll be going ashore now, Talbot."

"Aye, sir."

*   *   *

Ben finally found Captain Truesdell in a café that was so flyblown and filthy that they surely must have had difficulty attracting customers. There were, however, a number of customers in evidence. None of whom, Ben noticed, had plates of food at their tables despite the posting of signs that declared the place a café. It was enough to make a fellow wonder.

Wanderer's captain was engaged in close conversation with a thin, shabbily dressed man who had a look about him that said the prudent should be careful of turning their backs to him. The fellow, presumably a cargo broker although he certainly did not look like one, needed a shave and a haircut. And a bath.

"Mr. Cartwright," Truesdell greeted when he saw Ben come into the café, "join us."

"Thank you, sir," Ben said, taking the chair the captain indicated.

"We were just now speaking about you, Mr. Cartwright," Truesdell offered.

"Is that so, sir?"

"Yes, 'tis, isn't that right, Percival?"

"If this is your first mate Mr. Cartwright, it is," Percival confirmed. Percival—Ben had no idea whether that was the man's first name or last—had a voice that was somewhere between a hiss and a whisper.

"And what was it you were saying if I might ask, sir?"

"Oh, idle talk. That's all." Truesdell waved the question away, then turned to Percival. "Is there anything else you need?" he asked.

Percival gave him a grin and a cackle. The man's teeth were badly rotted, Ben saw. "No, I daresay you've taken care of everything. Except . . . you know."

"Aye. We'll do that later."

Ben concentrated on looking elsewhere in the dingy room since he so obviously was interrupting the tail end of a conversation here.

"Tomorrow morn, Captain. Here again at ten, then."

"So soon?"

Percival frowned. "Is there a reason to delay?"

"No, I suppose not."

"Could wrap it all up here and now if you please."

"God no, not here and ... everything. We'll talk about it tomorrow then. At ten."

"Ten will be fine." Percival nodded to Truesdell, but when he stood, it was Ben he looked in the eye for what seemed an unusually extended period of time. "Pleasure to meet you, Mr. Cartwright. Perhaps we'll meet again."

"Perhaps," Ben said. The response was socially obligatory but carried no truth in it. There was something about this Percival that he did not much care for.

Percival stood there for a moment looking at Ben, then turned and limped away. Now that he was in motion, Ben could see that his left leg was twisted and far shorter than the right.

"Are you here by chance, Cartwright, or was there something you wanted to see me about?" Truesdell asked. Ben thought the captain looked nervous, although nothing was said that would hint at a reason. It was just that the captain was not looking him in the eye now. That was unusual for Hiram Truesdell.

"I was looking for you, sir," Ben said, going into his questions about the orders to Jo-Jo that *Wanderer* be provisioned for so long a voyage.

Truesdell grunted and peered out the door toward the squalid, crowded streets of Port-au-Prince. He hesitated for a moment before speaking, clearing his throat several times first. "I, uh, you know how 'tis when a man takes t' the sea. Never know where the next cargo is goin', eh? An' the victuals are cheaper here than in the States. I just, um, thought it might be wise t' stock up heavy now. In case ... you know."

"But I don't know," Ben persisted. "That's the point. Do we have a cargo yet or not?"

"Well now, I'm not s' sure 'bout that, you see. Maybe aye, maybe nay. I'll know t'morrow."

"Does it have something to do with that man Percival?"

"Aye, that's right. So it does." The captain acted like he hadn't thought about that before, like he was grateful for a suggestion that he could pounce upon. "I'll be able to tell you then."

"Might I ask, sir, if Captain Stoddard gave instruction that I be in Boston by May?"

"There was . . . well, yes, Cartwright, your plans for the, um, event were certainly discussed with me by, uh, Cap'n Stoddard."

"Is there something wrong, Captain?"

"What d'you mean?"

"You look a mite flushed, sir. Are you having any dizziness? Fevers or a ringing in your ears, sir? Might you be coming down with the malaria?"

"I don't have the malaria, dammit," Truesdell snapped back at him.

"I only intended—"

"Never mind what you intended, Cartwright. G'wan now." The captain waved him away. "G'wan about your business. I'm sure you have some, so get to it, man. Don't be coming in here an' bothering me without cause."

"Yes, sir." Ben was perplexed, but obedient. He stood to go.

"Tomorrow," the captain said. "We'll, um, talk about this tomorrow."

"Aye, sir."

Ben left the café much more confused than when he'd reached it.

"Mr. Cartwright."

"Yes, Suggs?"

"There's a man t' see you, sir. I dunno who."

"Tell him to come aboard, Suggs."

"I done that, sir, but he's in a dory an' doesn't want to leave it. I dunno why. You want I should tell him t' go away, Mr. Cartwright?"

"No, I'll come see what he wants," Ben said. He capped the small jar of ink he'd prepared earlier and carefully dried the nib of his pen before laying it down on the chart table where he habitually sat to add to his long letters home to Elizabeth.

He left his correspondence folio where it was and ran lightly up the ladder to the deck. It was a fine evening, the sun down now but a soft twilight lingering. The sky toward the west was streaked with red and gold and purple beyond Ile de la Gonave. Red sky at night . . . it was impossible to avoid thinking about the old—but quite often reliable—saw. Red sky at night, sailor's delight; red sky in morning, sailor take warning. Tomorrow, Ben saw, was apt to be a delight.

But then all days were a delight now that Elizabeth was pledged to him. And he to her. He still marveled at the idea that so exquisite a creature as Elizabeth Eloise Stoddard could find favor with him.

"Where is—"

"There, sir," Suggs said, pointing toward the waist of the ship on the side opposite the wharf where she was secured, awaiting a cargo to load.

Ben mumbled a thank-you and ambled forward to the railing. He looked over the side of the ship, then broke into a broad smile.

"Belton. Is that you?"

The seaman waiting in a battered dory below seemed happy to see Ben. "Aye, sir, it's me a'right."

"Whatever are you doing here, man? And why won't you come aboard?"

"I'm here on captain's orders, Mr. Cartwright. And I've got no painter to tie up with. If I let 'er drift, I'll lose 'er sure, and then won't I be in for it, sir. So I figgered it best to stay where I be, sir, an' ask for you. Hope you ain't mad, sir."

"Not at all, Belton. It's good to see you again." Edgar Belton was one of the crew on the old *Pandora*. He'd always been one of Ben's favorites. For that matter, all the men on *Pandora* had been among his favorites. She'd been a happy ship and her crew a good one.

"Begging your pardon, Mr. Cartwright, but would you mind comin' down here so's we can talk without me having to shout at you? My throat's kinda raw and I'm getting dizzy from looking up so much."

"I suppose I could do that, Belton."

"Thank you, sir, because there's a message Cap'n Dawson wanted me to tell t' you, Mr. Cartwright."

"Give me a moment to fetch a ladder, Belton."

"Take your time, sir. I'll be here."

Ben had Suggs bring a rope ladder. Between them they secured the hooks onto the railing and lowered the device, which was much more rope than it was ladder. There was no wood in it, both the vertical supports and the steps being made of hemp. For anyone accustomed to climbing ratlines, though, it was no trouble to negotiate. Ben let himself down to *Pandora*'s dory while Belton used the sweeps to hold the little craft more or less steady against the tall, slightly curving hull of the *Wanderer*.

"Mind your step there, sir."

"Thank you, Belton." Ben took a seat on the aft thwart, and Belton immediately began to row away from *Wanderer*.

"Belton."

"Aye, sir?"

"Am I mistaken, or is that the boat's painter I see coiled and tucked away under the peak there?"

"Oh, I'd say you ain't likely mistaken, Mr. Cartwright." The man continued to pull strongly away from the ship, turning a bit now and angling out into the harbor toward a group of small ships riding at anchor. The tightly clustered masts made it impossible for him to make out the silhouette of any individual ship there, but he thought one of them might be *Pandora*.

"You said Captain Dawson has a message for me?"

"Aye, sir. He'll tell it to you himself, Mr. Cartwright. If that'd be a'right with you."

"I suppose I may as well go along with this mystery of yours. After all, I know you better than to suspect kidnapping, Edgar."

"Oh, per'aps you shouldn't be so sure about that, Mr. Cartwright." Belton winked at him, but would say no more on the subject while he continued to row hard for *Pandora*.

There were very few faces aboard *Pandora* that Ben did not recognize from his service aboard the ship. But then Captain Dawson managed to be both easygoing and adequately efficient. Unlike on most ships, there was very little turnover among his crewmen. Ben had to run a gauntlet of grins and greetings before he could get below to Dawson's quarters.

"Damn, it's good to see you again, Ben," the captain said, grabbing Ben's hand and pumping it. "I see you're all right. Good."

"Captain, I'm awfully pleased to see you too, sir. But I'm getting an impression here that things aren't entirely what they seem."

"Well, you never were stupid, were you?"

"Sir?"

"Ben, I hate to tell you this, but you won't be going back aboard the *Wanderer*. Nor into Port-au-Prince again either."

"Sir?"

"I'm not joking about this, Ben."

"I can see that you aren't, Captain. But—"

"Dammit, Ben, we'll kidnap you if we have to. The boys, those as served with you before, came and talked this over with me. Their idea was to simply go to war on your behalf. I convinced them that kidnapping would be better. I hope you'll understand."

"Sir, the only thing I understand right at this moment is that I must be imagining all this. Drunk or delirious or . . . I don't know what."

"Sit down, Ben. Give me an ear while I explain."

Up above, Ben could hear the sounds of *Pandora*'s crew grinding the squeaky old anchor windlass and preparing to make sail.

Emil Dawson was quite serious about this, Ben finally admitted to himself. *Pandora* was leaving Port-au-Prince even as they spoke, and the intention was that Ben Cartwright be aboard when she did. Like it or not.

"Sit, Ben. Please."

Mystified, but certainly more than a little curious, Ben sat while the anchor broke loose from the roadstead floor and the ship took on a new liveliness in the way she rose to the harbor swells.

"Good Lord!" Ben blurted. "Murder?"

"Now, calm down, son. I didn't say that. Not 'xactly."

"But—"

"What I said was, and what the boys heard was, that your Captain Truesdell hired this fella in Port-au-Prince to have his gang jump you. That doesn't *have* to mean what you think. Though o' course it could."

"You don't happen to know who this gang leader is, do you?"

"Don't know his name, but he's a white man, not a native. Skinny little weasel who's rich as the king o' bloody England but dresses like a beggar. Belton and Wallat was sitting close by him and his cronies in some saloon close by the harbor. Overheard talk between him and the pair o' buckos that were gonna do the dirty work for him. Wouldn't've made the connection between what they was hearing and their old first mate except this ringleader knew your old nickname in these waters. Those people knew you, right enough. Spoke o' the Devil from Boston. That made my boys' ears stand up for sure. Once they knew their Mr. Cartwright was in danger, they came a-running back here to collect the rest o' the crew and some cutlasses." Dawson smiled. "You should've seen them, Ben. Going to war on your behalf, they was. You'd've been proud of them."

Ben shook his head. He was having no small amount of difficulty taking this in. His own captain had actually hired someone to . . . To what? That was the question, wasn't it? Hired men—by way of that fellow Percival, obviously; and mustn't Percival and Captain Truesdell have been laughing up their sleeves when he walked in on their conversation earlier and made it all that much easier for Percival to identify the intended victim—hired men to do . . . *some*thing.

Murder? No. Ben couldn't believe that of Hiram Truesdell. But . . . a disabling injury? Even a permanent one? Or simply some injury serious enough to keep him from reaching Boston by May.

He could believe—not that he seemed to have much choice in the matter—that much of Captain Truesdell's loyalty to *Wanderer*'s owner.

Did Elizabeth's father hate him so very much as that?

Apparently.

But . . . this?

Now that he had a moment to think it all through, though, he couldn't even honestly claim to *know* what Abel Stoddard's instructions on the matter had been. It was possible—unlikely, but possible—that Truesdell misunderstood Stoddard's desires and had been exceeding the original intent. Or it could be too that Stoddard baldly, boldly, outright gave orders that Ben Cartwright not survive the voyage to return for a wedding that he opposed.

The truth, Ben realized, was that he very likely would never know the truth about what was said between Abel Stoddard and Hiram Truesdell before *Wanderer* left Boston for the southern seas.

Ben shook his head and turned to look at his old friend Emil Dawson. "I owe you much, don't I?"

"Owe? You owe me nothing, my young friend. I've owed you my life for all this time. This tonight was no more than a payment of interest on that debt."

"I'll settle for agreeing that we owe each other," Ben suggested.

"Done."

"It's just so hard . . ."

"Aye, it must be. But wasn't that your old ship? Aren't those your very people?"

Ben nodded and unhappily explained the chain of circumstances that had brought him here. "So you see," he concluded after the lengthy explanations, "it's really you that I owe for my happiness as well as my life. If you hadn't loaned me that copy of *Paradise Lost,* I never would have found the courage to go home, and never would have gained the joy of Miss Stoddard's favor." He smiled. "I left that volume of Milton with her, by the by. I hope you don't mind. It was something I thought she might enjoy, as we two seem to share more than I ever dared hope."

"Mind, lad? Hardly. Books are meant t' be cherished and passed among friends. An' anyway, this way you shall still have it to share. Your other possessions 'll soon be on their way t' Madagascar without you."

"Pardon?"

Captain Dawson fetched out a pipe and began to load it. "You mean you didn't know?"

"I've heard nothing of Madagascar if that's what you're asking."

"Aye, Ben, that was my question a'right. Interesting that the ship's own first officer hadn't been told when it's openly known in the port. Someone must've deliberately wanted to keep the news from you." Dawson used the flame of a candle to light his pipe, then leaned back again. "Truesdell's ship begins loading cargo t'morrow forenoon an' sails within a few days for Madagascar an' then on into the East Indies and the spice trade. Been some turn-around on the crew list, I hear, what with some not wanting t' be away from home all that long an' others wanting t' see new lands. 'Ve you ever been into the Indian Ocean, Ben?"

"No, that's a part of the world I've never touched."

"Hard on ships there, or can be. Bad storms. Wind an' wave like a man shouldn't never have to see. But good ports o' call. Cheap drink an' giggling women. Though o' course you wouldn't be interested in those." Dawson sounded almost regretful that he wouldn't be joining *Wanderer* on her voyage.

"If she's off for Cape Hope, then I shouldn't think she'll touch Boston before May," Ben mused.

Captain Dawson laughed. "No, but you shall, m' lad. You certainly shall be there without 'em."

Ben began to feel a little better at that thought. "You know, Captain, they're going to be a mite surprised when I don't come back aboard, aren't they?"

"Or not. Huh! Vicious damn fools might think that slimy little weasel and his pals did their deed an' fed you to the fishes."

"I hadn't thought of that, but you're right."

"Be kinda funny if Truesdell comes back from the Indies a few years hence an' finds himself facing a dead man, eh?"

"Yeah. Funny," Ben said sourly. But the prospect did have a certain amount of appeal at that.

"One thing sure, Ben."

"Yes, Captain?"

"*Pandora*'s found 'er wind now and she'll spread her wings. Feel her come steady na'. We're bound for Havana, lad." Dawson smiled, white smoke wreathing his head as he winked encouragement at his young friend. "An' you, Ben, are bound for Boston, eh?"

Boston, aye, Ben thought.

Not the way he'd expected. At this point he owned nothing but what was on his back. And a much traveled copy of *Paradise Lost*.

So long as he still possessed Elizabeth Stoddard's affections, though, he owned all he would ever require for happiness.

He grinned and stood. "Mind if I go on deck and look

to the set of your sails, Captain? I might be able to trim a bit more speed from the old girl for you."

Dawson laughed and said, "Good idea, lad. I'll join you."

Together they went topside into the fresh clean air of the southern breezes.

CHAPTER 10

I now pronounce you man and wife," the Reverend Mr.
Wickstrom intoned in a voice so solemn and funereal
that the occasion might well have been mistaken for a
wake rather than a wedding.

Ben heard a gasp from the direction of the bride's
family's bench. That would be Mrs. Stoddard, who had begun to weep even before the ceremony commenced.

As he bent to lightly and chastely brush Elizabeth's
lips with his own, he caught a glimpse of her father seated
on the aisle end of the front pew, his wheelchair hidden
away for the time being. Captain Stoddard gave all the
outward appearances of a man who was filled with pride
for his daughter—which he undeniably was and always
had been—and contentment with that daughter's choice of
husband—which he was not and never would be, to Ben's
certain knowledge.

He was a strange man, Abel Stoddard. When Ben returned from the south this month past, Captain Stoddard's
welcome was warm enough to almost be believed.

Window dressing, that was all it was. Window dressing applied for the benefit of the man's wife and daughter.

And never once, not by word or deed or implication, never once had Stoddard indicated to Ben that he was anything but pleased to see him. Never once did he hint that he'd not expected to see Ben Cartwright in Boston again.

Nor for that matter had Ben chosen to confront Stoddard on the subject. He'd had ample time on his way north to think that matter through. Elizabeth's happiness meant more to him than any other thing or thought or feeling in the whole of the world. Meant quite literally more to him than anything else. And an open breach between her father and her husband could only distress her.

Besides which, Ben realized, it would be pointless to make accusations that could not be proven. No matter what he might suspect of having passed between Stoddard and Hiram Truesdell when *Wanderer* sailed the previous year with Ben Cartwright as her first mate, there was no way any man but those two could positively know the instructions that were given.

And neither of them was likely to reveal those orders.

Murder, injury, abandonment—or simply placing half a world between Ben Cartwright and Boston come this joyous day—any of those was possible. And so was the possibility that Hiram Truesdell might have misunderstood or exceeded his master's wishes.

In the end Ben had determined that his best course in this matter was to pretend none of it ever happened. For the sake of all concerned, and for Elizabeth most of all.

When he'd returned, therefore, he only reported that he left *Wanderer* in Port-au-Prince and that the ship was proceeding to Madagascar and the East Indies.

Captain Stoddard had accepted that. Or appeared to. The man allowed none of his emotion, if indeed there was any, to show on his features, and now Ben was careful to be as sparing of outward feeling when he was in Stoddard's company.

Now ... now none of that seemed important any longer.

Now Elizabeth Eloise Stoddard was—

No!

Great God, no.

Now Elizabeth Stoddard *Cartwright* was his wedded helpmeet and boon companion.

And now Ben Cartwright's life, that of it which mattered, was free to begin.

"Wife," he whispered into Elizabeth's dear ear before he straightened to face the church full of well-wishers, "I do love you."

"And I you," she whispered back.

He squeezed her hand and straightened, and the two of them turned to proudly face their friends and their future.

Together.

Elizabeth half sat and half reclined, leaning her slight weight against him. He liked the feel of her there, warm and contented like a cat curled upon a hearth. Ben's arm lay protectively over her shoulders, and her right hand rested soft and trusting in his. It was also true, though, that his right leg was going to sleep. He smiled and shifted position a little to ease it, then with the other leg gently pushed off to start the porch swing in motion.

"Mmm. Hello there," she said so softly he could hardly hear.

Ben reached up to smooth and lightly pet her hair. "I thought you were napping."

"I think I was. Just for a second, though."

"Sorry I woke you."

"I'm not." She squeezed his hand. After a moment she asked, "Do you love me, Benjamin?"

"Beyond love. I adore you. You know that."

She sighed and wriggled happily against him as the chain-hung swing drifted slowly back and forth.

"Well?" he demanded after several moments of silence.

"Well what?" Elizabeth returned.

"Aren't you going to tell me?"

She feigned a yawn, making a show of covering her mouth with her palm and smacking her lips quite loudly. Ladies, Ben was discovering for the first time in his life, were capable of some thoroughly unladylike practices. "No," she said, "I shouldn't think that would be necessary. After all, you already know good and well what the answer would be. But if anything changes, I shall be certain to let you know."

"Fair enough," Ben told her. "In that case, madam, I shall stop telling you too."

"Oh, Benjamin. Please don't." She sounded startled and almost serious about it as she twisted suddenly around so that instead of leaning against him with her feet tucked half under her, she was kneeling on the swing seat to face him. She looked almost serious too, her eyes bright and wide and peering close into his. "Please, dearest, don't even tease about that. Oh, I couldn't bear it if I knew I would no longer hear you telling me of our love. Please, Benjamin, never never stop telling me that. Not even when we've been married a thousand years and I'm old and ugly and you're bored with me. Lie to me if you must, dearest, but never stop telling me that you love me. For as sure as God is in His heaven, darling, I shall never ever stop loving you."

"Elizabeth!" He caressed her cheek and leaned forward—even though they were in public; but then this was, after all, their wedding trip—and kissed her. "Darling. Don't fret so. You know I love you. You know I always shall."

"Even when I'm old and ugly?"

"Years may make you old, dear. But nothing could ever make you less than beautiful to me."

"Tell me, Benjamin. Please tell me again."

"I love you, Elizabeth Cartwright."

She looked close to tears of a sudden, her eyes becoming unnaturally bright with an unexpected welling of moisture. "Oh, Benjamin. I still get chills every time I'm reminded of my name. I'm so terribly, terribly proud to be your wife. Did you know that, my heart? Did you know that I love you?"

"I know," he said solemnly. "And I thank you for it, and I love you too."

Elizabeth sighed, mollified at least for the moment, and turned about to resume her posture curled against his side.

They sat like that in silence for some time then, swinging slowly to and fro and looking out across the gray, rolling swells of the vast Atlantic.

Sails dotted the horizon as boats of all size and description plied the short passage between Boston and Cape Cod Bay. From the seaside porch of the hotel at Rexhame they could watch the traffic, Elizabeth delighting to the many shapes and colors of the sails on the small, lightly scudding boats, Ben preferring the dignified majesty of the great ships instead. From this porch swing that had become almost a private retreat for the two of them each could find much in the view to enjoy, as they had been remarking quite happily to one another for the better part of the eleven days they had been in residence there.

"I do despise the sight of the sea," Elizabeth whispered after some considerable time had passed.

Ben's eyes popped open and he straightened a bit. "What did you say?"

"I said that I despise that ocean out there, Benjamin."

"But—But—I never—"

"Oh, I suppose I don't hate it really. But I do. Sort of."

"Am I supposed to understand that?"

Elizabeth reached behind her to find his face and touch it, her fingers encountering first his nose and then his right eye. He winced. "Oops. Sorry." She tried again and this time located his cheek and patted it.

"Surely, woman, you do not intend to make a comment like that and just let it drop there."

"That would be cruel, wouldn't it?"

"It would. Now please explain yourself."

"It is really quite simple, dearest. That great and beautiful and truly quite awful ocean out there is in competition with me. And in the long run, my heart, it will have more of you than I. When *Wanderer* comes home again, you will be leaving me for her. And I do not know if I can bear to be apart from you. I really and truly do not know if I can stand it. I mean . . . I thought I could. Mama spent all those years apart from Papa when Papa was at sea. And I've always known of your love for the sea. I've always known that my fate was to be a sea widow too." She turned again. "Oh, Benjamin. How can I explain this to you so that you will understand and not feel hurt? I love you more than . . . more than life. More than anything. And I would rather be your wife for one perfect moment, for this moment, than be empress of the world forever. I truly would. So it isn't that. But I can't . . . can't help resenting the sea, dear heart, because it is the sea that you love more than me."

"Elizabeth! I'm . . . shocked. I love you more than—"

"Shhh." She pressed a finger to his lips to stop him from speaking. "Hush, my dearest, before you say something you don't mean. And if you must know, darling, in spite of what I said a little while ago, I would much rather you tell me a harsh truth than the very prettiest of lies. I don't want you to give me assurances that aren't so. Please."

"No false assurances, Elizabeth. No pretty lies. Just simple truth. And simple truth, my dear, is that I love you more than that ocean or any ship or . . . anything, just anything else in this whole wide world. You have to know that, Elizabeth. You have to."

She smiled—sadly, he thought—and rose up to kiss him. "Thank you, dearest husband. I shall always remember that you said it."

"You don't believe me, do you?"

"I will believe anything you ever tell me, Benjamin, because I know you will never lie to me." She said it, but she did not sound as if she meant it. She was still smiling, but he could see that she was close to tears again, and this time they were not tears of joy, but of a bittersweet sort of sorrow.

"I love you, Elizabeth."

"I know that you do, dearest, and I thank you."

"I love you more than anything."

"And I you." She cocked her head to one side and for a moment looked deep into his eyes. Then she smiled again, truly smiled this time, as he could see in her eyes that she was by a conscious effort of will setting her concerns aside. She kissed him once more. Then she resumed her place tight against him and, patting his wrist, said in a bright and cheerful voice, "Look, darling. That little sloop over there. See how pretty she is."

"But not so pretty as you," Ben responded by rote. His thoughts, however, were far away from Rexhame and the idyllic spectacle that was spread out before them.

Ben lay awake, staring into the shadows while Elizabeth slept at his side. Beyond the billowing curtains, beyond the open windows of the hotel room, he could hear the low, muted, inexorably repeating sound of a light surf meeting rock and coarse sand. The sound of the waves was as rhythmic and as regular as a heartbeat. And seemed almost as much a part of him.

And that, he realized, was his problem.

Because Elizabeth was very nearly right. He did truly love the sea.

A boy growing up along the rugged coast of Massachusetts almost necessarily was drawn to the sea. It was livelihood, entertainment, teacher, and hope all mingled into one immutable, unknowable, great and unassailable entity. The sea fed those who followed it. Clothed them. Beguiled and cozened and ofttimes punished them. Its presence was pervasive, all encompassing. For all his life, one way or another, Ben Cartwright had been close to the sea. Physically, true, but close to it much more than by way of mere proximity.

And now ... now Elizabeth felt jealous of the sea and threatened by it.

Between the two of them, if choice he had to make, there could be no choice.

Elizabeth was his life. He'd said that. He meant it from the depths of his being.

And Elizabeth was jealous of the sea.

Ben kicked the sheet off him—he'd had it already pushed down to his waist—and would have gotten up to stand in front of a window in search of a breeze except that he was afraid he might disturb Elizabeth. She slept lightly and sometimes coughed in the night. She was so very, very delicate. Often he worried about her.

Tonight in particular, though, he did not want to disrupt her slumber. Tonight he wanted the solitude of the dogwatch in which to ponder.

Because soon, terribly soon, there were decisions of monumental importance that must be made. Putting them off would accomplish nothing, he realized. He knew that because he'd already tried it. Had been engaged in the practice virtually since his return to Boston before the wedding.

When he came back, he had of course known that he could not again consider employment as first mate of Abel Stoddard's *Wanderer*. Nor, for that matter, any other form of employment by Elizabeth's father.

It was possible, remotely so, that Captain Stoddard was innocent of the matter in Haiti, that Hiram Truesdell had misunderstood or exceeded his instructions.

But it was not possible for Ben to believe now that Captain Stoddard was a willing employer of his services. It was clear that his father-in-law would hire him as a grudging sop to the wishes of his wife and daughter.

Regardless of all else, Ben had too much pride to allow him to accept such charity. But, dammit, it was his responsibility now to provide for the comfort and well-being of this marvelous, elfin being who slept so innocently at his side, and in order to meet that responsibility, he was going to have to find employment.

Ever since his return from Haiti he'd been living on wages drawn against his months of service aboard *Wanderer*. He had earned that money without question. He'd been a good first mate, no matter Abel Stoddard's biased opinions. Which in any event never had related to Ben's competence as a ship's officer. Stoddard's ill will began over what should have been a mild disagreement and seemed to have grown with time, until now the man was entirely unreasonable on the subject of his son-in-law. The point, though, was that Ben had in fact earned his pay when in Stoddard's employ and so felt justified in drawing a wage he'd honestly earned.

That, however, was ended. *Wanderer* was God-knew-where off the coast of Africa, and even if Stoddard offered Ben another berth, even a ship of his own, Ben could not possibly accept.

Which meant that he must find another source of income.

Rather soon, too, if the truth be known.

His wages had been ample for ordinary purpose, but when he reached Boston, he had come ashore with nought but the things he was wearing and one change of small-clothes purchased with the few dollars Emil Dawson paid Ben for his "services" between Port-au-Prince and Havana. Ben had felt able to accept such from Dawson because it was a gesture of true friendship and caring rather than a scowling charity.

The pay drawn from Stoddard's accounts had refilled his pockets. But he'd had more than ordinary expenses ever since reaching Boston.

Apart from the expected, mundane everyday matters such as meals and shelter, there'd been clothing to buy, in particular a suit for the wedding. The tailor for that had come dear. And there'd been myriad minutia, picking nagging, individually wee, but in sum, expensive things like brushes and razors and strop and soap mug. One thing piled upon another so that now Ben's pockets were close to empty.

Why, this wedding trip—he had no idea how much it was costing. Or who, actually, was paying for it. It had all been arranged by Elizabeth and her mother. Ben supposed that eventually, somehow, he would have to pay. No, dammit, he wanted to pay. It wasn't a question of "have to." He wanted to, and he would. But he didn't know when. Or how.

He squirmed a little and stared intently into the darkness in search of the answers that eluded him.

Ever since he realized that he was finished with his service aboard *Wanderer,* he'd blithely assumed that once the frantic activity of the wedding was concluded, he would settle Elizabeth into ... someplace—he hadn't worked out precisely where or what or how—and that then he would find a berth aboard a good ship.

Certainly employment hadn't been a problem for him before, when he was on his own in the warm-water southern seas. He'd found more than enough demand for his services. And he was proud of the fact that his reputation made sailing masters from Newfoundland to Rio de Janeiro want to hire him.

Except for the one owned by Abel Stoddard, Ben Cartwright could sign back aboard any ship he'd ever served on and be welcomed with enthusiasm.

He knew that and he was proud of it.

He had, in fact, been counting on it.

But now ...

He groaned a little, loudly enough that he must have disturbed Elizabeth, because there was a momentary hesitation in the rhythm of her breathing before she resumed her quietude.

Now, he thought, the course of his future—no, *their* future—no longer seemed quite so clear to foresee.

If Elizabeth would be happier for him to forsake the sea and make his, their, livelihood ashore, then how oh how was he going to support and protect and take care of this wonderful creature who was his for as long as they both might live?

Whatever was he going to do now?

He hadn't a clue, except to know that whatever else might happen, he would cherish—and provide for—his beloved.

"I think Henry will be here in a few minutes, dear," Ben said. It was as gentle and subtle a way as he could think of to prompt her to hurry. He did not want to correct her. Exactly. But he did wish she would finish with the incessant folding and refolding of everything and simply close the trunk lid. It wasn't like one time was any different from the one before or the one next to come. Each attempt seemed quite identical to all the rest. At least in Ben's undemanding—so much nicer a way to put it than "haphazard"—masculine views on the subject of packing.

"That's quite all right, dearest. This won't take me but another minute." As she said that, she was surrounded by mountains of puffy cloth, pressed paper, and open containers.

Their time in Rexhame was coming to a close. The coach was to fetch them from the hotel late in the forenoon. The luggage would follow by way of a commercial carter soon after. If, that is, everything was packed and Henry was allowed to take it all downstairs.

Ben still marveled that he could have traveled halfway around the globe—all right, a quarter of the way 'round; but another quarter or for that matter a complete circumnavigation would not have needed any additional preparation on his part—with no more personal possessions that would fit into one small chest and a seabag. And at that, much of what he carried with him was more nicety than necessity.

Yet for a wedding trip of three weeks' duration and two score miles of travel, Elizabeth, dear and delightful and adorable Elizabeth, absolutely required a trunk, two chests, two hat boxes, a case, and three bags. Incredible.

Not that Ben objected. He did not. But he did, most admittedly, marvel at this level of necessity on his wife's part.

He smiled, thinking about that. His wife. The notion still both thrilled and amazed him. Thrilled because Elizabeth was such a treasure. Such a joy. So beautiful. So precious a companion. Amazed because from among all mankind she had chosen him, the most fortunate—and undeserving—of all male humans, with whom to share her life. That was doubly incredible.

"Can we talk, dear?"

"I'm listening, Benjamin." She picked up a dress she'd already folded several times, shook it out anew, laid it flat on the bed and once more began placing sheets of clean paper over and onto the cloth of the dress so she could recommence the process of folding and, eventually, packing. Her expression was firm and might be mistaken for annoyance, but he was coming to understand her well enough now to recognize the look as that of concentration rather than anger.

"It's about something serious," he said.

"Are you finally going to tell me what it is that has been bothering you for the past week?" She never once looked up from her packing, finally giving that dress a terminal pat and laying it into a compartment of the large trunk. She took up a shirtwaist and began preparing that. "Well, is it?"

"I didn't think . . . that is . . ."

"You didn't think I noticed, Benjamin dearest? Of course I noticed. Why, you've lain awake night after night."

"I hadn't thought I was disturbing you."

"Only in that I've known something is bothering you." She left her packing long enough to cross the room to stand in front of the chair where he sat waiting and watching. She bent down and gave him a soft, lingering kiss. "I love you, Benjamin. I shall try to be a proper wife and not interfere in your business. But I do love you. I do care about you. I hope you will discuss things with me, darling, any things at all, if you feel free to do so."

"I didn't mean to worry you."

"It isn't a matter of worrying me, Benjamin. I trust you to set the course of our lives. But I do expect to take interest in anything that concerns you. After all, anything that concerns you concerns me too now. And I want to be available to you for any discussion you may want to have." She smiled at him, touched his cheek. "So please do tell me whatever it is you've concluded, darling. And while you are doing that, sir, I shall finish with the packing." She turned and went back to her jumble of clothing and shoes and oddments of feminine apparel.

"I don't—" He wasn't quite sure how to go on. Certainly he did not want to give offense to Elizabeth or to her family. He didn't want to distress her. Indeed, he hoped that what he planned would please. But if it did not . . .

He cleared his throat loudly and tried again. "Your family has been wonderful, Elizabeth. Really wonderful."

"Mama and Papa think almost as highly of you as I do, dearest husband," she said. She was at least fifty percent incorrect in that assessment, but of course she had no way to know that. Ben, on the other hand, did.

"Yes, well, you know how highly I think of, um, them too." Half a lie perhaps, but also half a truth. He did in fact like Mrs. Stoddard very much. Ben liked to think that Elizabeth took very much after her mother, receiving little from her father's side.

Elizabeth flashed him a smile and began loading shoes into the largest of the three carpet-pouch bags.

"I wouldn't offend them for anything, dear. I hope you know that."

"Of course, Benjamin. Goodness." She opened a small case, inspected its contents and fastened the thing shut again before she deposited it tidily into a corner of one of the leather covered chests.

"Well, it is just that . . . you know, I've been thinking

about this a great deal the past few days, Elizabeth, and I've decided, well, when we get back home, dear, I won't be going back onto your father's ship."

That news was enough to make her stop her packing. She paused with a pale blue gown draped over her arm and a quizzical expression on her pretty face and stood as if frozen into that posture while she waited for him to proceed.

"What I think I should do, Elizabeth, is to open a shop."

Her eyebrows shot up.

"A chandlery, actually," he added. "I still love the sea. But I enjoy commerce too. A chandlery would keep me very much in touch with the sea. I'd be dealing with ships' captains and shipowners and the like. But of course I would be—"

He hadn't time enough to finish that sentence.

With a squeal and a half strangled shriek, Elizabeth dropped the elegant blue gown onto the floor and trampled over it as she ran to her husband and threw herself onto him, her arms wrapped tight about his neck and of a sudden her eyes filled with tears.

"Home, Benjamin. You'd be home with me, wouldn't you? Every evening, every morning. We could be together every, every day, my dearest heart. Oh, Benjamin! You aren't just teasing me, are you? Tell me that you aren't, darling. Tell me you truly mean this?"

Ben grunted and, wonderingly, returned his wife's hugs, albeit with more control and less frenzy than she was displaying at the moment. He'd been concerned that Elizabeth might be offended because of him choosing to separate their future from that of her father and her father's business affairs.

This particular reaction was one he quite frankly had not anticipated.

"Oh, Benjamin, my dearest Benjamin, this is the happiest thing that could ever happen to me. Apart from becoming your wife, that is. Oh, my love. You really would give up the sea for me? Are you sure you won't hate me for it afterward and resent me for costing you your love for it?"

"I'm not giving anything up, darling. That's the thing. I'm not giving up the sea; I'm gaining a wonderful new career that lets me stay with you."

"We really won't have to be apart for months and months and years and years at a time?" she asked joyously.

"Elizabeth Cartwright," he said solemnly, "we shall never have to be apart again. Not for so long as we both shall live." He smiled gently. "Now where might I have heard something like that recently?"

"Oh, Benjamin. The whole rest of our lives, dear, will be just like this wedding trip has been. We shall never have to lose the wonder of these weeks. Benjamin, I swear to you, darling, that I'm the happiest, most fortunate wife there ever has been. The very, very luckiest." Elizabeth's tears began to flow then. She was laughing and gasping, weeping and kissing him, all of them at very much the same time.

It was a response that Ben found not altogether unpleasant, although as a result of it poor Henry from the hotel had to climb the stairs twice before the packing was finally concluded and he could begin carrying things away, and Ben and Elizabeth came very near to missing their coach, and in fact would have been left in Rexhame had it not been for a patient and helpful driver.

CHAPTER 11

They sat side by side in the lattice-sided shelter atop the widow's walk on the roof of the Stoddard residence. Aside from the pleasure of the view from up here, this widow's walk and their own sleeping chamber were the only refuges of privacy that were available to them where they could talk or hold hands or simply be themselves without having to take into account the presence of others, for "the young people"—it was a phrase Ben was coming to despise—had been given quarters in the room that once had been Elizabeth's "until you get your feet on the ground."

The time when Ben's feet might be deemed comfortably on the ground would be very long in coming so far as either of the elder Stoddards would be concerned; Mrs. Stoddard, because she obviously and genuinely enjoyed the company of her daughter and son-in-law and wanted them to stay for as long as she could persuade them; Captain Stoddard, because he less obviously would never be willing to accept the notion that Ben Cartwright was fit to take care of Elizabeth. The captain, Ben long since realized, not only did not like his former third mate personally and in particular, the man was not yet willing to relinquish his daughter. Not even to a husband.

So for the time being—as short a time as he could manage, Ben swore—the Stoddard home was also the Cartwright home, and this rooftop sanctuary where a wheelchair could not travel had become a seat of great peace and comfort insofar as Ben was concerned.

Elizabeth sighed and nestled closer against Ben.

"Cold?"

"Huh-uh."

He tugged her shawl higher under her chin regardless. The breeze coming off the harbor was fresh, and he did not want her to take a chill. She seemed so delicate to him that he worried about her health even though she had yet to have so much as a case of the sniffles since they'd been married.

"Are you happy, Benjamin?"

"Am I with you?"

"You are not supposed to answer a question with a question. Don't you know that?"

"Do I?"

She poked him in the ribs with an elbow. Sharply.

"Ouch!"

"Did I hurt you?"

"Yes."

"Good." A giggle escaped past the veneer of false bravado, and she turned and offered her face for a kiss. He was pleased to oblige her. "Mmm," she muttered with a smile. "You taste like brandy."

"I stood treat for Mr. Cappelman and myself," he confessed. The price of the brandies hadn't been much, but it was money he had not intended to spend today. Now he wished he'd spent it on a pretty for Elizabeth instead of a dram for Cappelman.

"You did see him, then?"

"Mmm, yes."

"Oh, dear. It didn't go well, did it?"

Ben shook his head.

"Never mind, then. There are plenty of bankers in Boston, just as there are plenty of fish in the sea."

"I suspect there are rather more fish than bankers, though. And I seem to be running out of them."

"Fish?" she asked impishly.

"Them too." More fish at the table would have been welcome, actually. Captain Stoddard favored mutton, and so it was mutton that was served—incessantly served—at the Stoddard table. Once he had his own table, Ben often thought, he would issue an edict that no mutton should be brought into the house. Including on those occasions when the Cartwrights were playing host to the Stoddards.

But first, of course, he had to have his own table in his own household. And in order to accomplish that, well, he had to have a bank loan so he could sign a lease and acquire stock for the chandlery he planned.

"You sound discouraged, Benjamin."

"A little," he admitted.

"Please don't be."

He forced a smile. "Very well, then, darling."

"Tomorrow," she said.

"Tomorrow," he agreed.

"Did you show him the plans you've made? All the lists and . . . and . . . everything?"

"I showed him." Once they were back from the wedding trip and settled into the chamber that so recently had been Elizabeth's alone, Ben set himself hard at the task of preparing a business proposal so complete and thorough and sensible that no banker could possibly refrain from accepting the opportunity to make a loan on the chandlery. Every bale of rope that Ben thought he needed, in every size and grade, was listed; every spool of thread or sailmaker's needle; every gimbal, cup or candle. And of course he'd looked for a place to locate this most perfect of all possible chandleries.

And that was the rub. All the really good locations were already occupied and turning a good trade. The best Ben was able to find at anything like a sensible rate of rental was much too far from the waterfront, rather too small for the purposes he intended, and in truth not of very good construction or repair. But the building was the only one that Ben believed could be made to work at a profitable rate of return. The business judgment he'd learned at his father's side those years ago helped him avoid grandiose, pie-in-the-sky plans now, and so he confined his planning to that which he genuinely thought to be possible.

The silly thing about it was that if he'd prepared an overblown, hopelessly optimistic plan with the intention of leasing a waterfront site at exorbitant, ridiculously expensive rates, why, the same banks that were turning him down now very likely would have approved him for a loan. A loan fated to fail, of course, but a loan that would be approved. He believed that because banker after banker after banker told him that his proposed location was simply too far from the seat of trade to be viable. And no amount of argument or explanation seemed to sway them, not even when Ben expressed his conviction that low rates and fair dealing would be enough to draw custom and, once drawn, hold it. The bankers were adamant.

All of which, of course, was far over Elizabeth's pretty head, and so he resolved as he had throughout to refrain from bothering her with it.

"Benjamin," she whispered.

"Hmm?"

She kissed him, and he felt and electric thrill that had nothing to do with the cool of the salt-laden evening breeze. "Tell me."

"Tell you what?"

"Tell me again about our plan. Our future. Tell me what Mr. Cappelman said."

"Mr. Cappelman said the same as all the rest of them said."

"Then tell me what they've all said," she persisted.

"It's all quite silly. Boring, really. Not the sort of thing that's fit for a lady's ears."

"Please." She nuzzled the side of his neck and into

his throat. He could feel the warmth of her breath there. "Please, Benjamin."

What could a man do?

He began talking. Hesitantly at first, then more forcefully as all the pent-up frustrations leaped at this opportunity to surface and began pouring out of him.

And the most incredible thing was that Elizabeth, who should have been repulsed by anything so complex and unromantic as business, not only listened intently, she asked questions now and then that were insightful and intelligent to the point of being helpful.

It was a conversation that Ben had avoided for weeks, but which in the event proved to be stimulating and quite thoroughly enjoyable. So much so that the two of them stayed there on the roof talking until the wee hours and then had to creep downstairs in their stocking feet, hand in hand and both of them giggling like truant schoolchildren, in order to gain their room without waking Captain and Mrs. Stoddard.

"More mutton, Ben?"

"No thank you."

"Turnips?"

"Nothing, thanks. I'm fine."

" 'Liz'beth?"

"Nothing, Mama, thank you."

"Captain?"

"No thank you, Mrs. Stoddard." The formal address would have sounded stilted in many applications, Ben thought, but seemed somehow appropriate within this family.

Which, of course, was entirely unfair to Captain Stoddard. Just because Ben did not care for the man, it did not honestly mean that Stoddard was unworthy of the affection of others. After all, he doted on his wife and his daughter and undoubtedly would do anything, quite literally anything, within the scope of his powers to please them.

"You may clear the table now, Luther. We will have our coffee and dessert in the sitting room later."

"Yes'm, Miz Stoddard."

Ben quickly rose and helped Elizabeth with her chair. Luther was already attending to Mrs. Stoddard.

Coffee and dessert in the sitting room, Ben mused. That meant his and Elizabeth's evening would have to be postponed.

Not that there was anything particularly urgent in their plans. It had become their habit, though, before going upstairs, to sit together, Ben with his eyes closed and the worries of the day put aside, while Elizabeth read to him aloud from *Paradise Lost*. Milton's wonderful work had become her favorite every bit as much as it was his— particularly so once he confided to her the role the volume had played in his homecoming—and she delighted in reading aloud to him in her soft, melodious voice. They would spend half an hour or so with Milton, then either go up to the widow's walk if the evening was fair or retire to their chamber if it was not. Captain Stoddard generally disappeared into his study after dinner and would not be seen by "the young people" again until breakfast. Mrs. Stoddard would . . . It occurred to Ben that he hadn't any idea what Elizabeth's mother did in the evenings. She was rarely seen after the family meal. He just hadn't made any particular note of that before.

Now Mrs. Stoddard led the way from dining to sitting room, beckoning "the young people" to follow. Luther wheeled Captain Stoddard along behind without waiting to be told.

When they were all seated—Mrs. Stoddard in her usual chair, and Ben and Elizabeth together on the settee— Mrs. Stoddard nodded conspicuously at the captain. "Dear," she prompted.

Stoddard smiled benignly toward his wife and his daughter. His eyes, Ben noticed, did not touch upon the son-in-law.

"Ben," he said, looking at Elizabeth, "I have a proposition to make you."

"Sir?"

"I know all about this plan of yours to, um, open a chandlery. Excellent idea, that. Excellent. A young man with your skills and prospects should do well in a chandlery."

"Why ... thank you, sir."

"No thanks necessary. 'Tis a simple truth, eh?"

"Uh, if you say so, sir."

"Indeed I do. Fine prospects and a fine plan. But I'm told you aren't able to locate a banker to provide your capital. Is that right?"

"Yes, sir. Although I'm hopeful for a turnaround."

"Yes, well, you've found one."

"Sir?"

"I am prepared to enter a partnership agreement with you, Ben. Fifty-fifty. I provide the capital, you provide the management. We divide the profits evenly. After, that is, a salary commensurate with your, um, managerial skills. An ample salary, that is t' say."

Ben looked at Elizabeth, who was beaming. And at Mrs. Stoddard, who was nodding and smiling and looking at Elizabeth.

It took no great leap of intuition for him to understand how this "offer" had come about.

Elizabeth mentioned Ben's troubles to her mother. Her mother, almost certainly with Elizabeth's full concurrence, took the captain by the ear and informed him that he was about to go into partnership with his son-in-law. And there they had it. A fait accompli, and neither Captain Stoddard nor Ben with any need for participation in the planning stages of this coup.

Ben felt the blood drain from his head. He shot a despairing look at Stoddard, but the crippled old man did not see it for he was staring intently at his daughter. No doubt, Ben suspected, because if Stoddard had been forced to look at him at this moment, the truth would have shown in

his eyes, naked and ugly, and wife and daughter alike
would have to become aware of how Stoddard honestly
regarded him. And for the sake of Elizabeth and familial
harmony, neither he nor Ben wanted that to happen.

"No!" Ben yelped.

"Ben?"

"Dearest?"

Stoddard's fixated stare in the direction of his daughter wavered, and he came very near to looking directly at
Ben.

"Thank you for the offer, sir. It's kind of you." Kind?
It would have been, had the offer been genuine and not
one that was forced upon its maker. Ben and the captain
both understood that quite well. "But Elizabeth and I do
not require charity. Nor, sir, would I welcome a partner.
Our plans have no room for partnership, sir. So I must decline your generous offer, respectfully and with apprecia-
tion, but I must decline."

For a moment Ben felt almost a shared purpose with
Captain Stoddard, as if a measure of kinship.

But only for a moment.

Stoddard's expression clouded. His lip curled into a
sneer of distaste. But only briefly. Very, very briefly.
Quickly the man regained control of himself and—for his
wife's benefit and Elizabeth's—voiced regrets that he pa-
tently did not feel. Hidden within his tones Ben was sure
he could detect more than a little relief. And perhaps a
twinge of gratitude to this son-in-law whom he hated? Ha!
A strange pairing indeed it must be to place the two of
them on the same side of an issue. But on this one subject,
no matter the spoken offer, Ben and the captain saw very
much eye to eye.

"I trust you will accept my thanks, sir," Ben said,
"and grant me the freedom to go my own direction?"

Stoddard looked toward his wife, then at Ben. "Har-
rumph. Yes. Stout o' you, lad. Stout. Can't say that I
blame you, eh? 'Course I accept your wishes."

"Ben!" Mrs. Stoddard protested.

"You should understand," the captain quickly added, "that the offer stands if you should change your mind. No limit on it, boy. Any time you want t' accept it, just speak up."

"Thank you, sir."

Ben felt Elizabeth's hand creep into his and squeeze.

He had done the right thing. He was sure that he had. He hoped that he had.

Oh, Lordy, he thought. There really had better be a banker somewhere in the vicinity of Boston who would be willing to underwrite the creation of a new chandlery. Either that or . . . or Ben didn't know what he might have to do in order to meet his responsibilities to this wonderful wife of his.

Tomorrow, he thought. Tomorrow he would set out anew. He would find a banker and *make* the man believe in him. He would. If only because he had to.

Ben squeezed Elizabeth's dear hand and felt her gentle response.

"You may serve the coffee now, Luther," Mrs. Stoddard was saying.

"Yes'm."

Ben was in no humor for chitchat and coffee. What he wanted was to escape with Elizabeth to the sanctity of the widow's walk or into the pages of *Paradise Lost*. But he would put up with this other. Of course he would. For Elizabeth.

CHAPTER 12

For what was quite probably the first time in his entire life, Ben Cartwright stood on the timbered wharf in Boston harbor and looked out at the wheeling birds and majestic masts and bustling activity without experiencing a lifting, cheering joy at the beauty that was laid out before him.

Today the sights of the familiar old port brought him only a heavy and despairing heart. Because today when he looked out across the harbor, he saw not beauty but failure. Failure to launch the business that might have given him and Elizabeth their independence and their future. Failure because he was forced now to realize that the businessmen of Boston did not have faith in his judgment. Failure, worst of all, to keep the promise he'd made to Elizabeth when in dear and delightful Rexhame he had—foolishly, it now seemed—promised he would never again go to sea and be separated from her loving arms.

Failure because at this point Ben was forced to conclude that his choices were reduced to two. He could sign onto a ship and thus earn a livelihood for himself and his bride. Or he could remain under Abel Stoddard's roof and thus—certainly in his own mind and very likely in that of his father-in-law as well—accept a parasitic, beggar's way of life, turning over to Stoddard the rights and responsibilities of providing for sweet Elizabeth and her future.

In no way could Ben ever bring himself to do that. And so . . . No. That was a proud and defiant and good thing for a man to believe of himself. But it wasn't really true, because in his heart of hearts Ben knew that he would choose charity, even submission, to Abel Stoddard or to Beezlebub, if that was what was demanded of him to secure Elizabeth's life and well-being.

But, barring that remote extreme, Ben's choices now remained limited.

He could knuckle his forehead to Abel Stoddard. Or he could sign onto a ship in acceptance of his responsibilities as husband and head of household.

With a sigh he looked out now at *Belliaux,* a fully square rig sailing out of Eggemoggin, Maine. He'd heard a little about *Belliaux.* Like all square-riggers, she was said to sail poorly into the wind, and her master made up much of his profit by depriving his crew. *Belliaux* had the reputation of being a poor feeder. Still, bad as her men were treated, her officers were paid bonuses on the basis of performance and she was part of a growing fleet under one ownership, which meant there would be opportunity for someone who could get the job done.

And just this morning Ben had heard that *Belliaux*'s second mate slipped on a freshly washed deck—in the broad daylight of a fine day while the ship moved slow and serene across a gentle sea, which probably explained why the poor fellow hadn't thought to be cautious of the dampness on deck—and broke his leg when he fell.

Belliaux needed an officer as badly as Ben Cartwright needed a job.

Ben sighed once more. And resigned himself to have a word with the captain of *Belliaux.*

*   *   *

"Cap'n Cartwright, sir? Wait up a second, please, sir."

Ben stopped where he was and smiled at the boy who was pounding breathless and sweaty to him. "It's Mr. Cartwright, not captain, but I thank you for the thought, son. What can I do for you?"

"A gen'lmun, sir . . ." The lad reached Ben's side and stopped, bending over and leaning his hands upon his knees while he gulped for breath. "A gen'lmun, sir, asked me to find you. Said he'd pay me right handsome if I bring you to him ere he goes to his lunch, sir. A whole dime he said he'd pay, sir." His eyes widened at the thought of such munificence.

"Then by all means we must see to it," Ben agreed. The boy—he couldn't have been more than ten, if that old—was so solemnly intent on his mission as to be amusing to anyone not so passionately involved in the quest for his dime.

Ben had been about to descend a ladder to a punt waiting below to take him out to *Belliaux* at her mooring. Still, if someone was wanting to pay an entire dime just to find him, why, that trip—which Ben would have preferred to avoid anyway—could wait a little longer. He winked at the boy, then leaned out to call down to the man waiting at the oars. "Later," he said. "Something just came up."

"Aye, sir, whene'er ye please."

Ben waved to the boatman, then motioned for the boy to lead the way to this "gen'lmun" with the dime.

"Do you know who the man is who's so anxious to see me?" he asked as they walked.

"Yes, sir. He's Mr. Silas Pitt, sir."

Ben's stride lengthened, and before long the boy was having to trot to keep up with the pace.

Mr. Silas Pitt was a banker.

Not just *a* banker, but *the* banker, at least when it came to matters of ships and shipping in Boston, and for that matter along much of the northern Atlantic seaboard.

Mr. Silas Pitt was so exalted a banker that a young

man of Ben Cartwright's modest means would never have dared approach him without an invitation.

But if an invitation were once extended . . .

"Sir. Sir! Would you slow down a bit, please, sir? Please?"

"Sorry." Ben grinned over his shoulder at the scurrying youngster. And tried, without appreciable success, to curb his impatience to the extent that the tired lad might be able to keep up.

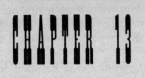

CHAPTER 13

W hatever in the world is this?" Elizabeth called from the porch of her parents' house.

"It's your husband, woman, demanding his rights. Did you or did you not promise to obey as well as honor?"

"I did, but—"

"Then come down here, Mrs. Cartwright, and join me."

"Benjamin! I'm not dressed."

"You look wonderful."

"But my hair isn't done. I haven't a hat. Benjamin. Really. I couldn't possibly be seen—"

"Luther. You there, Luther?"

"Yessir, Mistuh Cartwright?"

"Take a hat down off the pegs there, Luther. Any hat, it doesn't matter."

"Yessir?"

"Fetch down a hat and give it to Mrs. Cartwright, if you please."

Luther chuckled and hurried back indoors in search of a hat.

"Benjamin!" Elizabeth protested.

"No excuses. Come along now."

Fussing and grumbling but smiling nonetheless, Elizabeth allowed herself to be draped about with a hat, a parasol, and her handbag and virtually pushed down the porch stairs by Luther and by her mother as well, who had come out in response to the commotion in the street. Ben had no doubt that the window shades all along the block were hiding others who were just as interested in this spectacle.

And spectacle it was, Ben had to admit.

He'd shown up outside the Stoddard home riding in an elegantly grandiose maroon carriage with yellow wheels and polished brass lamps gleaming in the sunlight. The rig was drawn by a pair of handsomely matched bay horses and was driven by a nicely attired coachman with an only slightly battered top hat. There was even a footman—in this case footboy—clinging to a grab rail beside the luggage boot in back.

"But Benjamin—"

"Shush now, woman. Come along quietly."

The footboy hopped down from his perch and set a box on the ground to serve as an easy first step. Ben himself got down to escort Elizabeth into the grand vehicle.

"Do you like it?"

"Yes, of course, it's beautiful, but—Benjamin! Honestly. You haven't gone and bought a carriage, have you?"

He laughed and settled happily onto the leather upholstery at her side. "Of course not, dear. I haven't gone daft. Except over you, that is. I hired it."

"But—"

"We, Mrs. Cartwright, are off on a picnic."

"But—"

"No, don't worry yourself about a thing. There's a hamper of foodstuffs in the boot and a . . . a whatchamacallit—a set, sort of, with a cloth to put out on the ground and pillows for you to sit on, and napkins and tumblers and bottles of water and a set of plates and tableware and . . . just everything. You don't have to do a thing except sit where you are. These fine young men," he motioned toward the coachman, who was at least twice Ben's own age, and the footboy behind, "will take care of everything." He laughed. "I've bribed them, you see. I let them know that I've brought food enough for six. Which should be, I think, just about right for the four of us."

"But Benjamin, wherever are we going? There isn't a suitable picnic spot for miles and miles that I can think of."

"Oh, but my dear wife, there is one picnic spot that I can think of. Just wait until you see."

"We can't be away to all hours, Benjamin. Not without telling Mama not to expect us back for dinner."

"We can be back in plenty of time, darling. Not that I expect to be hungry again that quickly, but we should certainly be back in time to join the family for dinner."

"Benjamin. Surely a picnic will take just hours and hours, and—" Her protests were interrupted when the carriage drew to a halt on the waterfront only a few blocks from the Stoddard house. The footboy ran around to clip the hitching weights to the horses' bits, and the driver set his brake. "Why are we stopping here, Benjamin?"

Grinning, Ben helped her down onto the ground. With a bow and a flourish, he offered his arm. Perplexed, but apparently resigned at this point, Elizabeth accepted it, placing her own hand—ungloved, even though they were in public—upon his wrist. While they were doing that, the coachman and footboy were busy unloading baskets and bundles from the luggage boot and carrying everything into the cavernous interior of a cobwebbed and echoing warehouse that was built half atop solid ground and half on pilings extending over the water.

"Benjamin?"

"Allow me, madam." He led her proudly inside and to the middle of the huge, empty structure, to the place where the coachman was laying out a picnic while the footboy continued to carry bits of this and that in from the carriage.

"Whatever are we doing here, Benjamin? Now I'm serious about this. I really want to know."

Ben threw his head back and roared. About that time the coachman, now serving in an alternate capacity as waiter, managed to pull the cork from a bottle of sherry. The man poured tiny portions of the wine into stemmed silver goblets and handed one to Elizabeth and the other to Ben.

"Thank you, Bud."

Bud grinned back at him and stepped away, taking the footboy by the elbow and guiding him out of the warehouse to the carriage. Quietly Bud pulled the warehouse doors closed on his way out.

Once they were alone, Ben clinked the rim of his goblet against Elizabeth's.

"Welcome, Mrs. Cartwright, to the site of the new Cartwright Chandlery." He lifted his glass high in a toast.

"I can't—you haven't—oh, *Benjamin*!" With a squeal of delight, Elizabeth threw herself into Ben's arms, and the two of them hugged and danced 'round and 'round in the shadowy depths of the old warehouse, sherry and picnic and all else but this shared joy forgotten for the time being.

Ben swung the huge doors wide, the massive doors that opened directly over open water so that lighters, barges, even small ships could come directly alongside the chandlery—as soon as there was a chandlery, that is—for loading. Those doors, he was sure, would prove to be an advantage of immeasurable proportion because ships' masters would be able to save the expense and the labor of transportation for all their needs whenever they bought from Cartwright Chandlery. Ben was delighted with those doors, and his enthusiasm was clearly reflected in his voice when he tried to explain to Elizabeth the benefits that would be gained.

"Benjamin! I'm interested in all that too, dear, but I still don't understand how you managed to get all this."

He laughed and pulled her to him. "We, dear, not I. This is for us together, for our future."

Elizabeth came onto tiptoes to kiss him, then turned

so that her back was to him. She leaned against him, his arms tight around her and her hands pressed over his while they peered out over the busy harbor where boats and lighters scuttled back and forth like so many outsized water bugs. Ben rested his chin atop her head, enjoying this closeness, and then again tried to explain. But slower and more coherently this time.

"I was all set to go out and look for a berth aboard a ship," he admitted, "just like I told you I might have to do." He felt the press of her hands on his and the nuzzle of her pretty head against his neck. Elizabeth would have wanted him at sea even less than he now wished to be so far from hearth and home. "And this boy came running with a message," he went on, a note of wonder creeping again into his voice, "and the message was from Mr. Silas Pitt. You've heard of Mr. Pitt?" He felt Elizabeth nod.

"And when the boy took me to meet with Mr. Pitt . . . it was in his office, can you believe it? Me? In so exclusive a place as Mr. Silas Pitt's private bank? Why, an invitation there is . . . I'm rambling, aren't I?"

She laughed. Nodded. Squeezed.

"Anyway, a secretary met me and took me to an assistant, and the assistant escorted me right in to Mr. Pitt's very own private office—you should see it, Elizabeth, the carpet alone must be worth a fortune—and Mr. Pitt was there and he knew who I was. Can you believe that? He knew who I was."

"Of course I can believe that," Elizabeth retorted. "Everyone recognizes the most handsome and distinguished man in Boston."

It was Ben's turn to laugh and to give her a hug.

"Don't you dare stop now, Benjamin."

"Yes, well, as I was saying before I was so rudely interrupt—"

"Benjamin!"

He grinned, but gave in. "To make a long story short, dear, Mr. Pitt has heard talk from the bankers in town about my plan to open a chandlery and the price levels I think I can meet. I mean, my plan is a good one. Everyone has said that it was. Everyone agrees I should be able to attract custom. The problem all along has been to find a suitable location. And Mr. Pitt said he has faith in me and in my plan—did I mention that he remembers my father? Well, he does, he said so himself, he said he provided part of the capital when my father opened the shop here, that they were both young and eager and it was among the first commercial venture for each of them, Dad running the shop and Mr. Pitt loaning him the capital to do it—oh, but where was I?"

"Location," Elizabeth prompted.

"Yes, right, this location. Like I've found over and over before, the problem has always been location. And it seems that Mr. Pitt has only recently taken over management of this building. Which of course I've admired, practically drooled over, time and time again, except that everyone said it wasn't available and if it did come available would cost five, six times what it should be worth, even though with a location like this one and appointments like are here, the value should be enormous to begin with. But it turns out that Mr. Pitt—I'm not really clear on this point myself, whether he foreclosed on the building himself or one of his clients did—anyway, the building has only recently changed hands after Martin and Sons went out of business—do you remember them, dearest?"

She shook her head.

"Nice people, the Martins. They tried to operate a draying business out of the building here and buy and sell fish at the same time. That was why they'd wanted this site. But I gather they'd entered into the business unwisely. They were paying much too much for the building. Or so I'm told. Not by Mr. Pitt, you understand, he was quite circumspect about the whole affair, and I admire him for that. A banker has to be careful of what he repeats, after all. But of course I'd seen this place before and asked about it, and that is how I heard about the Martins and their troubles.

"So anyway, after Martin and Sons failed, Mr. Pitt came into a position of management that includes this building. And then he heard what I was looking for, you see. And Mr. Pitt is an experienced businessman. He understands that one doesn't bleed the cow and take the milk too. One or the other but not both, you see."

"Don't talk about bleeding, Benjamin. It makes me all goose-pimply."

"Sorry. What was I saying?"

"That Mr. Pitt knows not to ask more than a business can afford to pay."

"Right. Exactly. And the whole point is, Mr. Pitt found himself in need of a tenant for this building while we, dearest, were in need of a building. And he quoted me a rental that will be fair to both parties. And ... and I signed a lease. At once."

"But Benjamin, the money that will be needed to establish a stock of goods and put everything in order here—"

"That's part of the arrangement, Elizabeth. Mr. Pitt's bank will lend us the seed capital, just like he did with my dad years ago, and so he will earn interest on his loan at the same time that he is drawing a return on the rental. Naturally I had no objection to him providing the loan. Frankly, I was honored that he suggested it. After all ... Mr. Silas Pitt. Why, he is—"

Elizabeth turned in his arms to face him. "What Mr. Pitt is, dearest, is very, very fortunate to be doing business with the most wonderful, most intelligent, most romantic gentleman in all of Boston."

"What happened to handsome and distinguished?"

"Those too, silly."

He would have said something back to her, except Elizabeth had both arms around his neck now and was tugging at him quite insistently in an effort to bend him low enough that she could kiss him.

He decided not to interrupt.

CHAPTER 14

"Good night, Mr. Cartwright."

"Good night, George."

"Casey's already gone home. I hope that's all right, Mr. Cartwright."

"That's fine, George, thank you."

"Yes sir, well, good night, then."

Ben smiled as his clerk George allowed the expression of prissy disapproval to soften as he turned away and started down the steps from the loft where the chandlery office had been placed. George was a wonderfully efficient clerk whose books were not only in balance, but invariably immaculate and free of ink blots as well. But for some reason George was immensely jealous of John Casey, who was Ben's salesman, laborer, and general man-of-all-trades about the place. George was forever trying to find ways to bring poor Casey into disfavor and was forever reminding Ben or Casey or both of them that he was the one who had been with Cartwright Chandlery the longer. George had been the first employee Ben hired. That had been the better part of a year ago now.

Almost, in fact, a year to the day. Ben glanced at his

141

calendar and confirmed that the first anniversary of Cartwright Chandlery was only two days away.

Incredible, he thought. It seemed weeks, not months. And yet in another way it seemed forever. He could scarcely remember a life other than this one.

Certainly he would want no life other than this one.

The business was prospering. Already it was the third largest chandlery in Boston and was growing so fast Ben could barely keep up with it. Before long he would have to hire another man, he was sure.

And at home ... He laid his pen down and leaned back, simply wanting the moment to sit there in the silence of the still and darkening office while he appreciated the great gifts he had been granted.

In business less than a year, and already his note with the bank was paid within a few hundred dollars of being clear, and the lovely little house on Baldwin Lane was well within reach. They were leasing for the time being, but the owner had already said he would be willing to sell when Ben felt their finances made that possible.

And in the meantime, no home could ever have been happier.

Elizabeth was as radiant a wife as she had been a bride. She was sweet and kind, never an ill word, ever dear and supportive. She kept their home tidy and warm, and her kitchen was always cozy. Ben grinned and patted his belly. Still taut, thank goodness. But that would be due only to the lifting and stacking he was required to do each day at work. If ever he became so rich or so busy that he had others to do all the lifting, why, Elizabeth's wonderful cooking would likely turn him into a whale.

Whale! He uttered a brief exclamation of annoyance with himself for forgetting, and leaned forward to grab up his pen and quickly, before he forgot again, jot down a reminder that he must order more of those flensing knives that Charles Groening made. Captain Hartman of *Naiad* said they were the finest he'd ever used. Took an edge easier and held it longer than any other. And that wasn't the first such comment Ben had received back about the Weymouth smith's work. Quality. That was the thing, Ben knew. Combine quality and price and one couldn't help but prosper.

He wrote down the note. Post an order to Groening for. . . . what, five dozen? Seven, he decided. By the time the order could be filled, word of their quality would've spread among the whalers. Once that happened, seven dozen might not be enough. But it was, he decided, enough for this order. Moderation, he reminded himself. That was needed too, lest he allow himself to become carried away and grab for more than he could handle. That was the ticket. Quality and price for the customer, moderation for the merchant.

Ben had discovered an unsuspected talent for business, by jingo. And, more than that, a previously unsuspected pleasure in it. He was learning that it pleased him quite as much each morning to open the chandlery and survey this business that he had brought into being as it once had pleased him each day to walk onto a deck.

It pleased him to know that he was providing for his wife, and that his customers were treated fairly, and that his efforts gave employment to others beyond his own small family. He was quite frankly proud of what he was accomplishing here, and he took pleasure in that.

His stomach gurgled a little, reminding him that he hadn't paused for lunch today. Supper would be more than welcome this night.

Soon too, he thought. The clock suspended from the wall—positioned so that George could see it from his table—was in too much shadow to be easily read. That in itself was enough of a reminder that it was time to go home. He was either going to have to light a lamp or leave the office. And Elizabeth would fret if he were late. Better to leave the rest of this until tomorrow than to cause her any discomfort.

Quickly he cleaned the nib of his pen and put a stopper into the mouth of the inkwell, then laid a sheet of paper onto the ledger to mark his place and closed the heavy book. He took down his coat and high crowned hat and descended the stairs—it had taken him quite a while before he stopped thinking of stairs as a ladder, as the same structure would be termed when afloat—to the crowded floor with its shelves and bales and boxes of goods. To anyone unfamiliar with the chandlery, it would seem a vast and senseless jumble, but Ben and Casey and by now a good many of their regular customers knew where each and every item could be found. It was all more efficient than it appeared.

Ben made his way to the back and checked the big loading doors. As he expected, they were locked. Casey would have done that before leaving. And the latch had been set on the front door as well. That would have been George's thoughtfulness, to keep some customer from coming in at the last minute and interrupting Ben at his desk work.

Everything, Ben was satisfied, was exactly as it should be.

He was whistling a lighthearted tune as he let himself out and began the ten minute walk that would take him home.

"*What* is all this!" he demanded.

"We are having a celebration," Elizabeth said quite proudly. She was grinning fit to burst, for reasons that Ben hoped would soon become clear.

The kitchen, where they normally took their meals, had been abandoned for this occasion—whatever occasion it might be—and she had laid the dining room table with their very-extra-best silver and tableware, all the nicest pieces that had been given to them as wedding presents.

Fresh tapers burned in the wall sconces and in a pair of many-armed candelabra on the table. Overhead their modest little chandelier did its best to contribute light and sparkle to the display.

A roast of beef large enough to feed a small schooner's crew sat hot and steaming in a pond of rich juices, waiting for the master of the house to carve, and bowls of Ben's very-extra-favorite side dishes added their aromas to the scene. On the sideboard there were pies—not *a* pie but a pair of them, an apple and a berry, he guessed—and there was a crystal decanter of some ruby-colored wine close by Ben's place at the head of the table.

"Is someone coming for dinner?" He was quite sure he wouldn't have forgotten if they were having company. And anyway, the table was set with only two places.

Elizabeth giggled and shook her head.

"We've never used this room for just the two of us, have we?"

"Haven't we? I can't recall."

"Fibber," he accused.

This wasn't Elizabeth's birthday. Nor any other holiday that he could think of. It wasn't their anniversary or . . . anniversary. That was it. Of course. Elizabeth had this planned to celebrate the anniversary of the chandlery's opening. That had to be it.

Ben smiled, went to her and kissed her in thanks for her efforts. "I declare, darling, you are the most precious and thoughtful wife any man has ever had. I can't believe you remembered."

"Remembered?"

He explained.

Which brought a peal of laughter from Elizabeth.

"That isn't it, is it?"

She shook her head. "I'm sorry, Benjamin. I should have remembered. Can you forgive me?"

"Of course I— If that isn't what we're celebrating, woman, then what is?"

"Don't you want to eat first?"

"No, darn it. You have me curious now. Don't make me wait."

"You're sure, Benjamin?"

"Elizabeth. Really. You're standing there about to explode from wanting to tell me. I can tell. So do confess. Please."

"But dearest, this is so delicious, this drawing it out and making you suffer."

"If you don't tell me I'll—I'll—"

"You'll what, sir?"

"I'll thrash it out of you."

"Ha."

"Beg it out of you?"

"Never. Not until I'm willing."

"I know, then. I'll tickle it out of you." With a show of mock ferocity he started toward her, arms extended and fingers wiggling. There was one particular spot that only he in all the world knew how to find, where Elizabeth was desperately, hopelessly, helplessly ticklish. She squealed and backed away.

"Benjamin. Don't."

"Then tell me."

"I won't."

"You must."

"Beast." She was laughing and trying—but not very hard—to sidle away.

"Tell me."

"Later."

"Now."

"After supper, I think."

"Now." He grabbed her, sweeping her into his arms so that her feet came fully off the floor. "Talk, woman. Or I'll tickle you. I will."

"Be careful, dearest. Don't bounce me so hard."

"Bounce is it? Bounce? Tell me, woman, or I'll bounce you off the ceiling." He gently tossed her just enough that for half an instant she lost contact with his arms. Elizabeth squealed.

"Benjamin! Don't you dare drop me. You might hurt the baby."

"Ba—"

He was so startled that he very nearly *did* drop her.

CHAPTER 15

Time passes far too quickly when you are happy, too slowly when you are sad. Ben could remember a period when time passed slowly for him. But all of those memories were dim now and reached him only from a distance. With Elizabeth beside him, both of them aglow with the knowledge that soon they would be three, time sped by almost too rapidly for them to be able to savor and enjoy it.

Never could Ben had imagined being so joyous. Or so fortunate. He had Elizabeth. Soon they would have a child. And if those two facts were not miracle enough, the business continued to prosper as well.

Sailing masters from Halifax to Pawtucket were hearing comment about Cartwright Chandlery's fair prices and honest dealings. More and more of them were wanting to trade with Ben Cartwright, even if they had to go out of their way to do so. Ben received a tremendous amount of satisfaction from that. He understood for the first time—a deep down and genuine sort of understanding—the pride and pleasure his own father had received from the seemingly mundane and unexciting tasks of running a shop.

Providing service and creating employment were things a man could take pride in. That was not something he had been able to truly comprehend as a boy. The pleasures of business were a revelation to him. A most welcome revelation.

Good as that was, though, it was nothing compared with the joy Ben felt simply from being in the company of his dear and precious Elizabeth.

He woke before her each morning and without fail would lie abed while the dawn brought new light into their chamber. It was his great pleasure to prop himself onto one elbow and enjoy the sight of Elizabeth in her slumber as the soft light strengthened to reveal her innocent beauty, the lovely sight of her lashes curled dark and sweet against her cheek, the serenity of her expression, the curve of lips so vulnerable and soft. Sometimes his heart filled to overflowing and he could scarcely contain the love he felt for her. At those times a lump would form in his throat and it would take all his willpower to keep from disrupting her rest just so that he might see her smile upon waking.

Life truly could not be any better than this, Ben frequently—and fondly—reminded himself.

In the evenings it was their habit to withdraw to the parlor together. Ben would build up a fire to ward off the chill of the Boston nights, and Elizabeth would snuggle underneath a down-filled comforter in her favorite chair. She would trim the lamps as bright as they could burn and take out the battered copy of *Paradise Lost* that Ben gave her so long ago. Then, while he sat with his feet propped upon an ottoman, and a pipe wreathing his head with wispy halos of smoke, Elizabeth would read aloud so that they could enjoy together this magnificent work that had become so important to them.

And in recent months there had been an even more special joy added to their evenings, because it had become possible on occasion for Elizabeth to pause in her reading and beckon Ben to her. She would put the book aside and he would lay his palm against the swell of her belly while their unborn but already much loved child moved within Elizabeth's body.

That ability of the child to move, and for another to feel the motion, was something Ben would never in his wildest imaginings have been able to suspect. But that too was something that made him overflow with love and joy and pride.

Life was good. Truly.

"Mr. Cartwright, Mr. Cartwright, quick, sir, come *quick!*"

Ben bolted to his feet, shocked out of his reverie by the thudding approach of frantic footsteps and the near-panicked cries of a boy he recognized from the neighborhood.

"Quick, sir, quick."

Ben dashed out of the chandlery without so much as swerving aside to grab his coat off the rack.

"Doctor?" Ben stopped pacing and wrung his hands, as he had been doing repeatedly for the past half-dozen hours or so. "Is she . . . ?"

The doctor, a slender man with graying hair and bushy sidewhiskers, nodded solemnly. "They should recover satisfactorily, Mr. Cartwright. Both of them."

Ben's heart leaped. "Both?"

"You have a son, Mr. Cartwright. He is healthy and strong."

"And Elizabeth?"

"The delivery was hard on her. But I believe she will be fine now."

Ben reached for the back of the nearest chair to lean on, as for an instant there he felt actually faint with relief. He squeezed his eyes tight shut and offered up a brief, silent word of thanks. Then, unconsciously taking the doctor by the sleeve, he asked, "Can I see them now, please?"

For the first time the doctor permitted himself a smile. "Absolutely, Mr. Cartwright."

The worry Ben had been feeling through all those

hours vanished to be replaced by a thrill of intense, joyous exhilaration. Grinning now and wanting to hug someone—to embrace anyone, the doctor or the nanny or Mrs. Stoddard, even Captain Stoddard, if he proved to be the only one available—Ben let out a strangled whoop and raced up the stairs to the bedchamber where Elizabeth and their son lay resting from their ordeal.

Elizabeth *and their son*! How strange that phrase. And how wonderful.

Ben fairly flew up the staircase and down the hall. He paused outside the door for a moment to collect himself—with limited success, in truth, but he gave it an honest try—and then eased the door open as quietly as he could so as to not disturb Elizabeth if she happened to be dozing.

The first sight to greet him, however, was Elizabeth's prideful smile.

She lay, she and their *son* lay, swaddled chin deep beneath a fresh quilt, propped upon a mountain of down pillows.

There were others in the room. Ben knew that there were. He could not see them. Not yet. At that moment he could see only Elizabeth and the tiny, dark bundle at her side.

"Oh, my," he breathed. "Oh, my darling."

"Benjamin. Come meet your son." Elizabeth's voice was but a whisper. She sounded tired. And he had never seen her so pale and wan. But then the doctor had said something about the delivery having been difficult for her. Surely she wasn't . . . no, the doctor also said she would recover. That was the only truly important thing.

And his son. Their son. This child that was a creation of their love. The child was there at Elizabeth's side, squirming a bit. Even from across the room Ben could see the babe's coverlet wiggle and move. Once more there was that strange leap of a joy so great it was almost painful.

Ben tiptoed, grinning, across the rug to stand beside Elizabeth and simply marvel at the impossible miracle that had taken place here.

The child was . . . little. Red. Wrinkled. His skin was dark and mottled. His eyes were tight shut and his tiny hands knotted into fists. His lips, so incredibly small, pursed and he began to squirm about again. He was the most beautiful thing Ben Cartwright had ever seen. Most beautiful, that is, next to Elizabeth.

As Ben watched in utter fascination, the infant's little mouth opened and a cry rushed forth.

"Did I do something to scare him?"

Elizabeth laughed and shook her head. "No, Benjamin, I think he is just being bossy with us. Do you mind?"

Ben's only response was a vacuous grin. He was so completely entranced by the sight of his child, his son, that there was room within him for no other thought or feeling right now.

"Do you want to see something marvelous, Benjamin?"

His eyes shifted to meet Elizabeth's. "I already am."

"Thank you. But I mean it. Look here, Benjamin." She took the baby's tiny hand in hers and slipped a fingertip into the palm so that the little fingers clutched tight to her. She lifted the hand for Ben to see and, smiling, pointed to what she meant.

The fingernails. He saw at once that they were the source of her awe. And no wonder. "So perfect," he whispered. "Miniature and perfect." He frowned. "How do you trim a nail that wee? They're close to needing it already."

Elizabeth laughed. "I don't know, Benjamin. We both have much to learn, don't we?"

Gently, fearful of doing harm but unable to stop himself even had he really wanted to, Ben reached down and with the pad of one fingertip lightly touched first the child's impossibly soft and delicate flesh on the back of that tiny hand, and then, in the same motion, Elizabeth's finger as well.

"Oh, my dear, I can't . . . I can't—" He tried to swallow back an obstruction in his throat but had no success at all. "Are you all right, dear?"

"I will be," she said. "We both will be."

"Can I . . . can I kiss you?"

She smiled. "I would certainly hope so."

"And . . . him?"

"Yes. Both of us."

He leaned close. Tenderly bussed first Elizabeth's cheek and then the child's. He had never known that anything could be so soft as the baby's cheek proved to be.

"Benjamin."

"Mmm?" He was peering down at the child, at his son, at this second lantern to illuminate his life, the first and foremost being the marvelous, wonderful, incredible woman who had birthed this tiny recipient of so much awe and affection.

"I know what I want to name him, dearest. If you don't mind."

"Of course I don't mind." He said it without asking what name she had in mind. At that moment he would have granted her anything.

"I know we talked about naming him for your father and mine if he was a boy, Benjamin. But lying here, thinking . . . I believe I would like to name him Adam."

Ben smiled. He knew the origin of her impulse, of course. *Paradise Lost.* It already meant so very much to them both, in so very many ways. "Adam Cartwright. I like it. And a middle name?"

"I hadn't thought about that. Not either of our fathers, I shouldn't think. It wouldn't be right to honor one and not the other that way."

"No."

She hesitated only for another moment, then smiled. "Well?"

"Milton, of course. I should have thought of it sooner."

"Adam Milton Cartwright. It has a distinguished sound to it, doesn't it?"

Elizabeth nodded.

"You look happy," he said.

"I am." She reached up to take his hand and squeeze it. "After all, dearest, I have the two most distinguished and wonderful men in Boston, don't I?"

Inexplicably Ben felt his lip begin to tremble, and his vision wavered and swam through a sudden infusion of moisture in his eyes. "Oh, my darling girl. My dear son."

"Our dear son," Elizabeth said. "Our son Adam Milton Cartwright."

"Elizabeth."

"Yes, dear?"

He took a deep breath and tipped his head back, once more offering up a silent prayer. "Thank you," he said aloud.

CHAPTER 16

George."

"Yes, Mr. Cartwright?"

"Would you be kind enough to finish things here for me, please? We've a dinner engagement tonight, and Mrs. Cartwright asked that I not be late."

"Glad to, Mr. Cartwright." Far from being annoyed by the request, George looked quite pleased, accepting the responsibility as a compliment to his abilities rather than as an extra burden of time and labor. But he couldn't resist adding, "And don't you worry. I'll make sure Casey doesn't sneak away early while you're not there to see."

Ben smiled. "Thank you, George. I know I can count on you." More than five years, he mused, closer to six now, and George still maintained his one-sided feud with John Casey. Good thing the situation was laughable instead of intrusive. As it happened, though, Cartwright Chandlery had never been in a better position. Sales were so strong that Ben had been thinking lately about opening another location in New Bedford, his only remaining doubt being whether he would be able to adequately supervise a store so far away. Keeping on top of a second outlet

154

would require travel. And that would necessitate being away from Elizabeth and little Adam. He would be reluctant to do that.

Thinking about his wife and child brought a contented smile to his lips even as he left his desk and reached down the heavy coat and muffler.

Adam was becoming a sturdy, serious, intense little rascal, full of questions, and a keen observer of everything about him. At four years of age he already knew his colors and his alphabet and could sound out a number of simple words like "cat" and "rat" and "hat" when he saw them printed. Elizabeth spent much of her time playing with the lad, but playing at games that helped him to learn at the same time. And Adam was a quick one to learn. Ben knew he was prejudiced, of course. But even so, why, it was undeniable that Adam was a very bright child. And with *such* a marvelous mother too. Ben chuckled softly to himself as he buttoned the heavy coat to his chin and popped a furry, helmet-shaped cap onto his head.

"Don't be putting that muffler into your pocket, Mr. Cartwright. You know what Mrs. Cartwright said."

"George, you're becoming an old woman."

"That may well be, but you know the lady'd box my ears if I let you get out of here without a reminder."

"You exaggerate."

"Ha! Exaggerate or not, mind you put the muffler on before you step outside that door. And put it on proper too, not one of those over-the-neck-and-run jobs. Hear that wind howl? It's bitter out there this afternoon. And if you come down with something, it's me the lady'd blame. So do as you're told, Mr. Cartwright, or I'll not be responsible for the consequences."

Ben chuckled, but wound the muffler close around his neck so that his nose and eyes were practically all that would be exposed to the cold. As he was told. Huh, he grumbled quite happily to himself, it wasn't enough that Elizabeth held sway over the household. Now she was running the business too.

"Do I pass inspection, George?"

"So you do."

"Then good night to you."

The chief clerk smiled and gave him a final assurance that, "Don't you worry about a thing here, Mr. Cartwright. Enjoy your dinner."

"Thanks, George." Casey was working in the back of the huge, open building. Ben waved to him and to the two laborers who now worked under John Casey's tutelage. They waved back, and Ben let himself out into the sharp, cutting bite of the wind.

It was jolly cold, all right, he conceded. Good thing George fussed at him after all. The last Ben was outside had been at noon, and conditions hadn't been so bad then, but in the past few hours the temperature had plummeted and there was a wet, heavy snow accumulating wherever the ground was reasonably dry. Flakes as big as pigeon feathers so filled the air that it was difficult to see more than a few paces in any direction, and already ice rimmed the puddles in every rut or depression. Once the ground froze, the snow would pile deep if this kept up.

Ben ducked his head to shield his eyes from the force of the wind and plunged forward, taking his route by memory more than by mark. Lampposts and other pedestrians appeared before him like so many wraiths in the white, swirling air and disappeared just as quickly, like ships passing in a dense fog. He heard the rattle and creak of harness nearby and the rolling splash of heavy wheels cutting through mud, but never once did he get a glimpse of the team that was passing close by him on the road. Ben could not recall seeing a storm this intense in years. And never here in Boston within his own particular memory. The only comparable conditions he could remember experiencing would have been at sea far north in the Atlantic. He hoped the storm did not last long. The bark *Dannemara* was due to load a large order of goods in the forenoon tomorrow, and *Rainbow Chaser* was to take on another lot in the afternoon. A storm like this could throw the schedule off and make *Rainbow Chaser* miss her tide. Ben knew how little Captain Vale would appreciate that.

He hurried home as quickly as the conditions allowed, a matter of only minutes, but by the time he passed through the vestibule into the welcome warmth indoors, the end of his nose had been numbed by the cold and the tips of his fingers stung.

Mrs. Turnow, who acted as maid and nanny and lady's companion or any other capacity as required, met him at the door to take his wraps and scurry away with them into the kitchen. Whenever Ben might need them again, they would not only be dry, he knew, they would also be toasty warm. "Thank you, Mrs. Turnow."

"Aye, sir. No thanks necessary."

"I know that. But thank you anyway."

The woman, widow of a fisherman who'd been lost somewhere under the dark waters of the sea and who had been with them since not long after Adam was born, paused at the door as if she wanted to say something.

"Yes, Mrs. Turnow?"

"I'm a lady as knows her place, Mr. Cartwright. I hope you will agree to that."

"Indeed, Mrs. Turnow, I do."

"And I'm knowing that it ain't my place to be saying anything now."

"Go on, please."

"It's your missus, Mr. Cartwright."

"What is?"

"Your missus an' this dreadful weather is what I'm trying to say, sir."

"I don't believe I understand you, Mrs. Turnow."

"Mr. Cartwright, I've spent this live-long afternoon asking an' arguing an' finally begging Miz Cartwright to stay in t'night, sir. Ever since this storm came on s' bad, sir. She oughtn't to be out in a wind like this, I'm telling you. Not that it's my place to say anything. But I'll not stand by and allow that dear sweet woman to make herself ill, sir. Not even if you fire me for it on the spot right here an' now, sir. Which I freely admit you have the right to do if you feel you must."

"We'll have no talk about you leaving us, Mrs. Turnow. Now why is it that you think Mrs. Cartwright shouldn't go out tonight? Apart from the obvious, that is."

"Mr. Cartwright, you know the lady ain't been all that well ever since that dear child was born. You know the truth of what I say."

Ben nodded. It was true enough. Oh, there hadn't been anything specific, no particular illness or ailment that one could point to. Or that a doctor could treat. It was just that ever since the ordeal of bringing Adam into the world, Elizabeth never really quite regained her strength. Her vitality was unabated, as strong and as wonderful as ever. But she had always been delicate, and seemed all the more so since childbirth. That was why the Cartwrights had not been blessed with a brother or a sister for Adam. Dr. Jarman had warned them that she was too frail to safely carry another baby. A second pregnancy, he'd said, could mean the loss of child or mother ... or both. Ben had never been willing to take that risk, not even on those occasions when Elizabeth herself mentioned a desire that they have more children. Elizabeth and Adam were all Ben could ever possibly require for a lifetime of happiness.

"I'm telling you, Mr. Cartwright, that that little missus o' yours is sick more often than she ever lets on. Even to you, sir. Or to me either one. She puts on the brave face, sir, but she's hiding things from the both of us. I can tell. I can feel it in my heart, sir." Mrs. Turnow laid a bony hand over her own scrawny breast as if swearing an oath on the matter. Or simply locating her heart in the event Ben might not know where the things were to be found. "I'm that sure o' it, sir, that I'm speaking up here an' now though it ain't my place to do so. I'm telling you plain, Mr. Cartwright, to keep that dear lady indoors tonight an' don't be allowing her out into this cold an' wind, sir."

"Thank you, Mrs. Turnow. I'm sure you are correct. I'll suggest we stay home tonight."

"You can't just suggest it, Mr. Cartwright. Lord knows I been begging an' arguing this whole afternoon long. You got to put your foot down, sir. You got to tell that lady right out that you hadn't ought to go an' you just ain't going."

Mrs. Turnow looked so serious about it that Ben almost had to smile. "Thank you, Mrs. Turnow. I appreciate your loyalty, and I know Mrs. Cartwright does too."

"Yes, sir. Even if you fire me, sir, I had to say it."

"I'll go right now and speak to Mrs. Cartwright about it."

"She's in the nursery with Adam, sir."

Ben winked at the woman and took the stairs two at a time. Now that he'd had time to warm up from the bitter cold of the storm he felt exceptionally good.

"Pooh," Elizabeth said when Ben relayed Mrs. Turnow's fears to her.

"Pardon me?"

"Pooh, Daddy. Mama said pooh. Is that a bad word, Daddy? Is it?"

"It isn't a bad word, son. Mama doesn't say bad words." Ben swung Adam into the air, then turned him around and perched the child on his shoulders. To Elizabeth he said, "Adam has a point, dearest. Neither one of us knows just exactly what 'pooh' indicated in this particular circumstance."

"Pooh, my two darlings, means that Mrs. Turnow is worrying about nothing at all. Goodness, I should know how I feel, shouldn't I? And I am perfectly all right. Certainly no little bitty snowfall is going to keep us from going over to Papa's birthday supper. We shall simply bundle ourselves so deep in warm clothing that we can roll, roll, rolllllll," she reached up to pinch Adam's big toe, making him shriek with delight, "all the way to Mama and Papa's."

"It's awfully cold, Elizabeth."

"Pooh."

"But if you've been feeling poorly—"

"Benjamin. Really. Which of us should know better how I am feeling, Mrs. Turnow or me?"

There was no suitable response to that question. Not that Elizabeth wanted one.

"I am fine, Benjamin. And we did promise to be there. They will have been cooking this entire day long, and all the other guests will be on hand. It would be simply awful if his own family didn't care enough to come take dinner with him on his birthday."

"When we promised to be there," Ben reasoned, "no one knew there would be a storm today. And you know as well as I do that your father would be the last person—no, make that one of the last persons—in the world to want any harm to come to you. Much as I disagree with him about some things, dear, I've never doubted his affections for you and for Adam. He would be the first to ask you to stay home if there could be the least, littlest scrap of risk."

"But Benjamin, dear, that is what I am trying to tell you. Goodness, darling, I wouldn't think of going myself if I thought there would be a risk attached. But I don't. Truly. I feel fine. I have all along. Mrs. Turnow is merely worrying overmuch. You know it was a winter storm that claimed Mr. Turnow. That is the only thing that is making her so fretful now." Elizabeth came onto her tiptoes to give Ben a kiss in the shelf of his jaw and then with a squeal kissed the tender curve of Adam's knee. The child went into such paroxysms of giggles and squirms that for a moment Ben thought he might drop the boy. "Go on now, Benjamin. You'll want to put on a fresh shirt, I know, and Mrs. Turnow can dress Adam for the party while I change into something nice." She smiled sweetly. "Something nice and heavy if it makes you feel any better."

Ben sighed. "If you're sure."

"I'm positive."

"Mrs. Turnow says I should put my foot down and insist we stay at home tonight."

"If you put your foot down, dearest, you may get a sore foot. Personally, though, *I* am going to Mama and Papa's for the evening." And with that she was out the door. A moment later Ben heard her calling down the stairs for Mrs. Turnow to come dress Adam.

Ben frowned. There were times when he wondered if he should be more forceful with Elizabeth. But the truth was that he could bring himself to deny her nothing that was within his power to give. She did indeed have one strong point in her favor. No one but she could know how she felt. Mrs. Turnow could not. And Elizabeth had been right too—a point Ben himself had forgotten—that Evan Turnow and the rest of that crew died in a fierce winter squall somewhere on the Grand Banks.

One thing sure, though. Ben was going to absolutely insist that Elizabeth and Adam both be bundled so deep and secure that even their eyeballs couldn't become chilled.

He would put his foot down on that point if he had to. He really would.

"Doctor?" Ben looked up from his chair. Someone, he could not recall who, had brought it from the parlor to the upstairs hallway where he had been waiting in an anguished vigil for . . . how long? He had no idea . . . forever. His eyes were red-rimmed and stung from lack of sleep, and his cheeks were dark with beard stubble. His clothing smelled sour, and he knew he should go bathe, but he couldn't bring himself to leave that long. "Is she . . . ?" He could not force himself to ask the rest of that question.

Dr. Jarman shook his head. The movement was minute. It was enough to drive a spike of raw horror deep into Ben's chest.

"But she can't—" Ben was distantly aware of trying to rise from the chair, dimly aware that the doctor was standing before him—Ben hadn't noticed the man move, although he had come a half-dozen paces from the bedchamber door to the chair—pressing onto Ben's shoulders as if in an effort to keep him from getting up.

"I have to go in to her, Doctor. Please."

"Don't, son. There is nothing you can do."

"But I have to tell her . . . tell her—" Ben's voice broke. He sobbed and wrenched away from the doctor's grip.

"She is gone, Mr. Cartwright. I'm sorry, but she is gone. Please let the ladies take care of her now. They'll let you know when you can see her."

"But Doctor, you don't understand. I have to tell her . . . there is so much that I have to say to her yet. She can't go. Not now. Not before I tell her that I love her. Not before I tell her . . . good-bye."

Jarman motioned to someone—Ben couldn't see who—and Ben felt himself being turned, pulled, drawn away.

Elizabeth. Gone? He could not accept it. It was too much. Altogether too much. And too quick.

There was so *much* he needed to say to her. Assurances that he needed to give to her. Why, surely there were things she would want to tell him too. There was just so very much left unsaid that the doctor had to be wrong, just had to be. Elizabeth couldn't be gone yet. Not yet. They hadn't had a chance to prepare for . . . this. Hadn't talked about it. Why, Elizabeth and he talked about everything. Everything. Especially they should discuss anything as serious as this.

Elizabeth couldn't die, for God's sake.

Not without telling him.

Not without talking to him about it.

Not without . . . oh, God . . . not without him.

Dammit anyway. How dare she leave him like this? How dare she even think about going before him?

It wasn't fair. This way wasn't at all fair.

She couldn't . . .

He was downstairs. Somehow he was downstairs. He recognized the fact but had no recollection of being taken down the stairs. And he still had no idea who it was who had hold of his arms on either side. He thought about looking to see. Then knew that it didn't matter anyway.

Nothing mattered.

Except that Elizabeth was gone

No, dammit, she wasn't *gone*. She was *dead*. Not just gone. Dead.

Until death do us part. For some insane reason the phrase crept into his mind and refused to leave. Until death do us part. So good-bye, Elizabeth. Now we part.

Except he hadn't had a chance to say good-bye, and really they should have been allowed that, shouldn't they? Shouldn't they have a moment to smile and hold hands and make brave promises? Shouldn't they?

Ben could see faces floating in front of him. Worried faces. Sorrowful faces. Mrs. Stoddard. Mrs. Turnow. George Drummond from the chandlery. John Casey. The Browns from next door. The Warrens from across the street. Where had they all come from? How long had they been here? How long had it been since—

"So sorry, Ben."

"Please accept our . . ."

". . . loved by all who knew her . . ."

"Such a loss to the entire . . ."

The faces and the voices and the sorrows swam all together in a stew of half-sensed misery.

". . . so sad to hear of your loss . . ."

"Never knew anyone so decent and kind as . . ."

The numbing fog was a mercy. Ben knew that it was. It was perhaps the only thing in this experience that he did not resent.

". . . sweet child in the bosom of Abraham . . ."

Dear God. Elizabeth. I miss her. I miss her so much. Can't I tell her that, God? Can't I?

". . . good thing you still have . . ."

The voices all ran together into so much meaningless noise. But then without Elizabeth nothing made sense.

Without her there was no meaning. Likely nothing ever would have sense or meaning, not ever again.

It was difficult for him to breathe.

Not that he cared whether he breathed or not.

His chest rose and fell and he would have been quite as happy—no, happier—if it did not. If it simply stopped and he could—

Elizabeth!

He should have told her good-bye. That more than anything. He should have told her good-bye.

"Cartwright."

The voice was harsh. Accusing. Ben struggled to focus his attention for the first time since . . . since Elizabeth left him.

"Captain." His throat was raw, and his own voice seemed strange in his ears. He tried for Elizabeth's sake to call Abel Stoddard "Papa." She had wanted him to do that. Or at least to be able to speak to the man by name. Ben tried once again to bring himself to do it, for Elizabeth's sake, but as always before, he could not.

Even so, Ben's heart went out to the crippled old seaman. Abel Stoddard loved Elizabeth without reservation, as truly as he himself did, and that truth Ben could not diminish or deny. And the old captain had suffered a terrible loss now, just as surely as he had. "Captain, I—" He reached out, wanting to take Stoddard's hand, to touch him and to let him know that he too knew the depth of his pain and shared it.

Stoddard recoiled, snatching his wrinkled and liver-spotted hand off the arm of the wheeled chair.

"You son of a bitch," the old man snarled. "You killed her, Cartwright. You murdered my baby."

Ben blinked. The aura of unreality that had held him captive ever since Elizabeth died continued to surround him now. But he was sure—almost sure—that he heard Stoddard's words correctly.

"You son of a bitch," Stoddard repeated.

"I don't . . . I don't understand."

Stoddard struck feebly in Ben's direction, but Luther had already seen and rolled the chair backward so that the weak blow came far short of landing.

"Sorry, suh," Luther said. "I'm real sorry. 'Bout this and 'bout Miss Elizabeth too."

"I know, Luther. I know you are."

Luther wheeled the captain away, and the room full of mourners crowded in close around Ben.

Once more the fog descended over him. The blessed, merciful, pain-dulling fog.

Elizabeth, he moaned. Perhaps aloud or perhaps not. He did not know and did not care.

Elizabeth, I love you. Elizabeth, I miss you. And why oh why didn't you tell me good-bye, how could you leave and not even say good-bye? Dear God, I miss you so. . . .

CHAPTER 17

"Y ou sent for me, sir?" Ben's voice was dull and dis-
interested. As in truth he was. Since Elizabeth's
shockingly untimely death two months ago, there
was virtually nothing in life that interested him. He awoke
in the mornings. He dressed himself. Whenever food was
placed before him, he ate. He walked down to the chandlery each day and sat quietly at his desk. He did those
things only because he could think of nothing else that he
wished to do. Mrs. Turnow and Mrs. Stoddard took care of
Adam by turns, and Mrs. Turnow ran the household to
whatever extent it was run. George Drummond and John
Casey were taking care of the business. Ben wasn't sure,
but he didn't think the two men were even bickering
lately. Now for some reason Mr. Silas Pitt had requested
that he come to the bank. There had been a time when Ben
would have been nervous about such a summons. Now he
quite frankly did not give much of a damn what the powerful banker wanted.

"I did, Cartwright. Sit down." The old man's expression softened. "Please."

Ben sat without comment and gazed dully across the

broad desktop at this man who had provided banking services now for two generations of Cartwrights. Mr. Silas Pitt was a man in his early seventies, Ben guessed, with thinning hair and a complexion like bleached parchment. A scent of bay rum lay in the air around him, suggesting he'd stopped at a barber's on his way to the bank today.

Pitt waited for a long moment, obviously expecting Ben to ask the purpose of this meeting, but if that was his wish, he was disappointed. The foggy distraction that Ben had been experiencing ever since Elizabeth's death made this whole thing quite unimportant to him. All that was important now was that Elizabeth was gone. Nothing else mattered to him in the slightest.

"You, um, no doubt are wondering why I asked you here, Cartwright."

Ben didn't answer.

Again Pitt hesitated. From a detached and unbiased viewpoint where he was able to observe events as if he were invisible, Ben was distantly aware that Mr. Silas Pitt, the great and all-powerful banker to the whole of the northern coast, seemed unsure of himself, even embarrassed.

"I am sorry to tell you this, Cartwright. I must be frank with you. I have argued against this course of action, but my hands are tied on the subject. Do you understand what I am saying to you, man?"

"No." Hands. Ben looked down at his hands. His hands retained their strength. What they lacked, these hands that used to caress Elizabeth's dear cheek, was direction. What they lacked was purpose. What they lacked was the sweet softness of that cheek to touch.

"Can you hear me all right, Cartwright?"

Ben nodded. Silently.

Pitt cleared his throat and fidgeted on the big, rollabout armchair that dwarfed the old man's slight form. "Yes, well, as I was saying, Cartwright, this business is not to my liking. Before we get down to it, is there anything I can get you? Coffee? A pastry? Have you had breakfast yet?"

Ben couldn't remember if he'd had anything to eat today or not. Not that it mattered. "I don't want anything, thank you." He continued to examine his fingers.

Pitt cleared his throat again, more loudly this time, and motioned across the room toward one of the clerks, who, no doubt interpreting the gesture from long experience, went to fetch coffee and a tray of sweets anyway. Pitt waited until they were served before he continued with what was proving to be a painful task.

"Your, um, landlord, Cartwright, has, um, seen fit to terminate your lease."

There was a dark shading, dirt possibly, under the nail of the third finger on Ben's left hand. He thought about searching his pockets for some implement that would clean the offensive material away. But of course that would be rude. He remained silent and still.

"Did you hear me, Cartwright?"

"Yes, sir. The landlord wants his building back."

"There is a termination clause in the leasehold agreement. Do you remember that?"

Ben didn't respond.

"There is such a clause. But of course anything is subject to proof in a court of law. Not that I am, um, suggesting anything, you understand. But you are aware, I'm sure, that you could retain counsel, seek an injunction. If nothing else, you see, you could block the termination temporarily. Until your case is ruled upon in open court. Any reasonably clever lawyer should be able to string things out and keep the business open in its present location for, well, quite frankly, Cartwright, for perhaps several years. Certainly for a period long enough that you might be able to negotiate some accommodation from the, um, landlord. Or at the very least long enough for you to locate your business to new quarters.

"If I may say so, Cartwright, you've established a sterling reputation there. I am sure your custom would follow should you relocate. And I happen to know with some considerable degree of assurance that you would be welcomed as a tenant by other property owners along the harbor front. For, um, that matter, Cartwright—may I call you Ben?—for that matter it should not be impossible for you to obtain a loan for the purchase of a building of your own. Do you understand what I am saying to you, Ben? Do you?"

"Yes. Thank you."

"And, um, do you want to pursue any of those avenues? Do you have an attorney of your own? Or would you like for me to recommend one?"

Ben shrugged.

Pitt scowled, embarrassment giving way now to anger. "Are you not interested in the defense of your own affairs, man?"

Ben looked up from his fingernails and directly into Mr. Pitt's eyes for the first time since he'd been brought before the banker. "Thank you, sir. I appreciate your concern."

"Hmmmph. Seems my concern is greater than yours at this point, Cartwright."

"I'm sorry, sir," Ben said, not meaning it, but aware that it was what he was expected to say.

"I suppose I must go on then. Some time ago the person who is your, um, landlord asked to purchase your notes pledged against the Cartwright Chandlery. At the time I saw no harm in that, and there were sound business reasons why it would be to the bank's advantage. Never mind what those reasons may have been. In any event, Cartwright, the holder of those notes has, um, determined that he, uh, wishes to call for immediate repayment. Which you may recall is permissible under the terms of the note. It was my intention, Cartwright, to suggest that the bank—in effect, that I myself—extend a line of credit sufficient to cover those outstanding notes and, um, replace them. But your attitude here being what it is, man, why, I am not sure now that this would be a wise business course. Certainly it would not be if you intend simply to let the chandlery go without a fight. May I, um, ask what your intentions are at this point, Mr. Cartwright?"

Ben sighed. "I'm sorry, sir. I really don't know ... might I ask one thing?"

"Of course."

"Not that it matters, but—who is this person who is terminating my lease and my loans? I mean, I'd thought my dealings were with you and this bank."

"You did deal with me, of course, but I was, um, acting as an agent. It was all quite correct, I assure you. A favor done on behalf of one old client to benefit the son of another old client, so to speak. But of course you should have the right to know. The owner of the property that was leased to you, and the person who later purchased your notes, is, um, Capt. Abel Stoddard."

Ben nodded but did not comment.

"Does that ... is there anything you want to tell me, Cartwright? Or anything you want to ask?"

"No, sir. Thank you."

"Will you be seeking legal counsel?"

"I really don't know, sir."

"Frankly, Mr. Cartwright, I find it very difficult to believe that you can just sit there and accept the ruination of everything you have built here. You aren't angry. You aren't fuming or shouting or ... or anything. What kind of man are you, Cartwright?"

"I don't know, sir. Sorry." But within the privacy of his own mind Ben's response was more honest. An empty one, he might have said. If he'd cared enough to bother speaking out. "Thank you for your time and your advice, sir. May I go now?"

Pitt's expression became one of disgust, but the man's disdain held no sting for Ben now. Nothing did. "You may go, Cartwright. In fact, sir, please do."

Ben stood, the coffee and sweet rolls untouched on the gold-rimmed porcelainware that had been placed beside him.

He turned and without further comment walked away from Mr. Silas Pitt and the office and the bank.

"Mr. Cartwright, you have been drinking."

"No, madam, I have not. And if that is the purpose of your visit, then I suggest you leave."

"You are rude, sir."

"Am I?" Ben turned, went back to the chair where he spent nearly all his waking moments, sat and waited. If these people wanted to stay, they could do so. If they wanted to leave, that was fine too.

They were, obviously, a delegation of sorts. From the church, although the Reverend Mr. Wickstrom was not among them. There was Hankins, who was an elder of the congregation, and Mayberly, who was a deacon. This male contingent, however, was merely window dressing for the true delegates, who were Mrs. Clara Byner, Mrs. Maud Dorrance, and Mrs. Josephine Vold. Five persons, one expression. All their faces were pinched and disapproving.

Ben supposed he had this coming, though. Since the chandlery was taken away from him—no loss whatsoever in comparison with the loss he'd already suffered—he had lost the habit of bothering with the ordinary things. Like shaving or dressing or leaving the house. For the most part he simply sat in the parlor where once, for so many wonderful hours, Elizabeth used to read to him from the volume of *Paradise Lost* that he'd not opened since her death.

But he did not drink. Any such accusation was false. Mrs. Turnow could testify to that.

As for this delegation of prim and priggish ba— He grunted and lapsed back into lethargy. It didn't really matter what any of these people said or did. After all, nothing mattered any longer. Did it?

With a succession of clearly audible sniffs and snorts of disapproval, the church delegates helped themselves unbidden to seats in the Cartwright parlor.

It occurred to Ben that Mrs. Turnow was not on hand to flutter about offering coffee or cakes or whatever. In fact the housekeeper seemed quite curiously absent during this unusual event.

Well, he wasn't going to get up and offer to fetch and carry for them. If they wanted anything, they could damn well go and get it themselves. He ignored the visitors, picking up a pair of tweezers from the table at his side and using the pointed tip end of one tweezer leg to clean his fingernails.

"You really are being quite rude, sir." That sounded like Mrs. Vold. Not that Ben bothered looking up to see. He continued with what he was doing.

"Waldo?" one of the women prompted.

Hankins cleared his throat. And said nothing.

After a moment it was one of the women who unsheathed the knives. "Mr. Cartwright, it is our Christian duty, sir, to offer warning that we shall be forced to take action unless you change your ways."

Ben laid the tweezers aside and yawned. He swiveled his head about far enough to peer at Mrs. Byner, who seemed to have appointed herself spokesperson for the occasion.

"Your conduct is disgraceful, sir."

"Disgraceful," Mrs. Dorrance affirmed.

"It cannot be allowed to continue," Mrs. Byner said. "For the good of community and congregation alike, we must protest, Mr. Cartwright."

"For the good of that child is more like it," Mrs. Vold declared.

"That's right," Mrs. Dorrance agreed.

"A drunkard and sot has no business raising a child," Mrs. Byner said.

"Not when the innocent child's own loving grandparents are on hand to spare him the sight of an inebriate father," Mrs. Vold said. "The pain of having a drunk for a father is enough to scar a child through all his life, and there's no repairing damage once gone. Better that the child be raised by someone who will care for him and guide him decently."

"We are all agreed," Mrs. Dorrance said.

"The matter is quite settled," Mrs. Byner said.

"Either you mend your ways, Mr. Cartwright, or we shall be forced to take steps," Mrs. Vold said.

"Steps," Mrs. Dorrance echoed.

"In a court of law," Mrs. Vold continued past the echo.

"Consider this to be fair warning, sir," Mrs. Byner said.

"I do not drink," Ben offered by way of defense.

"Can you prove that, Mr. Cartwright? I doubt it."

"Mrs. Turnow would testify . . ." He looked about, but there was no sigh of Mrs. Turnow. She really should have been there. She could tell them that he was no drunkard. That little Adam had never in his entire lifetime, not before Elizabeth's death and never once since, seen his father in a condition other than that of complete sobriety.

"Would she?" Mrs. Byner asked, her expression something like that of a cat whose mouth is rimmed with bright yellow feathers.

Mrs. Turnow, Ben recalled, was a member of a number of the female societies that were connected with the Reverend Mr. Wickstrom's church. But surely Mrs. Turnow would not—

But Capt. Abel Stoddard would.

Ben knew that.

Stoddard would lie, bribe, do whatever might be necessary in order to exact vengeance upon him for the crime of loving Elizabeth and taking her away from her father's hearth.

The man had proven that well enough in the past.

And Ben simply hadn't cared.

But . . . to lose Adam too?

Would these people really and truly be cruel enough to take away from him the one bright . . . oh God, Ben thought. Adam *was* the one bright star remaining in his life.

Yet when was the last time he had held his son?

Tucked the child into bed at night? Held him upon his lap and read to him?

Dear Lord, Ben thought. These prissy, intrusive, arrogant fools were totally wrong in what they claimed. And totally right in what they implied.

Elizabeth was lost to him for all time except in cherished memory. There had been nothing he could to do prevent that. But if he were to lose Adam too now . . .

Surely he could at least do something to thwart that ultimate and final loss of life's meaning.

He shuddered, realizing and accepting the enormity of the selfishness he displayed in this state of withdrawal from life and from responsibility.

"Ladies," he said, "thank you for coming." He stood.

"But we've scarcely begun to explain to you what—"

"I beg to differ, ladies and gentlemen. You've accomplished more than you know. Now I thank you for your visit and ask that you excuse me. I have to go see to my son's needs. Good day to you."

With that he turned, leaving the parlor and a gaping church delegation behind.

By the time he reached the top of the stairs and turned in the direction of the nursery, he was running.

She was fighting back tears, and there was no comfort Ben knew to give her. Mrs. Stoddard had lost her only child. Now, almost as cruelly, she was losing her only grandchild. "We will miss you, Ben," she said. Her voice was strained and overly loud in a brave but failing attempt to maintain a facade of calm and control.

"Thank you. And I will miss you too." They both knew that the "you" in this instance was singular, just as her "we" of a moment earlier had been a fiction. Ben would miss Abel Stoddard not a whit more than the captain would miss him. As for the man's feelings toward Adam, Ben acknowledged and in a manner of speaking even approved of those. Certainly he understood them. But

Ben did not want to risk a court battle that might end in Adam being placed in the charge of his grandparents either.

Nor, truly, did he want to engage in an open fight with Stoddard regardless of who might ultimately come out the victor. Elizabeth had genuinely loved her father, and Abel Stoddard had returned that love in full measure. Out of sheer respect for Elizabeth, Ben did not now want to turn private distastes into public spectacle. Better, he felt, to handle things this way.

"Will you visit the grave before you go?" Mrs. Stoddard asked.

"I won't need to," Ben said, and then explaining, added, "There isn't any spot on earth or ocean so far away that it could take me away from her, you see. No matter where Adam and I go, ma'am, your Elizabeth will always be here in my heart. She is now and she always will be, for however long I may live. I see her in every sunrise. And even more I see her every time I look at our son." He reached down to touch Adam's dark, tousled hair as the child clung tight to his father's pant leg, shy from the enormity of knowing that they were leaving and could never come to this house again. "Can you understand that, Mrs. Stoddard?"

"I can, Ben. And so can he, you know." She didn't have to explain which he she meant. "That is what hurts him so, why he can't let his resentments lie. The pain is so much that he simply has to blame someone. It isn't you, Ben. Not really. It never was. Not even . . . before. Do you understand? Can you?"

That was a possibility he hadn't really thought of before. It was something he would tuck away in his memory to examine and to ponder in his night thoughts. Perhaps—he hoped it was true because at least then there would be rhyme and reason behind the ugliness—just perhaps Elizabeth's mother was right. "I'll try to understand it, ma'am." He smiled. Just a little. It was faint but it was a start. "For you. For her."

"Where will you go, Ben? You can't follow the sea.

He would find you. He won't ever let you be if you go back to the sea."

"I wouldn't anyway. It wouldn't be fair to Adam to be away from him so often. Whatever I do—whatever we do—it will be something that allows me to be with him."

"You are a good father, Ben. I know you were a good husband too. You gave Elizabeth joy." Tears began to flow down the woman's cheeks. "I cannot think of anything finer that could be said about any man than that, Ben Cartwright."

"Thank you, ma'am . . . Mother Stoddard. Thank you." It was the first time he ever called her that. It would also be the last. He bent, kissed her briefly on her powdered, tear-streaked cheek and turned away.

Mrs. Stoddard knelt to give the shy and apprehensive little boy one last, trembling embrace. And then, sobbing beyond control, she whirled and fled into the grand house that never again would be alight with love and happiness.

Ben took Adam by the hand and led him down the steps to the walkway and beyond to the coach that was waiting to carry them away. To places that neither man nor boy could even imagine today.

CHAPTER 18

Ben tried to close his ears to the hissing, clunking, clattering, splashing, thumping commotion. That didn't work any better than did his efforts to ignore the stink of smoke and cinders that filled the air. The plain and simple truth was that working as a deckhand aboard a sidewheel steamer was not in the same category of things as acting as first mate aboard a proud sailing ship. A proper sailing ship, for that matter even a poor ship, had dignity and character that a man could take pride in. A shallow draft steamer, on the other hand, was merely a utilitarian device that shuddered and groaned its ways from here to there.

Not all steamers, perhaps. Ben conceded that there were some genuinely grand boats plying the interior waterways. But the *Gaynell Malone* where he now labored could hardly be counted among them. It was lacking in certain of those niceties Ben always before took for granted. Niceties like ... a proper hull, decent hardware, a crew of professional caliber. Little things like that.

In his opinion, undoubtedly jaundiced though it was, the poor *Gaynell Malone* was little better than a haphazardly arranged collection of scrap lumber in search of a place to lie while rotting away. And the sooner it accomplished that deed, the better.

Unlike the commodious and garishly fancy grand stern-wheelers of the Missouri and lower Mississippi—Ben was unable to find true beauty in their squat and chunky shapes no matter how hard or how often he tried, the comparisons always falling short when he thought back to the graceful beauty of a tall ship under full sail—this poor relation of a side-wheeler hid its shame on stretches of shallow water the grander boats could not reach. The *Gaynell Malone* carried freight and an occasional passenger from Moline at the mouth of the Rock River upstream as far as the shabby little boat could drag itself, given the fluctuating levels of water and mud and obstruction.

It was not work a seafaring man could take pride or pleasure in. On the other hand, it was honest labor and paid an honest wage. Better yet, it was work that kept Adam close to Ben's side. The owner/captain of the *Gaynell Malone* had no objection to the child's presence aboard, and in fact seemed to enjoy the freshness and delight that were reflected each day in the youngster's eyes. For Adam, unlike his father, had neither prejudices nor bases of comparison between this and other boats.

Adam was entranced by all the sights around him. He could stand for hours in the prow of the sluggishly laboring side-wheeler, examining the flat, tepid flow of water beneath his feet, peering at trees and birds and lowing cattle on either side of the stream. This world of the inland waterways that Ben found to be so mundane and uninteresting was to Adam a source of great wonder and excitement.

Which, Ben considered now, was probably more a reflection upon the father's failings than it was a compliment to the son. For after all, little boys are supposed to be entranced by all they find new and wondrous. The shame was that this ability was so often lost over the years.

Ben paused in his self-appointed chore of coiling and stowing the springlines—everyone else aboard preferred to

leave lines ajumble and only bothered to sort out the kinks
and knots when a piece of cordage was needed in immediate use—and looked forward to where Adam was sitting
cross-legged on the splintered deck with a shingle and bit
of charred stick in his lap. The implements served in place
of the slate and chalk that otherwise might have been used.
Ben was determined not to let Adam forget the things his
mother taught him, and tried to school the boy in the evenings now and then.

The day was warm, just one more in the succession
of days—and of jobs—they had experienced since leaving
Boston and all its complications behind.

Ben wasn't complaining. Not really. So long as he
could be with Adam and keep the child fed and clothed,
why—

"Daddy, look, Daddy, look, Daddy, look, Da . . ."

Ben looked in the direction where Adam was pointing. There was a disturbance in the water over there. Ben
couldn't see what was causing the splashing.

"Look, Daddy, look, Daddy, lo—"

"Hush, son, it's just—no, by gum, it isn't either." The
length of greasy, fraying springline fell from Ben's fingers
and he began to run forward along the cluttered deck.

"Man overboard, Henry, all stop. Man overboard,
dammit."

Which was not quite a literal truth, but then this
seemed hardly the time for more accurate representations.
Never mind that the person who was thrashing about in the
river hadn't actually fallen from the *Gaynell Malone*. The
point was that someone seemed to be drowning off the starboard quarter.

"Man overboard," Ben shouted again as he jumped
onto a crate to gain height and dived cleanly out over the
railing, using the momentum of his run to help increase
the distance of the dive. He hoped.

Now if the dive proved far enough and he could recover in time to avoid the churning side-wheel only a few
yards aft along the starboard beam . . .

The river was colder than it looked. Ben hit the surface deliberately flat, sending a spray of water to either side. It stung to do it that way and drove the breath out of him, but it accomplished the purpose of keeping him on the surface so he could immediately begin a frantic swimming sprint, spurred forward both by the danger of the paddlewheel and by the need to reach the drowning figure just as quickly as possible.

He was conscious of the sounds of the paddles slapping onto the water—funny how loud and personal the noise was of a sudden—as the dripping blades flashed in the sunlight and marched inexorably upon him.

With a grunt of effort and a violent fluttering of his legs, he swam wide of the boat's approach, then paused to shake his head, clearing his eyes and trying to get his bearings again. Where was . . . there!

He stretched out flat to the water and began swimming hard for the pale head he'd spotted amid the splashing a dozen yards away. After only a few strokes he realized he'd lost sight of the figure in the water. He forced himself to slow and begin using a breast stroke so that he could hold his head high and look about him.

A swirl on the otherwise placid surface suggested the truth.

Ben gulped in a deep breath, ducked beneath the water and dove for the bottom. The water was murky, dappled by sunlight above but too full of silt and trash to permit good vision. Green and black shapes shimmered like moving shadows close to the bottom. A waterlogged branch swaying in the slow current beckoned like a human arm, for a precious moment making Ben believe he'd found the drowner, only revealing the truth when a frantic grab turned up rough bark where flesh should have been.

Ben kicked past the snag, twisting, searching, acutely conscious of how little time he had left in which to find the . . . there. Was it? Something pale. Something shifting and flowing. Cloth. A shirt? But was it . . .

He grabbed, missed, tried again.

There was resistance. He yanked harder. Felt an arm. He was sure it was an arm. Or a wrist. He could see now. It was a person. A girl. Her eyes were wide with terror, her lips pinched tight shut. She seemed to be caught on something, was being held beneath the surface by one of the countless snags that infested the rock.

Ben pulled himself down, struggled to find a purchase on the bottom, something against which he could push so as to gain some leverage and strength. His feet encountered only mud at first. Then something solid, he had no idea what. Did not care what it was. He took a firmer grip on the girl's arm, braced against the point of solid contact and pulled.

Cloth tore and came away. The girl came free of the snag, and Ben pushed her toward the surface, scissor-kicking his legs to follow her ascent.

Together they broke onto the surface. Ben treaded water while he held the girl's head up to ensure she would not slip under again. He could see now that she was older than Adam, perhaps ten or eleven, he guessed. She coughed, spraying water and sputum into his face. He laughed. That was all right. All right? It was wonderful. She was alive. She was breathing.

"It's all right now. You're all right. Grab hold of my shoulders. No, not like that, the shoulders. Leave my neck be, honey, so you don't choke me before we can both get to shore. That's better."

Her grip was tight but no longer panicked. He waited a moment so she could adjust to the idea, then slowly began to stroke for the bank, quartering into the current lest they be carried any farther downstream than they already had been.

Far ahead he could see the *Gaynell Malone* angled into shore. The boat, he thought, was riding at an awfully strange angle. But then surely that was only his imagination or perhaps some trick caused by perspective. One thing for certain sure was that he'd never seen the shabby little side-wheeler from quite this angle before.

"Are you all right, honey?"

"Y-Yessir." Her voice was timid and small. As they reached a sandbar and could stand again, she slipped off Ben's back and edged away from him. "You don't know me, m-mister."

"No, I don't, honey."

"Y-You don't know my papa."

"That's right."

"If my papa finds out I run off from my chorin' an' come here today, mister, he'll cane me sure."

"Oh, I'm sure he will be so happy to have you safely home that he won't do that."

"Mister, you don't know my papa. So I reckon I got to thank you myself now an' ask that you forgive me for not giving you my name nor fetching you home for a meal or pay or nothing."

"But—"

The girl whirled before Ben had a chance to say anything more. She scampered away into the brush that lined the river here. For a few moments he could hear the tramp and crackle of her passage. And then it was like she'd never existed. He was alone along the riverbank.

Shaking his head and chuckling to himself, Ben turned and began trudging along the bank to the boat that was waiting for him now with its prow nuzzling the shore like a pig pushed tight against a sow's teat.

Except for Adam, who understood that he was being praised for his alertness and who didn't particularly seem to care beyond that, the crew of the *Gaynell Malone* got quite a kick out of Ben's experience.

"I seen fish too little to be worth keepin'," Eddie Sherman teased, "but this here's the first'un I seen take one look at the fisherman an' run away."

"An' Ben, don't you know it ain't seemly to take a bath with your clothes on?"

"With some little girl too. You oughta be ashamed o' yourself."

"No, you done the right thing, Ben. Never mind about that little ingrate."

"She wasn't ungrateful really. Just scared of her daddy knowing what she was up to today. Smart kid, though. First thing she did was make sure I didn't know who she was. Then off she went. I'm just glad that Adam here saved her life." He reached down and ruffled the boy's hair. They were all standing on the riverbank at the moment. A bow line had been run from the boat to the bole of an oak sturdy enough to hold a first rate ship of the line, much less some dinky little pond-skimmer like the *Gaynell Malone*.

Ben declined an offer of a chew from Henry Tatum, who owned the boat. It never seemed to occur to Henry that Cartwright hadn't ever yet accepted a chew; the man continued to routinely offer his plug to whoever was standing nearest whenever he himself wanted to chew. "No thanks, Henry, but before you get back aboard, why don't you walk back this way with me for a minute?"

"Don't you think we ought t' be getting on now, Ben? Not that I regret stopping, you understand, but it's true we're losing time all the while we're tied up here. Losing steam too."

"I know, Henry, but there's something I think you ought to look at. It won't take but a minute."

"All right, Ben, if you say so." He turned to the others and said, "Don't none of you wander off anywhere."

"We won't." The other men took the opportunity to lie down on the soft earth in the shade of the great oak tree. A soft place to stretch out and some shade to do it in were both lacking aboard the *Gaynell Malone*.

"Now what is it you're wanting me to— Good Lord, Ben!"

"It isn't just me, then. I mean, I've never seen her from this angle before. But I wouldn't have thought she should be riding like that."

"Ought to? Huh. She wasn't riding all cockeyed and

heeling just this morning. Flat-bottomed thing like this hadn't ought to heel to start with."

Even as they stood watching, the boat slipped down another few degrees at the stern, taking on a definite list to port and settling deeper into the water.

"Damn," Henry muttered.

"I expect we'd better take a look," Ben suggested.

"You think?"

"Of course we should. Or . . . should we?"

"I dunno, Ben. Maybe we'd best all get clear. Just in case she's breaking up. You know?"

With his knowledge and past experiences virtually all drawn against a background of sail, it took Ben a moment to work that out. Then he realized what Henry meant. A steamboat has—obviously—a steam engine to drive it. And a steam engine is driven by a steam boiler. And a steam boiler filled with superheated steam being contained under high pressures . . . well, dunking one into cold water is not a particularly healthy notion. Or so Ben was told. There was still much he did not know about steam. And, frankly, much he did not really want to bother knowing.

The stern of the creaky boat settled a bit lower.

"What I'm thinking, Ben, is that all these snags and trash have finally scraped her apart. The bottom seams are coming undone, and she's breaking up on us." Henry scratched his cheek, turned his head and spat. He didn't look particularly surprised to see his old boat sinking before his eyes. Didn't seem especially alarmed either. "Let's get everybody clear, eh? Then if nothing happens, we can go back aboard after the boiler cools, right?"

"Whatever you think, Henry."

The man smiled. "What I think, Ben, is that you might've saved more than just one life today."

"Oh, surely it isn't all that big a thing."

"You ever see a boiler blow?"

Ben shook his head. "Not really. I've seen a boiler split once when a weld let go. Steam and water everywhere. Lot of noise. But I can't say I ever saw one really blow."

"Let's hope you don't see one today neither. If you ever do see it, you won't believe it. It's like a cannon shell, Ben, but more powerful. Like a whole cargo of shells going off all to once. Anybody that survives a drowned boiler won't never forget about it, I can promise you."

They walked back to the others, and Henry began herding everyone deeper into the woods. "Take Adam with you, would you please, Henry? I'll be right there."

Ben took a moment to step back onto the *Gaynell Malone* and fetch an oilcloth bundle from beneath what was laughingly referred to as the chart table in the tiny pilothouse that sat just forward of the machinery amidships. Passengers and crew slept wherever they could find space on deck, and shelter was of their own devising, but the crew was allowed to store their personal possessions in the pilothouse.

Ben was acutely conscious of the fact that the boat had settled to the point where now his ankles were awash even inside he cabin. And that the steam-filled boiler was only a few feet away, separated from him now by a plank wall half an inch or so thick. He was not going to abandon this bundle, though. It contained the much used and much loved copy of *Paradise Lost* that, other than Adam, was the only thing Ben had cared about preserving when they left Boston. He would not give it up now.

He also would not dawdle, though. It is one thing to tempt fate, quite another to thumb your nose at it. He grabbed the slim packet that contained all of his meaningful worldly goods and beat a hasty retreat for the safety of the woods.

"You shouldn't have done that, Ben."

"Oh, probably nothing will happen anyway. She's taking on water, but probably it won't be all that bad. She'll stabilize soon enough, and we can all go back aboard and—"

He was interrupted by an explosion that deafened all of them for a good five or ten minutes, and so powerful that leaves and even small branches were stripped from the trees for fifty yards in any direction.

Ben could feel the force of it bone deep inside his flesh, and anyone who'd been aboard the boat or even close to her would have been crushed by the almost inconceivable power.

His first concern was for Adam, who surely would be terrified to the point of hysteria.

But when he located the child, Adam was frowning and slapping his hands together, quite obviously intent on examining this odd fact of not being able to hear. He seemed much more interested in understanding what was going on than he was frightened.

Even so, Ben rushed to his son's side and picked the little boy up to hold him tight and know that he was safe.

Ben looked back at Henry Tatum, who shrugged and smiled and gave him a thumbs-up.

Henry, Ben realized, had been right on the money. It was a *very* good thing that circumstances had brought the *Gaynell Malone* and her crew ashore.

As for the future—they were all rather obviously out of jobs now—that could work itself out. The point was, they still had a future.

Ben hugged Adam close.

CHAPTER 19

Bank of Galesburg. Not that Ben and Adam might wish to think about banking here. But Ben had been wondering, mildly, what town this might be that they were passing through. All he had been sure of ever since they started following roads south from the twisted wreckage of the *Gaynell Malone* was that they were somewhere in Illinois. He had no particular destination in mind, just a general direction to take. He assumed that eventually they would come to the Mississippi and then he could look for work again. In the meantime the weather was fair. And he had Adam. That was as far-thinking and critical as he'd cared to bother with since Elizabeth died. Nothing else really seemed to matter very much.

"Hungry?" Ben looked down at his son.

The child shook his head without bothering to look up. He was concentrating his attention on a mud-speckled, bur-matted, homely old dog that was paralleling their course at a cautious but nonetheless interested distance.

Adam was fond of virtually all animals, an affection that was often returned. He could be considered a toddler still, and yet already he was developing a strong personal-

187

ity of his own. He was physically sturdy. And stubborn too. He would march along without complaint for as long as Ben wanted to keep going, and rarely did he mention wanting food or sleep. Sometimes Ben wished Adam would smile more. But then his loss had been every bit as great as his father's. If Adam chose not to smile ever again, it would not be in Ben to find fault with him for it.

"We won't look for our dinner until we've put the town behind us then," Ben said. Over these past few months he had developed the habit of talking to Adam as if he were another adult and not a little boy scarcely past babyhood.

When they were on the road, they normally found meals and lodging by stopping at farmsteads where Ben might exchange work for food and perhaps a shed to lie in. They did not seek handouts, and when any were offered— which was quite often, women tending to become misty-eyed and generous when they saw little Adam—they politely declined. The only food that will properly nourish a man, Ben explained to his son, is food that is earned.

In all the miles since they left Boston to begin wandering willy-nilly at the whim of road, river or breeze, neither of them had ever gone to sleep with an empty belly.

Adam sidled a little apart from Ben, maintaining his pace but moving closer and then a bit closer still to the old dog that had been walking with them since they entered the business district, what there was of it, of this farm community. Ben kept an eye on the child but did not call him closer. If the dog didn't want to be petted and fussed over, it would turn away on its own. And if it would welcome the attention, then Adam was in no danger from it anyway.

Ben slowed his pace to give Adam a little better opportunity to strike up a friendship. Not that that was easy to do. Because Adam made his own way, they already had to travel at a speed it had taken Ben weeks to accustom himself to. Walking even slower meant meandering along at a snail's pace. But they certainly were in no hurry. They had no appointments to keep. If wasting a few minutes here with an old dog would give Adam a moment of pleasure, well, why not?

The boy angled a bit more to his right, and the dog angled a trifle to its left, and shortly they were side by side.

"Why don't we take a break here, son."

Adam gave his father a big-eyed nod and a subdued smile, and immediately turned his full attention to the dog, rubbing its floppy ears and scratching beneath its chin and babbling to it in some nonlanguage that the dog seemed to comprehend just fine as it was wagging its tail and washing Adam's face and neck wetly. So much for thinking that the dog might not want to be handled.

Ben was in a fairly expansive mood. He had a few dollars in his pockets—he had been careful of their money since leaving Boston and the chandlery behind—and a yen for a good smoke. Tobacco was a luxury he rarely permitted himself lately, but today he felt the inclination.

"I'm going over to that store for a minute, Adam. Is there anything you want?"

"No, Daddy." Adam had to get up onto his tiptoes and, eyes squeezed tight shut, turn his head away to get the words out past the dog's ministrations.

"All right, then. You two stay there, please."

Adam nodded rather than risk being licked on the mouth while he was talking. Dog and boy were just about the same height.

Ben left Adam in what seemed rather good company and ambled across the rutted street to the porch of a general mercantile on the far corner. Ben's eye for commerce told him more than he really wanted to know about the store. Its location was good, and there was a loading dock on the side street where wagons could be drawn close in much the same way Ben had been able to bring good-sized ships alongside the big sliding doors at the chandlery. But this store needed paint and some trim work to give it an air of prosperity. Ben had always believed there is nothing that will draw custom like an appearance of success. People like to shop where others have been pleased before them. That attracts custom. The necessary and inseparable second requirement for success is to draw those customers back over and over again with a combination of fair prices and honest dealings. His formula was simple and direct and perfectly obvious. It also worked. And, sadly, it was sometimes amazingly rare in the realm of business dealings.

This store, Ben saw, was lacking, at least as regarded outward appearance. He was hardly in any position, though, to judge the proprietor on any other scale.

The store was empty when he stepped into it. He had lost track of the days of the week lately, but a look down the street outside would indicate that this was not a Saturday, when the farmers and their families would have been in town, nor a Sunday, when there would have been no stores open for business. A weekday then and therefore slow.

Ben stopped just inside the doorway to give his eyes a moment to adjust after the bright sunlight outdoors.

"Hello? Is anyone here?"

"One moment only, please, I be with you." It was a woman's voice. From quite close too. It startled Ben.

"Where . . . oh, there you are." She was balanced quite precariously halfway up a rickety, swaying stepladder and seemed to be trying to lift a rather sizable bundle onto a shelf over her head. "Here," Ben said quickly, "let me help you with that." He moved to the foot of the ladder and reached up.

"I get it. Just . . . oh!"

She slipped, nearly falling, and dropped the bundle.

The bundle proved to hold bolts, eight or ten of them, of blue chambray fabric of the sort popular for shirts and shirtwaists and similar articles of clothing. Ben had sold the same material in the chandlery.

The problem now, though, was that while no single bolt was particularly heavy, a bundle of eight or ten of them was heavy indeed. The burlap-wrapped bundle struck the side of his head, scraped painfully over his ear and hit his shoulder so hard as to numb it.

"Ouch!"

Through all that he retained presence of mind enough to grab the ladder to steady it and keep the woman from taking a tumble that could have been considerably nastier than a bump on the head, a stinging ear, and a numbed shoulder. The bolts of chambray hit the floor with a dull thump.

"Are you all right?" each asked at the same time, the woman's voice blending into his as if only a single sentence had been spoken.

And then, in every bit as much concert, "Yes, but are you—" Both stopped. The woman began to laugh.

"You are not hurt. Good. Excuse now, please." She came down to the floor and reached for the bundle of chambray.

"Let me get that," Ben said.

"I get it."

"Please. I insist." He took a moment to swing his right arm about, making sure it would still work properly after the blow to the shoulder, then picked up the cloth and, balancing it on the abused shoulder, went lightly up the ladder all the way to the top, considerably higher than the woman had climbed, where he was able quite easily to shift the bolts of cloth onto the shelf. "There?"

"Yes, perfect. Tak."

"Talk?"

"No, is . . . excuse me, please. Is a way to say thank you. But not English. Sometimes I forget. Please you will forgive?"

"Nothing to apologize for." He came back down to floor level. "Is there anything else you need put up there?"

"No. Thank you."

"Tak, you mean," he said.

The woman laughed and blushed. "I am sorry. Clumsy and I don't talk good. Throw things at you, make you work. You will not want to come to this store soon again."

Ben smiled. "Please don't apologize anymore. There really isn't any need for it. And I'm pleased I could be of some help. That cloth is much too heavy for you to be handling."

"Oh, not so heavy. But I do not go high enough on ladder. I know that. But I am afraid of being so high. Is silly, I know, but knowing does not make it any less," she paused and frowned, searching for the word she wanted, settling eventually for a compromise, "afraid-making. You know?"

"I know." He collapsed the stepladder and picked it up. "Where do you want this?"

"No, please, I can carry."

"Of course you can. But this time you don't have to. Now please tell me where I can put it. Over here?"

"Yes, there. How do you know that?"

"Because this is where I'd put it if it were my store."

A deep, unquestionably masculine voice asked, "You know stores, mister?"

Ben turned to see a large, heavily muscled blond man standing in the door that led out to the loading dock. "Yes, I know a little about stores. My father had a shop when I was a boy, and I've run a store of my own too."

The man grunted. "The boy I see you with outside. He is your son?"

"That's right. Why do you ask? He isn't in any trouble out there, is he?"

"No trouble. I see you. Now I wonder."

"This man, Gunnar, he come inside one minute ago. I bop him on head with the blue cloths, but he help me anyway." She sounded rather anxious about the explanation, and after a moment she slipped out of English and into whatever language she and Gunnar shared. Ben had no idea what they were talking about and, frankly, less interest. His concern at the moment was to see if they sold a decent grade of tobacco so he could have a pipe after supper tonight. There are times when a good pipe will soothe a man and ease his digestion like nothing else seems able to do. He spotted the display case he wanted and went to it.

When he looked up again, the man and the woman were heading toward him, both wearing very serious expressions.

"You would be interested to work?" the man asked. Behind him the woman said something in their own language, and the man responded sharply, cutting her off in a manner made perfectly clear by the tone of voice if not the words.

"Is there some problem?" Ben asked.

"No problem," Gunnar said. "You look for work?"

"I'm looking for work, yes, but I wouldn't want to cause an argument between you and your wife."

Gunnar blinked. Then began to laugh. "Wife? No, mister. That one is too ugly to find husband ever. Inger is my sister, not wife."

Behind him Inger flushed a dark, shamed red but she did not protest her brother's unthinking disdain.

Ben felt a flutter of sympathy for her—it was true enough that Inger was no great beauty, but she did not deserve being discussed with strangers as if she were of no more moment than a slab of bacon—but he managed to hold his tongue. He knew better than to enter into such intensely personal family relationships and difficulties as this seemed to suggest. Especially if he wanted to take Gunnar up on the offered job.

"So," Gunnar said. "You want work?"

"I want work, yes."

"You and the boy," Gunnar mused aloud. "No wife?"

"No wife," Ben confirmed.

"Dollar a day, mister. There is shed behind store here. You and boy can sleep there. No charge. Inger will cook for you, wash, all that. I pay you fifty cent a day net. Is agreed?"

"Agreed," Ben said. Fifty cents a day plus room, board, and laundry for the two of them. It seemed fair. Moreover it would give him a chance to let Adam rest and, staying in one place for a while, perhaps even meet some other little boys to play with. The child had never had any playmates. Stopping here in—it took Ben a moment to recall what the sign on the bank had said—here in Galesburg might be a good idea at that. And it wasn't like they had any better prospects in mind. Galesburg and this general merchandise store were adequate for the needs of today. Beyond that nothing really mattered anyway, as Ben had learned all too well in the past.

The big man shoved his hand forward to shake on the deal and seal their bargain. "I am Gunnar Borgstrom. She is Inger. You need anything, Inger will do. She will work or big trouble, yes? But you don't hit. If she needs, you tell me and I do it, not you. Now come, I show you where you sleep. Then there is work. Too much. You will earn your pay. You will see." He beckoned Ben to follow and walked away, leaving his maligned sister behind without a backward glance.

Gunnar Borgstrom proved to be a man Ben Cartwright found impossible to like but no real problem to work for. Borgstrom had only recently purchased the general store from his former employer and now was working hard to improve both the store and its reputation. What he wanted from Ben was hard effort, and that was something Ben was perfectly willing to give. Gunnar was also willing, indeed was eager, to listen to any comments or suggestions his new shop clerk might wish to make. All were heard out thoroughly, and in the long run most were adopted. Ben's opinion of Gunnar as a businessman was that he was cold and contained, but fair and scrupulously honest. He very likely would make a success of his store.

It was on the personal side of things where Ben disagreed with his employer so completely, especially as related to poor Inger. There too Gunnar was cold and controlled. But in Inger's case he did not seem fair. More accurately, perhaps, he appeared unfeeling toward his sister, whom Gunnar seemed to perceive as a mere female and therefore of little account.

Ben conceded that Inger was and never would be a beauty. She was younger than he had first thought, still in her twenties, although she had the appearance of a woman a good fifteen or twenty years older. She was tall and large-boned and looked heavy at first glance. Closer inspection showed that she was not fat, but she had a solid, chunky, beer keg build that gave that impression. She had a broad face and naturally red complexion beneath dull blond hair and huge, lake-blue eyes. Her eyes were really her lone good feature. Her hands were callused and cut from unceasing hard work, and she walked ponderously and without grace. At her age she had to be considered an "old maid" without hope or prospect of marriage.

Adam, however, adored her.

No one in Gunnar Borgstrom's household was apt to become idle, but Inger was never so busy that she could not find a moment to give Adam a wink and a treat, to bake especially for him the sweets that he liked best, to take him onto her lap for a hug and a pat, to kiss and tickle and squeeze him, to babble cheerfully with him in English or Swedish or singsong gibberish, to play hide and seek or even all-fall-down. Observing tiny Adam and big, awkward Inger play all-fall-down was something Ben could not do without having to run and hide lest he betray the ludicrousness of the sight by bursting into laughter and taking the risk of hurting Inger's feelings.

And hurting poor Inger's feelings was something Ben would never want to do. Lord knew she was hurt often enough and deeply enough by her own brother. Despite her size and appearance, it took no exceptional powers or sensitivity for Ben to quickly see how shy and sensitive Inger really was. She was easily wounded even though she tried not to allow her pain to show. She was big-hearted and caring. And homely as a mud-daub chimney stack.

Ben liked her, an emotion which he simply could not feel toward her brother.

In the weeks that followed his and Adam's arrival at the Borgstrom Mercantile, a pattern evolved in which Gunnar went out in the evenings after the store was closed—Ben had accepted Gunnar's invitation to accompany him on one of those excursions only once, and then had not chosen to participate in the activities; Ben did not necessarily look down on men who seemed to feel they had to prove their manhood in the pursuit of hard drink and harder women, but he had no desire to join them either—while Adam and Ben sat in the kitchen of the owner's quarters, Ben reading and chatting a little, Adam playing underfoot and Inger, as always, engaged in whatever work remained undone. For the most part that meant mending or ironing or baking breads and pastries to sell on the morrow. Often Adam chose to conduct his games close by Inger, and she would sing Swedish lullabies to him while she worked.

"How long will you stay here, Ben?" Inger asked on one such evening. She kept her eyes fixed on the seams of a shirt she was ironing for Gunnar. Ben noticed, as he had noticed several times recently, that Inger felt comfortable enough with him now to call him by his given name although she was careful to address him as Mr. Cartwright whenever Gunnar was within hearing.

He refolded his newspaper along the original creases and laid it gently down. It was a fairly recent copy of a Chicago weekly and could still be sold, but Gunnar did not mind him reading things so long as he took pains not to crumple the pages or smudge the ink. "I really don't know, Inger. I hadn't given it any thought. Why?"

"I only wonder." She smiled, reached down and patted Adam's cheek. He was playing close under her skirts so she did not have to go far to reach him. "I will miss you when you do go."

"We'll miss you too. Both of us. But goodness, we

don't have any plans to move on. Unless there's something we don't know about . . . ?"

"No," she said quickly. "Gunnar likes you. He told me this. That Ben, he is hard worker, Gunnar says."

"Huh. Not as hard a worker as you. Can't you sit down for a little and rest now, Inger? You've been on the go since well before dawn. I know for a fact that you have. I heard you in here taking something out of the oven when I woke up this morning." The lean-to where Ben and Adam slept was built immediately behind the kitchen at the back of the store building. The remainder of the owner's quarters, which Ben had never seen, although Adam was in and out of every square inch of the place on a daily basis, was upstairs and separate from a storage loft that took up most of the second floor.

Inger blushed and ducked her head shyly. "How do you know I was taking something out of the oven, Ben? Could I not have been putting something into oven?"

"Nope," he said cheerfully. "I heard the clank of the oven door and then I could smell what you took out. I think it was those wild currant buns that sold out today before I got a chance to try one."

"Do you like currants, Ben?"

"Very much."

"Then tomorrow I make more. Of those you will get, yes. I promise."

"You don't have to do that, Inger."

"Have to, no. Want to, yes. Tomorrow I will make the currant buns for you." She looked down and smiled. "You like them too, Adam, yes?"

The little boy grinned and nodded.

"Darn it, Inger, one second I'm saying you work too hard, the next thing I'm making more work for you to do. What did I do wrong here?"

She laughed and blinked and ducked her head. She was blushing again. Inger Borgstrom, Ben decided, was without question the most shy person he had ever in his life met.

He picked the newspaper up from his lap and carefully held it so he could read without wrinkling the paper. The background sounds of Adam chortling under his breath about something and of Inger's sadiron scrubbing back and forth over Gunnar's shirt were soft and soothing and gentle in the night.

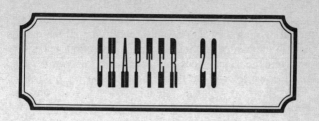

CHAPTER 20

O h!" There was the startled yelp and then, almost in
the same instant, a crash as something heavy fell
onto the puncheon flooring. "Oh, dear."

"Inger. Damn you, woman." The remainder of the ti-
rade was delivered in Swedish, which Ben could not understand and—hopefully—neither would any of the several
customers who happened to be in the store at the time.
Judging from Gunnar's tone, Ben was just as happy that
he could not understand the words.

Inger hurried to clean up the mess she'd made. She
had been carrying something into the store, probably more
of the bread she'd baked this morning, and accidentally
nudged a crate of eggs off the counter. Most of the eggs,
quite naturally, did not survive the experience. They also
made quite a mess.

Inger was still on hands and knees trying to scoop up
the sticky, oozing slop when Gunnar finished waiting on
the last of the customers and followed the man to the door.
Ben was more than a little surprised to see Gunnar push
the door closed behind the customer and slide the bolt shut
to lock it.

199

"I am sorry, Gunnar, please, I am sorry, please," Inger began, lapsing then into Swedish and trying all the quicker and all the harder to bring the mess on the floor under control, remaining on hands and knees and keeping her eyes fixed down toward the floor instead of on her brother.

"Stand up, woman," Gunnar ordered, voice and face both stony and stern. "Bend over, you."

Inger's usual practice of silent acquiescence broke as she began to tremble and shake quite violently. Tears streamed down her red, mottled cheeks, and she pleaded and loudly wailed in Swedish. Gunnar grabbed her roughly by the arm and yanked her bodily upright.

"Hold on, Gunnar."

"Quiet, Ben. This is not for you."

"I agree it's none of my business, Gunnar, but be fair about this. That crate shouldn't have been there. You set it too close to the edge. It wasn't Inger's fault that—"

"Shut up, Ben. You shut up now. Inger, bend."

Inger was shaking so badly now that Ben doubted she could have talked coherently if she'd had to. Not that anything anyone could say would likely reach Gunnar at the moment anyway. Gunnar did not wait for Inger to do as he ordered. He hauled her around so that she was facing away from him and slammed the heel of his hand hard between the shoulder blades to drive her forward. Still shaking, she allowed herself to be bent over the counter. She took a grip on the back edge of the counter with both hands, holding on so hard her knuckles turned white.

"Gunnar? What the hell do you think you're doing?" Ben demanded.

Gunnar unbuckled his belt, a two-inch-wide strap of heavy harness leather with a hefty brass buckle at one end, and pulled it off.

"You can't do that, Gunnar. Dammit, man, you—"

"I tell you already, Ben. This is not for you to say. Inger belongs to me. She will do as I say. Now you shut up."

Gunnar flicked the belt out behind him, poised himself for the strike, and then slashed Inger across the buttocks with vicious force. The leather whistled through the air and struck with a crack as loud as a bullwhacker's popping snake.

Inger's knees sagged, but she did not fall, nor did she cry out. She held grimly onto the store counter. Her teeth were clenched tight and she was pale. Ben could not believe that she was able to remain silent, but then he could not believe either that her own brother would do such a thing to her. And over a seventy cent crate of eggs? No.

Gunnar, his face grim and committed, shook out the makeshift lash and drew back to deliver a second blow.

His hand sped forward.

And abruptly halted in mid-delivery.

Incredulous, Gunnar looked around to see what had taken hold of his wrist.

Ben Cartwright, half a head shorter than Gunnar and at least seventy pounds lighter than the big Swede, stood there with one hand blocking the path of Gunnar's arm.

"No, Gunnar. Leave be," he said in a low and tight but nonetheless controlled voice.

"I tell you before, Ben. This is not for you to say."

"I'm sure you're right, Gunnar, but this time I'm making it mine to say. You put the crate where it didn't belong. This is not Inger's fault, and you'll not whip her for something that is at least partially your fault. I won't let you do that."

"If you get in my way, Ben, I break you in two. Now go 'way. This is with me and Inger, not you."

"I understand all that, Gunnar. I know this should be between the two of you, and I apologize for getting into it with you. I really do. But I'll not stand here and let you whip Inger for a simple accident. If it makes you feel any better, take the price of the eggs out of my wages."

"Is not cost. Is . . ." He struggled to find the word he wanted, gave up and said something in Swedish.

"I'm just telling you, Gunnar. You've always been fair before. Be fair now. Leave be." Ben released his hold on Gunnar's wrist.

"I could beat you, Ben. Break your back."

Ben took half a step back and nodded. "You're bigger than me, Gunnar. I don't doubt that you're stronger too. Maybe you can beat me in a fair fight or a foul one. One thing I know for sure, Gunnar. If you try and whip Inger anymore over that stupid crate of eggs, first you're going to have to prove that you can beat me."

Gunnar's eyes narrowed. "I am not afraid of you, Ben."

"I can see that, Gunnar. I know that you aren't."

"I try to be fair. You know this too."

"I know this too," Ben agreed.

"This one time, Ben. I let Inger off this one time."

"And I will pay for the eggs," Ben said.

"Yes. From your pay I will take."

"Good, Gunnar. That's fair."

Gunnar draped the thick belt over his shoulder and gave his sister a cold glare, then turned and stalked away out the front, leaving the door open behind him on his way out.

Inger, sobbing, slumped down onto the floor and without looking once toward Ben resumed the task of cleaning up the broken eggs.

Ben came upright on his cot, jolted out of a sound sleep by . . . something. He didn't know what. He blinked and rubbed at his face, wondering what it was that had wakened him. Then the noise was repeated, and he knew.

There was a crash and shouting and another crash. Ben leaped off the cot and fumbled on the nearby bench for his clothes. He didn't take time to dress, merely dragged on his trousers and shirt and hurried out the door still struggling with the buttons on his trousers. He made no attempt to find his shoes in the dark.

The kitchen door swung open to his touch, and the sounds reached him louder than ever. He could hear angry voices—no, one angry voice, Gunnar's—and panicked weeping and some dull, unidentifiable crunch, then the

sharper, recognizable sound of a slap. Inger cried out and
there was a sound like furniture being dragged across a
wooden floor.

Ben fumbled his way through the kitchen, found the
narrow enclosed staircase leading to the living quarters upstairs. No lamp or candle had been left burning, so he had
to feel his way along.

A door at the upper end was bolted closed.

"Gunnar? Open the door, Gunnar."

If Gunnar heard, he did not choose to respond. Ben
heard the moist, meaty sound of something hard, a fist or
a boot, thudding into living flesh, and Inger screamed in
pain.

Ben drew back and threw his shoulder into the door.
The locking mechanism shattered and the door burst open.
The first room, a cluttered sitting room with a rumpled bed
in one corner, was empty. The sounds were coming from
the room beyond.

A single candle in a wall sconce lent its feeble light
to the fray. A cot no better than the ones Ben and Adam
had been given was overturned on the floor, as were a
small table and the stand that had held the washbasin and
water pitcher which now, in many pieces, contributed to
the flotsam on the floor.

Inger, in a flannel nightdress and with her hair un-
pinned, cowered in a corner behind the upturned cot. She
had her knees drawn tight to her chest, and her arms were
held protectively over her head.

When Ben burst in, Gunnar stood poised on one leg,
his other foot drawn back. He was cursing, or so it
sounded, loudly in Swedish, while on the floor at his feet
Inger was pleading just as loudly in that same tongue.

Gunnar's foot lashed out, the toe of his work boot
driving into Inger's side between her hip and ribs. She
shuddered and squirmed, but there was nowhere for her to
hide and no way for her to escape. Gunnar had her trapped
in the corner there. Before Ben could reach him, Gunnar
kicked her again, this time catching her on the back of her

thigh. He leaned down and began pummeling her face and head while Inger frantically tried to ward off the blows with her elbows while she twisted and screamed.

That, however, did not continue long.

Gunnar's savagery was cut short by a powerful hand that appeared out of nowhere to take a firm grip in his hair and haul him rudely backward.

"What—"

"Turn around, Gunnar. I want you to see this coming."

"Damn you, Ben, I fire you now."

"Good." And Ben hit him.

The fist landed flush on Gunnar's mouth, splitting his lip and bringing a spurt of blood that quickly ran beneath his collar and turned the front of his shirt a bright scarlet.

Gunnar shook his head, drops of blood spraying to either side. "I warn you before. Now I break you in two pieces, Ben."

"Only if you can." Ben backed away into the center of the small room.

"See. Already you run. Ha!"

What Ben wanted was room enough to maneuver in. But if Gunnar wanted to think otherwise, he was welcome to his error.

"You surprise me one time, Ben. But you don't hit me again, never."

Ben waited silently for Gunnar to come to him.

And come Gunnar did, balling his hands into fists and rushing forward with a roar.

The man, Ben saw, fought like a bull, all brute force and straight lines. He was big and he was strong, but he lacked the rough-and-tumble experience of the years Ben had spent at sea.

Ben easily sidestepped Gunnar's initial charge, slipping just out of reach and staggering Gunnar with a clubbed fist over the big man's ear as he went surging by. Gunnar found himself on his knees wondering what had become of his much smaller opponent. With a snarl and a lunge he regained his feet and whirled.

Ben's quick left jabs stung Gunnar and brought tears into his eyes. A right pulped his nose and another closed his left eye with sudden swelling while blood from a split eyebrow ran into the eye as well.

Gunnar's powerful fists swept hard and wide in powerful blows one after another. If any of them had connected, Ben Cartwright would surely have been battered unconscious with a single blow. If any of them had connected.

Smaller, but as able as he was agile, Ben floated over, past and around Gunnar Borgstrom like a dragonfly, and Gunnar's wild swings were no more effective than if he'd been trying to hit tendrils of mist on a calm morning.

Within minutes Gunnar was bloody and staggering, both eyes swollen shut and his breath labored.

"Damn you. Damn you."

Ben set himself to end the punishment, taking a position immediately in front of Gunnar and gauging his timing to coincide with the big man's exhalations.

Just as Gunnar emptied his lungs, Ben put all his weight into one, knuckles-forward right hand that buried deep into Gunnar's solar plexus.

Stunned by the electrifying shock to the nerve endings there, and with the last vestige of breath driven from him, Gunnar collapsed like a marionette that has been cast aside. He dropped to the floor with a thump and lay there unconscious.

Ben turned away from him and was horrified to see that Adam had wakened and followed him upstairs. Adam was huddled crying and tear-streaked in the corner with Inger; and Inger, her face bloody and battered almost as bad as Gunnar's now was, was clutching the child to her breast and rocking back and forth to ease his fears while she crooned softly to him.

Ben rushed to kneel beside them and offer what little comfort he might be able to give.

*   *   *

"Bring me that towel please, son."

Adam jumped to obey, calmed by the activity and pleased that he was being asked to help. He ran across the kitchen to grab the towel his father pointed to and raced back to shove it into Ben's hands. "Thank you, son."

Inger reached out to stroke the boy's cheek. She winced a little at the touch of the cloth Ben was using to wash her injuries, but she did not cry out.

It could have been worse, Ben supposed. She would look like a purple All Hallow's Eve mask for the next few weeks, but there should be no serious permanent damage. There might be some scarring left there at the corner of her mouth and there above that eye, but he didn't think it would be very bad. Several teeth had been loosened, but he did not believe she would lose them.

"Has he done this before, Inger?"

She didn't answer. Which, he supposed, was an answer itself. Yes, Gunnar had done this sort of thing to her before, although whether from drink or in anger, Ben did not even want to know.

"I'm sorry if this hurts."

"Not so bad. But what you must think of me. I am much ashamed, Ben. I am so sorry."

"Hush now. I'm the one who's sorry. Sorry I didn't get up there sooner and keep this from happening."

"I will miss you, Ben."

"We will miss you too, Inger."

"You must go, please, before Gunnar comes down. Now, before morning."

Ben grunted and continued to wash the caked blood off Inger's face and neck. Adam proudly offered up the towel whenever Ben reached for it so that his father could tend to this woman he had come to love so much.

"Too late," Ben muttered after a moment.

"What is that, Ben?"

"I think I hear Gunnar moving around up there. I think he's coming downstairs."

Moments later they all could hear the impact of Gunnar's boot soles on the stair treads. The door pushed open and Gunnar blinked in the sudden light. Ben had lighted most of the lamps in the kitchen so he could see to Inger's wounds. If Gunnar objected to the waste of oil, they could discuss the matter any way Gunnar wanted.

"I fire you, Ben. Get out."

"Glad to," Ben said as he continued to gently dab at the myriad small cuts that he was finding. Inger, he noticed, had begun to tremble again at the sight of her brother.

Adam must have noticed too, for the boy bunched his small hands into fists and placed himself defiantly between Inger and Gunnar. Ben felt a welling of pride but could not say anything without running the risk of setting Gunnar off again.

"Get out now."

"When I'm done," Ben said calmly.

"All the way out of this city, you, or I have you arrested."

"Now that'd be a laugh, wouldn't it. Or won't you mind all your neighbors—and customers—all of them, Gunnar, knowing that you beat on women. That won't be very popular with the people I've met around here."

"No one will believe the word of a thief," Gunnar snarled.

"Thief, Gunnar?"

"You steal from me. I will tell everyone that."

"And they're supposed to believe you, is that it?"

"They believe me. Inger will tell them too. They will arrest you and—"

"No, Gunnar."

He stopped, incredulous.

"No, Gunnar, I will not," Inger said quietly but firmly. "I will not lie for you. Not this time. I will not hurt Ben for you, Gunnar."

"Ben, is it? Ben? Where is the Mr. Cartwright now? Do you shame me too, woman? Is that it? Is it not bad enough that you are clumsy, ugly, useless thing, now you must shame me too. Are you having baby, woman? How do you get this man to do that, huh? You tell him he must do this or lose his job? Huh? Everything else is not bad enough. Now you are hussy too. You would be a hoor except no man would pay you. You pay them. Like you pay this man."

"That's enough, Gunnar."

Gunnar glared across the room at Ben.

"You're a mean old man and I hate you," Adam piped in. "If you're mean to Inger again, my daddy will beat you up, you mean old man." The little fellow looked ready to try it himself if need be.

"Shut your mouth, you little bastard."

The blood drained from Ben's face. In one ill-chosen word Gunnar had managed to insult Adam, himself, and Elizabeth all at the same time. And of those three, insulting Adam or Elizabeth, either one, was beyond forgiveness.

Ben folded the damp cloth he'd been using to bathe Inger's cuts and laid it on the table. He handed Inger the towel and stepped around the chair where she was sitting so that he could better see Adam. "Son, I want you to stay right here beside Inger. I want you to protect her. Will you do that for me?"

Adam nodded and shot a withering look at Gunnar, clenching his little hands into fists once again.

"Gunnar, you and I need to discuss this. Outside, if you please."

"I don't go outside with you, damn you. You think just because you are—"

Ben's lips thinned into something that approximated a smile, although anyone who saw the expression would have had no difficulty in realizing that it was anything but. Certainly Gunnar did not confuse what he saw in Ben's face with anything like a smile.

"Because I'm what, Gunnar? Bigger than you? Stronger? Heavier? What happened to the man who was going to break me in two, Gunnar? Are you afraid to face me, Gunnar? But how could I have forgotten. Gunnar Borgstrom, man enough to beat women, too yellow to face a man. How little do they have to be for you to feel safe, Gunnar? Adam's size? Or perhaps a little smaller than that. You want to be safe, after all. It wouldn't do for you to get into a fair fight, would it?"

Gunnar was pale. His mouth gaped and worked, but no sounds came out. Ben could see how badly Gunnar wanted to bluster and brag and bully, but the danger was that anything he said he would most certainly have to back up, and Gunnar was neither able to do that against Ben Cartwright nor willing to try.

Gunnar had to either swallow a bitter pill or take another thrashing. He chose to swallow pride and manhood in one hard lump.

Gunnar turned and scurried to the door into the dark storefront. "Get out of my house, you," he snarled as he went. He reached the door and paused there to glare at his sister. "Your paid man will not be here to protect you long, Inger dear."

"Neither will Inger be here any longer to accept your mistreatment, Borgstrom," Ben blurted without thinking.

"You would take her? Good. Then I have you both arrested. Fornication is against the law here. Did you know that? If you take her with you, Cartwright, I have you both put in the jail. Have that kid taken away and put in county home. How do you like that, huh? You think I won't do it? I will do, all right. You can't come into my home and do these things, beat me up, violate my sister, maybe knock her up, who knows? Well, you find out now, Cartwright. I will get even with you."

"Inger is going with Adam and me," Ben said.

"Good. I will go find the sheriff now." Gunnar turned and lumbered quickly away before Ben might decide to chase him down and administer another whipping to him.

"He will do what he says, Ben," Inger whispered. She was crying again, and once he saw that, so was Adam.

"Gunnar won't do any such thing. I promise you."

"You do not know him, Ben. He will hurt you. Any way he can, he will hurt you."

"I'm not worried about that. Do you want me to help you pack, or can you manage on your own?"

"Oh, I cannot go with you, Ben. I cannot."

"You have to, Inger. If you stay and I'm not here to protect you, you know what Gunnar will do."

"It will not be so bad. I will heal. I have before. I will again this time too."

"There won't be another time, Inger. I meant that. And I meant it that you are going with us when we leave here."

"But Gunnar. He will go to the sheriff. He will do what he said. The law—"

"The law doesn't have a thing to say about a man and wife traveling together, Inger. We'll find a preacher and have him say the words. If you have a marriage certificate, no court in this country would care what Gunnar has to say or send you back to him."

"But Ben—"

"I'm not saying I will make you . . . I mean, uh . . . I'm not trying to—" He sighed loudly. "Darn it, Inger, I'll not make unwelcome demands. I mean . . . that is to say . . . well, Adam adores you, and I—"

She smiled, wincing only a little when the drying cuts at the sides of her mouth cracked open again. "I understand what you tell me, Ben. I know I am ugly and stupid and not meant to be a real wife. But I will do anything you want of me. Anything."

"The first thing I want, Inger, is that you never again call yourself stupid or ugly. You are a fine woman. I'll not have anyone saying otherwise. Not even you."

Inger resumed crying, and so did Adam.

Ben stood there a moment longer, trying to work out how all this had come about, almost without him realizing it. And out of his own mouth too. It was amazing.

Still, Adam did care for Inger and she for him. The

added responsibility of another traveling companion hardly seemed any burden either, compared with how he would feel if he allowed this poor, sad woman to stay here subject to Gunnar's erratic brutality. Far better this arrangement of convenience than to permit that.

"I'll help you pack," Ben said gently. "Then I think we should all leave. We want to be out before Gunnar returns."

Inger nodded and drew Adam into her lap for a moment, then resolutely put him down again and moved to do as Ben wished. She had said she would do anything for him. She meant precisely that.

Deputy Sheriff Horace Templeman caught up with them late in the afternoon of their second day, at a town called Gilson on the road to Peoria.

"Miss Inger. Ben." He tipped his cap to Inger and gave Ben an apologetic look. Both of them knew Horace. He and his wife traded at Gunnar's mercantile. "I'm sorry to have to be doing this, folks. I declare I don't know what's got into Max that he'd send me out on a complaint like this. I guess that dang idiot Gunnar talked him into it somehow." Maxwell Beck was the sheriff of Knox County. Ben and Inger knew him too, although not as well as they knew Horace.

"We understand, Horace. No hard feelings," Ben assured him.

"Look, Ben, you aren't going to make me do something silly like put 'cuffs on you or anything, are you? I wouldn't want to do that. You know. In front of the boy and everything."

"That's very considerate of you, Horace. If we have to go back with you, I'll give you my parole. No manacles will be necessary."

"Thanks, Ben. Thanks a lot."

"My pleasure, Horace."

Horace smiled. "You're sure taking this nice, the both of you. I wish everybody was this pleasant to arrest."

"You are placing us under arrest, then?"

"I got to, Ben. Gunnar swore out a complaint, and Judge Bennett issued the warrant, and Max told me I had to come after you and serve the darn thing. If you want to know the truth, I was hoping you'd have got clear of the county before I found you. I mean, you could've gone 'most any other direction, Ben, and crossed the county line by now. You should have thought of that."

"Oh, we thought about it, Horace. But if we'd done it that way, there would be warrants outstanding against us for . . . why, there is no telling how long something like that would stay on the books. I don't think I would like that. No matter where we went, it would make me feel like a criminal to know I was wanted by the police back here."

"I appreciate that, Ben, but gee, now I got to take you back to face charges."

"You won't mind telling us what the charges are, will you, Horace?"

"Oh, I got to tell you what the charges are, Ben. That's in the rules. Max is a stickler for keeping to the rules, you know." The deputy blushed. "I don't know that I can say this word in front of you, Miss Inger."

"The word you're uncomfortable with, Horace. Would it be fornication?"

"Ben, it would. I'm sorry to tell you that, but it's what Gunnar swore out and what the judge had to put down on the paper."

Ben took Horace by the elbow and drew him along down the street. "Tell me, Horace, have you ever met Judge Ricks?"

"No, I can't say that I have."

"Jim Ricks is justice of the peace here in Gilson, Horace."

"Is that so?"

"Um-hmm. He seems a fine old gentleman too. Judge Ricks was kind enough to perform a marriage ceremony yesterday evening. I think you should meet him. And see his record of that occasion."

"But Ben, that means—"

Ben smiled. "You know, Horace, I doubt Judge Bennett would enforce a complaint against a married couple. What do you think?"

Horace laughed and clapped Ben on the shoulder. "Why, Ben, you so-and-so. You and Miss Inger married. How about that. Why, I'm real happy for the both of you. Now I've got to quit calling her Miss Inger. She's not a miss no more, she's Mrs. . . . Ben, I hate to tell you this, but I've already put those warrants away and can't sneak a peek at them."

"And you've forgotten what my last name is, haven't you?"

Horace blushed and hung his head. "I have, Ben, sad to say. It isn't like I've known you very long, though. And I do like what I do know about you. I hope you know that."

"The lady's name is Cartwright, Horace. She is Inger Cartwright. Mrs. Benjamin Cartwright. You tell Gunnar that, will you, Horace?"

"I will, Ben, I surely will." Horace grinned and began walking with a spring in his step. "Mrs. Inger Cartwright. How about that?"

CHAPTER 21

B en lay wide awake, staring at the stars illuminating the black velvet sky that stretched wide above their roadside camping place. Adam lay sleeping at his side, and Inger just beyond him. The Cartwright family owned two blankets, and all three had to share them. Adam thought it all quite an adventure. And Inger did not complain. Inger never complained. Ben almost wished that she would.

She seemed so . . . grateful. She was so grateful for every tiny measure of consideration that she came near to making him uncomfortable.

Really she was taking this marriage thing entirely too seriously anyway. After all, it wasn't like it was . . . He closed his eyes and tried to ward off the pain that struck deep inside his chest every time these thoughts intruded into his mind. This pale and passionless joining was nothing like the wild, soaring melding of two into one that he had known with Elizabeth.

Elizabeth. Dear Elizabeth. How would she have felt about this? Would she have approved, knowing the kindness, indeed the genuine love, that Inger gave to their Adam?

214

Or would Elizabeth feel that her Benjamin had betrayed her?

Ben did not honestly know.

He only knew that he wished Elizabeth were still alive.

Not that he despised Inger. Lord knew that was not so. She was a kind and decent and honest woman, and she loved Adam dearly, and she would do her sincere best to make Ben a good and decent wife. Of that he never had to worry. Inger was a fine woman. If she was no beauty, well, it wasn't beauty that he asked of her. Nor much of anything else except as regarded Adam. Theirs was a marriage of need, not of joy. Inger needed protection from her brother's abuses. Ben needed a woman to serve as mother for his son. That was all there was to it.

But Elizabeth. Oh, God, Elizabeth . . .

He squeezed his eyes tight shut and tried to cry for her. But he could not. He felt so hollow and empty and dry within that he could no longer even cry for his beloved.

Even his memories of her dear features were becoming haze-filmed and indistinct, as if seen through fog or smoke.

Elizabeth. He had to put her memory behind him now. He knew that. He was married to Inger, never mind the absence of love. He was married to Inger, and it was to Inger Borgstrom Cartwright that Ben owed his loyalty this night and for all his nights to come.

He knew that, dammit.

And he resented it. Dear Lord, how he resented it.

He lay there warm beside his son and his wife and stared up at the cold and distant stars, and he wished it had been he who died instead of Elizabeth.

But of course it had not been, and now . . . now, dear God, how could he ever go on now that he knew Adam was safe and loved . . . and yet how could he not go on, because the responsibilities were his, for Adam, now for Inger too, even for the memory of Elizabeth. All of those were his, and a man must meet his responsibilities or no longer be able to count himself a man.

And yet . . .

He lay awake long into the night.

"Papa, Papa, Papa."

"Slow down, son. What is it?" Ben grabbed Adam under the arms and swung him high into the air, twisting him around and plunking the child onto his shoulders. "Tell me everything."

"I caught a fish, Papa, a big fish, and Mama said she will cook it for supper tonight, Papa, my fish that I caught, Papa, do you want to see my fish, Papa?"

"Do I want to see this fish that you caught? Oho, indeed I do, son, there's nothing I want more than to see this fish we will have for supper." Ben laughed with delight and praised the lad and made over him for his prowess as a fisherman of the very first class.

But there was a heaviness in Ben's heart too, for it was Inger and not Elizabeth who the boy so ingenuously, so unconsciously, called "Mama."

"Ben."

"Mmm?"

"Come. Sit, please. Here." She took him by the hand and drew him to the castoff rocking chair that she had rescued from the town dump and brought home for Ben to repair. Slowly, one article at a time, Inger was turning their rented cabin into a bright and lovely if not exactly elegant home. "Sit, please."

"Oh, Inger, you don't have to do this. I know you're as tired as I am."

"Sit," she insisted. She made him sit where she wished and then, his belly warm and full with the dinner she had made for them, and his shoulders aching from the labor of loading grain sacks onto barges for ten hours with scarcely a break, she began to knead and gently pummel the pains and the aches away under the influence of her massage. "You feel better for this, Ben."

"I know I do, but you—"

"But nothing. Be quiet now. It pleases me to do this for you. Do not deny me a pleasure, no?"

"I don't want to deny you a pleasure, no."

"So. Good. Thank you, Ben." She giggled. "Tak."

He smiled. "Are we going to start that again?"

Ben stretched, warm and content beneath the thick mound of quilts Inger made to cover their bed and Adam's. The thin, watery light of the dawn was already sneaking past the curtains, but that was quite all right. This was Sunday morning and there was time enough to lie lazy-cozy and half asleep here for another hour or more before they would all have to get up and begin preparing for the walk to church.

Cold walk too at this time of year. The snow was knee deep, old crusted snows from yesterday slumping and compacting and discoloring but being steadily replenished and freshened by the repeated new falls.

Never bad, though. Never storms like the one that had taken— No, dammit, he wasn't going to think about that again. He simply wasn't.

The snows here were really not all that bad, and the cold was nothing they couldn't cope with. Inger kept Adam bundled so deep inside mufflers and mittens that it was a wonder his little legs could move. She made Ben wear almost as much wool about his ears. Yet Inger herself hardly wanted to bother with so much as a scarf. She swore she was happiest and felt her best when the air was chill. She loved the winter. Called each new snowfall God's whitewash sent to beautify His earth. And whenever he looked out the windows at this time of year, Ben could hardly argue that point.

He yawned now and stretched again. He encountered Inger's warmth snuggled tight and trusting against him. She smelled of fresh-baked bread and wood smoke. She lay pressed close to him, her back to his chest and her legs arranged to match the curve of his so that they were like a pair of spoons placed one against the other.

Ben began muzzily to doze off. His arm slipped over Inger's waist, and in his state of partial sleep he pressed his face into the hair at the nape of her neck and hugged and gently rocked her.

"Are you satisfied, Ben?"

"With what?"

"With life?"

"Yes, of course." He smiled around the stem of his pipe. His feet were propped on an ottoman, and there was a copy of that very day's Springfield newspaper open on his lap. Adam was copying words onto a slate, and there was a smell of apple dumplings in the house. All of that seemed enough. More, in fact, than he ever bothered to think about. It occurred to him that his ambitions seemed to have died along with Elizabeth. How very odd that he hadn't ever until this very moment missed them. Or even so much as recognized their absence. "I am, Inger, but are you?"

"Yes, of course. For more I could not ask."

"But if you were to want something, what would it be?"

She shrugged.

"No, seriously. It's an interesting point. Other than this little house in Springfield, Illinois, Inger, what would you like to have? Someday, I mean, like if the Little People insisted on giving us their pot of gold. What might your dreams be? No matter how bizarre either. I want you to tell me. Anything at all."

"You will tell me if I tell you?"

"Yes."

She nodded and laid her needle and darning egg in her lap. "I listen, you know. I hear things. Read sometimes. And I think . . . I hear about the far west. Oregon, California. You know about these places?"

"I know they are very far away and there aren't many Americans there. But they say the government welcomes honest settlers. Would you really like to go there?"

"I think maybe yes. New country, new peoples, everyone starting over without the old memories. Yes, I think I would like that someday."

"Maybe we can do that, then. Someday."

"But not if you do not want, Ben."

"I wouldn't mind."

"You tell me now, Ben. Tell me what you dream."

He shrugged.

"You promised."

"So I did." He drew on the stem of his pipe and exhaled, the smoke hanging in the air above him and forming a ring there. "If . . . you know, someday—"

"I know."

"If it became possible, I don't know, I might—just might, mind you—might want to get into shipping again. Not as a sailor myself. I wouldn't leave you and Adam alone. But I wouldn't mind having something to do with the sea again."

"Would it be possible to do this thing in the western ocean?"

"Why, I suppose it would be. Hardly really thought about that before, but yes. There are ships that ply the Pacific. Not so many as to the east. But there is a little trade conducted with China and the Japans and Siam and the like. And of course there is Owyhee and the whaling trade. Ships call at the California ports. There are a few. I've never seen them, but I know of several. There is one that men say is magnificent. San Fran . . . Fran . . . I don't recall the name. San Fran-something-or-other. Goodness, now that's something I haven't thought about in years and years."

"Then perhaps we should go there, Ben." She smiled. "Someday, I mean."

"Yes, perhaps we should. Someday."

Inger returned to her mending, and Ben picked up his newspaper again.

"Mama."

"Yes, Adam?"

"Why do flowers grow?"

"To put beauty into the world, child."

"Why?"

"So that we can learn to appreciate the things that God has given us. So that we will know the most wonderful things of all are the things that are free gifts to us from our loving Father and not the silly things of this world."

"If God is my father, then who is Papa?"

"God is your heavenly father, but your papa is your everyday father." She smiled. "Papa is the father whose lap you climb into for hugs and kisses, ja?"

"Do both my fathers love me?"

"Oh yes, Adam. They both love you very much."

"I love both of them, Mama."

"That is good, Adam. That is very good."

"Do you, Mama?"

"You ask do I love both God and your papa, Adam?"

"Yes."

"Oh, yes, child." Tears came into her eyes. "I love them both so very, very much."

"Cartwright! Cartwright? Is there somebody here named Cartwright?"

"That's me. Over here."

"You better come quick, man. There's been an accident. They sent me to bring you."

"An accident?"

"I don't know anything more, mister. They just said I should run find you and bring you home because it looks pretty bad."

"No!" Ben blurted. He hauled back on the lever, taking the drive wheel off the belting leather and letting the big saw blade slow and whine to a halt. Long before the blade stopped spinning, Ben had abandoned his platform and run panicked from the mill, arms pumping and chest laboring.

An accident. Bad. An accident. Bad. The words repeated endlessly through his mind as he ran toward home.

CHAPTER 22

So many people were jammed into the small house that Ben had to push and shove his way through to reach the bedroom at the rear. The bedchamber was dark and shuttered and stupefyingly hot. A woman Ben recognized from the neighborhood was there, and several men. Inger lay pale and motionless with a sheet drawn high under her chin. She was breathing, but shallowly. She had been bandaged about the head. Bright blood stained the wrapping over her right ear.

"Clear the room, please. Haven't I made that plain enough, sir? The woman needs rest if she's to have a chance of recovery," an elderly man in a long outmoded suit of clothes said with a wave of dismissal. "Go on now. Out."

"I'm her husband," Ben told him.

The fellow cleared his throat and relented. "Be quiet then if you must stay. No commotion, if you please."

Ben dropped his voice to a whisper and tiptoed closer. "What happened?"

It was not the old man but one of the younger ones who answered. "Runaway," he said. "Something spooked

222

the team pulling Bud Carlson's big dray, and they bolted.
Bud wasn't even on the wagon at the time. He'd gone inside the store there on Center to tell them he had a delivery. Left the team alone. Next thing anyone knew, it was
a runaway. They ran 'round the corner onto Pond with bar-
rels and boxes and things flying off every which way."

"A barrel rolled clean over little Jessica Tighe," the
other younger man put in. "Broke her leg, they say."

"Hush, Billy, I'm telling this."

"Sorry."

"Like I was saying, the wagon come 'round onto
Pond real fast, the horses tearing along and the dray
bouncing and sliding. It was awful."

"Awful," the neighbor woman affirmed.

"Your kid and Mrs. Mehl's boy Freddy were playing
at something in the street there, and the woman—you say
she's your missus?"

"That's right."

"Well, she's a quick thinker, ain't she? She was
standing nearby saying something to Mrs. Mehl. When she
seen that the runaway was headed for the two boys, she
ran straight into the path of the team to grab up those kids
and toss 'em both out of the way."

"There wasn't time for her to get clear herself,
though."

"The off leader knocked her down and the wheeler
stompled right over her."

"Trampled," one of the men corrected.

"Whatever."

Ben blinked. Who cared about that, anyway?
"Adam," he said. "What happened to Adam?"

"That'd be the kid?"

"My son, yes."

"Kid's all right. Him and the Mehl boy are all right,
thanks to the woman there."

"Who are you folks?" Ben asked.

"We were passing by. We helped carry her home

here. She was awake then. She insisted she wanted to come home."

"First thing she asked was if the boys was all right."

"Then she made us promise we wouldn't take her off someplace where you wouldn't know where to find her. Made us promise we'd bring her home here."

"Mrs. Mehl showed us where you folks live."

Ben looked at the older man.

"I am a physician, sir. I heard of the incident and, ahem, volunteered my services."

"He isn't a very good doctor, if you want my opinion," one of the men said. "The way that foot is tore up, it should come off, certain sure. The poisons will set in, and she'll die inside a week. Mark my words. If you let this old quack have his way, mister, your woman will be dead inside a week. That foot has to come off."

The doctor—who looked more an impoverished pensioner than a practicing physician—made a face and tugged at the end of one of his mustaches. "Where did you take your medical training, sir, if I may be so bold as to inquire?"

"Huh. I've seen a thing or two. And everyone knows when there's an open wound like that, the limb must be removed. You risk the lady's life if you don't."

"And I tell you once again, sir, I—"

"Gentlemen," Ben said, breaking into what was rather obviously a continuing argument between them. He looked at the neighbor woman. "Is my son all right, Mrs. Mehl?"

"He's fine, Mr. Cartwright. I sent him to my house. My eldest is looking after him and Freddy. The worst either one of them suffered was some bruises and a little dirt. Thanks to Mrs. Cartwright here, praise the Lord." Mrs. Mehl rolled her eyes and lifted her palms heavenward.

"Thank you, Mrs. Mehl."

"Don't you be worrying 'bout that child. Not for a minute. He is fine right where he is."

"Thank you. Would you gentlemen consider doing my family another favor, please?"

"Glad to help out, mister."

"Would you please go ask all the, um, spectators out there to leave?"

"We can do that, sure."

Mrs. Mehl took the hint too and followed the gentlemen out of the room, leaving only Ben and the doctor. And a pale and pasty Inger lying motionless on the bed, her color little different from that of the sheets that covered her.

"Doctor, about what that man was saying—"

"Are you telling me you want the foot removed, sir?" the doctor demanded testily.

"Of course not. Why, I haven't seen how badly it was damaged. What's more, if I did see, I wouldn't have the professional competence to know what I was looking at."

"How refreshing," the little doctor—whose old-fashioned and fussy appearance did not, Ben had to admit, inspire confidence in the man's medical abilities—commented dryly. Ben could only hope that the fellow was a better doctor than he appeared to be.

"I'm concerned about my wife, Doctor. That's all."

"Trust me, sir. The lady's injuries are serious, but despite what that well-meaning gentleman said, quite frankly it is not the foot that concerns me. The foot will recover just fine. If, that is to say, there is sufficient time for it to do so."

Ben frowned. "And why wouldn't there be enough time, Doctor?"

"The wound on the side of her head, sir, is less spectacular but of much greater consequence. I have palpated the subdurum extensively." The old man exposed yellowing teeth in a wry smile. "That's the sort of mumbo-jumbo language we doctors use to impress fools like that one who just left. All that it means, sir, is that I felt of your wife's head. There is a fracture, a break that is to say, in the bone at the side of the skull. Just here." He pointed to the spot on the side of his own silvered head.

"And that is more serious than the foot?" Ben asked.

"I'm afraid so. Much more, in fact. And there is very little you or I either one can do right now but to wait and to pray. The danger, you see, is that the body will react to the indignity of injury by swelling. We have no idea what causes this swelling of the brain, but it happens. Not always, but it happens. If the swelling does occur, sir—your name is Cartwright?"

"That's right, Doctor. Ben Cartwright."

"I am Avery Barkoff, Mr. Cartwright. May I call you Ben?"

"Certainly."

"Thank you, Ben." Dr. Barkoff motioned Ben to a seat on the one chair in the small room, then perched himself onto the top of the chest at the foot of the bed where Inger kept their linens and a few other especially prized possessions. "Now. As I was saying, there are a number of possibilities. And several distinct dangers. Are you a pragmatic man, Ben? Can you handle truths even when they are harsh?"

"Everyone likes to think that of themselves, Doctor."

Barkoff smiled. "Carefully put, Ben. Good for you. In any event, sir, I shall be truthful with you. Your wife has been grievously injured. Her foot and ankle wounds, given sufficient time, will heal adequately well. I doubt she would even have a severe limp for any great length of time. If she manages to survive her other injuries, that is to say."

Ben did not at all like the direction this was taking.

"I was explaining to you the dangers of swelling of the brain tissue, I believe."

"Yes, sir."

"Extreme swelling would result in death, most probably without the lady ever regaining consciousness. That would at least be a swift and merciful conclusion. Worse possibilities exist, Mr. Cartwright. Lesser degrees of swelling could also result in lesser degrees of damage to the brain. The lady could live but become addled. She could even be rendered a lunatic by the injury. And one of the aspects of this sort of swelling that makes it so insidious, Ben, is that it can go virtually undetected at first. The patient can seem to recover, even returning to consciousness and a seeming recovery, then after a few days, even as long as a week later, lapse into fits or coma or irrational behavior. There are a few warning signs to watch for, Ben, and I will come as often as necessary, do whatever I must to help her."

"You are implying that measures can be taken to help if the swelling occurs."

"Am I, Ben?"

"You know that you are, Doctor."

"I compliment your intelligence, Ben. Should I now challenge your courage?"

Ben looked at Inger lying motionless—dying?—on that bed. "It isn't my courage that is at stake here, Doctor. Nor my life."

"No, I suppose not." Barkoff sighed and pulled a cheap and smelly rum twist from his pocket, lighting the ugly little cigar from a lamp someone had left burning on the dressing table near the bed. He coughed into his fist, then shrugged. "The simplest and best thing, of course, would be for the lady to waken with a headache and then fully recover. In the absence of swelling, even the broken plates of bone should mend back together in time, Ben."

"And if that doesn't happen, Doctor?"

"Let's cross that bridge if we come to it, shall we?"

Ben frowned but did not push the matter any further. It should be enough for the moment anyway to know that the doctor was not totally without resources if he should be forced to use them.

And anyway, Inger was a strong and vital woman. Surely she would be able to recover from these injuries. Surely soon the Cartwrights could pick up their lives and go on as if nothing had ever happened here.

*　　*　·　*

Ben came awake with a start, ashamed of himself for having dozed. His head snapped up and his eyes sprang open. He had no idea what time it was. Sometime in the middle of the night. His eyes burned from lack of sleep and his cheeks and neck itched where unaccustomed beard stubble grew. Three days and now into the third night, and there was as yet no change.

Inger lay as motionless and as pale as when he first walked in to find her like this. Her breathing continued shallow and thin, and her color had not improved.

Ben heard movement elsewhere in the house and did not have to look up to see who it was who entered the bedroom. A long shadow cast by the one lamp left burning on the dressing table was three times the height of the little man who cast it.

Avery Barkoff waved a cup of steaming broth beneath Ben's nostrils. "Here. Take this."

"Thanks." Ben accepted the cup without interest and set it aside.

"Drink it down, Ben. Take it like medicine. You need it."

"I will, Avery, I promise."

Barkoff looked at the other cups of broth he had brought in earlier. Ben had promised to drink them too. No doubt the promises were sincere. Each remained right there waiting for Ben to drink them at the earliest opportunity. "Right," the little doctor said without sarcasm. Ben was not the person here who mattered anyway. The doctor used the flame of the oil lamp to light a candle and held it close to Inger's face while he leaned near and examined her.

He unwrapped the loose bandage that covered the contusion on the side of the skull and felt of the wound. Instead of good solid bone beneath his probing fingers, there was a spongy resistance. He grunted and peeled back the lid of first one eye and then the other. "Ben, come over here a minute."

"Yes, Avery."

"See this?"

"Yes."

"Then look here. Can you see the difference?"

"Of course. This one is big in the middle and that one is little."

"Those are called irises, Ben. They should be the same."

"Does that mean . . . ?"

"I'm afraid it does. It certainly gives every appearance of it."

"How will we know for sure?"

"In the absence of consciousness, Ben, there is little indication possible. She cannot complain of pain or dizziness or double vision or loss of equilibrium. The only sure sign, I'm afraid, would be if she were to convulse and die."

Ben sobbed. "Avery, you can't know . . . all this time . . . how fine a woman she is . . . how little I appreciated or knew . . . Avery, you have to save her. You simply have to."

"There are no guarantees, Ben. Not of success and not of failure. The only promise I could make would be the attempt, not the outcome."

"I can't lose my wife, Avery, without having a chance to tell her . . . how much I value her. You can't let that happen, Avery. Please."

"There are men in my profession, Ben, who would think it foolish to attempt the relief of pressure on the living brain. I concede that the operation is a dangerous one. It involves drilling holes in the skull around about the traumatized point so as to allow the pressures an avenue of escape. It does not eliminate the swelling, you understand, but it allows the natural swelling to take place and then subside again without permanent damage. I won't try to minimize the dangers. The operation can be a complete success and yet the patient die anyway. Or a misapplication of the drill can pierce the brain and bring about instant death. Yet I've personally seen skulls in a colleague's office in England, skulls that lay buried underground for perhaps thousands of years, that prove the ancients performed surgeries much like I believe your wife needs. The skulls I observed showed complete healing and implied a long and full life for the patient after those crude surgeries were performed. Despite what most of my colleagues might choose to say now."

"I wouldn't know about any of that, Avery. The only thing I know is that I don't want Inger to die. And if she must die, then at least I want to be able to hold her hand and look into her eyes and talk to her and know that she is hearing and comprehending what I'm telling her. Is that possible?"

"I believe it is possible, Ben. But I cannot promise you that it is. You must settle for that, because it is all I have to offer."

Ben nodded. "You have to save her, Avery. At the very least we have to try."

"I'm going to go home now and sleep. I suggest you try to get some rest too. And drink that broth, Ben. Please."

"I will, Avery. I promise."

The little old man nodded and smiled and shrugged. "When I come back in the morning, Ben, I shall bring my instruments and several burly assistants to help hold the lady down. All I shall need from you is that you remain out of the way. Can you do that, do you think?"

"Of course," Ben said, not at all sure if he could, however.

Barkoff went to the door.

"Avery."

"Yes?"

"Have you ever ... I mean ... have you yourself ever performed this, um, operation before?"

"Successfully, you mean?"

"That's right."

"No, Ben, I haven't." And he was gone into the night.

*.   *   *

"Ben." "Avery."

Both had spoken at the same instant. Ben stood towering over the little physician who was in his shirtsleeves now, wearing a stained apron streaked with blood, his hands and forearms sticky with it.

"Is she . . ." "She is . . ."

Again both tried to speak at once. Barkoff held his hand up to forestall a third occurrence of the problem. "You can go in now, Ben. She is very weak, but she is awake now. You can speak with her. She will hear what you say and she will know. As I recall, that's what you asked for."

"But will she . . . ?"

Barkoff smiled. "I think so. No guarantees, Ben. But yes, I think she will recover now."

Ben looked up past the ceiling above them. "Thank you."

"Very sensible, Ben. God does not send bills."

By then he was speaking to an empty doorway, because by then Ben was halfway to his wife's bedside.

He dropped to his knees, took her hand and held it to his lips and his forehead. Through a misty, hazy film of water he could see that Inger's eyes were open. She was still pale, but not so pale as she had been. And there was clearly the light of life and of comprehension in her bright blue eyes.

"Thank you, God, thank you, thank you." He was crying. He felt stupid to be crying now that she was all right. That was probably about as stupid a thing as he could ever remember doing before. He was crying and he was clinging to Inger's hand—which she was squeezing in return now—and kissing her hand and then her cheek and . . . and he didn't know what all he was doing. What he did know was that Inger was alive and she would get well now and she wasn't going to die and all the regrets and recriminations of all the nights of his vigil over her, all those were for nought because now he could tell her, he could make up to her . . . oh, God, he could, he really could.

"Adam." Her voice was a whisper so faint he could scarcely hear it. He loved hearing it. He hadn't ever expected to hear Inger's voice again. "He is all right? The vagon, it did not . . . ?"

"The wagon it did not, my dear. Adam is fine. You are going to be fine. We all of us are going to be . . . oh, Inger. My dear and beloved Inger. How I worried when I thought . . . Inger, there's something I haven't told you." He hadn't told her because he himself had not known it. Not until these past few days. But now he did. He could not bring himself to confess to his wife that he had not known. But he could try to make up to her all that had been lacking before. "It frightened me so, my dearest Inger, when I realized that in all this time I never once said the words to you and . . . please forgive me, Inger. Please."

"Forgive, Ben? There is nothing to forgive, I know."

"But all this time, Inger, and I've never told you . . . Inger Cartwright, I love you."

She gasped, and for a moment he thought something had gone wrong after the operation, that perhaps Avery was wrong after all.

She began to cry too now. "Oh, Ben, my Ben, never did I think to hear from you those words, never. I love you so much. Since that first day when you walk into Gunnar's store I love you, but a fine man like you, I know you could never look at such an ugly lump like me, big stupid ugly Svenska like me. And then we are married and . . . and . . . oh Ben, I do love you so very much, I do."

And then Ben realized.

Inger. Dear Inger. He had not known he loved her before because to begin with he had not. And she, never complaining, knew that he did not. Yet even so she was dear and kind and giving.

So big a girl she was. She had to be in order to contain all that greatness of heart that was within her.

He squeezed her hand and kissed her. "Listen to me, Inger. Listen to what your husband has to say to you."

"Yes, Ben, I listen."

He smiled through the tears that were coursing down his cheeks. "I love you, Inger Cartwright. I love you very much."

"Never has anyone been happier than I am right now, Ben. Never."

Ben felt a hand on his shoulder. It was Avery Barkoff standing over him and motioning him away. "She needs rest now, Ben. She's been through a lot, you know."

"I will be fine," she said. "Now."

Barkoff acted as if he did not know what she meant by that, and perhaps he did not. Ben had no idea if Avery had been standing there very long or, for that matter, if what he and Inger said would have had meaning to anyone other than themselves.

The important thing, though, was that he was in love with his wife and she with him, and soon she would recover and they would once more be a family. But a closer and happier family than ever before. He was sure of that.

"Come along, Ben, please. I have some broth waiting for you."

"Good, because I'm awfully hungry for some reason."

Ben pressed Inger's hand, gave her one more kiss. "Sleep now, my darling. We'll talk more when you waken."

"Yes, my love. Anything you say." Her smile was . . . dear heavens, he realized. When Inger smiled like that, she was beautiful, truly beautiful, with the genuine beauty of her innermost nature shining through onto the surface to render all else unimportant. And in Ben's eyes she would forever more be beautiful to him.

"I love you," he told her.

"You are a lucky man, Ben," Avery said as he pulled the door closed behind them.

"Yes."

"It would have been a tragedy to lose the two of them."

"Two, Avery? I don't understand."

"You don't, Ben? Surely you . . . dammit, Ben, even if Mrs. Cartwright didn't tell you, surely you aren't so blind that you haven't noticed it by yourself."

"Noticed what, Avery?"

"I take it back. You really are that blind." Barkoff shook his head. "In another three months, Ben, four at the most, I'm going to bill you again for the delivery of your child."

But Avery Barkoff lied about that. It was nearly five months before Inger gave birth to a healthy, strapping, lusty baby boy.

CHAPTER 23

W hat's that, son?"

"A leaf, Papa."

"It's a very pretty leaf. Is it for Mama? No? For me, then. No? But if it isn't for either of us, Adam, who could it be for?"

The youngster giggled and shyly approached the basket where his baby brother lay kicking and wiggling. "Can I give it to him, Mama, can I?"

"Yes, of course, Adam. Just don't let him eat it, please. Little ones put everything into their mouths, so you must watch out for him."

"I will, Mama, I promise."

Ben put his arm around Inger's shoulders and drew her closer. He pushed off with his feet and the porch swing creaked back and forth, the sound of the chain links loud on the hooks overhead. It was a fine, fair evening, warm for the time of year, and Ben was enjoying being outdoors with his family after being cooped up inside for the past several months.

"Adam is so good with him, isn't he?" Inger observed.

"Quiet, woman. You're distracting me."

"From what am I distracting you, mister?"

"I was sitting here looking at you trying to decide which part of you is the most beautiful. Would it be your hair, cheek, nose, eyes? I can't decide. All of you is so beautiful."

Inger blushed and slapped him on the wrist. "You are cruel to say these things to me, Ben. You tease me."

"No, I love you."

"Sometimes I almost think you mean what you say to me."

"Good, because always I do mean it when I say such things. You are beautiful. And I do love you."

Inger sighed and leaned her head against his shoulder. "So lucky am I." She heard the baby giggle and sat up so she could see what he and Adam were up to. Little Eric was reaching for the leaf Adam waved over him. Inger smiled.

"Get it. Get it, Hoss."

Ben laughed and leaned forward. "What was that, Adam?"

"I told him to get the leaf, Papa. See how close he is? He can get it if he tries hard."

"What did you call Eric?"

"Hoss, Papa. That's his name, isn't it?"

"No, my sweet," Inger said, laughing. "Your brother is named Eric Haas Cartwright. Eric for my papa, and Haas was my mother's maiden name." She smiled fondly at Adam. "Never mind, dear. To you it means nothing."

"Mr. Lewis calls his bay gelding Hoss all the time," Adam pointed out.

"So he does," Ben agreed.

"An' brother Hoss is awful big."

"Yes."

"I like calling him Hoss better than Eric."

"Whatever, son."

"Why is my name Adam?"

"For the first man. The first son named for the first

man. And Milton for a very wonderful poet and author who wrote about that Adam."

"Can I read what he wrote, Papa?"

"Certainly, as soon as you can sound out the words, the big ones too. You've gotten lazy about your reading lately, but when you can sound out even the big words, you can come to me. I will let you read from the book I keep."

"The special book, Papa?"

"Yes, the special book."

"I'm going to learn to read the big words real fast, Papa, so I can read the special book."

"That's nice, son."

"I'll read the book to Hoss."

"That's good."

"I'll get my slate and study now." He jumped to his feet, the leaf fluttering forgotten onto the porch floor. "Stay there, Hoss. I'll be right back." And he dashed inside with a thump and a slam, leaving Eric wriggling and cooing in his basket.

"Wild Indians would be more quiet," Inger said.

"But not half so much fun."

"This book, it meant much to you and Elizabeth, yes?"

"Yes," Ben said. "Very much. Do you ... do you mind me keeping it?"

Inger smiled and touched his cheek. "No, my darling. I am glad you have something of her. More than Adam, I mean, although nothing could be more wonderful than to have her son beside you."

"You are truly a marvel, Inger Cartwright. I don't think there is a jealous bone in your body."

"But Ben! How could I not be grateful to your Elizabeth? She gave you Adam and she gave you great joy. This I know because it was so terrible when you lose her. She loved you, and so do I. I want you always to be happy, and I am glad you were happy before we met. I would change not one thing of your time with Elizabeth. Except for her not to die."

"Even though—"

"Yes, Ben, even so."

He hugged her. "I do love you, Inger. So much." He reached for his pipe and slowly began loading it, musing aloud as he did so. "When Elizabeth died, I didn't want to live on without her. I thought sure I could never find love or happiness again after loving her so much and being so happy with her. And then I met you and even then I didn't appreciate you because of old sorrows. Inger, you've taught me so much about what it means to be truly loving, truly giving. You've given me Eric—"

"Hoss," she teasingly corrected.

Ben made a face and then went on. "Seriously, dear, I owe you so very much that I can't begin to tell you how grateful I am to you for these lessons. And for your love and devotion. I was not whole until I met you, Inger. Thank you."

There were tears in Inger's eyes. Ben kissed them away. They were interrupted by Adam's thundering return and a startled squeal from Eric, who had been drifting into a nap until Adam arrived with a slate and bit of chalk stuck under Eric's nose.

"Watch me, Papa. Watch me write."

"What will you write, son?"

"Our names, Papa." A moment later he asked, "Mama, how do you spell Hoss?"

Patiently she told him while her husband rocked them back and forward on the hanging swing and man and wife held hands in the gathering dusk of a late winter's evening.

"Are you all right, Ben?"

"Yes of course, dear. Why do you ask?"

"You are restless."

"No."

"Yes."

He shrugged. "Maybe just a little."

"You would tell me about?"

"I'm being silly."

"No. Now tell me."

"It's just ... oh, I don't know. I have a good job. This is a nice little home here. You and the boys are perfect. No one could ever want for more than I already have right here with you and our sons."

"Yes, Ben, all of this is true. Most especially so the part where you say the boys and I are perfect. So what is lacking that you think you are being silly now?"

"It's just ... actually it's your fault, Inger."

"I knew that would be so, Ben. You did not even have to say this part."

"Well, it's just that here lately I've been thinking that a good job is all well and good. But a man never gets anywhere by working for the other fellow. You know?"

"Yes, this is true, I know. And you are not a man to sit by while others do. This too is true, my Ben."

"So I've been thinking ... sort of ..."

"Shipping, Ben? Perhaps another chandlery?"

"I'm not thinking of going back to Boston."

"But San Francisco maybe, yes?"

He grinned. "Am I that transparent, my dear?"

"To me, Ben, yes. You are."

He laughed, crossed the room and swept her into his arms. "I do love you, Inger Cartwright."

"Good. Do not change that, Ben. Not even a little bit, no."

"I haven't any plans to." Then he sobered. "We have it nice here. If you don't want to risk making a trip like that, we won't go. I mean, it isn't like we have to go. We can stay right here. Save our money and one of these days open a little store. We really don't have to give up everything we've built here, you know."

"But I want to see California too, Ben. I told you this a long time ago, no?"

"You told me of course, but—"

"One thing I ask of you, Ben."

"Yes?"

"When we get to California and find our home there, I would like to have more babies. Boys, girls, lots of babies. The boys will all help you in the business, and the girls will all marry rich, wonderful men who love them."

"I can't think of anything I would like better, my dear."

"And then we will grow old together in California with our grown babies close around us and grandbabies to rock on our laps and spoil so much that their mamas and their daddies are angry with us."

"Perfect," he declared.

"When do we start, Ben?"

"I suppose we should plan everything very carefully. We could, I don't know, start next spring perhaps?"

"Next spring? Bah! Why wait? We have one perfectly good spring starting just now. We don't have so much to take. Sell most things and carry little. It is the best way, you know. Most trouble is from the people trying to carry too much with them."

"Inger, how would you know all that?"

She gave him a triumphant smile and pulled away from his embrace long enough to find her knitting basket. In it she had, in addition to the obvious yarns and implements, a thin, buckram-covered volume with white lettering on the cover. *Removing to Oregon, a Sojourner's Guide,* by Smythe.

"But how . . . ?"

"I buy it two weeks ago. You must read it, Ben. On the boat would be a good time."

He shook his head. "On the boat?"

"But of course, where else? We go first down the Illinois to the Mississippi. Then on the Missouri. Then to someplace called Sa'nt Joe. There we buy wagon and ox team and join a group of others, hire a guide. It is all in this book, Ben. You will see."

"Two weeks ago," he said.

Inger laughed. "I would have bought earlier but it took me a week to find the book I want."

"I really must be transparent."

"Only to me, only because I love you."

"In that case, madam, please keep it up." He wrapped his arms about her and kissed her quite thoroughly.

"Oh, Ben, this is so exciting."

"That kiss?"

She giggled. "That too."

"But I know what you meant. I just hope it won't be too hard on you and the boys."

"Nothing is too hard so long as we are all together," Inger said.

"To California," he said, raising an imaginary goblet high in a toast.

"To our family," Inger proposed.

Together they laughed and hugged and danced giddily around the tiny parlor.

CHAPTER 24

Ben walked wide around these strange and exotic beasts about which he knew so little and upon which so much depended. The intricacies of sails and rigging were second nature to him. But the whys and wherefores of oxen?

"What are their names?"

The seller nearly choked. "Names? Mr. Cartwright, oxes don't have names. Though I 'spect you'll name 'em all soon enough, but not the sorta names you'd be wantin' the wife an' them kiddies to hear. But names? Mister, would ya name a tool? Would ya name that wagon there?"

Ben smiled. "Actually, friend, I just might, much like I would most certainly name even the smallest and meanest of boats if that were all the ship at my disposal. In fact, I shall name the wagon . . . Egbert. For no reason at all. Adam. Where are you, son? What is the brown ox's name, Adam?"

"Doesn't he have a name, Papa?"

"That is what we are determining now, son."

"You mean I get to name him?"

"Yes, you do."

Adam dashed to the front of the yoked six-up and stared into the ox's huge, soft eyes as if for inspiration. "I think this one's name is Ichabod, Papa."

"Ha. You've been reading Mr. Irving, haven't you? Good for you, Adam. Shall we call Ichabod's yokemate Irving, then?"

"Yes. And the white one is Washington."

"I think the speckled one should be called Sleepy," Inger put in with a laugh.

"What about you, Eric? What do you say?"

The baby gurgled and bounced in his mother's arms. It was a good thing Inger was as sturdily built as she was because young Eric was quite a chunk. But a laughing, happy, outgoing chunk who hadn't yet met a stranger.

"What was that again, Eric?"

"Hoss said that ox's name is Adam, Papa."

"Oho, named it for his favorite brother, did he?"

"He did, Papa. I heard him."

"Yes, Ben, I'm sure that is what I heard too."

"Adam that one is, then. And shall we name the last ox Eric? We certainly can't call it Hoss. People would get awfully confused to see Egbert being drawn by an ox named Hoss."

Adam burst into a giggle fit. The man who sold them the team and wagon shook his head and no doubt departed with the impression that he'd just done business with an entire family of lunatics. But then he was a dour soul with no sense of fun, fun being a commodity Ben was getting much practice in with Inger of late.

"As soon as we get to the wagon park, Adam, you can paint Egbert's name on the tailgate."

"Can I, Papa? Thank you."

Ben helped Inger and Eric onto the seat of the tall wagon with its spanking white canvas and proud red wheels. Adam scrambled up to sit beside them, and Ben picked up the whip and goad the seller had thrown in with the deal.

"Gi'yup," Ben barked, as he'd been taught over the

past few hours. "Gi'yup, boys, haw." He tried an experimental snap of the whip and managed it without knocking off his newly acquired broad-brimmed hat in the process. He didn't make any noise either, but he thought it something of a triumph simply to know that he hadn't hit himself or anyone else with the lash.

Despite their new owner's shortcomings, Ichabod, Irving, Washington et al leaned forward into their yokes, and the wagon wheels began to turn.

All that remained now was to load the new wagon and get into line with the others in the Johnston train. When they first arrived, they hadn't appreciated how lucky they were to find this one last train making up; most of the year's movers had long since made their start, and the Johnston party of forty-two wagons would be undoubtedly the last train out this season.

"California, here we come," Ben called out with a tip of his hat westward. Adam went into another giggle fit, and Inger waved and shouted too.

"California, here we come."

"Halloo, you'ns. Halloo an' welcome." The greeting was warm enough, even though the thirty-seven wagons of the Johnston train were a filthy and bedraggled assortment. They were, Ben conceded, a far cry in appearance from the gaily painted collection that pulled out from Missouri those long weeks earlier. On the other hand, this no longer handsome assemblage was trail hardened and capable. But badly in need of rest and refitting, which was what they would be able to accomplish now at Fort Laramie.

Ben had walked forward to the head of the train so he could determine what was up. Adam was quite proudly in charge of the team, which, in truth, would follow behind the wagon ahead with dogged and docile persistence unless forcibly turned off from the line of march. Adam's presence, although he didn't know it, was more a matter of proud participation than any need for real control over the team.

"Roll in an' welcome," the man from the fort was saying. "We got a smith for anybody as needs. An' you'd be wise t' check the set o' your tires. Don't forget, what you've covered this far is the easy part. Past here's where things turn serious."

Everyone said that, and Ben supposed it was the truth. But really, how bad could it be? The oxen were pleasant creatures and no bother. One simply yoked up in the morning and traveled until evening and then did the same again tomorrow. And tomorrow and tomorrow and tomorrow. Eventually one was where one wanted to be.

So far, at least, the travel had been tedious but far from difficult.

"Have the Ballards already pulled out ahead of us?" Leonitis Johnston asked of the man from the fort.

"Who?"

"Tom Ballard, Asa Finch, the Huckleys, and the Carters. We started out forty-two wagons, and one fellow whose wife went off her nut turned back a few weeks out of St. Joe. Ballard and those others were mule-drawn and didn't want to hold to the pace of our oxen. They pulled ahead, oh," he turned to the nearest of his train members, who happened to be Ben, "what would you say, Cartwright? Three weeks ago?"

"About that," Ben agreed.

"Right. They pulled ahead and said they'd come on at their own pace and meet up with us here at Laramie. But I don't see their wagons anywhere."

The man from the fort scratched his neck and pondered. "No, mister, we ain't seen sign of no four mule-pulled wagons. You, uh, didn't pass no wreckage or see no smoke in the sky, did you?"

"What are you implying? Hostile Indians? Be serious, please."

"I ain't implying nothing. Just telling you, mister, we ain't seen no four mule wagons here ahead o' you."

"How odd," Johnston said.

"Those Indians were friendly," Ben said.

"Of course they were."

"You seen Injuns?" the man from the fort asked.

"Friendly ones, yes. They were a mounted party of perhaps two dozen. They stopped and visited with us. We gave them a little sugar and tobacco, and they were quite content."

"An' this Ballard, he'd of got along with them the same as you done?"

"You know Tom and Asa," Ed Pugh put into the conversation. "They likely would've got their backs up and chased them Indians off if it was them the redskins was trying to beg off of. Tom was pretty big-mouthed on the subject of how Indians oughta be taught their place an' made to stay there."

"Huh," the man from the fort said, turning aside to spit. "If they ain't here yet they ain't likely t' get here. Either they's got lost or they's got dead. You ain't real apt t' find out which."

"I can't believe—"

"Look, them people took their chances. They knowed what they was doing. An' if they didn't, they anyway should've. Forget 'em, you won't never see or hear of 'em again, most like. Now . . . what can we do for you'ns?"

It was beginning to get through to Ben just what a strange and cruel land this was they were crossing. So alien to everything he had ever known, yet in its own way so exciting and beautiful too.

And they said the great prairies were only a tune-up for the magnificence yet to come.

A man in this country, Ben was already learning, could stand just as tall and breathe just as deep as a sailor far out at sea.

Leonitis had things well in hand here. Ben turned and went back to join his family. He wondered, though, just what he should tell Inger about the Ballards and those others. Inger had been particularly fond of Tom Ballard's wife, Nina.

But then, surely nothing bad really happened to them.

Surely they'd only chosen to go a different way or to bypass Fort Laramie for reasons of their own or . . . something. Surely.

The rationalization sat uneasy on him, and as soon as he reached his own wagon, he climbed onto the driving box and grabbed Inger and Eric in a tight hug.

"Is everything all right, Ben?"

"Yes. I suppose." With a sigh he sat down cross-legged on the ground beside Inger's supper fire. He pulled out his pipe, peered for a moment into the empty bowl and decided he could wait until later for his nightly smoke. Something less than nightly of late. He was running short of tobacco, and there wasn't exactly a store handy where he could replenish his supply. The train—still called the Johnston train, for no particular reason except perhaps inertia—was somewhere southwest of the big salt lake.

"Mr. Drummond again?" Inger guessed.

Ben nodded. Then smiled. "He's harmless, of course. Good thing too. But I must admit that sometimes I wish he'd taken the Oregon road with the others."

The train had split weeks earlier, most of the wagons, including Leonitis Johnston's, holding to the north, bound for the rich farmlands of Oregon, an even dozen others striking out across the dry, alkaline flats toward mountains so distant their very existence had to be taken on faith, and beyond them to California. Of the California travelers, only the Cartwrights were drawn by dreams other than that of gold. Rumors were circulating that gold had been found in the north of California, and the lure of gold, Ben was learning, can do strange things to people. On the other hand he supposed he should be grateful for the rumors, true or not. Otherwise there would have been no others to travel with him and his family across this lonely, arid path through the wilderness.

"Well, I don't care what he says," Inger declared. "I cannot see a child go hungry, Ben. Not when I have food to share. Why, I could not eat if I refused to do something, Ben. I could not."

He took her hand and squeezed it. "Lucky for us we don't need Drummond's permission for what we do."

"Yes, isn't it," she said with a smile, recognizing that she had her husband's approval to go ahead and do as she wished.

"Pete is just in a lather for fear we'll run out of supplies before we get over the high passes into California. He's worried about it being so late in the season. He isn't a bad man, though."

"I know that, Ben. And I am not a bad woman."

"True."

"And I will not see a child go hungry."

"No."

"I will take from our own things only. Not much. But even a little will help. You saw, Ben. Could you sleep tonight if we did nothing?"

"Probably not, Inger, probably not."

In his mind's eye he too could still see the miserable degradation of the pathetic, louse-ridden band of Indians they had seen camped beside a tiny rill of barely potable water late this afternoon.

Pah-Utes, someone thought they were. Whatever that meant. Ben knew nothing about Indian tribes. What he did know, the same thing that Inger knew, was the sight of extreme poverty.

The Indians—be they Pah-Ute or some other, it mattered not at all—were nearly naked, their only possessions seeming to be a few stone tools, a few weapons made from flimsy sticks, and a very few baskets. The adults were naked save for thongs about their waists supporting loincloths made of rabbit or gopher skins. The children hadn't that much covering for their emaciated bodies. Many of the smaller children had bellies that were distended and swollen from a state of chronic, acute hunger. The children seemed all open sores and huge eyes.

Inger's heart had been touched by their plight. Anyone's surely must be. But Drummond, who had appointed himself leader of the California group, argued and ranted that they could waste no supplies on a bunch of filthy Indians. If anyone had food to spare, Drummond declaimed, it should be divided among the other white families who might well need it if the train were caught in the mountains by early snow.

Ben could not argue with Drummond's logic, but he could not forget the sight of those hungry children either. Certainly he could not tell Inger that she should turn her back on human suffering, no matter what Drummond or anyone else said. There are times when logic simply is not enough reason to overrule one's heart.

"Cartwright. Where are you, Cartwright?"

"Here, Pete."

"Come over here a minute, would you?"

Ben got to his feet and winked at Inger. "Wait here, all right?"

"He only wants to argue, Ben."

"Then we'll let him argue. It won't hurt anything. Won't change anything either." He took a moment to squeeze her shoulder and to glance at Eric sleeping in his basket nearby. Adam was in Ralph and Lillian Kuntz's wagon playing with their three boys. "Coming, Pete."

He ambled slowly across the compound to Pete Drummond's wagon and helped himself to a seat close to the fire there. The evening air in the desert was chill, no matter the heat of the day, and at night a fire was welcome.

"Would you like a little tea, Ben?"

"That would be nice, Emily, if it's no trouble."

"No trouble at all, Ben." Emily Drummond was a handsome woman, patient and serene in the face of her husband's intensities. She poured a steaming cup of tea for her guest and then withdrew before he could compliment her on the brew. More than the compliment, though, he wanted to ask what mix she had used so Inger could duplicate it. All of the wagons were low on coffee and real tea by now, and so they all made do with whatever herbs, leaves, and bits of bark the women could gather locally. It was amazing how much variety even a desert will yield when one begins paying attention to it.

Ben enjoyed his first cup of tea and was working on a refill while he listened with silent fortitude to a repetition of Pete Drummond's earlier arguments. Pete, Ben sometimes suspected, enjoyed the sound of his own voice a trifle overmuch. Not that Ben intended saying so. He could at least give the fellow the courtesy of hearing him out. Then he and Inger could do as they thought best on the subject of—

A piercing scream resounded from somewhere out in the night.

Ben leaped to his feet, his cup of tea spilling unnoticed down his trouser leg and into the dirt.

"That sounded like Inger," he blurted.

The scream rang through the cold air again, and Ben began running blindly into the night in the direction the sound had come from.

CHAPTER 25

Inger! Are you all right? Why are you bending over like that? What happened? Did someone—"

"Ben, please. Give me minute to catch my breath." She sounded all right to him, but she was holding herself rigid and half bent over. He knew something was not as it should be, but he did not know what. "I am sorry I startled you. All of you."

Close at Ben's heels were the other men of the small train, most of them armed with the rifles and pistols that long since became habitual adornment in this harsh land, almost as commonly worn as hats or shoes.

"Was it those Injuns, missus?" someone asked.

"Please do not be alarmed, please," Inger said.

"Inger, dear. What is it you're carrying there?" She had a small burlap sack in her hand. He had no doubt whatsoever about what would be in that. She quite obviously had been carrying surplus food out to those Indians. But he could see that she was holding something else too. A stick, it looked like. She was keeping one hand pressed tight to her side as if she'd been running for a very great distance and had developed a stitch, although of course that was not possible in rugged country like this was and at night. "What is it, dear?"

"Is nothing. Really."

"Damn," one of the men said. "That's a spear. I seen one o' them Injuns carrying one just like it this afternoon."

"Let me see, Inger. Please." Ben held his hand out.

Reluctantly she gave him the article.

"It really is a spear."

"It is only a stick for throwing at rabbits," Inger insisted. "Do not make so much of it."

"Did one of them throw it at you?"

"I came upon them in the night without warning. Of course I startled them. They did not mean to hurt anyone. They were only frightened. One of them threw this to defend himself and then he ran away. He did not mean harm."

"Filthy bastards. Let's get 'em." That was Guy Jenrette's voice. "All you with guns follow me an' we'll—"

"Mr. Jenrette," Inger snapped. "You will do no such thing. I mean it. Was my fault. And anyway no harm was done."

Ben wasn't so sure of that. Inger was still holding her side, although she'd straightened up now and was standing at her full height while she admonished Jenrette. In the starlight he wasn't sure, but thought there might be an unnaturally dark stain on her dress beneath the palm of her hand.

"Please, everyone. I startled the Indians and they ran away. They startled me as well and that is why I screamed. I am sorry if I bother you all, but everyone please go back now. Please."

After a moment the men reluctantly complied. Pete Drummond was the last to turn away and leave. He eyed Inger's bundle suspiciously but chose not to confront her. After all, he had no real authority and he likely could see that Ben was in no humor to be ordered about at the moment. Right now all of Ben's attention was on his wife, and Drummond chose not to interfere. "If you need anything—"

"Thank you, Pete. We'll let you know if we do."

"Yes, well, I suppose a man's got to do what he thinks best."

"That's right, Pete. Good night now."

Drummond grunted unhappily but turned away and lumbered back in the direction of his wife and his supper.

"Seriously now, Inger," Ben said when all the others had gone. "Are you all right?"

"Is a scratch only. The point stuck in just a little. It is not bad."

"Let me see."

"Not here, Ben. I would have to open my dress. I cannot do now. Later. When we are in wagon. I will wash it then, and you can see. It is a scratch. No more."

Ben hefted the spear and examined it more closely. It was only a slender wand of some light wood, its tip scraped to a point and hardened in fire. It was crude and primitive and so light in weight that he would not likely bring down a coyote, much less any creature as large as a deer. Or a human.

"Do you want to keep it for anything?"

"No, of course not."

He would have tossed it into the brush, but she stopped his hand. "No, Ben."

"Why not?"

"He will need it back if he is to hunt, no? If he is to feed his babies?"

"Inger, you are a marvel. I swear you are. All right, we'll ... I don't know ... stick it upright in the ground so he can find it come morning. How would that be?"

"Have you forgotten, Ben? The children."

"Inger, surely you don't want to go over there still. What if they—"

"Ben!"

He sighed. "All right, but I'm going with you. And

make plenty of noise. We don't want to frighten anyone and have them start throwing spears again."

With Inger carrying the sack of food and Ben holding the absurdly primitive little spear, they made their way through the darkness toward the Pah-Ute camp.

itter anguish soured Ben's stomach and brought hot
tears to his eyes. He tried not to show the range of
emotions that churned inside him, threatening to
overwhelm and bear him down into a maelstrom of regrets
and recriminations.

The truth, though, was that he had faint hope left.

It all seemed so . . . stupid. Senseless. Wasteful.

Inger lay dying.

And from what? From a minuscule prick of the skin.
A wound so slight she might have gotten worse had she
pinched her finger in a hinge.

That seemingly inconsequential break in the skin
caused by a skinny, frightened Pah-Ute festered and rotted,
and now the inside of the wagon box stank of pus and pu-
trefaction. Its sweetish, sickening odor greeted Ben's wak-
ening each morning and haunted him on his pillow each
night.

Dark, angry whorls and streaks of poison showed red
and purple beneath Inger's skin, radiating outward from
the place—no larger even now than a thumbnail—where
the spear point had penetrated, spreading like so many evil

255

vipers as they carried their death-dealing poisons farther and farther inside her body. Flesh that was once firm and vital was discolored now, become puffy and swollen and ugly.

And she was in pain. She was in horrid, terrifying pain. She never uttered a word of complaint, choosing to lie drenched in cold, oily sweat with her jaw clamped so hard against screaming that she trembled and shook as if freezing. She could force herself to accept her pain with stoic resolve, but she could not keep the man who loved her from seeing that pain and sharing it. Inger would not let herself cry, but Ben could cry for her, and he did.

And all of this from so silly a thing as a pointed stick thrown not with malice, but from a fear of noises in the dark. The whole thing would have been, could have been, should have been . . . laughable.

Ben wished he and Inger could laugh about it together. Walk side by side and talk about it and laugh about it and hold hands while they walked and talked and laughed.

Instead he clutched her dry, limp hand between his and tried to will his own healing life forces into her wasting body.

So quickly had the poison spread into her system and began wasting her that she seemed to be sinking into the bedding as if she were carved of ice and now had begun to melt.

Her strength was failing too. Only a few weeks and Inger could no longer sit up unassisted or feed herself or even tease with the children. If only that Indian hadn't . . . if only they'd seen the danger in time to use a cauter or . . . if only the poison centered in a limb that it would be possible to remove and . . . If only.

Ben despised the words "If only."

"Ben? You in there, Ben?"

"I'm here, Ralph." Ben felt the side of the wagon give to Ralph Kuntz's weight. But gently. Ralph was considerate. He thought to ease his weight onto the step so as to avoid jarring Inger within.

"It's Pete, Ben. He says—" It was plain that Kuntz did not want to finish what had to be said. The message disturbed and perhaps embarrassed him.

"I know what he's saying," Ben said. "The train has to move on. I've seen the clouds up there. Already there is some snow. If you don't move now, and quickly, you risk being caught in the passes. Everyone would very likely perish if that were to happen. Twelve wagons, fifty-three souls. All are in danger if the train doesn't move now." Ben shook his head. "Make that eleven wagons and forty-nine souls."

"You have to come, Ben. You'll die if you stay here." They were camped on a broad, pretty field beside a river. Truckee Meadows, someone said it was called, and offered a reference in a guidebook to prove it. Even then there was some argument about that, because they hadn't had anyone to guide them since they split away from the Oregon party all those many miles back. The one thing that was not in contention was the mighty, majestic presence of the Sierra Nevada mountain range that stood over them to the west, and that lay between them and the latter day Promised Land that was California. This river and the meadow beside it lay in the afternoon shadow of the great mountain range, and high to the west the clouds were dark and forbidding. There was snow in them. The wagons had to move and move at once or run the very real risk of being buried, along with the people who inhabited their meager shelter, in the high passes yet to come.

"I can't move her, Ralph." The people of the train were not insensitive. They were anything but. The men were sympathetic and the women even more so. Already the train had delayed here three days longer than they really shoud have in the hope that Inger's condition might improve so she could go on. Or that she might quickly worsen and die and be done with it. "It's too much for her."

"We have to go on, Ben. We have to."

"I know that. I agree. The train can't wait any longer. But I can't go, Ralph. The movement, all that jolting, would be too hard on her. It would kill her."

"She's dying anyway, Ben. When it happens . . . it will be a blessing. I'm sorry, but that's the truth."

"I love her, Ralph. I'm grateful for every day I have with her. I'll not cut those days short."

"Dammit, Ben—"

"I know. You are very kind. Both of you. And I know your advice is well intentioned, possibly even very sound. It is just that I can't accept it. I have to stay here with Inger."

"Lil said you'd feel that way."

"She's a bright lady, that wife of yours. Thank her for understanding, will you?"

"She said . . . I don't know how you'll take this, Ben, but hear me out. She has a point."

"What is that, Ralph?"

"If you all stay here, Ben, you risk the children too. Let Lillian and me take them with us. Come spring you can join them. You know we'll take good care of them. They fit right in with ours anyway. And you can join them, Ben. First thing the passes open come spring."

Ben smiled a little. "If I'm alive then, you mean."

Kuntz nodded solemnly. "That is what I mean, Ben, yes."

"You're right. Lillian does have a point." He sighed. "It would be for the best, wouldn't it?"

"Yes, I think it would. You might survive a winter here alone. But with two small children to look after. Well . . ."

"You know, of course, that I'm still hoping there will be two of us to winter over."

"Yes, of course."

"But . . . not four. I think not four."

"I know that isn't an easy decision for you, Ben. But I think it's best for Adam and Hoss."

"Eric," Ben corrected absentmindedly. Kuntz seemed not to hear. "Did Pete say when the train is moving?"

"We're, uh, yoking up now, Ben."

"I think that's the smart thing to do, really." Ben held onto Inger's hand, leaned down to swab her forehead and throat with a bit of cloth.

"You, uh . . . Pete is thinking to use your oxen, Ben. Since you won't be, that is." Many of the wagons were being pulled by teams that had been reduced by death or injury or simply because the oxen that had drawn them wore out and would need weeks in which to recover their strength and allow sore feet to heal.

Ben's initial reaction was that what was his was his and to hell with Pete Drummond and his officiously arrogant manner. But in truth, those cattle were needed. The eleven wagons that were going on to California still faced the highest and most severe passes of the entire journey.

"All right, Ralph. Tell Pete he has my permission to use the oxen."

"Thanks, Ben. I'll tell him."

"One thing, Ralph."

"Yes?"

"On the other side—I want you to take charge of my oxen, please. And if next spring I don't . . . that is to say—"

"I'll sell them if need be, Ben, and give that money to your boys."

Ben nodded and swallowed back all the other things he wanted to say and knew he shouldn't.

He looked down at Inger, peaceful while she was enjoying the blessed escape of sleep. After a while he felt the shift of weight once more as Ralph stepped down off the wagon and was gone.

Beyond the thin canvas of the wagon cover he could hear the bustle of the train making up to leave. Probably he should go fetch the boys in and wake Inger and let them say their good-byes.

Probably.

He didn't know yet if he could bring himself to do that.

God, how he wished none of this had ever happened.

Ben straightened, icy water dripping from the bucket onto the smooth stones underfoot. He shaded his eyes with his free hand and watched a huge vee formation of geese honk and clatter their way south, their wings spread dark against a slate-colored sky. There was a bite in the air to match that of the water, but the two were equally clear and invigorating as well. It was good to be alive on a crisp morning like this.

Funny—or not so—how much he appreciated life while Inger lay dying.

Funny—or not so—how differently he felt about his own mortality now as opposed to the morose withdrawal he had wished for when Elizabeth died. But then he had learned so very much about life and love from each of them.

And this time—thank you, God—he was able to sit with Inger, talk with her, enjoy loving her all the more even while he was in the process of losing her. This time they had time together.

Inger knew she was dying.

They talked about that, of course.

Once the first tentative, hesitant exchanges were made, the subject became an open one, and one that Inger accepted much more readily at first than he. Ben railed against her death. She chose to prepare herself for it with quiet dignity.

"You will bury me please in the gray dress I wore when we married."

"That? I didn't know you still even had it."

"Oh, but yes."

"You have other dresses that are so much prettier."

"I have no other that does so much to keep you in my heart, though. It is the one I wish to be buried in. It is in the bottom of that little chest there, Ben. No, to the left.

Yes. It is wrapped in paper. When the time comes, if we know soon enough, my Ben, I will help you put it on me."

He nodded. It was all he could manage at the moment.

"The boys know that I love them, but please you tell them for me anyway."

"Yes."

"And you know that I love you, but this I want to tell you anyway. I am the most blessed and fortunate of women, for I have known the love of Ben Cartwright. I have never been pretty or delicate or fair—no, Ben, do not interrupt, please—I have never been any of these things, and I am awkward sometimes, but not stupid. I have known what and who I was, and never did I think that a man so wonderful as you could love me. Even when circumstances caused you to marry me, I never dreamed I would have your love too. Then you gave it, and it was like the sun rose to warm only me each morning and to light my world alone. You have brought to me joy, Ben Cartwright, and there is no thing more grand or wonderful to me than this privilege I have had to be your wife. This you must know."

Another time she told him, "You must make to me a promise, Ben. I know you will grieve. You love me, and it is healthy for you to have sorrow. You will miss me and sometimes you will be angry with me for leaving you alone, and that too is as it should be. But one thing you must not do, Ben. You must not pity yourself. When Elizabeth died you allowed sorrow to become self-pity, I think, and that is not good. Adam and Eric need you, and you cannot indulge yourself in pity so that you are not able to give them love."

And again, close to the end, she whispered so faint he could hardly hear, "Do not be afraid to love again, my Ben, for you are a good man and have much love to give. Know that I love you and want your happiness now and always. Tell my sons I love them."

They had nine days alone together at the Truckee

Meadows, and those days were bittersweet, sad but loving too.

He dressed her in the shabby dress she'd worn the day she ran away from Gunnar to be with him and Adam, and he buried her atop a knoll from which one could see the jagged, snowcapped Sierras to the west and the lush bottomland spread out below.

His sorrow was great, but the pity he felt was solely for Inger and not for himself. It helped for him to know that even though she was gone, he did not have to stop loving her. For that he could never do.

CHAPTER 27

Ralph and Lillian Kuntz had talked about looking for him in the spring when the passes opened once more, but Ben could see no reason why he should winter alone at the Truckee Meadows when his sons were only a few hundred miles distant on the other side of the Sierras.

The boys deserved to know that Inger was gone. They were entitled to the loving message she left for them.

Besides . . . their father was lonely. He wanted to see them, touch them, hold them in his arms and share his tears with them.

The children were entitled to their time of sorrow, and so was he. Ben understood that now as he had not when Elizabeth died. Perhaps even more important, he and Inger had had time together. They had known. They had talked. They held hands, and even as she slipped away from him, they had a deep and abiding love to share. They were able, in sum, to prepare.

Ben's grief was every bit as deep this time. The difference was that it was not paralyzing. Now he knew and appreciated the gifts that Elizabeth and Inger had given him: his two fine sons. He wanted now to be with them as quickly as possible, and spring was a very long time to wait.

The second day after saying his good-byes to Inger, Ben made up a small pack out of the supplies in the wagon. There was not much he would carry. A hand ax and knife. Flint, steel, and burning glass. Flour, salt, and lard. The cash that he and Inger intended as the seed money for a mercantile venture in this new land. Copy of Milton; he would rather have left the food behind than *Paradise Lost*. Rifle—he'd bought the thing in St. Louis and fired it only once, that being when the man at the shop showed him how to load it—and two blankets. Those things were few, but weighed more than he would have thought possible. They would, he hoped, suffice to meet his needs until he breasted the passes and reached California.

He could have tried to take the wagon across. There were enough loose oxen about, creatures that had been abandoned for being footsore but which now were recovered enough to work again, that he could have made up a team and more left over. But already the country he could see to the west was dusted heavy with snow. He doubted a wagon could make it through, and a man on foot would be able to travel faster as well as through harsher conditions than a wagon's wheels would permit. Better to leave the wagon here. If he wanted, he could come back in the spring to capture the loose roaming oxen and reclaim his property.

God, it was lonely here. He missed his sons.

Delaying further would be without purpose. Inger was gone. There was nothing he needed to say to her grave that he had not already said while she lived.

He picked up the blanket-wrapped bundle, took one last fond look toward the mound where Inger lay, and began the slow, uphill trek along the path the others had taken before him.

Such natural beauty Ben had never seen. Not anywhere. Not even in all his years at sea had he found any sight to compare with this magnificence.

Automatically, quite without conscious thought, his head turned and his mouth opened in anticipation of commenting on the extraordinary view.

But Inger was not there.

Ben felt foolish and empty and mildly ashamed of himself that he could have forgotten, even for that instant. But, oh, he wished that he could share this with her. Inger would have loved it. She found joy and excitement in the shape of a flower petal. What would she have said had she been able to share this with him now?

The lake was so bright and pure a blue that it fair dazzled the eyes. Beyond it were white, jagged, spire-tipped mountain peaks. One after another after another of them marching north to south.

That knowledge was somewhat daunting, however beautiful, because Ben had thought twice already that he was climbing into the last pass and must surely be breaking soon onto the western slopes of the Sierras. Now he could see that the mountains he had thus far conquered were only the foothills of the continent's great and rugged spine. At this point his journey was scarcely begun, although he had thought it nearly finished. That was daunting, true, but it did nothing to take away from these majestic vistas.

Beneath his feet the great forests of ponderosa pine—Inger's guidebook had spoken of those; Ben chided himself now for not tucking her book into his pack along with *Paradise Lost*—swept thick and dark down the slopes toward the great lake.

He had no idea how large the lake must be. The faint wagon tracks he had followed to this point angled toward the south end of the lake, which he could see far below him and to his left. To the north, though, the jagged, irregular shoreline stretched interminably into the distance. There had to be an end to the water. Somewhere. But from this vantage point Ben could not see it. The lake ran quite literally for miles and miles at the bottom of a deep valley suspended high in these fantastic mountains.

The crystalline waters were so placid now that they acted like a mirror of gigantic proportion, reflecting the distant peaks, the dark-streaked avalanche chutes, the vast sweeps of forest that from so far away looked like a soft black-and-olive carpet on the mountainsides. Each sight and nuance was twinned, one master set laid out in splendor and a faithful duplicate lying in the still waters below.

Far above, the sky was streaked with bold white lines where cloud formed a ripple pattern upon the sky, and there to the north by northwest Ben could see another weather line, this one lower and gray and hazily indistinct but moving swiftly beneath the plates of high, bright cloud.

He frowned, because beautiful though the scene was, had he been at sea he would have been concerned. That frontal line was moving too quickly for comfort. The color did not seem particularly threatening—at least it would not have been so in the waters of the Atlantic—but in his weather experience speed of movement quite often is an alarum of danger. And this weather front—it was too soon to tell if it should be considered a storm front—was moving very quickly indeed.

Oh, but the views. Fantastic. Wonderful. The lake, the mountains, the magnificent virgin forests.

Apart from the few scratches and scrapes at Ben's feet where wagon tires had left their puny signature, man had as yet made no impression upon this country.

Probably that was part of its appeal.

Here Ben felt as an explorer must feel when he comes upon a vista no human eye has ever seen before, when his feet tread onto ground no human foot ever touched before him. This country was untouched, untrammeled, unsullied by rooftop or chimney, by ax or shovel, road or ruin. No trash littered the forest floor here and no smoke showed against the buttermilk sky.

Ben felt like Adam. Not Milton's Adam, but God's. All he lacked was Inger's Eve to make him whole.

If only he could tell her. If only she could stand at his

*side with the rising breeze in her face and share with him
this beauty.*

But then ... perhaps ... she was?

Ben lifted his face into a freshening wind and closed
his eyes. The only scent on this crisp, clean air was a faint
hint of pine sap.

He breathed deeply of it, savoring the aroma of the
pines like a connoisseur might delight in the flavor of a
superb wine held long on the tongue.

His brow knitted, though, as a sharper scent cut into
that of the pine pitch. Ozone some called this crisp, biting
undertone of odor. It was a scent, or perhaps a feeling, that
made the hairs at one's nape prickle and stand upright. It
brought Ben's eyes open.

And then they opened wider.

In the moments, little more than seconds, since last he
had glanced to the north, the line of swift cloud had swept
nearly the entire length of the huge lake.

Now it was rushing down upon this high ridge where
Ben stood puny and helpless before it. Far from being gray
and pretty and benign, at this distance he could see the
storm's true colors. They were dark and ugly and frightful.

Below him the tops of great pines twisted and writhed
as the leading winds lashed and tugged at them. Small
branches cracked and were strewn through the air in the
swift-rushing van of the weather front. Saplings were
whipped into quick submission or were broken clean away
from their tender roots. Miniature whirlwinds fluttered and
churned. All the distant views of lake and mountain were
swept away, obscured by the pervasive gray and white of
the storm.

Ben could smell dust on the air now, and moisture.

What once had seemed a pale and inoffensive gray
now showed itself to be a dirty, wind-whipped white.
Snow. Blinding, driving, swirling flurries of it that danced
and writhed and curled within the body of the onrushing
storm.

Ben went pale.

He had seen storms before. He had faced the icy gales of the North Atlantic and the great, clawing hurricanes of the southern seas. He had seen snow. Immense flakes of it. Wind-driven spikes and spicules of it. Coarse granules and wet lumps of it.

Never had he seen anything like this. Never.

Its speed and ferocity alarmed him and sent his blood to pounding through his veins. He needed shelter from this storm. He knew enough to recognize that. There was no belowdecks here. No indoors. Not even a wagon cover to huddle beneath.

He was a man alone in a strange wilderness—and a wilderness that was beyond his own ken or experience, at that—with only two blankets to cover and warm him.

He needed shelter. He needed fire. And he needed them at once.

The leading winds struck him with bone-numbing cold and a force so great that it rocked him off his heels and he had to stagger backward two paces before he could regain his balance and, leaning into the vicious force of the cold blast, fight ahead like a man wading against a strong current.

He had the impression—perhaps silly, but nonetheless strong—that if he hadn't been anchored by the weight of his pack and rifle, he might have been knocked off his feet. The wind was that strong.

Before he had gone a dozen more paces, his ears and the tip of his nose stung and burned. Much longer, he knew, and they would go numb. Once that happened, he was in danger of losing them to frostbite.

He had to get out of the wind and the cold, and he had to do it now. Otherwise there would be no one to tell the boys that he and their mothers loved them.

Worse, there would be no one to find him and carry him back down to Inger's side for burial.

He had to take shelter.

Now!

CHAPTER 28

Cold. C-Cold. Very cold.

Ben's hands trembled. His fingers, too numb to feel, he had to operate by sight now that his sense of touch had largely deserted him.

He huddled in the lee of a brush and rock pile. It was poor shelter but it was all he could find. He had one blanket wrapped around him like an overcoat. The other he draped over his head and shoulders like an undersized tent as he bent low to the ground.

What he needed the most right now was not direct shelter, but a source of heat outside his own body.

He needed a fire.

He *had* to have a fire.

With a fire he could warm himself. With a fire he could melt snow to make tea. Simply hot water to drink and thus warm himself if that was all he could manage to find. With fire he could make up a crude dough for the stick-bread that he intended as his staple until he reached California and safety.

But without fire ...

Without fire he could die.

Almost certainly would die.

And because of this interminable, insidious, incessant, miserable, stinking damned *wind* he could not seem to make a lousy *fire*.

Shuddering and trembling, he tried again. He held the blanket tight to the ground, willing it to stay in place there, just for a minute, just for a matter of seconds, just long enough, please. He held the blanket down to seal out the omnipresent, intrusive damned wind, and in numbed hands clutched flint in the fingers of the one hand and steel in the palm of the other.

He struck, and a fan of sparks sprayed onto the charred black tinder he had prepared long ago and kept sealed in a tin with a tight-fitting lid.

The sparks rattled onto the scrap of tinder—so delicate and gossamer thin it would have made a spider's web seem indestructible in comparison—and began to glow. Trembling, Ben leaned closer and with aching lips pursed, he blew, fanning the bright yellow-red curl of incipient fire.

The glow caught and strengthened. Ben wrapped a handful of dry, shredded bark loosely around the carefully charred tinder cloth and, hoping against hope, began to gently blow again. If the tinder coal became hot enough and the bark took flame, then—

A gust of icy wind whipped beneath the blanket edges, lifting and billowing it off Ben's shoulders, scattering the threadlike filaments of bark and exploding the delicate tinder like a puff of smoke.

The coal was gone. And Ben's hope with it.

He had only one more small scrap of tinder. Thanks to the wind, he had used all he had brought. And there would be no more. It takes fire to make tinder. It takes tinder to make fire. Without one he had no hope of creating the other. And if this last bit of tinder did not catch . . .

He would die.

Without fire he would die.

It was as simple as that.

Flint and steel cannot produce fire without the presence of some form of prepared tinder, for no naturally occurring substance is sufficiently flammable to take flame from so small a spark.

Patiently, slowly, Ben reassembled his fire-making tools.

He set the burning glass aside. If the day had been cloudless, he could have made fire with that regardless of wind or temperature. But the day was no longer cloudless, and he would not survive to see sunlight again if he did not manage to start a fire now.

He shredded more dried fibers from the inner lining of a bit of tree bark. Tinder was needed to take an initial coal from the spark. Something more substantial was needed if that hint of fire were to grow into true flame.

He placed his lump of flint and half-moon firesteel just so. He drew the blanket once more on top of him and tried to anchor it there with stones piled onto it for as far around as he could reach.

Finally, shaking as much from fear as from cold, he twisted open the lid of his tinder can.

The bit of black fluff, still bearing the weave and texture of the burnt cloth it was made from, lay like a wisp of down. Tinder could be made from many substances. This, like most of Ben's experience, happened to be made of linen that was airlessly fired, much like an extremely delicate form of charcoal. It was no heavier or more substantial than goose down. But it was brittle. The tiniest jar could shatter it and render it useless. The least disturbance and it would disintegrate.

Gently, carefully, Ben lifted his last hope for survival from the can. He held it cupped in his palm. If he burned his hand in the process of making fire, well, that was something he would gladly risk.

He held the flint above the tinder, positioned it as best he could to ensure that sparks from the flint would be directed down onto the dry and immensely flammable tinder, finally took up the steel and held it poised to strike.

He took a deep breath . . .

And gasped aloud as a vicious blast of cold wind tore the blanket off over his back and sent it streaming out in front of him.

The bit of tinder so carefully placed was whipped out of his palm to disappear, leaving behind nothing but steel and useless flint.

Rage and frustration warred within Ben, but he did not give them vent. Rage and frustration would serve no purpose.

Nor, he supposed, would they have done any harm.

Still, he would not give in to base impulse. He simply would not.

He sat where he was for a moment, then patiently—uselessly—replaced the empty tinder tin, the flint, the part circle of steel, finally the burning glass with which he could have made fire and thus more tinder. If only there were sun. If only he could survive to see the sunlight again.

He knew he could not.

What he could do—all that he could do—was to accept his fate with dignity.

He retrieved both blankets and drew them tight around him, pulling a flap of heavy wool over his head so as to block as much snow and retain as much body heat as possible.

Back to the wind, then, and head bowed, Ben sat somewhere high above the great lake of the Sierras and waited for either the end of the storm or the end of life.

He wished he could have seen his sons one more time.

"No!"

Ben came to his feet with a defiant, angry bellow.

No, he would *not* sit huddled beneath a blanket and wait for the end of life. He simply would not.

This storm might kill him yet, but it would have to

take him out spitting and scratching and fighting against it tooth and toenail. It would not take him meek and mild.

Walking warmed a man, didn't it? Stamping one's feet? Jumping up and down? Fine. He would do all of those things. He would do them all at the same time if he had to.

What he would not do was allow himself to die without a struggle. Every man dies. Ben Cartwright did not intend to do it easily.

He took up his things and began walking. He could see no bearings or reference points through the impenetrable veil of blowing snow, but he had a seaman's sense of navigation.

Ahead in the direction he had been traveling he knew there were only the lake and more mountains, these peaks higher and more severe than any he had yet seen.

Behind there were miles and miles of pine forest and empty country. But behind him too there was the potential relief of a lower elevation where the temperatures might not be quite so extreme. And back there too was the wagon, with all that implied of shelter and safety.

Even if that safety were illusory, illusion was quite enough for the moment, because right now the fact of having a goal was much more important than the utility of the goal once it was attained.

Cold, possibly freezing to death, but angry now and grimly determined, Ben Cartwright turned and began a blind and probably hopeless attempt to retrace his path through these mountains.

The Sierras could kill him.

But dammit, they could not make him quit.

CHAPTER 29

Ben lay shivering. He stretched toward the warmth and sneezed when something tickled his nose. He could smell ... what? Smoke. Grease. Something else that was musty and ammoniac, like the sharp but not really unpleasant scents of an old barn.

He smiled a little, remembering where he was.

Why, there wasn't a barn within ... who knew? Five hundred miles? A thousand? Perhaps there were barns in California. It was a pity he hadn't lived to find out.

Was he dead yet?

He really didn't think so. Certainly, though, he was hallucinating. Well, he'd always heard that freezing was a pleasant enough death. Sort of like going to sleep, they said, once the cold numbed the brain. That must be what was happening to him now.

Odd, though, that he thought he could smell things. Hear things too. Like voices murmuring low and deep around him. Angels waiting to carry him on high? Or demons lurking in the shadows? On the whole he would rather the angels.

Smell, sound, even heat.

He squirmed and wriggled, reaching out toward the heat he could have sworn he felt.

"Ow!"

He bolted upright into a sitting position, eyes staring in disbelief and his finger stinging from the burn it received when he put his hand into the fire.

He was . . . Lordy, he hadn't any faint idea where he might be.

In a low hovel of some sort, some rounded shelter sort of thing little more substantial than a brush arbor but built low to the ground like a large basket overturned.

A fire burned bright and cheery in the middle. The walls of the crude little shelter were so porous that there was only a real sense of heat immediately beside the fire. Just a few feet away and the cold crept in.

Dark faces and bright, glistening eyes surrounded him. Ringed tight about him and stared at him with both fascination and . . . wariness? Not quite fear, but bordering it, he thought. Indians, in any event. Nearly naked despite the snow and frigid temperatures without.

Ben glanced down. He had been laid out on a pallet made of pine branches and one of his own blankets. The other blanket, pushed aside and disarranged now by his movement, had been laid over him.

The Indians were scrawny, filthy, scarecrow creatures. He thought they looked wonderful.

"Hello."

A young man said something back but in a guttural, explosive tongue that held no meaning for Ben. As, presumably, his greeting meant nothing to him.

The young man said something more, held up a finger as if in admonishment—or warning?—and turned to crawl out of the hut through a door flap no more than two feet tall. Snow and cold air swirled inside when the flap was pulled away. The young man going out into the force of the storm was wearing nothing but a loincloth held up by a leather thong.

When he was gone another man, slightly older, spoke,

and two women quickly responded. One of them pressed into Ben's hands a cup made of willow withes woven tightly together and sealed with pitch. The beverage was a warm herb tea of some sort. He drank it, the slight warmth of it spreading through his stomach almost instantly.

The other woman handed him a dough ball that he suspected was made of the flour, sugar, and lard he had been carrying with him. The mixture was uncooked. It tasted quite perfectly wonderful.

He smiled and nodded and thanked them even though he was sure they could understand no more of what he was saying than he could comprehend of their language.

"Thank you. You are very kind. Thank you." He bobbed and bowed and smiled, figuring that message would be clearer to them than the words could be. "Thank you."

The door flap was pulled aside and the young man returned, bringing a middle-aged man with him. The others in the hut moved quickly aside to make room for this newcomer, and Ben guessed that the older man was a person of some substance. He had the remains of a blue shirt covering his shoulders and much of his chest, and there was a steel knife in an untanned leather pouch hanging from his waist thong. That was the only appurtenance of modern society that Ben had yet seen among these people, barring the blankets that he had brought with him.

"You," the older man said, obviously struggling for words half familiar and possibly long forgotten. Where he might have picked up a little English, Ben could not imagine.

The man reached over and touched Ben's wrist. He nodded. Motioned around the interior of the flimsy little hut. Patted his own chest and smiled. "You."

It was intended as a welcome, Ben guessed. "Thank you," he said. "Thank you very much."

"You. Woo-man. You." The man pointed to his own mouth and mimicked the gesture of eating.

"Yes, thank you," Ben said, nodding and holding up

what was left of his dough ball to show that, yes, he had been fed already, thanks.

The Indian shook his head. He appeared frustrated with the inability to communicate. "You. Woo-man. You." He swept his arm away and pointed. Ben had no notion what direction he might have been pointing. After all, Ben had been quite thoroughly unconscious when he got here. Wherever here was. "Woo-man. You."

The man gestured toward a clutch of small children sitting half hidden behind their mothers and again made the eating motions. Ben did not understand.

The Indian grabbed a pointed stick from another man nearby and made as if to throw it. "Woo-man," he said forcefully. "Woo-man. You."

Across the hut one of the Indian women took a crudely carved wooden spoon and acted like she was stabbing herself in the side. Then she shook herself as if shaking off the annoyance of the wound and reached inside an imaginary bag or basket to bring out an imaginary treat that she handed to one of the children who was sitting cross-legged beside her. The youngster, a little girl, pretended to eat. Her smile afterward was quite real.

"Woo-man," the older Indian said. "You."

Comprehension finally burst through. His woman. Inger. And these people. These were the same people, or anyway part of the same tribe, that Inger fed.

Dear Lord, these were the same people who killed Inger.

Except of course they didn't know that they killed her, and hadn't honestly wanted to kill her.

Inger herself, Ben suspected, would have approved of the trade-off. Their spear had killed her. Now their presence was saving him. It was an exchange that Ben could not approve, but he knew Inger would have.

A wave of sadness swept through him at the thought of her. Then it passed, to be replaced by the needs of the moment.

"Thank you," he said. "Thank you."

Later, much later, he would learn through gestures and in groping, halting, imprecise attempts to communicate between him and his hosts that the Pah-Utes had come to the Truckee Meadows to find oxen abandoned by white travelers and left there on the lush grass. The impoverished and nearly weaponless Pah-Utes were able to capture the docile beasts of burden, whereas wild game of any size easily eluded their rabbit sticks and thrown rocks.

Ben was not entirely sure, but he thought what he was being told was that the Indians watched him for nearly a day, waiting for him to die in the snow so they could strip his body of the mysterious possessions he carried. But he stubbornly refused death, and finally a latecomer recognized him as the man who with his woman had fed the children, and a decision was made to take him down from the mountain to warmth and shelter.

That winter he had more than ample time to improve on the cairn he had erected over Inger's grave. He did not speak aloud, though, to tell her about the things that had happened since she died. He suspected he didn't have to.

CHAPTER 30

Ben stood with one foot propped on a fallen tree trunk, surveying what he still believed was the most beautiful sight in the world. The great lake that Ma'hundi called Tahoe was spread out far below him. The distant peaks still were starkly white with snow. But the melt was well under way now. Soon the passes would be open. Soon he would be able to follow the trail around the south end of Tahoe and climb the final slopes that separated him from his sons. That reunion could not come soon enough to suit him.

But today was sufficient for today, and today was very good indeed.

He had a cape of elk skin over his shoulders to warm him, and his belly was full with good meat and with the greens and wild onions that the women were gathering now in the meadows far below. Spring came earlier down there. Here winter lingered.

He needed powder and lead when he saw civilization again. After all this time the Pah-Utes did not seem to comprehend the relationship between ammunition and the rifle. Ben hadn't had the rifle with him when the Indians found him. It was only later that it was discovered dropped in the snow and half buried. Ma'hundi would have used it as a pry bar or cudgel if Ben hadn't rescued it from the headman and put it to better use.

One thing. After this winter Ben had learned to become adept with the rifle and with the revolving pistol that salesman in St. Joe talked him into. Now he was glad he'd brought them.

As for the wagon, well, it could stay where it was. All of last year's abandoned oxen were long since either roasted and eaten on the spot or slaughtered and dried. The Pah-Utes had enjoyed their most comfortable winter in living memory. At least that was what Ben thought they told him. His grasp of their language still was no better than theirs was of English, and that was marginal at the very best.

The wagon could have stayed almost where it was anyway.

Ben had had the entire winter to think this through. And to fall almost as much in love with this magnificent country as he had been with Elizabeth or with Inger.

Why, there really was no need for him to go to California except for the boys. Certainly he was under no pressure to settle there, and he had reached several conclusions during the dark winter nights with his Pah-Ute friends.

If indeed there was gold in California, men would be swarming to the new discoveries. There would be wagon trains by the score and wagons by the hundred this season and for some time to come, where just last year there had been no more than a dozen trains, or so Leonitis Johnston was told last summer.

Now all of that would be changed.

And it occurred to Ben that a man who wanted to establish a trading venture could do worse than to establish himself at the Truckee Meadows.

It would be months before the first wagons could arrive from Missouri. In that time he would be able to cross into California and reclaim his sons.

Together they could return to this wonderful country.

Ben had it all worked out in his mind. Oxen should be cheap at the California end of a one-way road. Only those who intended to farm in the new land would have any use for the beasts. Ben and his sons should be able to buy them cheap and bring them back over the Sierras to the Truckee. There the emigrants with their footsore and weary oxen coming in off the arid, barren desert to the east could exchange those worn-out creatures for fresh ones. They could buy or trade, however they pleased, and press on over these highest and most difficult passes with fresh livestock to pull them. While they were doing that, Ben could simply turn the tired oxen onto the rich grasses along the Truckee. By the time the next train came along, those once worn-out beasts would be recovered and be ready for sale and useful employment again. The idea appealed to him in its simplicity.

He could also buy a stock of merchandise in California of the sort that road-weary emigrants might want for themselves. Dried meats and fruits, perhaps. Coffee, tea . . . he would have to see what was conveniently and inexpensively available and then make that sort of decision.

Why, if this thing with the oxen paid off, there was no reason why he couldn't expand on his business. There was a wide, rich world of grazing land available here on the hills and in the valleys east of Tahoe. He could lay claim to it—Lord knew, no one else seemed to want anything to do with it—and raise cattle here himself. Horses or mules too, if he wanted.

Why, there was practically nothing a man couldn't accomplish in new country like this.

The Cartwright family, father and sons, would be the first to take up land here. It would be an idyllic place for boys to grow up tall and strong and proud. Ben could teach them himself. And they would meet others every year as the wagon trains passed through. They would not be totally isolated from society, and here . . . here they had more than society could ever hope to offer.

There were woods to roam and streams to fish. There would be work aplenty, and that was to the good. A man needs work. It is what strengthens and defines him.

They could build a house . . . Ben knew exactly where he wanted to place it. There, where he had first stood and looked out in awe at the splendor of Tahoe and the Sierra Nevadas. He would build their house on that very spot. He already knew what he wanted it to look like.

And they would claim land. A great, sweeping tract of it. After a winter with the Pah-Utes, he knew the best land for grazing and the best for timber and the best if they should choose to put in a crop. They would take up the land—and protect it from being despoiled— starting at that high ridge and running south all the way down to the creek where he and Doheetsu shot the buck deer with the huge, odd-looking ears. And from the eastern shore of Tahoe all the way down to the lake where Kla'kat taught him how to make a fish weir.

Ben was excited now as he looked out over this magnificent land that he intended to make his home. And his sons'.

He breathed deep of the clear, sweet air, and his chest nearly burst with the power of the land.

A rancho—isn't that what the Mexicans over in California called such?—a rancho such as this one, and never had there ever been any rancho to compare with it, a rancho such as this one deserved a name as grand as it was.

Ponderosa, Ben thought as he gazed fondly at the huge, majestic trees that seemed the very symbol of the beauty and richness he found here.

The Ponderosa rancho. He smiled.

With God's grace, Ben thought, there would be Cartwrights on this Ponderosa now and for all time to come, because this is where he would build, this is the legacy he would leave to his sons, this Ponderosa ranch.

The Cartwright saga continues!

If you enjoyed *The Pioneer Spirit*
by Stephen Calder, be sure to look for the
next novel in his BONANZA series,
THE PONDEROSA EMPIRE,
available in November 1992 wherever Bantam
titles are sold.

Turn the page for an exciting preview of
THE PONDEROSA EMPIRE by Stephen Calder.

Ben Cartwright straightened, coming upright from bended knee and reaching down again to brush the dirt and bits of loose gravel off his trousers.

Everything here was as tidy as he could make it. The fence was tight again after a winter of abuse and would keep out browsing deer or grazing cattle, either one.

The carved stone was straight and the lilac bush he'd planted behind it looked like it might be established well enough this season to thrive and for the first time come into flower. Both the headstone and the bush had been brought across the mountains from San Francisco.

The stone read:

INGER BORGSTROM CARTWRIGHT
Beloved Wife and Mother
May 1822–September 1848
Slumber Sweetly

Ben would have preferred to be more specific with the dates, but he simply hadn't known what the exact date was when she died in his arms that September day nearly seven years earlier.

Seven years. It seemed so much longer. And yet in another way it seemed there had hardly been time enough to blink an eye or catch his breath.

He looked first at the headstone with a cascade of freshly gathered early wildflowers at its foot, then up toward the magnificent Sierra Nevada mountains looming so close above.

Inger hadn't lived to share with him the great beauty of those mountains, she had died here at the base of the foothills, but he knew she would have loved the high country every bit as much as he did.

They had shared so much in the short time they'd had together. Their tastes and hopes and joys had been so very much alike.

And Inger would have been proud of what Ben and his sons had built here.

Elizabeth would have been proud of that too. Ben could not honestly decide if Elizabeth would have shared the joy he found in this mountain splendor. Elizabeth had been a child of city and sea. Probably she would have, though. Certainly she would have been willing to share whatever life he chose, whether that proved to be in Boston or here.

He was a lucky man, Ben Cartwright told himself now. Thinking about the two women whose love had enriched his days brought him much more joy than sadness.

For many reasons.

Ben smiled as he looked down from the knoll where he himself had placed Inger's grave that heart-wrenching day so long ago. He was looking at the two primary reasons why memories of his dear Elizabeth and of Inger were still so strong, and yet even in their absence so joyous. Because down there ambling along the banks of the Truckee River were the sons those two wonderful women had given him.

Adam was thirteen now, dark and lean and quick in

both body and mind. Elizabeth Stoddard Cartwright had been Adam's mother.

At his side now—always at big brother's side, it seemed—was cheerful, sturdy, laughing Hoss. Eric Haas Cartwright, really, but Adam long ago corrupted his baby brother's name into something more to his liking. At this point Ben supposed seven-year-old Hoss would be indignant if anyone were to begin calling him Eric. After all, whatever his infallible guide and mentor Adam wanted was law so far as Hoss would be concerned.

Oh, they were wonderful boys, Ben thought with pride and pleasure.

While their father watched from the knoll, the two youngsters stopped, bent, straightened again. Ben could see that they were in close consultation about something. He wished he were able to eavesdrop on their conversation.

Hoss threw something into the creek. Adam shook his head and then patiently spoke with his brother for a time, finally demonstrating, and then Ben knew what they were about. Adam was teaching Hoss to skip pebbles off the water.

From this distance it appeared that Hoss's enthusiasm exceeded his ability. What he lacked in dexterity Hoss tended to make up by way of determination. In this particular matter, though, Ben suspected a certain amount of technique would be required. Unless, that is, Adam knew of some magic that would allow his brother to shortcut the normal learning processes. Ben was convinced that if such a method were physically possible, Adam would surely invent it.

In the meantime, though, Hoss would just have to keep trying.

The blocky little boy, built square and solid, so that he almost looked chubby although there wasn't an ounce of fat on him, laboriously peppered the surface of the Truckee until finally he was rewarded with a splash that might—if the observer were in a charitable frame of mind—be considered a skip.

Adam grinned broadly, said something to Hoss and patted him on the back, and little Hoss squirmed and preened in the glow of his big brother's approval.

Together the boys started off again in the direction of the lush glade where Ben had left them with their fishing lines and willow poles and picnic makings.

The boys always insisted on coming along whenever Ben came down from the mountain to tend to Inger's grave, but they rarely joined him on the knoll itself. Ben suspected Adam kept his distance because the memories of Inger were so painful to him. Adam had no real memory of his own mother, but he had adored Inger and admitted that it was she who was in his mind when he thought about his mother. Hoss, of course, stayed away because Adam did. He had no memory of his mother, nor even of the succession of sympathetic and warm-hearted pioneer women who had taken care of Adam and Hoss in those earliest days.

The wagon train Ben and Inger and the boys came westward with had to go on or risk becoming snowbound that fall, even though one of their number lay dying of a festered wound. Ben sent the boys on ahead with helpful friends then, but insisted on remaining behind with Inger despite the danger to himself. They had had long, peaceful days to share their love, the time made all the more precious because they both knew that Inger was dying. They had talked and held hands and made the most of what time they were given. Later Ben nearly died too as he tried to cross the Sierras alone in winter. It was only the intercession of a band of Pah-Ute Indians that saved him.

He had spent that winter learning from the Pah-Utes. And becoming ever more captivated by the majesty of the great mountains.

When spring released him from the bondage of its grip, he had hurried west to California to find and reclaim his boys. And then came right back here to these mountains he had come to love so very much.

The land he took up then would be his home for however many days he had left to him, he swore.

And if he were lucky, his sons would love it as much as he and continue on this land long after Ben Cartwright's time was past.

Ah, but that was a serious matter to think about.

And today, despite the nature of their visit here at the Truckee Meadows, today was a far from serious day.

Today, like the other days when Ben came down from the mountains to Inger's grave, was a break from the dull and normal routine of ranch life, and gave the boys a chance to get away from home for a day on horseback with their father.

Ben was always glad for the company. And for any other excuse to spend time with his sons.

He stood on the knoll a moment longer, enjoying the bright sunshine of a fine spring day, then let himself out through the gate he'd installed two years earlier and started down toward his two fine boys.

By the time he reached the meadow and started across it toward the grove where the boys were fishing, he could hear the intrusion of a persistent noise from the emigrant trail downstream.

If wagons loaded with movers and gold seekers were arriving at Truckee Meadows this early in the season, then Missouri and the plains must have had an exceptionally mild winter just past, he realized.

Surely no one could be this far west so quickly.

Why, he wasn't ready for them.

He hadn't brought the oxen down off the foothills. Hadn't prepared the vast quantities of dried meat that would be needed, nor yet sent his own wagons across into California to bring back flour and salt and coffee.

Why, he simply wasn't at all ready.

Surely no one could have made it this far yet.

Yet there someone was. Even as he rejected the possibility of travelers reaching the Meadows this early in the year, Ben could see the lead pair of a mule-drawn light wagon burst out of shadow into sunlight on the open, grassy sward.

The mules pulled steadily in a smooth, easy-swinging trot, one team after another, until there were four lightly loaded rigs in view, each carrying five or six passengers, and none of them seeming burdened by much in the way of supplies or equipment.

Adam and Hoss heard the jangle of the harness and came up the creek bank to see. Ben increased his pace to join his sons. The boys saw him and hurried to meet him halfway, positioning themselves one on either side and close to their father. They stood together there to greet these months-early newcomers from the east.

"Bless you, Mr. Cartwright, you're everything they told us you would be."

"Frankly, Mr. Hamer, I'm not sure how I should take that. Not until I know everything you were told."

The leader of the party threw his head back and roared. "That's a good one, Mr. Cartwright. Not till you know all we were told, ha ha."

"Seriously, Mr. Cartwright," the man's missus put in, "we appreciate all you are doing for us. Why, I declare, any gentleman who invites twenty-three perfect strangers to dinner without warning must be a saint."

"Why, thank you, Clarissa, for implying that I am perfect," Hamer teased.

"Charles!"

"You are the one who said that we strangers were perfect, Clarissa, not I."

"Mr. Cartwright, I ask you. Whatever shall I do with him?"

Ben chuckled and accepted the reins of his horse from Adam. With this interruption in their down-valley outing, the boys had been dispatched to bring the mounts in from grazing. Ben noticed that Adam had gone to the trouble of saddling and tightening the cinches on all the horses, not merely his own. Ben was pleased with the display of thoughtfulness.

"Son," he said now, "why don't you and Hoss ride ahead and tell Mr. Malloy we'll be having company tonight. It wouldn't do for us to show up with this many extra and not give him a bit of notice."

Adam sat up straighter on his saddle and he tried his best to appear serious and responsible and mature . . . but the telltale upturning curves of a poorly hidden grin kept flickering in and out of view at the corners of his mouth. Being sent off like this up the lonely mountain road from the Meadows to home—alone save for the responsibility of his baby brother—why, this was heady stuff indeed. "Yes, Pa. Should I take the rifle, Pa?"

"Yes, I think probably you should, son."

Adam stifled an incipient yelp and walked—swaggered was closer to the truth of it—to the side of his father's horse to take down the short-barreled mountain rifle that was hung from the pommel of the saddle there. His chest puffed out to mighty dimensions as he lifted down his father's "possibles" bag with powder, ball, and caps and slung the leather bag over his own skinny shoulder. Not for a moment would he have considered hanging the heavy bag from the horn of his saddle.

Chunky little Hoss scaled the side of his horse—Jean-Pierre DeMarigny, the Ponderosa's foreman, had tied on some knotted thongs that the boy could use like a rope ladder when he wanted to climb the heights into his saddle—and was ready and waiting by the time Adam mounted, his dignity impeded only a little by the rifle.

"Count on me, Pa. I won't let you down," Adam declared.

"We," Hoss corrected with a show of mild indignation. For after all, he was a part of this mission too.

"Right. The two of us won't let you down, Pa."

"I know you won't." Ben restrained an impulse to remind Adam to take care of Hoss—Lord knew, no such reminder was needed—and bit back another, even stronger inclination to tell the boys to be careful on the road.

The children set off up the well-marked and perfectly visible wagon road that would take them to the Ponderosa Ranch headquarters, Adam leading the way at an easy lope.

Ben noticed with a mix of pride and pleasure that the boys, even little Hoss, rode as if they were part of the horses, as if somehow they had become perfectly natural, perfectly balanced outgrowths that rose from the backs of the equines so that man and horse were blended into one creature.

Ben himself, coming to riding as an everyday means of transportation relatively late in life, after a youth spent on the decks of ships at sea, knew that he would never experience such a mastery of horsemanship as his young sons already found to be as normal as breathing.

"Are you sure they will be all right?" Mrs. Hamer asked in a nervous tone of voice.

"Ma'am?"

"Should you have let them go alone like that, Mr. Cartwright? I mean, if the older boy fears he may need a firearm . . ." Her eyes were wide and worried.

Ben smiled. "There isn't anything or anyone that would harm them, Mrs. Hamer, I assure you. Not within fifty miles, I wager. Carrying the rifle makes Adam feel that much more grown up. He's at that age, you see, when he's wanting to leave childhood behind but isn't quite yet ready. You will understand that when the time comes."

Mrs. Hamer blushed a little and quite involuntarily touched the slightly bulging front of her dress. "You are a very perceptive gentleman, Mr. Cartwright."

"No, just an experienced one." He took Mrs. Hamer's hand and helped her back onto the box of her husband's wagon. "Best we should be getting along now if we want to get to the Ponderosa in time for supper." Ben mounted, and the wagons rolled slowly forward while Ben rode close beside the box of Hamer's lead rig.

"Ponderosa," one of the men in the party said. "I thought that was the name of a tree."

"So it is, sir. It is a tree that I particularly admire, graceful and yet sturdy and true. That is why I chose to name my home for it."

"They tell us you're the only whites this side of the Sierras, Mr. Cartwright," another said.

"Oh, there was a time when you might have been able to say that, but a few folks have chosen to settle on this side of the mountains since I came. There is a small settlement to the south, and right here at the Truckee Meadows there is seasonal occupation when traders come across the passes with wares to sell to the emigrants and the gold-seekers."

"Like you, Mr. Cartwright. I'm surprised you don't keep them away."

Ben laughed. "To tell you the truth, sir, I don't think of them as competitors. More like unofficial partners who take some of the load off me and my sons."

"But I thought that was your business, Mr. Cartwright, trading with the travelers on the California road."

"It was, more or less. At least to begin with. This was where I happened to be, and that was the business that was available to me. Mostly, though, I chose to stop here because this is where my wife is buried—on that knoll up there, actually—and this is where I found a peace and a beauty the like of which I have seen in no other place. The business aspects, such as they were, came afterward.

"For some years, you see, travelers abandoned livestock on these meadows. They turned loose any stock too weak to attempt the passes to the west. And because of this, the Indians came here each fall to claim the recovered oxen and mules and whatnot for their winter meat. Those same Indians saved my life when I found myself alone in the mountains after my wife died. We've become friends, those Indians and I. They know they are always welcome at the Ponderosa now, and my sons and I are welcome in their shelters." He smiled. "But it was the trade you asked about, wasn't it? Sorry.

"That first year, I went over to California early and brought back some food that I might sell to the emigrés. And there were some oxen in the thickets too, animals abandoned earlier and long since fully recovered from the fatigue of travel. An ox hauling a heavy wagon from the States will be footsore and thin by the time it reaches the Meadows here, you see, but given a few weeks to recuperate, it will rebound completely to good health. Well, I soon realized that I could trade fresh oxen for tired ones. Two worn-out animals for one fresh one. Then in a few weeks when another train came through, I would have two fresh oxen to give in exchange for four tired ones. Give four, take in eight. Give eight, take in sixteen. You can see that in no time at all I had oxen to spare. Oxen to sell and oxen to slaughter for jerky, both to sell and to give to my friends the Indians. And there were other creatures too. Dairy-bred cattle too emaciated to go any farther but still living and able to recover; calves whose dams had lost their milk; colts whose mothers died along the trail; any number of such things.

"Before long I was in the business of raising livestock as well as of trading with folks on the road. At this point I am quite frankly concentrating on livestock for the future. Not just oxen, but horses, both saddle and draft stock, and beef cattle, even a few head of dairy cattle. I have more than enough grazing land here on the Ponderosa. And timber too, if there should ever be a means to transport timber from this side of the Sierras over to the gold-mining country. In any event, I believe my sons have a good prospect on this land I've taken up for their future."

"They say you own half of California, though, Mr. Cartwright. How is that?"

Ben laughed. "It's a bold claim, sir, and I wish a true one. If you want the full truth, though—and I'm not ashamed to give it—I have no idea how much of California, or any other state or territory, I might own. The thing is, I've always believed in the honesty of my fellow man. And I am pleased to be able to tell you that I've rarely been disappointed. No one has ever left here without food enough to carry him across the mountains. That would be cruel and greedy of me, and I don't want to think either of those things about myself. I've always been willing to give a man whatever he needs, and if he is able to repay me later, that will be fine. It is something we can think about at that later date. Fortunately, a good many of the people who've taken advantage of this find themselves in excellent circumstances once they are established in California. Some of them have repaid me with shares in their ventures. Mines, banks, mercantiles, what-have-you." He grinned and added, "Would you believe, sir, that I own a one-sixteenth share of a barber cum bathhouse cum funerary parlor in a place called Doolin's Gulch? I have a letter somewhere that so informs me, although I can't claim to have seen any cash dividends from this joint venture quite yet."

The gentlemen and two ladies in the Hamer party laughed.

"You, uh, you still have that policy of allowing no one to leave without sufficient supplies to reach California, do you?"

"Yes, Mr. Hamer, I do."

"And, um, what guarantees of repayment is it that you require, sir?"

Ben could see easily enough where this conversation was leading. "Don't worry yourself about it, Mr. Hamer. You and your people will be just fine now."

Mrs. Hamer and the other lady, a Mrs. Cumberland, seemed unnaturally bright of eye now, Ben noticed. As if they might be on the verge of tears. It occurred to him that perhaps these travelers, who were on the plains many months in advance of what was normal, were in poorer shape than he'd realized.

Because their mules seemed to be in excellent condition, he hadn't thought to question the state of the humans in this small group. Now he reconsidered that oversight and realized that the wagons were virtually empty save for a few items of luggage. There was little evidence of edible supplies in any of the four Hamer wagons.

"You know," he said, "I'll bet those mules could handle a spritelier gait than this, at least until we start to climb. We're hours away from my ranch, but I can't see any need for us to dawdle and make the time longer than it has to be. What do you say we quicken the pace just a little, eh?"

Charles Hamer snapped a whip above the backs of his leaders. On the seat beside him his wife once again touched her belly.

Ben hoped that darn cook Malloy put plenty on the table this evening. Humph. First, he supposed, he should hope that that darn Malloy was sober enough tonight to cook something for these poor folks. One of the few drawbacks of being so far off from everything and everyone else was that it was difficult to find help worth hiring, Edgar Malloy being a particularly telling case in point. The man was a drunkard and sometimes a problem, although when sober he was as good a cook as could be wanted. And anyway, Ben did not have the heart to turn Malloy out. The fellow was bad enough here where alcohol was seldom to be found; Ben was afraid to think what might happen to him if Malloy carried his self-destructive habit with him to one of the gold camps where liquor would be readily available to him.

"You're in for a treat tonight, folks," Ben promised the emigrants. "Just wait until you see my home place." Of a sudden he found himself as eager to arrive there as Hamer and his party obviously already were. "Just wait."

CODY'S LAW

Matthew S. Hart

❏ **GUNMETAL JUSTICE** 29030-4 $3.50/$4.50 in Canada
Texas Ranger justice is about to catch up with a ruthless land baron and his henchmen. A showdown's coming, and Cody will have to ride into hell to end the trail of tyranny.

❏ **DIE LONESOME** 29127-0 $4.50/$5.50 in Canada
Two hundred Winchester repeating rifles have been stolen from an army supply depot. Undercover and alone, Cody has the brains to set a dangerous trap, and the guts to use a beautiful saloonkeeper as bait. But someone is desperately waiting for a chance to plug this lawman full of lead.

❏ **BORDER SHOWDOWN** 29371-0 $3.50/$4.50 in Canada
A band of ruthless desperadoes is spreading a reign of bloody terror...and Cody comes up with an ingenious plan to bring these hard cases to justice. It will take every ounce of courage Cody possesses to bring the culprits to justice.

❏ **BOUNTY MAN** 29517-9 $3.50/$4.50 in Canada
All Cody wants is to get his uncle, a notoriously ruthless bounty hunter, out of Twin Creeks. But when a posse of hired killers shows up to spring his relative's prisoner, Cody and his uncle must join forces—or watch Twin Creeks drown in a sea of blood.

❏ **MANO A MANO** 29670-1 $3.50/$4.50 in Canada
Cody is drawn into a deadly contest beyond the Texas frontier when a beautiful singer is kidnapped. But in the scorching heat of the Mexican desert, Cody has no authority, and the ultimate law is fixed on the blade of a bowie knife.